conqueror's moon

Also by Julian May

THE SAGA OF THE PLIOCENE EXILE

THE MANY-COLORED LAND

THE GOLDEN TORC

THE NONBORN KING

THE ADVERSARY

A PLIOCENE COMPANION

INTERVENTION

THE SURVEILLANCE

THE METACONCERT

THE GALACTIC MILIEU TRILOGY

JACK THE BODILESS

DIAMOND MASK

MAGNIFICAT

BLACK TRILLIUM (WITH M. ZIMMER BRADLEY & A. NORTON)

BLOOD TRILLIUM

SKY TRILLIUM

THE RAMPART WORLDS

PERSEUS SPUR

ORION ARM

SAGITTARIUS WHORL

conqueror's moon

THE BOREAL MOON TALE: BOOK ONE

JULIAN MAY

ACE BOOKS, NEW YORK

An Ace Book
Published by The Berkley Publishing Group
A division of Penguin Group (USA) Inc.
375 Hudson Street
New York, New York 10014

First American edition: January 2004
Previously published in Great Britain in 2003 by Voyager Books.

Library of Congress Cataloging-in-Publication Data

May, Julian.
  Conqueror's moon / Julian May.—1st American ed.
    p. cm. — (Boreal moon tale; bk. 1)
  ISBN 0-441-01132-2
  1. Feudalism—Fiction. I. Title.

PS3563.A942C66 2004
813'.54—dc22

                                    2003061723

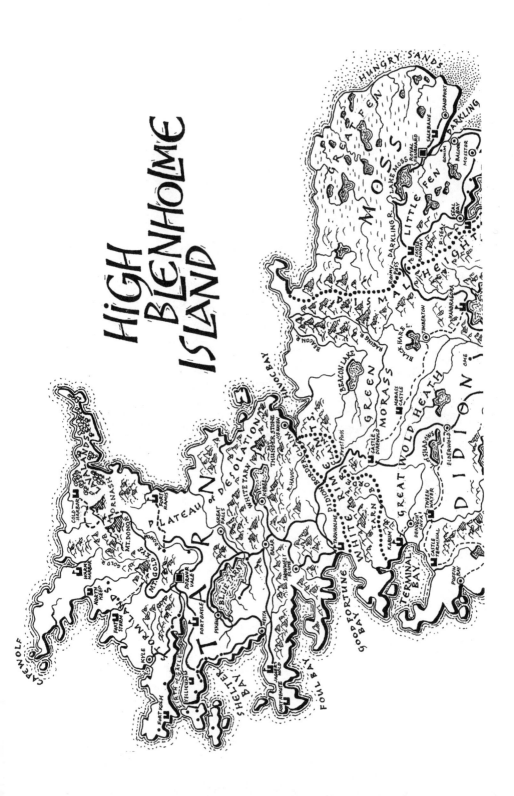

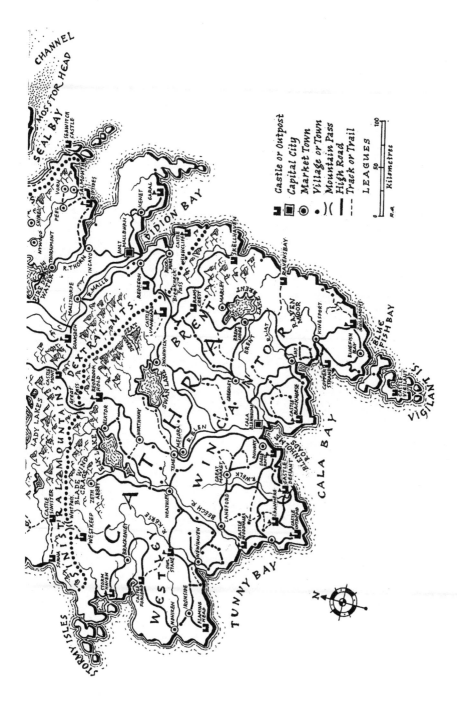

THE TWELVE MOONS RHYME SUNG BY CATHRAN CHILDREN

Snow Moon, Storm Moon, winter fast.
Wind Moon, Green Moon, spring at last.
Milk and Blossom follow after,
Then comes Thunder, God's own laughter.
Corn and Harvest bring their boon,
But Hunters curse the Boreal Moon.
Last of all the Ice Moon drear
Doth bring the end of Blenholme's year.

Each of my successors may pose to me one
Question before singing the Deathsong, and I
will answer true.

—Bazekoy, Emperor of the World

prologue

The Royal Intelligencer

In obedience to a command from the throne commuting my death sentence, the Lord Chancellor of Blencathra banished me to the continent two years ago, with an adequate stipend that will continue so long as I keep my mouth shut. Left unsaid was what would happen if I did not. Cutting off my pension would doubtless be the least of it; and I fear it's only a matter of time before my silence is ensured by more economical means.

Well, if I'm caught, so let it be. I value my life, as every man does, but there's also a great fatigue having nothing to do with bodily weariness that tempts me to release my grip and allow all the burdens to fall away.

But not yet, I think. Not quite yet.

For prudence's sake, every morning I perform a shortsighted windsearch encompassing a dozen leagues or so round about my dwelling. I've not yet found anything or anyone suspicious. The one minor sigil I managed to take away with me from the palace at Cala Blenholme remains under my bed in a locked lizard-wood box. It's called Night Preserver, one of the non-hurting sort, hardly worthy of the Lights' notice, primed for defense against assassins dispatching me in my sleep. But a truly competent cut-throat would have little difficulty getting at me during waking hours, so of late I have had to review my situation and decide whether or not I want to retain control of it, or surrender at last.

Surrender is such a seductive option when one is very old.

My years number four score and one, and I'll certainly die soon of something, whether it be the infirmities of age or foul play. But shall I go unregarded and unsung, in the manner that I lived most of my life . . . or is there a more amusing option?

The gold of my royal pension has bought me a comfortable house in southern Foraile along the River Daravara, five rooms furnished well, with a peg-legged manservant to cook and keep the place from getting too squalid. This is a pleasant land, warm throughout most of the year and kind to old scars and bone breaks, where the breezes blow soft and musk-fragrant, and folk having arcane talents such as mine are so rare as to be the stuff of peasant legends. But I never before lived a tranquil life, and perhaps my attempt to do so now lies at the root of my present mental unease. Tranquillity, to one of my stripe, is boring. No one is so pitiable as a derring-doer put out to pasture, no one so frustrated as a tired old spy without an audience to impress with his cleverness.

When I first arrived in this over-placid exile, I spent some time each day overseeing my old haunts, especially Cala Palace and its ants' nest of scheming courtiers and retainers. Not for curiosity's sake or with any hope of learning fresh secrets, but out of a pathetic longing for those hazards and intrigues that once caused my blood to sing even as my stomach wrung itself like a bile-soaked sponge.

The diversion was a dangerous one, for I am no longer the peerless scryer I used to be, and my own unique talent shielding me from other windwatchers is fading fast, like the other arcane abilities I inherited, all unknowing, from my strange ancestor. If Cathran magickers should catch me spying on the palace, my blood would surely be forfeit. I had to ask myself if this rather tepid species of fun was worth the risk. At length, I decided that it was not.

But the pleasures left to me are so few! I am too frail of body to ride or hunt or even explore the tame jungle surrounding my house. My traitor stomach rebels at rich food. Expensive wines and liquors only put me to sleep without gladdening my spirit. And not even the cleverest bawd from the local house of joy seems able to rekindle the sweet fire in my nethers. There's really only one source of delight left to me now.

Mischief.

The telling of secrets.

The tearing away of masks.

Why provoke trouble in piddling small ways, when one has the potential to bring on a grand firestorm that will rock a kingdom? Why not stir my sluggish passions by reliving the old dangerous life I loved?

Sitting here on my shaded porch above the languid tropical river, with only indifferent birds and my grouchy housecarl Borve to take note of my labors,

I shall write it all down. At the end, if God wills that I finish, I'll return to the island and publish the story myself. It will be supremely gratifying to revel in the ensuing scandal. Why should I care then if my reward is the sharp blade belonging to an agent of the Cathran throne, cutting my scrawny throat?

Highborn or low, the people of High Blenholme would all know who I am at last.

I was born in Chronicle Year 1112, in the Cathran capital city that was called simply Cala in the days preceding the Sovereignty. My name is Deveron Austrey. Although rumor had it in latter days that I was the by-blow of some wizard, the truth is that my father was a harnessmaker in the palace stables, as was his father before him. This would have been my work as well, had not fate decreed otherwise. My mother was a laundress, and my memories of her are scant, for she died in childbirth when I was five, taking her unbreathing babe with her. Apparently, neither of my parents showed any evidence of arcane talent. My own didn't evidence itself until I began crossing the threshold of manhood, and I was slow to recognize it for what it was.

My father perished of wildfire fever when I was eleven years old, so I became apprenticed to my grandsire, irascible and half-blind, but still one of the most ingenious leather-workers in the royal household. I had not a tenth of his artistic skill, but I labored dutifully at my trade, urged on by the occasional smack on the ear, one more among scores of insignificant crafters in the stables, until an alert head groom took note of an odd thing.

Horses were uncommonly docile when I fitted them out in harness. Even the most fractious destrier gentled when I took him in hand, and before long I was the one called to saddle up the huge, evil-tempered stallions trained to fight in tourneys with hooves and teeth, as well as the mettlesome coursers preferred by Prince Heritor Conrig and his high-spirited young band of Heart Companions. My gift with horses was really a species of wild talent, the first to manifest itself.

The second talent to bloom was nearly the death of me.

When Prince Conrig was an unbelted youth of nineteen, not knowing what else he was, and I was twelve, still working with leather but also filling in as an undergroom, I had occasion to lead His Grace's skittish horse to him before a hunt. He spoke to me kindly, and after looking him in the eye I dared to answer back with what I thought was an innocent observation.

Horrified by what I told him so casually, the prince thought at first to have me killed. (And told this freely to me later, as he swore me to secrecy with a formidable oath.) But even then I possessed a glib tongue and a winning manner, and after close questioning and deep thought, Conrig realized that I could be supremely useful to him in a singular way. So he made me his fourth footman, in time dubbing me Snudge because of my artful sneakiness, and thus my later patrons also styled me.

My crabby grandsire, deprived of a useful dogsbody by my promotion to the royal household, predicted that nothing good would come of me aspiring beyond my God-given place. He died a few months later, by which time I had completely forgotten his dire prophecy. Whether it was true or not I leave to the judgment of those who read this tale of mine.

I was Royal Intelligencer throughout most of my life. I fought and fled and skulked and snooped and committed red murder and magical mayhem in the service of King Conrig Ironcrown and his three remarkable sons. I was condemned and reprieved by another of that family, who continues to rule peaceably enough in the wake of the Sovereignty's dissolution.

I was perhaps the most humble of their arcanely talented servants, but so insidious and necessary that I witnessed—and even secretly helped to bring about—many a regal triumph and defeat. That was in times long past, four thousand leagues to the north, on an island where sorcery was once taken for granted and inhuman presences still share the world with mankind.

Continental readers unfamiliar with my former home may appreciate a brief description of it, and they would also do well to consult a map as the story unfolds. Others may skip directly to the first part of the tale, here following.

High Blenholme, an island in the Boreal Sea, is a rugged, roughly oblong landmass with a broad northwesterly extension. It is about four hundred leagues in width and measures roughly six hundred leagues from north to south. Blenholme means "moon island" in the old Forailean tongue. At that northern latitude, a trick of the eye makes the heavenly orb seem much larger than normal at certain times of the year, and so the moon enjoys a prominent place in local religion and folklore.

What with the wildness of the waters surrounding the island, the reefs and frowning precipices that guard its approaches, and the Salka, Green Men, Small

Lights, and Beaconfolk who haunted the place in prehistoric times, High Blenholme was shunned by Continental explorers and would-be settlers until the mighty invasion fleet of Bazekoy the Great sailed into Cala Bay, and he himself planted his standard at the mouth of the River Brent. That portentous event marked Year 1 of the Blenholme Chronicle.

The emperor's heavily armed, disciplined forces drove the sluggish Salka monsters beyond the central mountain ranges and the Green Men into the Elderwold. The Small Lights were only a minor threat to humankind and learned the virtue of staying inconspicuous, while the mighty Beaconfolk unaccountably gave no resistance at all to the invasion. Perhaps they were in the mood for fresh amusements!

Bazekoy named the fertile southern part of the island Blencathra ("moon garden"), and it soon attracted hordes of farmers, herders, and hunters from the teeming mainland. The discovery of iron ore in the west and rich copper deposits along the River Liat led Bazekoy to establish mining and smelting operations, and even facilities for manufacturing weapons and armor to further his continental conquests. By the time of the emperor's death in Chronicle Year 62, Blencathra was a thriving province, exporting not only metals but also grain and many other kinds of valued goods to Foraile, Stippen, and Andradh, and even to other nations more distant.

After Bazekoy's incompetent successors allowed his empire to disintegrate, Cathra became an independent kingdom—although still attractive to continuing waves of immigrants from the politically turbulent Continent. Over the next thousand years the entire island was gradually taken over by humankind and most of the surviving Salka forced into the fens or the dreary Dawntide Isles far to the east.

Geography divides Blenholme naturally into four realms; but Cathra, south of the dividing range, has always remained the richest, most populous, and most fortunate.

The second kingdom to be established was Blendidion ("moon forest") in the north-central part of the island, more austere of clime and having soil mostly thin and poor. It was settled in the mid-500s by rude barbarian adventurers from Stippen, who subdued the scattered Cathran settlements, then married into them. The vigorous newcomers exploited Didion's vast woodlands and established their fortunes through forestry products and shipbuilding. The land also possessed valuable furs and deposits of tin, which it exported to Cathra as well as to the Continent. In time, it became a prosperous, loosely knit nation of quarreling dukedoms and isolated robber-baronies owing reluctant fealty to the Didionite monarch at Holt Mallburn.

The windswept northwestern peninsula of the island was explored late in the Seventh Century by marine marauders of Andradh who called themselves Wave-Harriers. They discovered gold nuggets and valuable opals along the pebbled shore of Goodfortune Bay, settled the area, and defended it successfully against the navies of Cathra and Didion, which lacked the Harriers' fighting prowess at sea. Later, the Andradhian incomers discovered the sources of the gold—enormous living volcanos whose effusions warmed certain rivers and created temperate valleys in what was otherwise an arctic wilderness. Sulphur deposits from the geyserlands and saltpetre exuding from rocks in the White Rime Mountains inspired an anonymous alchymist to invent tarnblaze. That eerie weapon, immune to magical defenses, ensured that the upstarts now calling themselves the Sealords of Blentarn ("moon pool") and their descendants would keep their bleak but wealthy homeland safe against all attackers.

The fourth island kingdom, tiny Moss in the chill northeastern marshes, was born almost by chance in Chronicle Year 1022. Originally a precarious outpost of Didionite sealhunters, fishermen, and amber-traders, the fortified castle of Fenguard came under the control of a mighty sorcerer named Rothbannon Bajor. He had acquired Seven Stones from the Salka, sigils carved from moonstone capable of high sorcery that drew their power from the Beaconfolk. This man's demands for tribute from the locals, enforced by hideous atrocities, energized the Didionite authorities, who condemned Rothbannon to death in absentia and sent a warship to carry out the sentence.

Warned of his impending fate by friendly Salka shamans, Rothbannon invoked the dreaded Beaconfolk and used one of the Seven Stones to whistle up a gale that drove the man o' war onto the Darkling Sands, where all but a handful of the expedition perished. The self-styled Conjure-King of Blenmoss ("moon swamp") then demonstrated other of his formidable powers to the awestricken survivors of the shipwreck and afterwards sent them home to Holt Mallburn in a leaky fishing smack, carrying a list of non-negotiable demands.

The King of Didion paid substantial tribute to the terrible Conjure-King for decades; but when Rothbannon died, his successors proved much less adroit in the art of extortion, since they were afraid of the perilous Seven Stones and the Beaconfolk who empowered them. Didion stopped paying tribute, but decided that reconquering Moss was more trouble than the place was worth. After all, the Mossbacks would have to sell their sealskins and amber to *someone*—and the traders of Didion were always ready to do business.

The four kingdoms of High Blenholme on occasion squabbled viciously but never went to war—until 1128, when my tale begins. I was at that time sixteen years of age, and had served Prince Heritor Conrig as a fledgling snudge and secret talent for four of them. We were more than master and man, for I alone knew what it was that set the prince apart from ordinary mortals.

Or so I believed.

It was a peculiar time. For three years, in a manner unprecedented, the volcanos of Tarn had been in a state of intermittent eruption, filling the Boreal skies with a haze of dark ash that folklore named the Wolf's Breath. The phenomenon had previously been very rare and of brief duration, albeit much dreaded in Didion, where prevailing winds carried the ash-clouds eastward, casting a pall over the land that invariably resulted in a failed harvest.

A Wolf's Breath persisting for three years in a row was a signal calamity, and Didion was finally pushed to the brink of famine. The mighty Sealords of Tarn also faced ruin, since a great proportion of their food was imported at high prices, and they had been forced to abandon most of their goldmining operations until the poisonous exhalations of the eruptions should cease. Even fertile Cathra produced scarcely two-thirds of its usual abundant crop of grain. This was sufficient to feed its own people, but left a diminished surplus available for trade. Only sorcery-ridden Moss, being foggy and poverty-stricken most of the time anyhow, seemed to suffer not a whit from the Wolf's Breath.

Which was suspicious on the face of it . . .

Many blamed Conjure-King Linndal of Moss for the misfortune, saying that he was taking vengeance on King Achardus of Didion for having refused to consider Linndal's daughter Ullanoth as a fit bride for his second son. Others said that the Tarnians themselves had triggered the dire event by grubbing too much gold from the bowels of their mountains, so that hellfire seeped up to fill the empty space and spewed forth sky-darkening smoke. The Brothers of Zeth in Cathra, being more learned in science and wishing to instill hope, maintained that the eruptions were a natural distemper of the earth and would surely cease once the subterranean integrants regained their equilibrium.

But the eruptions did not cease.

As catastrophe overwhelmed his country, Achardus of Didion squandered his assets in a desperate attempt to buy food and ward off insurrection among his starving subjects. Eventually, the market for the nation's raw timber, furs, and tin was glutted. Prompted (as was thought then) by conniving mainland shipbrokers, Didion began building vessels of war. These found an all-too-ready market on the Continent, where the powerful nations of Stippen, Foraile, and Andradh nursed expansionist ambitions.

In Cathra, King Olmigon Wincantor had taken to his bed with the ailment that would ultimately end his life. His Privy Council, riven by factional disputes, was at first unwilling to take effective action, even when Prince Conrig, the able heir to the throne, forcefully pointed out the potential dangers in the situation. What if the Wolf's Breath blew for a fourth year—or even a fifth? Starving refugees from Didion were already attempting to cross the passes into Cathra. If numbers of them broke through, the rapacious Continental nations, who had long coveted High Blenholme's natural riches, would probably take advantage of the resulting chaos and launch an attack on the island.

In order to forestall this peril, Prince Heritor Conrig presented his father and the Council with an ingenious plan, which they finally accepted. That the immediate consequences proved disastrous was not the prince's fault; he was overruled by his conservative elders in the scheme's implementation. In the wake of the débâcle, he conceived yet another bold stratagem. But this time he determined to carry it out himself.

one

Conrig wincantor, prince Heritor of Cathra, Earl of Brent, and Lord Constable of the Realm, ate without much of an appetite, picking at the cold roast beef, eel pie, and fine white wastelbread. He had no stomach at all for the cress salad with scallions or the dessert of pears seethed in cranberry cordial. The prince's only dining companion was his older brother Vra-Stergos, newly ordained Doctor Arcanorum in the Mystic Order of the Brothers of Zeth. No pages served them. They had come to Castle Vanguard on a secret mission, and their presence was unknown to the ordinary inhabitants of the northern fortress.

Their meal had been set out in a small chamber lit only by a glazed loophole, adjacent to the castle solar where the council of war was to take place. Neither of them said much, but the prince could not help but notice how Stergos's eyes lost their focus from time to time, and how he would sometimes hold his head motionless as though listening, even though this arras-hung cubby where they supped was as quiet as winter midnight on Raven Moor.

Finally Conrig said, "Gossy, is there something amiss?"

The alchymist had been sitting like a man frozen, his wine cup poised halfway to his lips. Now he gave a sudden start and set the drink down with a shaky hand. "I don't know." His voice was fretful, but then Stergos had always been a worry-wart. "I think I sense a presence somewhere close by, someone possessed of the talent. I said nothing earlier so as not to spoil our dinner."

"Perhaps Snudge is watching us, trying to read our lips." Conrig flashed an exasperated smile. "Damn his impudence! But he means no harm. I'll admonish him and box his ears later."

"I wish you'd left that boy behind at Brent Lodge," Stergos complained. "It was unwise to bring him along on this crucial mission. Wild talents aren't to be trusted! He can't be windwatched so I never know exactly what he's up to. Deveron's been badly spoiled by your overindulgence, Con. He needs discipline. At sixteen, he's quite old enough to enter the novitiate at the abbey—"

"No," said the prince with a firmness that brooked no argument. "Deveron Austrey is mine, not Saint Zeth's, and I alone will command his loyalty, erratic though it sometimes may be. You must never tell your mystical brethren or anyone else that the lad is not a common man. Is that understood?"

"Yes, but—"

"I need my personal spy, my snudge. He sees things other talents do not—not even you, reverend brother. Folk are wary in the presence of a professed alchymist and windvoice, but who pays any attention to the youngest of the prince's footmen?"

"He still thinks of his aptitudes as playthings! One of these days he'll make a slip and reveal what he is to the wrong person. I'm only trying to protect you, Con."

"I know, Gossy. Search the wind one last time for intruders, then you must leave me while I gather my wits for the council." The prince spoke evenly, hiding the concern that suddenly touched him. There *was* someone watching. He felt it, too. Drinking down the last of his watered wine in a single pull, he arose from the table. "This cramped room is depressing. Come. Let's go into the solar. I'll look at the scenery while you exert your magic."

They left the inner chamber and stood near the solar's huge leaded-crystal window, a marvelous thing made of hundreds of polished small panes, each one perfectly transparent. It was Duke Tanaby Vanguard's particular pride, facing westward so as to give an expansive view of Demon Seat and the lesser peaks in the Dextral Range, silhouetted now against a glaring sunset sky that struck jewel-bright reflections from the collection of silver wine ewers, gilt flasks of ardent spirits, and glass cordial bottles set out by the window for the council attendees.

Stergos cupped both hands over his eyes and stood still, ranging outward. He had been shaved bald for his ordination a moon ago on his thirtieth birthday, and now his head had sprouted fine golden fuzz that gave him a childlike air, even in his imposing crimson robes. Slight of body and round-faced, he had always seemed younger than Conrig, although five years separated them. The two brothers were devoted to one another, in spite of the differences in their temperament.

At length the doctor lowered his hands. "It can't be that knave Deveron riding the wind. It's another—a mind far more adept—but God knows who it is. It seems that all of the noble guests down in the great hall have done just as Duke Tanaby bade them. None of their retinues include alchymists, windvoices, or other folk of talent, and Vra-Doman Carmorton and the rest of the duke's own magickers are temporarily exiled to the town. Their scrying powers are meager, and they're much too far away to see into the castle. As far as I can tell, the only practitioners in all of Vanguard are the young intelligencer Deveron and myself. And yet I'm positive that someone oversees us!" Stergos smote his brow in vexation. "Ah, if only I were not newly frocked, I might serve you more competently, Con. But overseeing is so much more difficult than windspeech—"

"Never mind, Brother. All will be well." The prince paused, turning away to stare at the spectacular vista outside the window. "It may be that I know who could be watching. If I'm right, she has no evil intent."

The doctor's face stiffened in dismay. "Of course! I didn't think of *her*. God's Breath! If only there were another way for us to—"

"You must not even hint at such a thing, Gossy," Conrig chided him. "If we gain at last what we have sought for so long, it will be because of her help."

Vra-Stergos only shook his head, not daring to say more for fear of offending his brother by casting aspersions upon the co-author of the great new scheme. The accursed woman might even be *listening* from a far distance as well as watching! Such a feat was alleged to be impossible, but who could tell with Mosslanders? The devilspawn were said to be part Salka, and might very well share the monsters' inhumanly strong talent.

"Everything is ready for the meeting," Conrig said. "I have the wafers secure in my purse, and no one has meddled with the wine."

Stergos's eyes flickered. "Is there no way I can dissuade you from using them?"

"I respect your misgivings, but you know there was no alternative. Go now and wait with our Heart Companions in the tower. I'll join you as soon as the council is over and tell you everything. Take the hidden stairs."

"May Saint Zeth guide you." Stergos touched the golden gammadion amulet of his order hanging at his breast and returned to the inner chamber.

Conrig waited for several minutes and then followed. The latch that opened the concealed passageway was in the curtain wall next to the necessarium, beneath a stone shelf holding a lavabo, a crock of scented softsoap, and fine linen handtowels. He pressed a knob and a low doorway swung open. After listening for footfalls and hearing none, the prince ducked inside and closed the door behind him. Much of the castle and its six great towers could be stealthily accessed via these 'tween-wall passages and cramped spiral stairways. The things were full of cobwebs and dead insects and rat turds, poorly lit by the occasional inward-looking peephole or narrow slits or oillets in the exterior masonry. Only the duke's family and their most trusted retainers knew of the secret warren's existence. Conrig and Stergos and their poor simple brother Tancoron and their sisters Therise and Milyna had used the passages as a playground when they were children visiting their godfather's castle.

The prince went quickly to the musicians' gallery above the great hall, thinking to watch the diners at the high table without notice and perhaps discover something of their mood. The small balcony was empty and deeply shadowed at the rear, with only a few discarded pages of music lying on the floor among the benches. There would be no entertainment for the duke's guests this evening and no dawdling over the meal. Conrig crouched behind a balustrade with upright members carved fancifully into Green Men and other rustic demons and studied the scene below.

Cresset-lamps and candles had been lit, but the lowering sun still shone through tall narrow windows, casting bars of red-gold light across the sixteen people sitting on the dais. The conversation was low-pitched, even along the sideboards where the knights and retainers ate, with only an occasional burst of nervous laughter from the younger ones.

Following the prince's instructions, Duke Tanaby had summoned the council attendees to table early, saying there would be only simple fare, and cautioning them against heavy drinking that might cloud their brains when such would be sorely needed later. Most of the high lords and great barons, Conrig noted with approval, were following Tanaby's example of sobriety and drinking water from the castle's renowned mineral spring—although Parlian Beorbrook, who was Earl Marshal of the Realm, and his lone surviving son Count Olvan loudly demanded refills of their bumpers of mead. Not even Vanguard dared deny them.

Numbers of the noble guests seemed to savor their meal as little as the Prince Heritor himself had done. Old Baron Toborgil Silverside had scarce touched the slices of meat on his silver trencher-plate, and the hovering pages found few takers for the steaming tureen of carp in nettle broth and the bowls of garnished frumenty and platters of apple and cherry tarts that were the final courses.

Neither Duchess Monda nor any other of Castle Vanguard's ladies were present. The only woman there—and her seated at the duke's right hand, by Bazekoy's Blazing Bones!—was the redoubtable Baroness Zeandrise, the Virago of Marley. She was still clad in her stained green doeskin riding habit with a divided skirt, and wore no veil and no head ornament but a glittering jeweled pick nearly the size of a dagger, transfixing her coil of frowsy grey hair.

Conrig knew that the baroness had only ridden into Vanguard at the last moment, when he and Tanaby had nearly despaired of her arrival. Her manner at table was taciturn and forbidding in spite of the duke's best efforts at hospitality. The prince had debated long with himself before including the Virago among those invited; but his godfather told him to swallow his southern prejudice against a belted female, reminding him that warriors of her sex were far from uncommon among the Didionite barbarians. And besides, Zeandrise Marley commanded fifteen knights and nearly a hundred mounted thanes . . .

He noted stout Count Munlow Ramscrest and his allies Bogshaw, Cloudfell, and Catclaw. And there were Tanaby's sons, Swanwick, Hawkhurst, and Grimstane. The wealthy mountain barons Kimbolton and Conistone, with estates bordering those of Beorbrook, were holding close conversation with their powerful overlord. At the far end of the table on the left sat Viscount Hartrig Skellhaven and his cousin Baron Ingo Holmrangel. Their seaside castles and fleets of armed cutters defended Cathra's far northeastern coast, and they were themselves rumored to be little better than pirates.

"So all of those invited did come after all," said a soft voice behind Prince Conrig.

He felt the hairs at the back of his neck prickle as a draft of chill air brought a familiar, green-fen scent of vetiver.

"It bodes well for the enterprise," the voice continued, almost purring with satisfaction. "For you know that not even I could compel their alliance. Of course, they haven't accepted your proposal yet, but I believe that the odds are strongly in your favor—and your plan for taking care of any nay-sayers is most ingenious."

Still crouched low, Conrig dared not turn around. Suppressed fury tightened his throat. A Sending here? Now, at this critical juncture? Was the woman mad?

"If you're seen," he hissed, "I'm ruined! My brother Vra-Stergos is hidden away with my other Companions in the repository tower, and your Sending could only be attributed to *me!*"

"No one will see or hear me, my prince." She spoke with a hint of mockery. "Your accession to the throne is safe, untainted by any whiff of magical talent."

He craned about and saw a cloaked and hooded figure standing in a dark niche. The face was invisible, and the glowing moonstone sigil that enabled the Sending was out of sight. Slowly he withdrew from the railing and climbed to his feet, keeping well out of view of those below, and went to her. "Why are you here?" His whisper was brusque, to hide the fact that he had been badly startled.

"I come with good news, as well as some of less happy portent." Her hand reached out and caressed his cheek. "Affairs in Didion have fallen into place just as we hoped, and you may so inform your council of war. King Achardus will remain at the palace in Holt Mallburn during the crucial time. He has scant motive for traipsing abroad among the faminelands listening to the wails of hungry peasants or the mutterings of mutinous vassals. His sons Honigalus and Somarus are another matter, however. Both have taken ship to the south, probably to seek help from Stippen or another Continental nation in countering your blockade in the Dolphin Channel. Beynor and three senior members of the Glaumerie Guild are accompanying the Didionite princes. My dear brother is playing some game of his own, and he's probably being well paid for it. He has used a sigil to cast a strong spell of couverture over their vessel, and I cannot penetrate it."

Conrig muttered a quiet oath. "But you *will* be able to find out what they're up to?"

"Eventually. It may become necessary for me to empower another of my own Great Stones in order to learn his plans, but I hope I can use alternate means. The most powerful sigils are activated only through atrocious suffering, and their conjuring puts the user deep in debt to the Lights."

He felt the familiar thrill of dread at her mention of the awful Beaconfolk. "Lady, must you invoke those dire creatures? Is there no other manner of sorcery that will serve our purposes?"

"None so effective. I call upon the Coldlight Army as rarely as possible, since they're notorious for twisting petitions and conjurations to unwelcome outcomes. But we must find our what Honigalus and Somarus intend. They are the real power behind Achardus's throne, and they have powerful friends on the

Continent. It would do you small good to triumph in the north while disaster strikes the southern underbelly of your unborn Sovereignty."

"No," Conrig admitted reluctantly. Most of the Cathran navy was at sea, enforcing the blockade against Didion, and the capital city of Cala on the south coast would be vulnerable to a lightning assault from mainland ports.

He was silent, considering other things that her words had brought to mind. Then: "Advise me, if you please. None of these council attendees, not even Duke Tanaby or the earl marshal himself, knows that the Edict of Sovereignty was as much your idea as mine. Would you have me tell them?"

A patronizing laugh. "I'm not the one who covets the ancient glory of Emperor Bazekoy, my prince. Warriors mistrust sorcery, and for good reason. It's best that they know nothing of our earlier . . . strategic consultations, for that might taint the sanctity of your great vision and weaken your authority. You must certainly tell your council of war how I intend to assist the invasion, and my reasons for doing so. But keep the rest secure in your own heart. The unification of High Blenholme is your own dream, after all, and none but you can fulfill it."

He felt sweat start out on his brow, not from doubt of his own abilities to persuade and command the others, but in a belated flush of apprehension at where this alliance with her might eventually lead.

"They will ask—my godfather and the earl marshal, at any rate—how you and I came to this marvelous friendship. Lady, what am I to tell them? They know we could never have met face-to-face. And even though we have made some use of my brother's arcane talent—"

"He has *always* been our go-between! You must convince the others of it. And see that Vra-Stergos is also convinced."

"I'm sure my brother has suspected that I possess the talent, that you and I bespoke each other through magical means long before your Sendings appeared to Gossy and me together at the hunting lodge. He's a timid soul, and he no doubt put the notion out of mind for fear of what the consequences would be. Nevertheless, my brother won't tell an outright lie about my talent, even to protect me. It would violate his vows to God and Saint Zeth."

"Then you must ensure that he does not officiously strive to tell the truth," she snapped, "while you say what you must to the duke and the earl marshal, and charge your own conscience. And if the new-hatched Doctor Arcanorum will not let be, then you must silence him."

"He's my older brother!" the prince exclaimed in horror. "I love him!"

"He is a man born with the talent, whose voice carries on the wind and whose mind solidifies the Sending. And by that token he is ineligible for your precious throne of Blencathra. As are *you*, Conrig Prince Heritor, if your vaunted truth be told."

"But I didn't know!" His whisper was desperate. "Not until—"

"Until I came," she said, unaware of the real state of things and knowing nothing of Snudge. "And I showed you how the audacious dream of your youth might be fulfilled. You listened well to my secret counsel, and your scheme prevailed. The Edict of Sovereignty was proclaimed. That its fulfillment was cruelly bungled by imbeciles was only a temporary setback. With my aid you shall set all to rights. And in the end who will care that you possess a small portion of the talent, or that a few necessary falsehoods were told in your great endeavor's fulfilling?"

He could think of no way to counter what she had said. Gossy would understand. He must understand . . .

"Very well. Leave me, then, lady. Be assured I'll do what is best."

Again she touched his cheek, smiling, then vanished. The scent of vetiver remained, sweet and woodsy.

Prey to unspeakable thoughts concerning his beloved brother, he crept back to the balustrade and looked down blindly on the hall for a few minutes more, until Tanaby Vanguard announced to the nobles at the high table that it was time to go to the solar and begin their conclave.

two

They entered in an untidy crowd, the Virago and seven other great barons, three viscounts, three counts, and Parlian Beorbrook, the kingdom's chief military officer, all of them caring nothing for the niceties of precedence as was the way of easygoing northerners. Last came the host of the clandestine gathering, who slammed the tall double doors firmly behind him and shot its twin bolts into place.

"His Grace will join us in a moment," Tanaby Vanguard said, nodding towards another closed door that gave onto the inner chamber. He wore a simple houserobe of russet velvet, a thin man with finely drawn, unreadable features, whose nose jutted like an axe-blade. Chestnut hair thickly streaked with grey fell to his shoulders. Unlike most of the other men, he was clean-shaven.

Beorbrook spotted the table of drinks by the window and strode to it purposefully, hauling his dented old silver cup out of his belt-wallet. "Is that a Snapevale Stillery flagon that I spy?"

"Leave be for a moment, Parli," said Tanaby, "until the Prince Heritor arrives."

"How sober do we have to be for this bloody mystery confab anyhow?" the earl marshal muttered. He was a hale man in early middle age, broad rather than tall, with muscular legs grown bandy from horseback riding, and enormous gnarled hands. Blue eyes cold as an Ice Moon sky were sunk deep beneath shaggy black brows. His beard was also black, although his hair had gone snow-white. He wore a doublet of dark blue leather, intricately worked, having stiff sleeve-wings that emphasized his extraordinary shoulders. His chain of office was conspicuously absent.

"You must decide the need for a clear head yourself," Tanaby told his long-time friend. "As for blood, there may be quantities of it in the offing if we here decide so."

The marshal gave a grunt, and some of the others exchanged wary glances or small grim smiles. Except for Vanguard, none of those present were intimates of the prince. They knew only that he favored some sort of retaliatory strike against Didion, and as Lord Constable of the Realm had the power to lead one even if the Privy Council balked—provided that the king himself did not expressly forbid it. Tanaby's carefully worded messages bringing these northern nobles to a secret meeting had sparked battle-fever in some and skepticism in others, but all had agreed to listen to the prince and decide whether or not to support him in the undertaking.

A fire burned in the broad greystone hearth, before which were sixteen common stools, arranged in a semicircle. In the middle was a single collapsible field-chair fashioned of carved walnut and faded brocade, fronted by a small table. All of the usual furnishings of the solar, save for the sideboard with the liquor, had been removed.

"I realize we aren't here for a cozy chat, my lord duke," drawled Lady Zeandrise, eyeing the comfortless seats. She still had spurs on her booted feet. "But is it necessary for us to perch like a gang of tomtits on fenceposts during this conference?"

There were a few chuckles. Tanaby said, "The unusual arrangement, dear Zea, was meant to evoke the *lack* of coziness we may expect to experience if we agree to participate in the prince's venture."

"I see." The baroness kept a straight face. "Well, it's been a dull year in Marley. The harvest's safely in and ample enough in spite of the Wolf's Breath, and my knights and thanes are restless and in need of distraction." She glanced out the window at the spectacular sky. "A pity we only get these magnificent sunsets when the volcanos belch."

Old Baron Toborgil Silverside said, "King Achardus of Didion and his starving people must take faint comfort in such beauty."

"Famine smite the lot of them dead," growled Beorbrook, "and may a hundred thousand vultures shite their bones!"

"And so let it be forever," Count Ramscrest added, in a voice hard as granite.

A respectful silence fell over the group, for everyone knew that the marshal's two elder sons and Ramscrest's youngest brother had been in the ill-fated royal delegation presenting the Edict of Sovereignty to the King of Didion. Ramscrest's brother had left a widow and three small children. As for Beorbrook, only his third son, Count Olvan Elktor, untried in battle at twenty-one and thick as two oaken planks, was now left to inherit the most strategically important duchy in all of Cathra. There was small hope that Olvan would ever fill his father's boots as earl marshal, and it seemed likely that the office and its great perquisites would pass out of the Beorbrook family with Parlian's demise.

All at once the door of the inner chamber was kicked open with a sharp rap and Conrig appeared. The Prince Heritor was dressed all in black, as was his custom, and his wheaten hair and short beard looked almost coppery in the ruddy light, a strange contrast to his dark brown eyes. He had two magnums of wine tucked under each arm and a corkscrew dangling from his right hand.

"Good evening to you all, my friends, and thank you for coming. Be at ease, and let there be no idle ceremony." When they continued to stand motionless and uncertain, he said to Vanguard, "Godfather, help me cope with these bottles, which I brought specially from Brent Lodge for this gathering. It's a brisk new Stippenese vintage from the Niss Valley that will quench our thirst without dulling our wits. Time enough for ardent spirits after you've all listened to my proposal and made up your minds about it."

They relaxed then, and there were low-pitched words of greeting to Conrig from the older nobles and diffident nods from the young ones. Cups were drawn from velvet or leather pouches and held out for filling by the prince himself, who called each person by name and made casual talk. Lady Zeandrise had her weathered hand kissed by the royal winebearer and pursed her lips tightly to forestall a smile.

Finally Conrig poured into Tanaby's own simple beaker of waxed honeywood and let the duke do the honors for him. The prince's silver cup was lined with gold; a great amethyst formed part of the stem, a talisman against drunkenness . . . and poison.

"A toast," he said quietly, lifting his drink. "To the good sense of those here present, which must determine whether the plan I propose will be acceptable or die aborning."

"To good sense," Tanaby echoed, "but also to daring." He had already been taken into Conrig's confidence and knew some details of the scheme, but had withheld judgment of its merit pending this consultation with the others.

They took their seats in a poorly concealed aura of excitement, with the Prince Heritor seated on the folding chair and the others spread out on either side. Young Baron Kimbolton put more wood on the fire. The sunset was rapidly fading.

"Do you like the wine?" Conrig inquired pleasantly.

Most voiced their approval. Count Munlow Ramscrest grimaced and shifted his great bulk so that his stool creaked ominously. His oversized mantle, trimmed with black wolf fur, spread around him like a sledge robe. "I would as lief take honest Cathran mead any day over foreign grape-gargle. Still, it does cut the phlegm."

The others roared with laughter.

But then bluff Ramscrest asked the prince flat out, "Your Grace, does this plan of yours involve mere punitive strikes against Didion, or would you wage open warfare?"

"I intend to mount an invasion," the prince replied, "and seize Holt Mallburn, and force Achardus to accept the Edict of Sovereignty or have it stuffed down his gullet."

Ramscrest's face, as homely and full of bristles as that of a boar, broke into a beatific smile. He said, "Oh, yes. Yes indeed!"

Some of the others began to exclaim and call out questions, but the penetrating voice of Parlian Beorbrook cut through the clamor like a brazen trumpet. "And what does the King's Grace think of this brave notion?"

They all fell silent.

The prince set his cup on the small table before him, rose, and began to pace slowly back and forth in front of the fire. He was five-and-twenty years of age, over six feet tall, well-built, and fine of feature as his father, King Olmigon, had been in his youth; but no one in the room would dispute that Conrig Wincantor far surpassed his sire both in strength of character and in mental acuity. In recent years the king had become capricious and vacillating, prone to following dubious advice from certain favored members of his Privy Council, and shunting important matters aside while he dithered over some triviality.

Olmigon had agreed to Conrig's Edict of Sovereignty proposal only after months of dispute. It was the king who had made the disastrous decision that the royal delegation bearing the Edict to the court of Didion should be small and accompanied only by a token force of warriors; and it was the king, a fine naval tactician in his prime, who had decided that Cathra's response to the delegation's slaughter should be a sea blockade rather than a land invasion of the northern kingdom.

Conrig said, "Before answering that question, Earl Marshal, I must impart to you melancholy tidings. Since you've been busy for the past months keeping Great Pass secure from bandits and Didionite incursions, you may not know that King Olmigon has lately experienced a worsening of that abdominal rupture which has so long afflicted him. The royal alchymists are zealously applying both natural science and sorcery, but the latterday weight-gain of my father makes treatment more difficult than in past years." He took a poker and pulled the smoldering logs together so that they might burn better. "King Olmigon is in great pain much of the time. He continues to conduct important state business from his bed, however, refusing medicine that he fears might dull his mind, even as the suffering itself prevents him from straight thinking. Queen Cataldise is at his side day and night."

Dying! They all had the identical thought.

The prince turned about and let his eyes rove slowly over those seated. "However, my lady Maudrayne has sent to Tarn for a healer of special talent, and if God wills, the King's Grace will be restored to health. I command you not to broadcast tidings of his sad disability beyond this room. Only keep him in your prayers."

And remember who it is that will succeed to the throne of Cathra when Olmigon does sing his Deathsong.

Nods and murmurs.

"It was my personal decision," Conrig continued, "as well as that of a certain other high-ranking member of the Privy Council, not to trouble the king with this new matter until I have consulted with you all and determined whether or not the invasion proposal is practicable. As Lord Constable of the Realm, acting with the covert approval of Chancellor Falmire, who is the only one of my father's advisers with the brains to understand the situation, I have the power to summon this extraordinary council of war. The persons I chose to invite are those in a unique position to render service to Cathra—to redress the atrocious insult done to our kingdom by Didion, and assure the security of the entire island."

Whisperings. None of them were fools. Unlike the intrepid northerners, who had always borne the brunt of defending Cathra's border, the lords of the south had grown complacent and soft from long years of martial inactivity. They were businessmen, tending to their varied commercial ventures, not fighters. With the coming of the Wolf's Breath, worried by the decline in their private fortunes and too shortsighted to understand the potential danger from the Continent, the southerners were in no mood to spend money re-equipping and training their knights and thanes as an invasion host.

"As you all know," Conrig continued, after a pause, "the impetus for the Edict of Sovereignty came originally from me. From my youth I have idolized Emperor Bazekoy the Great, who unified the nations of the mainland, brought civilization to our own island, and chose to die here for love of it. It has long been my dream to bring all of Blenholme together and return it to the glory of Bazekoy's time."

"The Emperor," Munlow Ramscrest grumbled, "has been dead for over a thousand years . . . most of him, at any rate! And the Blenholme of his day no more resembles our own than children's fables resemble the sacred Chronicle."

"Count Ramscrest speaks the unwelcome truth, as usual," the prince conceded, to universal amusement. "Our world is more densely populated and our politics more complex. Nevertheless, even the marble-domes on my father's Privy Council eventually agreed that the time was ripe for a move to Sovereignty. Three years of the Wolf's Breath have brought tragedy to Blenholme—but also an unprecedented opportunity. Didion is at the brink of civil war. The gold-coffers of the Sealords of Tarn are near empty with the closing of the mines. Even in Moss—"

"Who cares about Moss?" Baron Wanstantil Cloudfell sneered. He was a haughty beanpole who dressed with great elegance and affected a foppish manner. "Let the Conjure-King use sorcery to make the sun shine on his stinking swamps, and may he have much joy in the fulfillment. My prince, don't tell me you'd bother taking that soggy nest of magical mountebanks into the Sovereignty!"

"As it happens, Lord Cloudfell, the kingdom of Moss would play a crucial role in unifying Blenholme."

"The hell you say!" Beorbrook exclaimed. "Does this scheme of yours depend on vile Mossback enchantments, then?"

The prince fixed the earl marshal with a level look, saying nothing, until the veteran general looked away, his jaw clenched and his brow like thunder.

"Hear His Grace out, Parli," urged Vanguard. "It's true there are arcane elements in his plan, but no invoking of the Beaconfolk or anything else an honest warrior could scruple at. Carry on, Godson."

"Very well," said the prince. "As you know, the three Wolf's Breath years have by no means left our own land of Cathra untouched. Our fields have produced significantly less grain. Our exports to Tarn, our favored—and wealthy—trading partner, left almost nothing for Didion. That nation has been forced to import foodstuffs from the Continent."

"And the required coin of payment," said Count Norval Swanwick impatiently, "is Didionite warships. Yes, yes, and all of us know what use Foraile and Stippen might make of them. Your Grace isn't the only prince harking back to Bazekoy's days of glorious conquest. The emperor was, after all, a Forailian by birth."

"It was to squelch such harkings," Conrig said, "that I pressed for the Edict of Sovereignty." And he quoted from memory. " 'For the benefit and security of all Blenholme, and to thwart those Continental opportunists who might think to take advantage of the current natural disaster afflicting our island, the Kingdom of Blencathra extends its merciful hand to the suffering people of its neighbor, Blendidion, and vouchsafes it prompt paternal succor and relief, as Blendidion acknowledges vassalage in the new, benevolent Sovereignty of High Blenholme, and accepts Olmigon Wincantor as its Liege Lord.' "

"But they didn't, did they?" Viscount Skellhaven pointed out, with sour satisfaction. "Not without a Cathran army and a train of grain wagons coming at them over Great Pass along with your precious Edict."

Even though he had ridden into Castle Vanguard on horseback like all the others, he wore salt-stained seaboots, the wide pantaloons favored by sailors, and a silk scarf tying back his long hair. His attire was of good quality but shabby, as if to reinforce his perennial pose of being ill-used and unappreciated by the Crown.

Beorbrook said, "We all know how the King of Didion responded to Cathra's declaration of Sovereignty. He killed our people and stuck their heads on pikes above Mallmouth Bridge for the crows and seagulls to eat, and fed their poor bodies to the crabs." The earl marshal tossed off the remainder of his wine, and his son Olvan hastened to bring more, then served the few others who lifted their cups with all that was left in the last bottle.

"It was six months ago that my sons and the others died," Beorbrook went on. "The Crown's blockade of Didion isn't working—no offense, Skellhaven!—because there's too much water to cover and the bastards are better sailors than we are. Now that Achardus knows for sure we're out to topple him, you can be sure that he'll be on the lookout for a land invasion as well. I can assure Your Grace that the Didionite mountain fortresses beyond Great Pass are manned and alert, in spite of the terrible conditions prevailing in their lowlands. If need be, King Achardus will rally the timberlords from Firedrake Water. Their thanes and stump-jumpers fill their bellies with venison and wildfowl rather than dearly priced bread, and they're in fighting trim despite the Wolf's Breath. It's only in the valley of the River Malle and in the large coastal cities that folk are starving. Now, it seems to me that we've already missed our best opportunity to strike at Didion. We should have been poised to come at them from both sea and land if they refused to accept the Edict of Sovereignty."

"The King's Grace deemed such a course too expensive," Conrig said, smiling without humor.

"Of course he did," Skellhaven said bitterly. "Same reason Ingo and me never get the brass we need to do a proper job patrolling the northern sealanes! The king won't raise taxes on the rich merchants and trader-lords who curry his favor."

Count Norval Swanwick climbed to his feet. Vanguard's son and heir was an experienced battle-leader who had often fought at the side of the earl marshal, defending both Great Pass and the Wold Road to Tarn. "May I speak, my prince?"

"Please do, my Lord Swanwick. All of us know that you and your valiant brothers have fought many a skirmish against Didionite robber-barons and Green Men. I have great respect for your opinion."

"Here's what I'm afraid will happen if we invade Didion by land: At the first hint that we're on the move, their arcane talents as well as their best fighters will rush to meet us at Castlemont beyond Great Pass. Even if we're aided by the magical flummery of Mossland's Conjure-King, we can't hope for any element of surprise. The country in that region is so open, they'll see us coming from leagues away. And there are no strongpoints between the frontier and their Castlemont fortress where our forces might safely encamp to beseige the place."

Many spoke up in agreement.

"Furthermore," Swanwick went on, "the earliest we could launch an invasion is in spring—late next Wind Moon, when the mountain snows will have melted and the mud dried. But by then our granaries will be sore depleted after winter.

I'm sure Your Grace realizes that there will be no chance of foraging in the faminelands of Didion as we march eastward toward Holt Mallburn. Even if we're victorious at Castlemont, enemy forces could easily sever our supply line over the mountains while we engage the main host of Achardus."

There were gloomy comments from the others. But the prince cut them off with a ringing voice. "We *can* take them by surprise!"

"How?" asked Swanwick.

"I would not lead a large army but a smaller, swift-moving force of some five hundred picked warriors. We would penetrate Holt Mallburn in a lightning raid and seize Achardus, his entire family, the court officials, and the merchant-lords who control the nation's commerce. And we would not invade Didion in spring . . . but within five weeks, when they have no reason to expect us. My plan is not to march through Great Pass and then battle our way two hundred and sixty leagues through the enemy heartland. I plan to invade through Breakneck Pass, above this very Castle Vanguard, along a route less than one-third of the distance to the Didionite capital. The road is admittedly more rugged, but also more meagerly defended."

"Over Breakneck?" the earl marshal exclaimed in disbelief. "There *is* no road—only a poor track that is often little more than a goat-path! And in late Boreal Moon we would risk fierce rains and washouts, snowstorms driven by hurricane winds, or—God help us—those sudden ice-mists that freeze a man and beast to glazed statues before they realize their mortal peril."

The pass in the eastern reaches of the Dextral Range was indeed a shortcut to Holt Mallburn, but so steep and hazardous that only couriers, smugglers, and the bravest of legitimate traders made use of it. Almost all land commerce between Cathra and and its northern neighbors was through Great Pass, north of Beorbrook Hold.

The prince said, "The Wolf's Breath has upset the seasons of our island in many ways, significantly delaying the onset of winter in the high country. Favorable weather will prevail over Breakneck Pass at least until Leap Day of the Boreal Moon. I have been assured of it."

"By the Conjure-King of Moss?" Lady Zeandrise inquired softly.

Conrig continued without responding to her. "Our fighting force will consist only of mounted warriors, lightly armored for the sake of speedy travel. We'll have no foot soldiers. Strong mules and ponies will carry supplies in the rear. We'll move very quickly once we cross the frontier and strike without warning. There is only one small mountain outpost between Breakneck Pass and Castle Redfern, and the fortress itself is poorly sited, vulnerable to a surprise attack during fog."

"Fog!" Beorbrook's eyes narrowed. "And we can count upon fog?"

"Oh, yes," the prince reassured him. "And not the dreaded freezing mists, but a warm concealing shroud, through which our army will ride on muffled hooves, led by friendly guides. We'll seize Castle Redfern and use it as a staging area for the main assault upon Holt Mallburn, after we have briefly rested."

"What of Redfern's windvoices?" asked Baron Bogshaw. He was a hulking presence whose face was disfigured by a livid diagonal scar from a swordcut that had blinded his left eye. His lands, like those of Ramscrest and Cloudfell, lay along the mountainous frontier between Cathra and Didion. "And the foe may have talented ones posted at their outpost as well. Once they spot us, they're sure to windspeak the alarm, even if our covert crossing of the pass is successful."

"Any Didionite windvoices along our line of march to Redfern will be silenced before our arrival," said Prince Conrig. "And so will those at the castle."

"Ah . . ." A soft sound from many throats.

"However, it will be up to us to make certain that no ordinary foemen escape and give warning in a commonplace manner. When we leave Redfern, we'll move like ghosts through the mist, down from the mountains to the Coast Highway leading to the capital. We'll cross over the great Mallmouth Bridge—its gate will be opened for us by our magical ally—and when we reach the inner city we'll set selected parts of it afire as a distraction, using tarnblaze bombshells that each one of us will carry. A portion of our force under Lords Skellhaven and Holmrangel will press toward the quay, where they'll use their nautical expertise to seize or destroy whatever ships are tied up there or moored in the harbor. The rest of us will take the palace, capture King Achardus, his two sons, and the other royal officials, and force Didion to surrender to the Sovereignty."

"Great God!" said old Toborgil Silverside. His sunken eyes were shining. "What a glorious feat that would be!"

"We're to accomplish all this under cover of fog?" Munlow Ramscrest was dubious. "In a strange city notorious for its twisted maze of streets?"

Conrig inclined his head. "As I've said, we will have guides. From the summit of Breakneck Pass to the raised portcullises and open barbican gates of Holt Mallburn itself."

Ramscrest persisted. "What manner of guides? Creeping Mosslander wizards bearing magic lanterns?"

"Nay," said the prince. "I may not speak of the guides to you yet, but I'm assured of their assistance. They are to meet us at the top of Breakneck Pass, and if their aspect provokes mistrust among you, then I pledge to abandon this enterprise forthwith."

"It's magic, true enough," said Lady Zeandrise, her mouth quirked by a roguish smile, "but not so outlandish as to put off our knights and thanes, eh, brothers? Fog, eldritch pathfinders and gate-openers, cold steel, and hot tarnblaze! A lightning thrust into Didion, and Holt Mallburn waiting like a sleeping babe . . . Can we be sure King Achardus will be in residence?"

"Oh, yes," said Conrig dryly. "He's there now, and he has little incentive to leave his stronghold. At least it's well stocked with food and drink." There was scattered laughter among the council, for the gigantic Didionite king was an infamous trencherman. "As we prepare to sally forth from Castle Redfern, I'll be kept informed by windspeech of the king's precise whereabouts, as well as that of the merchant-lords and our other special targets. My brother Vra-Stergos will accompany the expedition, as will Duke Tanaby's trusted alchymist, Vra-Doman Carmorton." He said nothing of Snudge.

"And will these good Brethren also use windspeech to transmit reports of our daily progress to the Conjure-King?" Skellhaven inquired archly.

Conrig paused, then spoke with reluctance. "King Linndal of Moss has nothing to do with this plan. Most of the time he is raving mad and confined to his rooms. He spends his lucid days voicing Salka sorcerers in the Dawntide Isles, trading arcane secrets. Our Mossland collaborator is another."

"Who?" Beorbrook demanded.

"His daughter, Princess Ullanoth." The prince took up his cup and sipped from it, but his eyes did not waver from the skeptical face of the earl marshal.

"And what does this benevolent lady ask in exchange for her good offices?"

"That Moss receive First Vassal status in the Sovereignty, with a reasonable guerdon paid annually, and that we support her claim to the throne of Moss above that of her younger brother, Beynor."

"It seems a modest enough boon," Lady Zeandrise remarked. She frowned, then added, "Perhaps too modest."

Beorbrook addressed Vanguard. "Did you know of this, Tanaby? Your royal godson consorting with a Mosslander witch?"

"I knew," the duke replied stolidly. "An unlikely ally, perhaps, but the Lady Ullanoth is a powerful sorceress, and there seems no good reason for her to contemplate using us treacherously."

Munlow Ramscrest exploded in a coarse guffaw. "Why should we give a mule's fart who rules that godforsaken corner of our island? Fens and frogs and peddlers of hocus-pocus and gimcrack amulets! Let the Conjure-Princess have the poxy place and welcome. As for her bribe, we can wring it out of vanquished Didion."

Baron Sorril Conistone, a middle-aged peer who was famed for his scholarly bent, had remained quiet as the prince set forth his plan and the others made comments, seated on a stool at the far left of the blazing hearth where he was almost lost in shadow. Now his deep voice rode over the laughter that had greeted Count Ramscrest's remarks.

"Your Grace, are you certain that this Ullanoth will require nothing more of us?"

"She has asked for no other thing, Lord Conistone," Conrig said. "I swear it on my honor as Prince Heritor of Cathra."

Zeandrise Marley remarked, "Without the lady's help, we're flat skinned, my lords, having not a hope in hell. Do any of you know a better plan?"

"If we're to venture an invasion at all," said Baron Tinnis Catclaw, "then it must be in the manner described by His Grace. The scheme is a goodly one, to my mind, although I would wish it not so dependent upon the whims of an alien sorceress."

Someone sighed.

"And how are we to pay for this grand enterprise?" Viscount Skellhaven asked, not bothering to hide his ill will. "Certain lords and their knights will loot Mallburn Palace of its treasures, while my fighting sailormen and I merely torch the Diddly waterfront. Are we supposed to be content with the spoils of empty warehouses, worm-eaten scows, and burnt-out hulks?"

"Our mission is not to pillage the city," Conrig declared. "It is to seize it and to force the capitulation of Achardus, his state officials, and the powerful Guild of Merchants. This I vow to do. This I *will* do with the aid of you stalwart northerners, who are familiar with mountain terrain and the battle tactics needed for a swift and stealthy assault against an unsuspecting foe. As for your material reward, it will be more than generous. I'll not forget those whose bravery helped cement the Sovereignty of High Blenholme. This I also vow, on the head of Emperor Bazekoy the Great."

Skellhaven's thin lips stretched in a disagreeable smile. "A very impressive oath, Your Grace. Please don't take me wrong. I'm a poor man, only concerned for the welfare of my followers. All too often the Crown has made fine promises to us and then . . ." He shrugged.

"I am not King Olmigon," Conrig said. A few of them drew breath at his lack of respect, but he turned away from Hartrig Skellhaven and let his gaze sweep them all. "The time has come, my friends, for you to decide. Please say—beginning with you, dear Godfather—whether you will join me in an invasion of Didion."

"I will come," said Tanaby Vanguard, "along with one hundred of my knights and thanes."

"And I with forty," said Norval Swanwick. "Plus farriers, cooks, and leeches well able to fight."

"Ramscrest pledges sixty mounted warriors and twenty sumpter-mules well provisioned."

"The Virago of Marley will follow you with a force of eighty mounted men," Zeandrise declared, "plus thirty stout pack-ponies and their armed drivers."

"My festering leg precludes my personal participation," said Conistone, "but I will send my four sons, ten knights of my household, twenty fighting thanes, and five farriers."

The others chimed in their assent one by one, some charged with eagerness and others, like Skellhaven and Holmrangel, with an air of having been coerced, until the number of warriors pledged reached well over four hundred, with a wholly adequate supply train and remounts. The last to speak was Earl Marshal Parlian Beorbrook.

"Your Grace," said he, "I am a cautious man, but not an ignorant one. I've read the Chronicle from beginning to end, the histories of more than a hundred Cathran rulers. But none of them, I think, will be the match of you if you can pull off this mad stunt. I pledge thirty knights, the same number of fighters mounted on sturdy coursers, and fifty mules loaded with goodly fodder for man and beast . . . and I pray I'll live to hail you Sovereign of High Blenholme."

The council of war surged up from their seats and cheered.

Conrig nodded in ironic acknowledgment of the backhanded compliment. "Your agreement to my proposal gladdens my heart, Earl Marshal." He opened the ornate black velvet purse that hung from his belt. "I have here wafers of the most exquisitely flavored pyligosh, which I will share with you all as a token of our new fellowship."

Almost solemnly, he handed out the rare small sweetmeats, each of which was wrapped in a green cloth square and tied with golden cord. "Please eat them now to symbolize our unified resolve—and then let's see what manner of liquid cheer Duke Tanaby has set out for us. I, for one, am now in need of refreshment stronger than wine."

The nobles sprang up from their stools and crowded toward the laden sideboard, leaving only Zeandrise Marley to stand before Conrig, holding her wrapped tidbit. She spoke in a voice that was almost inaudible.

"My prince, do you know why I am called the Virago?"

He smiled. "I was told that when your wealthy young husband died, and you were left childless, a certain uncouth mountain lord came a-wooing. You spurned him, and he returned with an army to press his suit. Whereupon—"

"I rallied the knights and thanes of my barony and whipped the britches off the whoreson. And I defeated another force led by my late husband's saucy cousin, who tried to lay claim to my fiefdom through some trivial point of law. After that, Vanguard gave me the warrior's belt with his own hand, and I've held Marley against all comers for the past twenty-two years. I'm a hard woman, Prince Heritor."

Conrig bowed his head in acknowledgment, still smiling.

"And I think you're a hard man." She held up the green-wrapped sweetmeat. "What would have happened to those who opposed your invasion scheme? Would they have been given wafers wrapped in a different color of cloth—or with cord tied in a special knot?"

He stepped closer to her, and for an instant something flickered in his handsome face. She stood her ground and his ambiguous expression was transformed into a broad grin. He unwrapped his own wafer and bit into it with evident enjoyment. "Absolutely delicious. And much more efficacious against noxious substances than drinking-cups with amethyst talismans. That's just a silly superstition, as any alchymist can tell you. You may ask my brother Stergos, if you doubt me."

Her eyes widened. "So it was the wine."

"Which I partook of, along with the rest of you. The effects of the subtle poison would not be obvious for at least two days, when the unfortunate nay-sayers were well on their journey home. Thus no suspicion would fall upon me or Tanaby Vanguard—who, by the way, knew nothing about my precautionary measures. Earlier, I pressed him to take prisoner anyone who opposed my plan, but he wouldn't agree to it. My godfather is too trusting and chivalrous. But then, he doesn't aspire to be the Sovereign of High Blenholme."

"And such a one must be ruthless?"

"Very." He rested both hands on her shoulders in a gesture that might have passed for affection. "Are you going to tell the others what I did?"

Her worn face remained calm. "No . . . I won't tell them. But I think it would bode well for our future comradeship—and the Sovereignty—if *you* did."

They stared at each other without speaking. Then he took her arm and led her gently toward the waiting table of drinks where the others were gathered. "I'll think about it, my lady. And you won't forget to eat your wafer, will you?"

three

S nudge had sensed the mysterious overseeing presence, too, while carving the joint of roast beef that had been sent to the repository tower for the evening meal of the Heart Companions. Unlike his royal master and the Doctor Arcanorum, he knew he'd probably be able to trace and perhaps even identify the watcher if he could just get to the tower roof and do his search under the open sky.

The apartment where the prince's party had been secreted took up the third and fourth floors of the tower. The third floor, holding the castle's extensive library, was the most attractive, having tall windows and a wide hearth with wood blazing cheerfully, and numbers of cushioned chairs and benches in an open area surrounded by rows of stacks. Conrig and his three closest friends among the Heart Companions—Feribor Blackhorse, Tayman Owlstane, and Sividian Langford—had turned it into their common room during the two days preceding the council of war, while they kept their presence secret from most of the other castle inhabitants. The prince had the chief scribe's office for a bedchamber, and the three young counts slept on cots laid out between the shelves. They used the big central table for eating and drinking and playing at boardgames and dice.

The fourth storey of the tower, just beneath the now-untenanted guardroom that had a door opening onto the roof, was normally used by the duke's controller of accounts, and for document storage. It was low-ceilinged and crowded with coffers of parchment and racks of tax-rolls. Vra-Stergos elected to spend most of his time in a partitioned nook up there, where he had privacy for his arcane studies.

Snudge and the four young armigers serving the prince's Companions and the alchymist also slept in the accounts room, but they were obliged to remain below for most of their waking hours, waiting on the nobles or the prince.

This evening, Snudge and the other boys finished clearing the table after the Companions' supper, gobbled their own, and put the soiled platters and leftovers outside the door for the castle staff to dispose of. Count Tayman, a genial West-leyman of two-and-twenty, challenged the other Companions to a session of picture-dice and called upon two of the armigers to serve them that evening while they gamed.

"Saundar and Belamil will play lute and flageolet," he said, "and keep us well-supplied with refreshments. Mero, Gavlok and Deveron may take their ease after turning down the beds and laying out fresh garb for tomorrow."

"Yes, my lord," the boys chorused. The lucky ones darted off among the bookshelves to open up the beds of the noblemen, which had mattresses of doubled bearskin, silken sheets, and pillows stuffed with eiderdown.

"I'll fix the alchymist's bed while you take your ease at the fire, Gavlok," Snudge volunteered after they had finished, looking for an excuse to go upstairs. "Maybe I'll take a nap before His Grace returns and has need of me."

Stergos's quiet, studious squire gave him a grateful smile. "I thank you, Deveron."

"You're such a kind fellow, stable boy," sneered Mero, who served Count Feribor Blackhorse. "Be damned sure we'll tell Prince Conrig you're lazing away in the sack if you're not down here on the spot when he returns."

The armiger was a burly redheaded youth who had just turned nineteen, nearly as tall as his formidable master. But where Blackhorse was so slyly sadistic that you might pass off his cruelties as unintentional, Mero was a flagrant bully who used his position to terrorize the pages and servitors back at Brent Lodge, the prince's hunting residence, where they had lived for the past month. Mero was usually more circumspect with the armigers of the other Heart Companions and with Gavlok, the bookish lad who served the Doctor Arcanorum, confining himself to verbal assaults. When Conrig had unaccountably chosen Deveron Austrey, his young footman, rather than a nobly born youth as bodyservant on the secret mission to Castle Vanguard, Mero was incensed, as though the presence of a commoner—even one who could read, write, and reckon—in the royal party were a personal affront. He had been imprudent enough to complain to

Count Feribor. The blackened eye he received for his pains was now a muddy yellowish-green. With fine illogic, Mero had sworn to revenge himself on the upstart footman, but a suitable opportunity had not yet presented itself.

Snudge hurried up the iron staircase to the accounts room. He'd have to act quickly on the roof; the alchymist would not be attending the council of war and might return to the tower at any moment. Rummaging in his pack, he found a small roll of cloth containing short lengths of wire of varying thicknesses, cunningly bent, tools he well knew the use of.

The door leading to the guardroom stair was locked, but a brief fiddle with one of the wires caused it to snap open. Snudge bounded up the steps and dashed through an armory crowded with compact defense engines—mangons and ballistas and catapults—along with wicker baskets of rocks, vires, and other missiles, stacked braziers, buckets of charcoal, cauldrons of solidified pitch, and crates of spherical iron bombshells packed with tarnblaze, having lengths of tarry cord protruding through their nozzles. The door opening onto the roof was only latched.

Outside, he saw the sun descending behind jagged black peaks while the snow-covered slopes of Demon Seat glowed pink with lavender shadows. The air was dead calm. Smoke from the castle chimneys and from buildings in the town beyond the outer ward and the curtain wall rose straight in blue-white columns. The first spunkies, like infinitesimal earthbound stars, began to sparkle in a patch of marshy waste ground below the castle's knoll. He heard a dog bark. Someone down in the inner ward cursed a squealing horse. The shrill laughter of women came from the covered colonnade around the castle spring.

Snudge clapped hands over his ears, shut his eyes, and let the wind bear him away.

And immediately found watchers. Not one, but *two!*

Then came the difficult part. He felt himself sinking to his knees, finally flopping prone as the strength drained from his body and empowered his mind. He followed the thread of the first watcher, whose windsign he recognized too well, for hundreds of leagues northward.

The scene seemed hazy, as though obscured by thin gauze, since he viewed it at such a great distance; but the details were clear enough. Snudge seemed to soar over flats of black quicksand exposed at low tide toward a ramshackle castle nestled between crags above a misty estuary. The place was Royal Fenguard, seat of the rulers of Moss. This time there was no blocking cover-spell at the terminus of the trace, as had invariably been the case when he attempted to spy on her previously. Invisible as the wind, he seemed to pass through the bubbly glass of an illuminated window in the tall south tower.

And saw her: Ullanoth sha Linndal, daughter of the Conjure-King, only eighteen years of age but having the imposing presence of one much older. She was standing motionless in the middle of a room crowded with books, alchymical apparatus, and arcane objects of unknown function. On one side of her stood a tall candlestick, but the indistinct object it held was not a candle, although it glowed weakly.

The sorceress wore a flowing gown of leaf-green satin, the skirt and sleeve drapes gold-embroidered in an elaborate pattern of bulrushes. Her long unbound hair, almost luminous in the candlelight, was a strange pale hue—silvery with the kind of faint rosy undertone found in the lining of certain seashells. The narrow face had prominent cheekbones, an elegant long nose, and milk-white skin. Her eyelids were closed to enhance her oversight of Castle Vanguard, their thick dark lashes resting upon her cheeks.

After a time her thread of watching snapped and she opened her eyes. They were large as a doe's and at first appeared to be green, but almost immediately their color changed as the sea does in late evening, becoming slate-grey, and then turning to an uncanny black. She smiled and refreshed herself with a drink from a golden cup, then took down a long cloak of midnight blue that hung from a wall peg. Donning it, she pulled its hood closely over her bright hair. Finally, she pulled something from the bosom of her gown—a small pendant on a chain that shone with the same faint radiance as the object on the candlestick.

At one wall of the room was a peculiar piece of padded furniture that resembled a narrow couch raised on end by means of a frame. It was tilted at a sharp angle and had rails at the side and a footrest to keep one from slipping off. Ullanoth arranged herself upon this and gripped the neck pendant tightly. Her mouth moved in soundless speech as she pronounced some elaborate spell, and even though Snudge could read lips, the words were incomprehensible to him.

He watched in awe. The small pendant in her hand blazed up like some miniature greenish lamp. Its nature was impossible to discern. The princess uttered a deep groan of pain. Her body seemed to shimmer, expand . . . and become two identical cloaked forms: a true body and a Sending, floating in mid-air beside the slanted couch. It was a rare magical talent, far beyond the abilities of the Brothers of Zeth, and Snudge knew of it only through reading occult books that he regularly borrowed—without permission—from the library of the Royal Alchymist back at Cala Palace.

The Sending drifted down until it stood upright, looking perfectly natural. The body on the couch, on the other hand, lay as motionless and pallid as a corpse. After glancing about the chamber, the Sending frowned as if it had forgotten something, then gestured at the tall candlestick with the faintly glowing object atop it. There was a brilliant emerald flash. The interior of Ullanoth's tower vanished from Snudge's oversight, as impenetrable to his scrying as it had always been before this night.

He knew, without knowing how, that the Sending was no longer inside the tower. It was flying on the wind directly toward him like some unseen wraith. But how had she managed to windwatch him when no one else could? He braced himself, too astounded even for terror, expecting her to materialize in front of him there on the roof.

Expecting quick death from a sorceress furious that he had spied on her . . .

But no. She had not been coming at him after all!

He smothered an oath as the Sending soared down into the great hall of Castle Vanguard and disappeared into the heavy shadows at the rear of the musicians' gallery. An instant later Prince Conrig slipped out of the secret passage and began his scrutiny of the diners below him, not knowing Princess Ullanoth was there.

Snudge had windwatched her with Conrig twice before, when she came to Brent Lodge and conversed with the prince and Stergos. The boy had not realized then that her body was a magical simulacrum until she herself spoke casually of the miracle in her conversation with the brothers. After each visit, the double had returned to Fenguard, where it disappeared behind a shielding spell infinitely stronger than the puny sort Snudge himself was capable of spinning. He had never before been able to oversee the Mosslander princess in her home because of that spell.

With the subjects of his viewing now close by, Snudge watched with less effort as the prince was accosted by the cloaked woman. He read his master's lips easily during the ensuing colloquy and wished he could know what the shrouded witch said about Vra-Stergos that caused the prince to blanch in dismay. But all

that it would be awkward to explain their friendship to Duke Tanaby and the earl marshal, since the two of them had never truly met face-to-face.

"And then came the most puzzling thing. His Grace and the lady spoke of *you*, my lord." Snudge hesitated. "The prince said, 'My brother will never tell a lie, even for me.' The lady spoke. Then the prince said, 'He is my brother. I love him.' And his words seemed weighted with anger and fear."

"Damn her!" the doctor whispered, knowing what Ullanoth must have told Conrig. His face twisted like one in pain. "Is there more?"

"Only that His Grace said he would do what was best. Then the Sending left him . . . and so I went in search of the second watcher."

"A second—!"

"Aye, my lord. And one who is apparently far more adept than the lady, for he can perform two magical actions at once. He's hiding somewhere within the castle stables, well-covered by some superior spell so that I was unable to locate him precisely, much less identify him. He watches the council of war."

Stergos uttered a moan. "Oh, God. Oh, God. And I perceived nothing. *Nothing!* What are we going to do?"

"If I may suggest—"

"What?" The doctor's dismay turned to alarm as the boy explained.

"Let me go down through the 'tween-wall passages and see if I can find this fellow. Perhaps he's visible to the naked eye, even though windsight can't scry him. He may be a wild talent . . . just like me! He must be someone in the entourage of one of the lords, for you know the duke didn't allow any casual travelers or other strangers to enter the castle during this secret gathering. Since he's in the stables, he may be disguised as a horse lackey. If he is visible, he could pretend to be drunk or sleeping and no one would suspect what he was doing."

"If he should discover you—" Stergos broke off fearfully. "He must be a talent of great power, Deveron, to exert two magical functions at the same time. Even Ullanoth gave some hint to me of her watching, although I couldn't be sure of her. But not this unknown—working his sorcery practically on top of us! If he's spying on the council, he must be a mortal enemy of our prince. He might not hesitate to kill you."

"He won't realize I'm a danger to him. Not if I just seek him out and give him a casual glance. Just another housecarl without an adept bone in my body."

"It might work," Stergos said grudgingly. It was a sore point to him that Snudge's wild talent was imperceptible to the anointed of his Mystic Order, to say nothing of the fact that the boy was capable of identifying even the smallest modicum of talent in others.

"Shall I go, then? I won't get lost. I've already explored most of the passages on this side of the ward. I did it last night, while you were all asleep. I even made a dark lantern for myself out of an old pewter tankard and a candle."

Stergos sighed. "I might have known . . . Very well. Do your best to find out who the villain is, or who he pretends to be. Be quick about it and don't take any dangerous chances. His Grace and I will decide what to do about him."

"Yes, my lord."

"If only I could watch over you . . ."

But that was impossible. Even though Stergos, like most of the Zeth Brethren, had the ability to scry over short distances, Snudge's wild talent protected him from any sort of magical surveillance, a fact that particularly delighted Prince Conrig at the same time that it dismayed his brother.

"I'll take great care, my lord. Don't worry about me."

"Oh, all right," the doctor grumped. "But if you get into serious trouble, bespeak me at once and I'll do my best to help you."

"Of course, my lord." He bobbed his head and slipped out of the cubicle, leaving Stergos full of misgivings but at a loss to know what else to do.

four

The boy made his way to the area where the armigers had laid their straw-stuffed palliasses. He rummaged in his pack for a moment, then hurried to the opposite side of the tower. Three document presses stood there. The left-hand one had a few ancient crocks of dried-out ink on its lower shelf. Snudge pushed them aside so he could creep in and touch a small stud at the rear of the cabinet, causing a low door to slide soundlessly open. When he was safe inside in the dark he paused for a moment, then struck fire with his talent, lighting the wick of the candle inside his lantern.

It was cleverly made. A fat waxen stub was affixed to the wall of the tankard. Tiny vent holes poked into the base kept the flame burning when the tankard's hinged lid was shut. If the lid was more or less held open by a thumb, a beam shone out. The only problem with the thing was that a section of the handle tended to get uncomfortably hot after a while; he'd wrapped it with a strip of leather, but he still had to watch how he gripped it.

Snudge crept down the constricted spiral stairway and paused for a moment to look through a peephole into the library. The three Companions were dicing and drinking. Count Sividian cursed his luck while the two younger lords cackled and jeered. The four armigers were out of eyeshot. Snudge prayed that none of them had discovered the library's own door into the secret passage, and continued down.

He had a fair distance to go. Castle Vanguard was an enormous place, almost oblong in shape, with a tower at each corner and two more sited midway along the extensive northern and southern wings. The repository tower lay across the ward from the kitchen tower, which overlooked the stable area as well as the brewing and baking buildings. In order to reach the stables unseen, he'd have to traverse half the castle's perimeter, moving through the south wing past the great hall and the southwest tower, then beyond the solar, the west gatehouse, and the chapel, into the northwest tower. From there he would enter the massive north wing, in which the kitchen tower was emplaced. When he emerged at the base of that tower, he'd be forced to abandon the safety of the secret passages and make his way openly to the stables. He was unable to use his talent to hide and simultaneously follow the watcher's trace.

He set out, moving quickly enough through the familiar passages, treading in his own dusty footprints (and those of Stergos and the prince), pausing only for a moment to peep into the solar, where he was amazed to see his royal master pouring wine like a pageboy. Then he came into places he had never been, and several times made wrong turnings. There were no more footprints now save those of the rats. He heard rustling noises now and again, but never caught sight of the creatures.

Inside the gatehouse wall he abruptly came to a dead end in a nook with small unglazed loopholes, full of spiderwebs and bird droppings. The only egress led outside onto a parapet where machicolations fronted the west barbican, above the top of the massive main gate. He cracked the door open and peered cautiously out, then withdrew with a curse. He dared not risk it. It was still bright twilight. Both the northwest and southwest towers were manned by guards, and one or more of the men would be certain to see him crossing. He couldn't muddle the minds of several people well enough to hide himself unless it was full dark. But if he waited until then, the council of war might come to an end and the windwatcher cut off his surveillance.

He nearly gave it up, but almost by accident he pressed the proper stone in the mold-encrusted wall. A slab swung up, and he saw a black tunnel barely large enough for a man to worm through. Dust lay two fingers deep inside.

"Codders!" he whispered in disgust. It looked as though no one had gone that way for a hundred years. Even though he had not yet reached his full growth, he was a well-built youth with broad shoulders. What if he ended up wedged in there like a cork in a bloody bunghole?

Had to try.

A footman, even one serving a prince, owned no such luxury as a kerchief. So he used his small dagger to cut out the fustian lining of his black livery jerkin and wrapped that around his mouth and nose. Then, pushing the lantern ahead of him, he started to wriggle through. His eyes watered fiercely, and as the dust thickened in the meager air he feared he would smother. He pressed on, coming at last to another stone slab. It pivoted easily. He thrust his body through the opening and fell onto the floor of yet another passage, letting loose a huge sneeze. The lantern clattered as he dropped it and its candle went out.

"Shite!" he moaned, and lay still in the dark, first listening and then casting about with his talent to determine whether he had been overheard. When nothing happened he struggled to his feet and felt along the wall until he found one of the interior peepholes. He could see nothing through it, but smelled candlewax and incense. A chapel storage room, no doubt, windowless and deserted.

He giggled. "Lucky again, Snudge!" Found the lantern, rekindled it with his talent, dusted himself down as well as he could, and started off.

Suppertime for the stablehands: chunks of black bread, hot mutton pottage thick with barley and onions and carrots, cannikins of strong brown Vanguard ale, famous in the north country. The duke's men and the grooms and horseknaves of the visiting nobles were gathered together around a flaming brazier in the small arcade between the smithy and the saddlery, cursing the kitchenboys for ladling portions deemed too small and loudly demanding more ale when the first barrel was emptied.

Snudge dodged past that well-lit area into a shadowed corridor beside the granary and hay-store, where he came upon a stack of iron-bound wooden buckets. He had turned his mutilated jerkin inside out to hide the prince's silver stallion blazon, and no one would think to question a scruffy waterbearer wandering about. He took a bucket and slouched openly to the spring-shelter out in the midst of the ward, dipped up a small amount of water from the basin, and headed into the area of the stables where common-born visitors were lodged at night. It was there that he believed the windwatcher was lurking. Almost immediately he met two head grooms in Marley livery, who eyed him with disdain.

"You, knave!" called one of them. "Where do the upper servants dine?"

Snudge bobbed his head humbly. "In the kitchens, messire. Straight past the smithy yard and to your left, within the middle tower."

They strode off without another word, leaving Snudge with his heart pounding. He slipped into an alcove hung with coils of rope, put down the bucket, and closed his eyes to search closely.

Perhaps down that corridor to the right . . . His mind's eye could perceive no human form in any of the chambers, but there seemed to be a strange blur among the packsacks and fardels and other baggage belonging to some lord's train. The boy concentrated his oversight on the mundane objects near the blur. The room was dark, but he was finally able to make out a heraldic device stamped on a small leather coffer—a lymphad with the sail furled and oars over the side, flying a death's-head flag: the arms of House Skellhaven.

Ha! Had the spy had come in from the east coast, with or without the knowledge of the piratical viscount?

An idea suggested itself. Since there was small likelihood that the watcher would recognize his own talent—not even Vra-Kilian, the Royal Alchymist, had managed to do that—Snudge decided to blunder into the room like an oafish servitor and hope for the best. The water provided a suitable excuse. Perhaps the spy would be so engrossed in his work that he wouldn't even notice an intruder.

Snudge ignited his improvised dark-lantern, which he had hung from his belt like an ordinary tankard, and hoisted the bucket. The first dormitorium, with its door wide open, was untenanted. So was the second. The third chamber was closed but not locked, and when Snudge opened the door and held high the lantern he stopped short in astonishment.

"Futter me blind!" he whispered, almost letting the bucket fall to the floor.

At the far end of the dark, shuttered room, which was strewn with baggage, the wavering shadow of a human form was dimly visible on the wall.

A shadow without a body to project it.

Open-mouthed, Snudge advanced a few steps, sweeping the lantern from side to side. The movement of the light caused the shadow to change shape. "Who's there?" he cried, without thinking.

"Why, it's only me, laddie—Jasiko, a man of Lord Skellhaven's! Who might you be?" The voice was like dry oak leaves crushed underfoot.

The windwatcher had appeared in the blink of an eye, and Snudge was aware of an insistent mental whisper telling him he had only imagined the bodiless shadow. The magicker was mind-mashing him!

He was a wiry little old fellow bald as an egg, with a deeply lined face, as though he had experienced great pain. He wore the dirty white pantaloons, waxed leather jacket, and folded high boots of a sailor. Around his neck hung a short gold chain with a square stone pendant that glowed as faintly as foxfire. The sorcerer's eyes were golden-orange, like an eagle-owl's, and the boy had never seen their like in a human head. Within them shone the glint of talent, the same fugitive spark perceptible to him in the gaze of anyone possessed of arcane ability: easy to discern in Stergos and the other alchymists and windvoices of his acquaintance, more elusive but nonetheless a tell-tale sign in the eyes of certain others, such as Prince Heritor Conrig Wincantor.

"I'm . . . Oddie, the scullion," Snudge said.

"What do you want?"

The boy lifted the bucket. "Here's w-water for washing. I'll just put it here and go."

The spy started toward Snudge, an ingratiating smile spreading his furrowed lips. His teeth were decayed brown stumps. The pupils of his amazing eyes expanded until all trace of their fiery color had been obliterated by blackness.

"Bide a moment, lad. I'll take the bucket." He held out a hand, striding quickly through the scattered chests and packs of Skellhaven's retainers.

Snudge felt a terrifying splinter of ice prick his throat. He cried, "Oh!"

"Don't be afraid." The sorcerer spoke in a wheedling tone. His eyes had become gleaming jet beads, enormous and compelling. Magic stiffened Snudge's tongue and rendered him mute. He felt his fingers freeze. A wave of cold began creeping up his arms. His feet tingled painfully, then lost feeling and seemed rooted to the floor. Snudge's mind screamed:

Damn you! You won't! You won't do that to me!

He drew arcane power from somewhere, fending off frigid paralysis, and flung the iron-bound bucket overhand, dealing the spy a glancing blow on the side of his head. The man blinked, breaking the spell of encroaching ice for a moment, but kept coming. The fatal cold took hold of Snudge again, and he hit his adversary in the face with the hot lantern, which promptly went out. The sorcerer tottered and crashed over backwards onto the wet, slippery stones, visible only because of the faint gleam of his amulet. Snudge leapt on top of him, using his fists. Neither of them uttered a sound.

The small man struggled like a mad thing in the dark, exerting uncanny strength. Straddling his adversary's torso, Snudge felt sinewy fingers seize his neck. Thumbs with nails like steel pincers dug in on each side of his voicebox, bringing pain and roaring dizziness and a red fog pulsing behind his eyes. He couldn't breathe. His pummeling fists had no effect. He fumbled desperately at his waist, found his little dagger, and grasped it in both hands as he felt death closing in on him. Time for one strike—only one—and instinct or something else taught him the appropriate place to drive in the blade, the sure route to the sorcerer's heart. He knew how to thrust up under the breastbone, bury the dagger to its hilt, and twist . . .

Then came an abrupt relaxation of those claw-like hands, the melting of the muscle-fettering ice whose power he had kept at bay for a few critical seconds.

The eerie glow of the sorcerer's pendant showed Snudge a face contorted with incredulous rage. His heart torn and stilled, the spy bucked upward in a last spasm of agony as all thinking ground inexorably to a halt. There was a rattling exhalation of breath, followed by a blare of windspeech:

Beynor!

A call?

How did the boy do it? How? How? How?

Each soundless demand was fainter than the last, until there was only silence on the wind. The furious glint of talent in the sorcerer's eyes dwindled to blank nullity and his soul fled to an inaccessible place, leaving only dead flesh and bones behind.

The glow of his pendant winked out.

Snudge took a shuddering breath. For a time be did nothing but draw in sweet air, resisting a powerful urge to spew up his supper. Then he fumbled for the fallen lantern, found and lit it, and stared in wonder at his handiwork.

A human being once alive was slain by him, as dead as a crushed ant or an arrow-shot stag or a chicken with its neck wrung. He felt no remorse, no fear, no sense of relief at escaping whatever perilous enchantment had threatened him— only an empty numbness. Almost without thought he pulled out his blade, wiped it on the wad of torn fustian lining he had crammed into his belt-wallet, and sheathed it. Blood oozed forth from the small wound, not as much as he would have expected. It slowly soaked the man's linen shirt, but was kept from leaking onto the floor by the waxed leather jacket.

The pendant on the sorcerer's breast had become a square of ordinary translucent stone, blue-white in color, curiously carved.

A moonstone sigil.

Snudge had read of such a thing in one of the books purloined from Vra-Kilian back at Cala Palace. Sigils were rare artifacts of the Salka monsters, having conjured into them the power of the Beaconfolk. The only human beings possessing them were members of Moss's Glaumerie Guild, a league of master sorcerers. A sigil could generate a single magical function. This one had obviously produced the strong covering spell of invisibility, but one that could be penetrated by the wearer's windsight, as ordinary couverture could not.

After a moment's hesitation Snudge unfastened the gold chain, slipped off the sigil, and thrust the thing into his wallet. The valuable chain he replaced on the dead man's neck, buttoning his shirt and jacket over it.

Snudge was not *that* kind of thief.

He took the body by the arms and dragged it over the water-splashed floor into a corner. A few pallets of stuffed sacking had already been laid out as beds for Skellhaven's men. He arranged the corpse in a fetal curl on one of them, face to the wall as though sleeping, then pulled off the seaboots and set them neatly to one side. He used the wad of fustian to mop up the spilled water as well as he could. Perhaps the floor would dry before anyone else came. He put the sodden cloth into the bucket.

Now I must search, he thought, strangely calm, to see whether any talented person heard the sorcerer's death-cry.

Shutting his eyes, he became one with the wind again, seeking any trace of awareness, any thin strand of oversight focused on the dead man, exploring nearby first, then outside the castle, and finally sweeping along a narrow path three hundred leagues northward to Royal Fenguard. The effort drenched him with sweat and weakened his muscles so that he almost collapsed. But no magical adept watched from afar, and no ordinary person had heard the brief commotion in the stable and started out to investigate its source.

Deveron Austrey, mankiller, opened his eyes. After his strength returned, he stepped into the dim corridor and used the lantern to examine his clothing, making certain there was no trace of blood. Then he started back to the repository tower, moving slowly like one half-asleep, taking the bucket with him until he could abandon it safely inside the secret passage.

five

Prince conrig and Vra-Stergos sat together in a dark part of the ducal library sectioned off by tall stacks. The Companions' drunken picture-dice game was still proceeding noisily out in the middle of the great round room. The armiger named Saundar Kersey played the lute while Belamil Langsands sang "Brown-Eyed Wenches of Garveytown" in a sweet young tenor. A clock-candle burning atop a nearby reader's carrel indicated that the ninth hour after noon was three-quarters past. Conrig had only just returned to the tower from the solar after the council of war ended. He described to his brother what had transpired at the meeting.

Stergos listened without comment, his brow furrowed and his hands clasped tightly in his lap. When the prince finished, the alchemist continued to sit without speaking.

"Don't you have anything to say, Gossy?" Conrig was puzzled. "The great enterprise is on! What's wrong?"

Stergos made his decision. "Con . . . you know that I would never do anything to harm you, or to endanger your great dream of Sovereignty."

The prince stiffened. "Go on."

"Young Deveron perceived someone windwatching us. Without my permission, he followed the trace to its source and discovered Princess Ullanoth overseeing Castle Vanguard. He identified her positively. She was not protected by any shielding spell."

"We knew she had to be the one," Conrig said impatiently. "What does it matter, since she knows our plans already?"

Stergos was staring miserably at his hands. "Deveron saw the princess fashion a Sending. He saw it travel here and meet you in the musicians' gallery, and he read your lips as you conversed with it. The boy told me of this, unaware that a Sending can appear only to the talented."

"So." Conrig met his brother's tear-filled eyes. "Now you know."

"What I have suspected but tried to ignore, not being willing to accept the truth. You have the talent, but not in its full power, or Vra-Kilian would have identified it in you as he did in me. How Ullanoth discovered your secret, I have no idea."

"She might have spied on me and caught me doing something . . . imprudent." Conrig gave a great sigh of resignation. "When Snudge innocently found me out four years ago, I considered killing him, but decided he was too valuable to waste— a wild talent unknown to the Brethren: to Vra-Kilian, damn his prying! From time to time, when we were alone, the boy would attempt to teach me magical tricks. I mastered a few: moving small objects a few inches, kindling a flame without a tarn-stick. Ulla might have seen me do such a thing. Or perhaps the magic of the Beacon-folk guided her. She Sent herself to me many times and helped me formulate the scheme of Sovereignty." He shook his head. "I never thought to ask her how she knew of my talent. I was bedazzled by her cleverness, by the prospect of being able to invade Didion with her assistance." And by her beauty . . .

The brothers sat without speaking for some minutes. The squire finished singing his bawdy ballad and began a more plaintive air, this time accompanied by another youth playing the flageolet.

"Vra-Kilian bespoke me not half an hour ago with unsettling news about the invasion," Stergos finally said. "I'll tell you about that in a moment. But first I must assure you with all my heart that I will never betray your secret. Never! Poor Tancoron and our sisters are barred from the throne by Cathran law. The sons of Father's older sister Jalmaire stand next in the succession, so if you were ineligible, the next king would be our wastrel cousin, Duke Shiantil Blackhorse."

Conrig's laugh was bleak. "Shi-Shi—and what a calamity for Cathra he'd be! At least his younger brother Feribor is a stout-hearted warrior and a loyal Heart Companion. But that lummox Shi-Shi cares for nothing but swiving and drinking and gambling. He probably can't even *spell* Sovereignty . . . The fool would end up as Vra-Kilian's puppet. The Royal Alchymist is not happy at the prospect of losing political power when Father dies."

"No," Stergos agreed.

Conrig said softly, "Gossy, what would you do if Uncle Vra-Kilian or another Brother of Zeth in authority over you should ask you the dread question about me under oath?"

"I would die rather than admit your talent," Stergos said without hesitation. "As a matter of fact, since Deveron confirmed my worst fears about you, I've been trying to decide which poison to carry with me on a contingency basis. Something quickly lethal but not too agonizing." He shrugged. "I do hate pain."

Conrig threw his arms around the doctor. "Forget poison, dear brother! Just tell me if Kilian dares ask about me, and I'll whack off his perfidious, self-righteous head."

"Oh, no!" Stergos was genuinely horrified. "That would be sacrilege!"

"Let me worry about impudent wizards, Gossy. In the new Sovereignty, I'll decree that talent will *not* be a bar to kingship, and we'll have nothing to fear from the likes of Vra-Kilian. Now! You said that he bespoke you earlier."

"Yes. The king has learned about your scheme to invade Didion with the aid of the northland lords. The Lord Chancellor revealed it to him."

Conrig stifled a curse. "Falmire—that faithless old weasel! Why did I ever trust him?"

"Father ordered Vra-Kilian to demand of you how the council went, which lords have agreed to support your venture, if any, and all details of your strategy. Con . . . Vra-Kilian also told me that our father remains gravely ill. The Tarnian shaman summoned by your wife greatly eased his pain, but could do naught to heal the underlying disability."

"But the king is not approaching the brink of death?"

"Vra-Kilian believes he is not, but the barbarian healer thinks otherwise."

"I dare not tell Father of our plans via your windvoice. God knows what he would do with the intelligence. He might very well forbid the invasion outright, misunderstanding the role Ullanoth would play. I must be there in person to persuade him that she is a true friend to Cathra . . . Gossy, I want you to bespeak Kilian immediately and say that matters are not firmly settled here. That's the truth, for we intend to work out details of organization and logistics at another meeting tomorrow. Say that I'll set out for Cala within a day and inform our father with my own lips how the council went."

"But if the Royal Alchymist presses me—I can't lie. I *do* know what was decided at the council."

Conrig took hold of his brother's shoulders and fixed him with a gaze of steel. "Tell Kilian I forbade you to talk about the matter to any soul save our father the king. Tell him you swore a solemn oath to me. *And now do it!*"

Stergos's round face had gone greasy with perspiration in the candlelight, and he clutched his gammadion amulet of Saint Zeth with a frantic hand. "I swear it! I swear to tell no one about the council of war."

"Gossy, be strong," The prince eased his grip, and his voice became both earnest and compelling. "I know how Vra-Kilian has overawed both of us since childhood—you, especially, because of your mystical vocation. But we are no longer boys to be cowed by the threats and blusterings of our mother's brother. One day soon, I'll be king and you'll be my Royal Alchymist, while Kilian will be banished to Zeth Abbey and spend his days conjuring worms off its rose bushes."

The young doctor's eyes widened. "I? The Royal Alchymist? Brother, do you mean it truly?" Plainly, the amazing notion had never occurred to him.

"Of course I mean it," said Conrig, chuckling softly. "Who else could serve me better in arcane matters? And now you must go to your sanctum upstairs and windspeak our former nemesis with no more ado, while I have a word with our godfather about tomorrow's activities."

The prince would have risen from his seat, but Stergos said, "Wait! I have other important news to impart." Then, haltingly, he told of Snudge's further magical researches and the boy's deadly encounter with the spy in the stables. "Deveron returned over an hour ago. He's up in the accounts room now, keeping windwatch on the corpse as I bade him."

"So the body has not yet been found?" Conrig asked grimly.

"Nay, unless it happened after I left Deveron. Numbers of Skellhaven's carls have taken to their beds since the deed was done, but none seemed to have noticed that anything was wrong with their comrade. The lad was careful to arrange the dead sorcerer in an attitude of sleep. Fortunately, the man did not soil himself as he expired, and there was little blood."

"Hmm. We'll have to find a way to get the body out of there before dawn. Our godfather could manage it. Some of his trusted men could pretend the fellow was wanted for some transgression and haul him away. If it was done cleverly, I think few of the aroused sleepers would be aware that the prisoner was no longer alive . . . Would the corpse have passed already into rigor mortis?"

"Probably not completely. He could be dragged easily, as if drunk."

The prince nodded, his face troubled. "It's going to be sticky, dealing with Skellhaven. He could be entirely innocent in this matter, and I *need* him for the invasion. But his castle lies near the border, and he has longstanding grievances against the Crown. If he's sold out to Didion . . . Curse it! It's quite possible that the dead sorcerer was one of those Glaumerie Guild members Ullanoth told me of, who accompanied the two Didionite princes and Prince Beynor of Moss on a voyage south from Holt Mallburn." He gave Stergos a hurried account of the presumed reason for that trip, adding, "The ship could have put in stealthily near Skellhaven, dropping the spy off, and he might have contrived to join the viscount's party as it rode to Castle Vanguard."

The alchymist said, "You realize this presupposes Prince Beynor knew in advance of your council of war."

"Another ugly little mystery! Damn all magic! Who would have thought that a Mosslander wizard would ally himself with Didion?"

The doctor permitted himself a rueful smile. "Who would have thought that a Mosslander witch would ally herself with Cathra?"

The prince flung out his hands, conceding the point. "Yes, you're right, of course. But it's done, and without her help the invasion can't proceed . . . What we must determine, if it's possible, is whether or not the man Snudge killed was able to pass on crucial details of our council of war to his master before he died."

"Perhaps not. According to Deveron, the spy was still windwatching when the lad entered the sleeping chamber. You know that a magical practitioner may perform only one operation at a time. Deveron insists that he perceived only those windspoken words that I related to you—the name Beynor, and the question "How did the boy do that?" I believe the man was astonished that a mere lad, apparently untalented, could have known he was spying with arcane powers. Then he died, saying no more. Deveron detected no other watcher, and he—he is superior to anyone I know in that particular talent."

"Yes. But perhaps the sorcerer windspoke Beynor earlier, before Snudge arrived."

"I think it unlikely. The man would not have wanted to miss anything transpiring in the council of war, and lip-reading requires great concentration. I believe he would wait until the council ended before sending news of the outcome to his master. Also, I don't think Beynor would attempt to scry us himself, knowing his agent was on the spot and able to do it with so much more efficiency.

Watching from a great distance is very taxing, if done for more than a few minutes at a time. Most persons of talent, including myself, cannot manage it at all."

"Well, we must pray our secret is safe, Gossy." The prince rose. "I must go to Duke Tanaby now. I'll take Snudge with me. You retire to your place above and bespeak Kilian. If you are able, also do a search from time to time to determine whether Beynor or any other magicker save Ullanoth is overseeing us."

Stergos sighed. "I'll do my very best, but you'd better have the boy search, too. He's so much better at it than I." He went out into the central room of the library, where the gaming was noiser than ever, nearly drowning out the two armigers singing "Strawberry Lips."

So now there are three who know I have the talent, Conrig thought, staring at the flame of the clock-candle. I suppose I'm safe enough for now. All of them have strong reasons to keep the secret. But the possibility of eventual betrayal remains.

Which one, I wonder, is most likely to give me away—my beloved brother, the conniving Mosslander princess, or the stable boy who owes his life to me?

six

Snudge had anticipated the prince's command to search for other wind-watchers. Sent down from the accounts room by Stergos, he reassured Conrig that he had detected no magical surveillance of the castle. The dead body was also undisturbed.

"But I didn't mean to kill him, Your Grace. The fellow gave me no choice. He—"

"Your rash action could have very grave consequences," the prince said sternly, cutting off the boy's excuses. "I'm afraid you can no longer serve as my fourth footman."

"Oh," said Snudge. His face had gone dull. "Am I to be sent back to the stables, then?"

Conrig's eyes were twinkling. "On the contrary. You are to be made an armiger. Since you've proved yourself my loyal man in armed combat, shedding enemy blood on my behalf, I have no other choice. It'll mean a great deal of tedious practice with weaponry, and learning music and other gentle arts you might think are a waste of time, but that's the way it goes if you want your knight's belt at twenty. You'll also have to think up a suitable blazon for yourself. Perhaps an howlet or a bat or some other furtive creature. A rat wouldn't be quite the thing."

Snudge's features were transfigured by joy. "Your Grace, how can I thank you—"

"Enough. We'll talk about it later and think up a plausible reason for you to've stopped the Mossy bastard's heart. But follow me now. There's still work to do tonight."

The two of them set out openly for the duke's private apartments adjacent to the southeast tower, there being no longer any reason to keep the prince's presence in the castle a secret.

"You look a bit grubby," Conrig remarked, as they hurried through the echoing corridors. Most of the castle had already retired. "And why aren't you wearing your livery jerkin?"

Snudge explained about ripping out the coat's lining and worming through the dusty tunnel. "I didn't think you'd want me looking like a tatterdemalion when we visited the duke, so I put on my second-best."

"And how did you know we'd visit the duke?" asked the prince sharply. "Were you eavesdropping on Stergos and me?"

The boy managed an apologetic grin. "Only to be sure the Doctor Arcanorum gave you a complete account of my adventure."

"Rascal!" But the prince was smiling, too. "And did he leave anything out?"

"Only this," Snudge said, pulling the sigil out of his belt-wallet. The translucent stone caught the torchlight glow, but there was no sign of the uncanny internal luminescence. "I didn't tell my lord Stergos that the sorcerer used this amulet to make himself completely invisible—and imperceptible to arcane viewers, including me. I located him by following the thread of his windwatching. This thing enabled him to watch even though he was hidden. With it, he could perform more than one magical action at a time."

"What the devil is it?" They stopped and the prince examined the moonstone closely.

"A rare kind of magical tool. I read about them in a book that I . . . borrowed from the Alchymical Library back at Cala Palace." He replaced the sigil in his wallet.

"Stole, more likely," the prince growled. "Why didn't you hand the thing over to Stergos? I should think he'd want to study it."

"I believe he would have destroyed it, rather than try to find out how it worked. It's a thing empowered by the Beaconfolk, called a sigil."

"Bazekoy's Ballocks! You young lunatic—throw it down a jakes-hole before it does us a mischief!"

"It's dead, Your Grace," Snudge reassured him. "At least for the moment. While it functioned, it shone with a weird light, which vanished when the spy who owned it died. When we return to Cala Palace to prepare for the invasion, I'll search through more of Vra-Kilian's books. Perhaps I'll discover the sigil's secret."

"It takes power from the Beaconfolk! You don't dare use it. You must get rid of it!"

"But think of the opportunity that may then be lost to us." The young voice was cool and persuasive, for all that Snudge's eyes were dark-rimmed and his face sallow and oddly blotched, as though with some illness. "The Lady Ullanoth doesn't hesitate to command the Coldlight Army, knowing the danger. I swear to you that I'll only study the thing, not attempt to use it. But if you insist that I throw it away, of course I'll obey."

"Well . . ."

"One day we may need the sigil. Trust me."

"Trust! That's what *she* always says!"

"But I have only our best interests at heart, Your Grace, while the Lady of Moss . . ." He trailed off.

"Out of the lips of babes," the prince muttered. "Very well. Keep the cursèd thing. But you'll have to risk pilfering Vra-Kilian's magic books yourself. No way dare I command my basilisk uncle to lend them out, even to me."

"Yes, Your Grace."

"And keep your mouth shut when we're in Vanguard's chambers, unless I invite you to speak."

"Yes, Your Grace."

They continued on to the ducal apartments. Two guards were posted outside, who saluted as the prince and the boy approached.

Conrig said, "Tell my lord duke I would speak with him."

"At once, Your Grace." One of the guards went inside and returned almost immediately. "Please enter."

Tanaby Vanguard wasn't alone in the sitting room. Earl Marshal Parlian Beorbrook sat drinking with his old friend at the fire. An unrolled parchment map of the Dextral Mountains lay on a low table between them, held open by a decanter of ardent spirits, a silver bootjack, a heavy jeweled dagger, and a candlestick.

"Welcome, Your Grace," Beorbrook said, with a certain ironic attitude. "We were just about to invite you to join us."

"To query me about Lady Ullanoth," the prince said equably.

Beorbrook glanced at Snudge. "Perhaps the lad should wait outside."

"Deveron is my man, and he stays."

The earl marshal hoisted his black brows. "Does he indeed!"

Snudge bowed and retreated to a bench in the shadows. Only the small fire and the candle on the table lit the room.

The duke lifted the decanter. "Will you join us in a wee noggin, Godson?"

"Gladly." Conrig drew out his cup, sipped the fiery liquor, and said, "Much better than Stippenese wine! Did both of you eat your wafers?"

They nodded. Beorbrook's smile was now openly wicked. "Clever trick, with the poison. But I think Skellhaven was the only dubious one in the pack."

"You guessed?" the prince asked.

"I'm the futterin' earl marshal. I'm supposed to be sharp. Made certain that all of them munched up the antidote goodie, too. Your blockhead godfather, here, was going to save his and give it to the duchess. Dear Monda has a sweet tooth."

The prince paled. "Saint Zeth! I never thought—"

Vanguard waved a hand. "Let it be. We're all playing a dangerous game . . . And speaking of games, I think you'd better tell us how you made the acquaintance of Lady Ullanoth."

"In a moment, Godfather. But first, I immediately require three strong men, well armed, whose loyalty and discretion you trust absolutely."

"Any of my household knights will serve," Vanguard said. "What's going on?"

"There's a dead man in the stables, lying in a far corner of the dormitorium where Viscount Skellhaven's lackeys are bedded down. The body must be taken away at once and brought to a prison cell or some other secure place, where Skellhaven will be asked to identify him and explain his presence here. The man was both a magicker and a spy, scried out by my brother Vra-Stergos as we held our council of war."

"God's Breath!" exclaimed the duke. "This intruder oversaw us and read our lips?"

"Apparently. As an ordained Brother avowed to peace, Stergos did the only thing he could think of, sending young Deveron to confront the villain. There was a struggle, and the spy was killed."

"By your *serving boy?*" The earl marshal shot an incredulous look at Snudge, who sat expressionless.

"He is more than that, my lord. As I said, Deveron is my trusted man." To the duke: "Godfather, the matter is urgent."

Vanguard went to the door and told the guards, "Summon Sir Myndon, Sir Tiralos, and Sir Naberig. Be quick."

When he returned, he asked permission of the prince to question Snudge, and so did the earl marshal. But the boy only confirmed what Conrig had said, adding that he had made his way to the stables through the secret passages, which the Doctor Arcanorum had sketched out for him from childhood memories.

"But—weren't you afraid to confront a sorcerer?" Beorbrook asked.

"We don't know that he was one, Earl Marshal," Snudge dissembled. "More likely he was just a wind practitioner particularly adept at scrying. A skinny little fellow, but he came at me like a wildcat. I clouted him with a bucket, and then we fought, and he ended up stabbed."

Beorbrook grunted. "Too bad. It would have been useful to question him. As it is, we'll make do with Skellhaven, as His Grace suggested. Go back to your seat, lad." He turned to the prince with hooded eyes. "This is a serious development, and we can only hope that the invasion hasn't been betrayed. Could this fellow have been an agent of the Conjure-Princess?"

"Hardly," said Conrig. "Why should she bother, when she herself helped draw up the plan of action? In my opinion, he came from Ullanoth's younger brother Beynor, who knows she covets the throne of Moss. According to their laws, the reigning monarch may appoint his or her successor. Thus far, King Linndal favors the son, whose arcane powers are supposedly stronger than those of his sister. This is why Ullanoth decided to make her bargain with me." He paused, then plunged into the lie. "As to how she and I first met, it happened in Thunder Moon, a few weeks after the murder of the delegation to Didion. Stergos and I were taking our ease in a stone pavilion at Brent Lodge after a boar hunt, looking out at a great storm approaching from across the lake. Suddenly the Lady Ullanoth appeared before us in the form of a Sending."

"That's a kind of living ghost, is it?" the earl marshal asked.

"Not really. The apparition is quite solid. To Send requires extraordinary talent and strength, such as none of our own alchymists possess." He lifted his shoulders and smiled. "My brother explained the process, but I have forgotten the details. The lady proposed an alliance, and we discussed the matter at great length while the storm raged around us."

"This was your only meeting?" Vanguard asked.

"Nay. She came again, and we refined the scheme and discussed every aspect of the invasion, and agreed on the terms of her benefice and guerdon should the venture succeed. She even helped to select the nobles I would invite to participate in the enterprise, including Skellhaven."

There was a loud knocking at the door. The prince said, "May I take the liberty of instructing your knights, Godfather? I've worked out a way the body might be removed without raising suspicion among the others in the dormitorium."

"Go ahead," said the duke. When the prince went to the door and was out of hearing, Vanguard spoke to Beorbrook in a low voice. "What do you think, Parli?"

"Disturbing, this Beynor knowing about the council of war. Makes you wonder if Ullanoth has other fish to fry. We'll have to talk to the doctor, but I reckon he'll back up his brother's judgment."

Both of them had completely forgotten Snudge, sitting motionless in the darkened room.

"The two princes were close as lads," the duke recalled. "Young Con always the cleverest, knowing what he wanted and often not scrupling at how he got it."

"I'll say! That damned wine . . ."

"Aye. But that ploy might have been my own fault. I refused to detain any nobles who opposed the invasion."

"And now it's on, for better or worse, and maybe compromised already. Bloody hell."

"Well, we still have the option of turning back at Breakneck Pass," the duke said. "I daresay the witch Ullanoth will keep a close magical eye on events in Didion over the next five weeks. She'll know if we're expected by the foe, and give us warning."

"If it suits her," the earl marshal said cynically. He fell silent as the prince returned.

"I told them to bring the covered body to the gatehouse armory," Conrig said. "Let's fetch Lord Skellhaven and have a look at it."

"I've never clapped eyes on the wanker in my life," said the seagoing viscount. "Look at him. Just another underdeck swabbie." He bent forward suddenly and spread open the body's blood-stiffened shirt, where a yellow gleam had shone momentarily in the torchlight. "Booger me! What kind of lackey wears a heavy golden neckchain like this?"

Vanguard and Beorbrook exchanged glances. If Skellhaven did know the identity of the spy, would he have called attention to the betraying chain?

The viscount unfastened the gold from around the corpse's neck and held it closer to the armory's sputtering wall torch. "I'll tell you something about this bauble, Your Grace. It's Mossbelly-made. Nobody else uses twisted-wire links like these, and the thing's worth a pretty penny."

Conrig said, "My lord, did anything unusual take place before you set out to Castle Vanguard, or on the journey?"

"Hmm. We had a problem at one inn a day's journey from here. A dozen or so of the lads got royal gut-aches after eating rabbit pies that'd turned. They moped and moaned and browned the hedgerows all the next day riding into Castle Vanguard. Some of 'em still feel a mite seedy."

Conrig addressed the duke and earl marshal. "My brother Stergos has told me that when a man is ill, he is more susceptible to the spells of a magicker. Perhaps this fellow"—he tapped a dead shoulder—"did away with one of your retainers and took on his identity."

"It's possible," said Skellhaven. "Those few who weren't sick were in a rare kerfuffle for doing all the extra work and might not have noticed a clever stranger. I sure as hell didn't."

"We'd like to believe that." Conrig's face was carefully neutral.

The nautical lord's eyes blazed. "Huh! So you think I might be in league with Didion, do you, Your Grace? Well, you're wrong! I hate the whoresons and their fancy ships that sail rings around our own while the Diddlies raid our coastal settlements and rape our women. And now that the Wolf's Breath's laid the scum low, I say let's drag 'em kicking and screaming into the Sovereignty! Civilize Didion once and for all. If you don't trust me to join your invasion, so be it. But you'll be losing the services of some of the best fighters in the north country."

The prince said, "Ride with our force, Hartrig Skellhaven, and welcome."

The viscount gave a curt nod. "Can I keep the gold chain?"

Conrig and Snudge returned to the darkened library just as the nightwatch called the midnight hour. The great room had grown cold and the fire burned low. Moonlight shone through one of the long windows. The three Heart Companions were snoring among the stacks and the armigers had disappeared upstairs.

"Go to your own bed now, Snudge," whispered the prince. "I'll disrobe by myself. You've done well this day and I won't forget it. You're looking rather ill. If you think you might suffer bad dreams over the killing, take a good tot of spirits for a nightcap."

"Thank you, Your Grace. Do you think I should watch Lord Skellhaven to be sure—"

"I believe he's an honest man, by his own lights. Don't worry about him. And for heaven's sake, don't strain yourself with any more windwatching tonight."

"The body—"

"The duke will see to it. We'll say the man died of virulent colic brought on by the dicky rabbit pie. Off you go, now."

The prince entered his improvised sleeping chamber. The great bed with its brocaded tester and coverlet had to have been disassembled and brought in piece by piece, for it nearly filled the entire scribe's office. There were tarnsticks on a sidetable beside the candle and he struck one. The thing flared, then died. Damp, probably. Conrig cursed and scratched another against the wood of the table. When it also refused to light, he used his talent to ignite the wick, closed the door, and removed a silver flask from his trussing coffer. He tossed back a hearty swig of malt liquor and sat down on a stool to pull off his boots—

Froze as he felt the presence, smelled the warm green scent of vetiver.

The bed hangings parted, and a lovely narrow face peered out. Her eyes shone like green jade, and her long wavy hair was the color of pearls, covering her bare breasts like a silken shift.

"You!" he exclaimed, starting to his feet. "Were—were you watching again?"

Smiling, she put up a warning finger. "Hush. We don't want to disturb the others, my prince. I saw you with Vanguard and Beorbrook and Skellhaven, but I did not eavesdrop, for I cannot do lip-reading. My lips are fashioned for other purposes."

"Great God, lady—!"

She had left the bed, naked as a fish, and was unfastening his doublet, easing it off, opening his shirt. "All has gone perfectly, hasn't it? And now you shall tell me everything and then claim your reward." She opened her arms and the veil of shining hair fell to each side. "I assure you that my Sending enjoys every attribute of my true self."

The prince felt the blood rising within him. He had to force the words from his throat. "I—I am a married man, and faithful to my vows."

A laugh, sweetly scornful. "Your sharp-spoken Tarnian wife has given you no children during your six years of marriage, and for some time you have secretly despised her."

"That's not true!"

"You have even considered putting her aside, now that the alliance with Tarn is no longer crucial to Cathran state policy."

"How did you know—"

"I know so many things about you." She embraced him. Her mouth was hot and tasted of exotic honey. "Are you afraid of me, Conrig Wincantor?"

"No," he lied, and crushed her to him, returning the kiss.

Snudge lay on his pallet in the room above. He had drunk a fair amount of ardent spirits and his talent was extinct as a result, useless as a blown-out taper. But his mind's eye still saw a wrathful face, a wide-open mouth full of rotten teeth, ferocious magic glittering in jet-black eyes. He sensed his own doom approaching, cloaked in paralyzing frost, and his windvoice screamed.

Damn you! You won't! You won't do that to me!

His dagger vibrated with the last drumbeat throb of a stricken human heart. He heard the frenzied windcry—*Beynor!*—and those eyes bright with dreadful life turned flat and dull and dead, only to open again and threaten and freeze and die once more.

He prayed for sleep, but it would not come.

seven

The king had already closed his eyes when Vra-Kilian Blackhorse came into the royal bedchamber in Cala Palace, scowling like the wrath of God, and commanded everyone to withdraw. The hovering courtiers and Princess Maudrayne and her red-bearded barbarian shaman went out obediently, but Queen Cataldise had no fear of her imperious older brother and refused to budge.

"I won't have you upsetting the King's Grace, Kilian," she said, gentle but inexorable. "He has just taken a sleeping draft. Any news of our troublous son Conrig can wait until morning. Please go away and let us be."

"It's all right, Catty," murmured the king. His eyes opened and he beckoned the Royal Alchymist to come close. The two men were the same age, five-and-fifty; but the monarch was a pale and flabby ruin of a man once stalwart and handsome, while the wizard retained a well-muscled body beneath his scarlet robes, and his close-cut black hair and tidy beard were barely touched with grey.

"I have no news from the Prince Heritor," Vra-Kilian said dourly. "Stergos was adamant that Conrig would reveal to you the results of the war council's deliberation only face-to-face. He's leaving Castle Vanguard on the day after tomorrow, but he has at least three days' ride ahead of him, perhaps more if the weather turns bad."

The king gave a groan of dismay. "It's my own fault. He doesn't trust me, and small wonder . . . but I can't wait for him. Every day's precious now! I must set out for Zeth Abbey while I still have the strength." A hand crept out of the bedclothes and gripped that of the alchymist with surprising vigor. The sick man struggled to rise while both Kilian and Cataldise hastened to restrain him. "Windspeak Abbas Noachil at once. Tell him to expect me. I *will* make the pilgrimage and ask my one Question!"

The alchymist's dismayed gaze met that of the queen. She shook her head. "He's spoken of little else since you left us earlier this evening, Brother. Since . . . the Tarnian healer delivered his final diagnosis."

"Your Grace," Kilian said to the king, "your duty to Cathra is to regain your good health, not endanger it by undertaking a long and arduous journey for such a fanciful reason. Abbas Noachil would be the first to tell you that this so-called oracle—"

"Nevertheless," the king interrupted. "I intend to make the pilgrimage."

"I forbid it," said Vra-Kilian. "You are gravely ill. As the Royal Alchymist, charged by Saint Zeth to preserve the spiritual and bodily life of the King's Grace, it is my obligation—"

"Be silent!" said Olmigon in a voice abruptly loud and resolute. Kilian blinked in amazement. "The cavalcade will leave Cala Palace tomorrow morning at first light. I've already commanded the Lord Chamberlain to make all preparations, and you countermand my orders at your peril, Brother-in-Law! This is one time you'll not get your way. Furthermore, you'll accompany us on the trip to the abbey so I can be certain you don't get up to mischief with the Privy Council while I'm gone. Now get out of here and leave me in peace."

Vra-Kilian inclined his head. "As you command, sire." Radiating glacial disapproval, he swept out of the chamber.

"Catty?" whispered the king, when the door had closed.

"Yes, my dearest love." The queen came to him, setting straight his nightcap, which had fallen awry with his exertions, and patted his hand before putting it back beneath the coverlet.

"You don't think I'm being fanciful, do you?"

"Of course not."

"That Kilian! Thinking he could forbid me to do something. The man takes too much on himself."

"He's only thinking of your welfare," said the queen.

"Huh! He makes fun of the oracle. Probably Conrig would, too."

"You must do as you think best, husband."

"Yes. I'm the king."

She kissed his cheek. "High King of Blencathra and absolute monarch of my heart."

He let out a gusty sigh. "Conrig said he'd make me Sovereign of Blenholme. The young idiot!"

"I think not," Cataldise said firmly.

"So you take the boy's part, do you?" He spoke with more disappointment than anger.

"Conrig is an extraordinary young man, not a boy. You know that for the truth. Our son is not always tactful, I must admit, but he has a remarkable grasp of statecraft."

"Damn him! Everyone thinks he's brainier than I am. You'll never catch Kilian or Falmire patronizing *him* in the Privy Council meetings the way they do me."

"You are wise in your own way, husband. But Conrig's arguments for Sovereignty were cogent and impressive. Even those members of your council who opposed him conceded the logic of his position—as you did, in the end. It wasn't Conrig's fault that . . . King Achardus responded to the Edict in an uncivilized manner."

Olmigon turned his face away from her. "I made a terrible mistake, Catty, promulgating the Edict without a show of force. I realize that now. The slaughter of the delegation lies heavy on my conscience. And the sea blockade's a failure, too, even though Tothor Dundry and his lick-spittles in the Admiralty are too stubborn to admit it. Last week I conferred with other fighting captains—bluewater sailors, not parchment-shuffling peacocks—who weren't afraid to tell me the truth. There's calamity brewing. I can feel it in my bones. I've never had such a horrid premonition before. Conrig thinks he's so clever, trying to organize a land invasion of Didion. But what if he's misread the situation and the real danger threatens us from the sea? What then?"

"The Question you would ask of the oracle," the queen said in a soothing tone, hoping to distract him. "Will it pertain to our son's proposed war against Didion? Is it your desire to assist Conrig in some way, perhaps by asking how such an enterprise might best succeed?"

A mulish expression darkened Olmigon's face. "Maybe. Curse the boy! Why did he have to go behind my back, plotting with Vanguard and Beorbrook?"

"They are the best military leaders in the kingdom," Cataldise replied placidly. "He wanted their advice and needs their approval and assistance."

"But I'm the king." His words were slurred, and he fought in vain to keep his eyelids open as the sedative drug took effect. "I'm the king, Catty. I don't give a

damn if Con loves me. But he has to respect me. The Question . . . I'm going to
know what'll happen! . . . Ask old Bazekoy . . ."

"Yes, love," said the queen. "Tomorrow we'll be on our way. But for now, go
to sleep."

Olmigon Wincantor, High King of Blencathra, set out on his pilgrimage during
the last week of the Hunter's Moon, after leaving with the Lord Chancellor a writ
commanding Prince Conrig to await his return before undertaking any military
action against Didion.

The cavalcade was a modest one. Queen Cataldise and Conrig's wife, Princess
Maudrayne, shared the great coach with the ailing king. Drawn by eight strong
horses, it had wheels two ells in diameter and was hung from steel blade-springs
to give a more gentle ride. The spacious interior was padded leather, with a bed
for the invalid set up along one side and places for the women on the other,
together with compartments for all manner of necessary supplies. The Royal
Alchymist, the king's valet, and two lords-in-waiting occupied another coach that
followed, and a third bore the Master of Wardrobe, two of the queen's ladies-
in-waiting, a tirewoman to deal with the fine laundry, and the Royal Cook. At the
last minute, Princess Maudrayne's chief lady-in-waiting had come down with the
grippe and could not join the party, so one of the queen's ladies was commanded to attend her. Ten knights of the household rode horseback at the head
of the procession, and at the rear was a contingent of the King's Guard and a
dozen minor retainers.

The procession moved northwestward over the excellent Cathran highroads.
Vra-Kilian estimated that it would take ten days to travel the three hundred leagues
to Zeth, moving slowly but steadily. They would press on well into dusk, when
spunkie lights rose from the hedgerows and swales and danced in the ground-
mists, until they reached a suitable castle or large manor house, whose resident
windvoice had received advance notice from the Royal Alchymist of the king's
imminent arrival. The train would continue on its journey at dawn the following
morning.

It passed through Wincantor Duchy's stubbled grain fields, now with cattle
and sheep turned out in them to glean fallen corn and enrich the soil with their
manure. Further north, the acreage was striped black and green, burnt-over fallow
fields and those sown with winter wheat. In the orchard country of the Blen River

valley, mills were crushing fruit and barreling the juice, filling the air with the luscious scent of fermenting cider and perry. The last crops were being harvested from the market gardens, and farm wagons loaded with cabbages, beets, carrots, and onions trundled south toward Cala, pulling onto the verge to allow the king's party to pass in the opposite direction. After crossing the great bridge at Heathley, the train came into hill country, upland pastures where the island's finest bloodhorses were bred, and rougher places where sheep grazed.

At every town and village along the way, free folk and serfs gathered along the roadside in silent respect. But no one cheered and no children strewed the way with autumn flowers, for Olmigon was not a ruler beloved by the commonalty—nor by the burgesses and nobles, either. He was apparently fated to be remembered as a remote, self-absorbed king of no distinction, controlled by venal and self-serving advisers, loved only by a handful of intimate courtiers, most of his children, and the two royal women who attended him on this final pilgrimage.

Olmigon himself was not unaware of this melancholy state of affairs but had always managed to shunt it aside—until the Tarnian shaman dared to pronounce his death sentence. At that point inspiration had come to him, vivid as a bolt of lightning. In asking his one Question, foolish old King Olmigon Wincantor believed he had one last chance at glory.

Ironically, he was correct.

The road steepened and became more narrow as the entourage left settled lands and approached the looming ramparts of the Bladewind Crags, which gleamed white in the hazy sun. By the tenth day of the journey, the route had become little more than a rutted, rocky track. From time to time the royal coach lurched violently, causing the sick man to utter soft moans. But when the queen and princess bent over him they saw that he continued to sleep soundly.

"Red Ansel's medicine is still doing its good work," Princess Maudrayne said, touching the king's brow. "There is no fever or sweating. Let us check the belly-binding."

"The healer should have come with us," Queen Cataldise said resentfully. "You should have insisted. What kind of a doctor abandons his patient?"

"Ansel had done all he could for the King's Grace. He was urgently needed at the bedside of the Tarnian ambassador's small daughter. If need be, Vra-Kilian can windspeak him for medical consultation at any time."

"It's not the same thing," the queen fussed. "His obligation is to my husband and to the Crown, who will be paying his fee as well as his traveling expenses—not to a mere sick child."

Maudrayne said coldly, "A man such as Ansel Pikan is not a hired hand nor a common doctor to be ordered about like a servant. In my country he's reckoned a mystical healer of the highest degree, more revered than your Abbas of Zeth. He came to Cala because I besought him from the bottom of my heart—not because of any promised stipend. Yes, I intend to reward him well! But I will do it from my own treasure. Is that quite clear? And if Ansel chooses to use his healing powers on a mere sick child in the meantime, that's his business and none of the Crown's."

"Hmph!" said the queen, unmollified.

The women were not friends, as happens often enough with wife and husband's mother, but thus far on the long journey they had contrived to keep peace between themselves for the sake of the dying man whom both of them loved. Cataldise Blackhorse was of ancient Cathran stock, a small person, deceptively mild in demeanor, rosy-cheeked and stout but with iron-colored eyes and a will to match. She was the one who had begged Olmigon to appoint her brother Vra-Kilian to the post of Royal Alchymist. The king had been unable to resist her plea, to his lasting regret. Until Conrig came of age and became Lord Constable, Kilian had dominated the Privy Council through sheer force of personality. The prince and the wizard had been at loggerheads ever since, with Olmigon frequently caught in the middle.

Princess Maudrayne Northkeep was the favorite niece of Sernin Donorvale, the dauntless First Sealord of Tarn. Tall as a man, with high breasts, curling auburn tresses, and piercing blue eyes, she was so lovely that Conrig would choose none other from among the eligible Tarnian maidens—in spite of her reputation as a short-tempered hellcat with a tongue like a rapier. Their mating had been a clash of titans, wildly ecstatic at first, then tempestuous as the Prince Heritor became obsessed with achieving the Sovereignty of Blenholme and spent less and less time with his demanding wife. Of late, their relations had been not so much stormy as detached and ominously formal. And Maudrayne knew why.

Her apparent inability to conceive a child had frightened and infuriated the princess. Her temper soured and her desperation grew as Conrig's ardor cooled. He still treated her with respect, but they bedded joylessly now, only in hopes of engendering an heir to the throne. Oddly, as the princess became estranged from her ambitious husband, she drew closer to the morose and suffering king—two tormented souls who had begun to fear that they had failed in their duty through fault of their own.

Maudrayne now carefully uncovered Olmigon's abdomen and examined the stout truss contrived by the Tarnian healer that now confined the ruptured bowel to its natural place. Then she restored the king's garments and the covering. "All is in order with the binding. His Grace seems much improved the last few days, no doubt buoyed up by anticipation."

Queen Cataldise gave the younger woman a hard glance. "And what will happen when his hopes are dashed? My husband would have been content to remain safely in Cala if your uncouth witch-doctor had kept a tactful tongue in his head."

"Ansel only spoke the truth," Maudrayne retorted, "as must all of his kind. The King's Grace asked plainly how many days were left to him. In my home-land, the dying have a right to know this, so that they may put their affairs in order. It's a stupid Cathran custom that healers should lie to the patient about impending death, out of misplaced kindness."

"So you say, madam! And I say *your* custom is cruel to deny all hope of remission or recovery. Is your precious Ansel a seer as well as a physician, to state positively that my royal husband will surely die within two moons—making him determined to undertake this vain journey that can only hasten his demise and perhaps disrupt the peace of the realm?"

"Red Ansel is indeed a seer," Maudrayne shot back. "A mighty practitioner of both natural and supernatural science. He did the king good service, and only an ingrate would speak ill of it. As to the pilgrimage, if it comforts Olmigon's uneasy heart, how can it be vain? I thought you approved."

"Approve? Bah! Any educated person knows that the Promise of Bazekoy is only an ancient superstition. No Cathran monarch for the past three hundred years has given the oracle credence—only my poor simple-hearted darling. Yet I could not distress him by telling him so."

"The king has a right to ask his Question. So said Abbas Noachil himself, when windspoken by the Royal Alchymist. Call it superstition if you dare, madam. I say this pilgrimage will give the king consolation in his final days."

"And shorten his life!"

"He knew the price and accepted it. So must you. If his Question receives a clear and felicitous answer, it may bring solace to the Cathran people as well as to His Grace."

"If we only knew what he intends to ask!" the queen fumed. "But he won't say. What if the oracle stands mute? Worse, what if it's only some ancient charade once countenanced by the Brothers of Zeth, but now, in this more enlightened age, become mercifully obsolete?"

"The king *will* ask his Question," Maudrayne repeated. "Abbas Noachil conceded him that right, but he did not say whether there would be an answer. Thus it is with all prayers. And yet we continue to storm heaven, madam—you and I as well as the king."

She fixed her mother-in-law with a challenging stare, and Cataldise had the grace to look away, abashed.

"I never counseled my son to put you aside for barrenness," the queen said in a low voice. "Nor did the king. Both you and Conrig are young. There is time for you to have children."

"That's true. Remind your son of it! Ah, God—if only I could put my own Question to Bazekoy! I know what *I* would ask. But the emperor's oracle only speaks to a dying ruler of Cathra. The rest of us can only petition the unseen, silent God and try not to despair."

eight

The cavalcade arrived at the gate of Zeth Abbey at the end of a dreary, overcast afternoon. The animals and most of the travelers were bone-tired and covered with grey dust, the latter a legacy of the Wolf's Breath. The periodic bouts of falling ash had afflicted this region of the kingdom more than the parts farther south, strewing the ground with pale patches like thin frost, even after summer thunderstorms and the soft rains of autumn had washed much of it away. In a fine paradox, the ash greatly enriched the soil; but only when the Wolf's Breath ceased to dim the sun would folk reap its benefits.

King Olmigon had roused as the coach covered the final league of the journey, taking both water and nourishment and declaring that his pain was much diminished. When they rolled into the abbey, his mind was clear and his spirits high. Abbas Noachil, a stooped ancient with shrewd, bird-like eyes, stood in the forecourt with all of the resident Brethren to welcome the royal party.

Supported by the two lords-in-waiting, Olmigon alighted from the carriage, then settled into an open chair-litter that would be borne by four of the red-cowled Brothers. The queen and princess flanked him and the Royal Alchymist hovered behind. Olmigon was dressed in a loose gown of white velvet, having a hood edged with blue fox fur. As befitted a pilgrim, he wore no crown and no ornament. A wooden disk with the gammadion's voided cross burnt into it hung from his neck by a leather thong. His hair and beard were a dingy yellowish color and sadly sparse, and weight-loss occasioned by the rigors of the trip had left his face seamed and wrinkled as a withered apple. His eyes were opaque hazel pebbles sunk in rheumy pits.

"God's peace and the blessing of Saint Zeth be upon you," Abbas Noachil said. "Who are you, and why have you come to this holy place?" The question was a formality, because the Royal Alchymist had windspoken the progress of the procession to Noachil every day it was en route. But it was necessary that the king make his unusual request with his own lips.

"I am Olmigon Wincantor, High King of Blencathra." His voice was little more than a whisper, but without tremor or hesitation. "I have come here, where Bazekoy the Great, Emperor of the World, breathed his last, in order to ask my one Question and receive a true answer, as is my right. Know that my own body is failing, and I am prepared to sing my Deathsong at any time, and grant me prompt audience so that my request may be fulfilled."

"Enter the Abbey of Zeth," Noachil said, lifting his staff in blessing, "and follow me to the imperial sepulchre."

The assembled Brethren began a solemn chant, and the king was carried up a shallow flight of stairs and into the cloister that led to the emperor's mausoleum, which was built of native limestone like the rest of the abbey. At the bronze doors decorated with scenes from Bazekoy's life, a waiting Brother gently restrained Queen Cataldise and Princess Maudrayne.

"No lay persons may enter during the questioning," the abbas explained. "Later, you royal ladies may venerate the emperor's ashes and pray to his spirit, but for now I ask you to accompany Prior Waringlow to the guest-hall."

A brief look of resentment crossed the face of the princess, who had made no secret of her desire to view the mysterious oracle. But Queen Cataldise said, "Come, Daughter," taking her elbow, and they went away.

Abbas Noachil said to the king, "Your Royal Alchymist, Vra-Kilian, may attend the rite, if you wish."

Olmigon said, "No! And I command that no man will hear my Question or know the answer until I deign to reveal it. Not even you, Father Abbas. I pray you conjure up a spell of couverture to shield me from windwatching during the consultation."

"It shall be done."

Kilian opened his mouth as if to protest, then shut it with an audible click of teeth and spun on his heel to follow the women. He had tried to ascertain the king's Question many times during the trip, without success.

Noachil lifted his staff and smote the bronze door three times. It opened of itself, revealing a vaulted interior lit with scores of candles that burned within blue glass vessels hanging from gilt chains. The stone pillars of the shrine were iridescent black iris-stone from Foraile, and the floor was a complex mosaic of lustrous gold and white tiles. At the far end of the mausoleum, which might have been thirty ells square and at least that in ceiling height, rose a dais with a titanic statue of the emperor, carved from marble and lit by azure lamps. The brothers carried King Olmigon to the statue's feet, where a marker was embedded in the floor.

"Beneath this plaque lie the ashes of Bazekoy's body," said the abbas. "You may pray for a time, if you desire."

"Is it here that I pose my Question?" the king asked, seeming rather disappointed.

"No. That will be done in the chapel to your right."

"Then let's get on with it," Olmigon said peevishly. "Time enough for prayers later. The pain's coming on again, and I don't want to pass out before getting what I came for."

Noachil was not offended. In fact, he smiled. "So might the emperor himself have said, in your place. He was never known as a patient man."

He made a sign to the bearers and they carried the king to a dim alcove, shut off from the main chamber by a wrought-iron gate. Unlocking this, the abbas went to a low altar that held a domed golden reliquary about two feet high. On either side were large candlesticks surmounted by blue glass cups with chill flames burning inside. After the brothers had backed off reverently through the gate and retreated out of sight, the abbas unlocked the reliquary and swung its doors wide.

Inside was a sizable crystal urn full of liquid, in which floated a human head.

"God's Teeth!" whispered Olmigon.

Abbas Noachil made a brief, almost playful obeisance to the altar. "Good day, Imperial Majesty. I trust you continue to rest in peace. May I present Olmigon Wincantor, High King of Blencathra, here to ask his alloted Question ere he sings his Deathsong. If it be God's will, give him answer." The abbas handed the king a silver bell, directing him to ring it when he had finished, and withdrew from the chapel.

Olmigon felt no awe at this supreme moment, only a quizzical detachment. Could the head actually be real? It seemed made of wax, with an inhuman translucence to the flesh. The eyes were closed. Abundant hair, grey and slightly wavy, floated from beneath an archaic crowned helmet ornamented with rubies and huge blue pearls. Bazekoy the Great had a neatly trimmed moustache and thick sensuous lips that almost seemed to smile. Like so many Foraileans, he had a broad, snub nose.

"But your body burned in its funeral pyre," the king said softly. "So how came your head here? If this really is your head . . ."

The eyes opened: very large, very blue like the candleflames in their sapphire cups.

Is that your one Question, Olmigon Wincantor?

The king started like one touched by a burning coal. "No! My God, no!"

A judicious nod. Then I'll answer gratis, for you're the first to seek my counsel in three centuries, and I thought I might have been forgotten! . . . A dream of strange Lights instructed me to render up my life here, on the island where my great conquests began. I came to this place, as directed, when it was a mere hermitage, and my warriors prepared for me the traditional funeral pyre of my people. But before my body was burned the resident wizard secretly removed my head and preserved it, so that I might literally fulfil a rash promise made on my deathbed. That impudent magicker was the one you name Saint Zeth, and I hold him no ill will, for through his boldness I was able to advise and console many a Cathran ruler face-to-face . . . until the times changed. Times do change, Olmigon! And a wise man accommodates himself and doesn't cling to worn-out ways and customs. A truly great man, on the other hand, not only accommodates, but uses change to get what he wants.

"So said my son Conrig." The king winced at a momentary stab of pain in his guts. "Damned ambitious pup! Wants to be Sovereign of Blenholme—wants glory, like you had."

Bazekoy smiled. *You're jealous, old man.*

"How dare you speak to me like that!"

Jealous! Because your son's vision is greater than yours could ever be. Because he overrode your pissy-arsed objections and forced you to issue the Edict of Sovereignty. Admit the truth of what I say!

"I—"

It was a small-minded attempt to exert power that led you to overrule Conrig's plan to send a well-armed delegation to King Achardus. Sheer bloody-mindedness— or else malice, wishing his ploy to fail. Do you deny it?

"I came here hoping to help my son!"

Nonsense. You came hoping to justify yourself—to Conrig and to history.

Olmigon took a furious breath, intending to defend himself against the oracle's insults. But a terrible wave of agony swept over him, making him writhe, squelching his pride and leaving any notion of defiance in tatters.

You are dying, the apparition said implacably. *Stop deceiving yourself. For most of your reign, you've been a silly fool, surrounding yourself with councilors such as your brother-in-law who flattered and manipulated you to their own selfish ends. When you were finally obliged to admit the Prince Heritor to your Privy Council, you were frightened by the strength of his character and the boldness of his plans. And envious! For shame, old man.*

"I thought the Sovereignty scheme was imprudent. So did many of my advisers. It was both risky and expensive—"

Ah! Now we come to the truth of the matter. The merchants and the great lords whose wealth depends upon them resisted any plan that would raise their taxes— especially during the Wolf's Breath time, when their profits are already curtailed. Never mind that unifying the island would make it a stronghold against southern enemies. And do away with the wasteful small disputes among the four kingdoms that have cost both money and human lives over the past hundred years.

"All kings don't have to be empire-builders." Olmigon's eyes were watering treacherously.

So. Would you have your son's great dream of Sovereignty die with you? Do you intend to forbid the invasion?

"Not if it has a real chance of success. What do you take me for?"

Is that your one Question?

"No . . . no."

Then ask it, old fool.

Olmigon wiped his eyes with a palsied hand and pulled himself upright in the chair. On impulse, he had revised his original elaborate query to one that was starkly simple. "All right, damn you! Here it is . . . Can my son Conrig succeed in uniting High Blenholme in a Sovereignty?"

There was a long silence.

"Well?" Olmigon said. "Are you going to answer? Are you real or only some bloody conjurer's trick? Will Con be able to do it?"

Only if you rise from your deathbed to assist him, said Bazekoy's head.

"What?" the king cried. "Are you toying with me? What do you mean?"

The Question is answered. Now leave me in peace, Olmigon Wincantor. If you have other questions, ask them of your son.

The emperor's gleaming blue eyes closed.

The king gave a final bellow of impotent rage, then slumped back in mingled despair and puzzlement, tears coursing down his cheeks. The small silver handbell fell out of his hand and struck the floor with a sharp chime.

nine

What the devil kind of answer was *that?*" exclaimed Prince Conrig. "Was the cursèd thing mocking you?"

"I don't know," Olmigon replied wretchedly.

They were alone together in the royal bedchamber in Cala Palace. The caval-cade had arrived home around the eleventh hour, but the queen had refused to let Conrig visit his greatly weakened father until he had been put safely to bed. She would have forced the prince to wait until morning, but Olmigon would not take any sleep-inducing or painkilling medicine until he conferred with his son.

"Sire—you're certain the head of Bazekoy was real?" Conrig could not hide his skepticism.

"No, I'm not sure!" croaked the king, in a feeble fury. "But the damned thing opened its eyes and looked at me, and its lips moved, and it had a snotty, over-familiar manner at odds with any fake the Brethren might have rigged up. It was no puppet, I tell you! And if it was a sorcerer's illusion, why did it insult me and then answer the Question with such casual ambiguity? Surely the Brothers of Zeth would have wanted to placate me with some soppy reassurance, rather than drive me daft with a riddle."

But the oracle couldn't possibly be real, the prince told himself, feeling a pang of terrible presentiment. If it spoke true, then the great scheme's attainment depended not on Conrig's own meticulously planned strategy, but on this weak-willed, foolish old man who had already thwarted a bloodless victory over Didion.

" '*Only if you rise from your deathbed to assist him,*' " Conrig quoted. "What do you think it means, sire? Are we supposed to take the reply at face value, or are the emperor's words only a metaphor for impossibility?"

"I didn't want to ask Abbas Noachil for his opinion, nor Kilian, either. The oracle's answer is *mine,* Con—and yours! We must puzzle it out ourselves, king and king-to-be. It's important. I'm certain of it."

Conrig was silent, searching his father's ravaged face as his own mind was racked by turmoil. He had come to the king's bedchamber this night resolved to have his way at any cost—to persuade, to browbeat, to do whatever was necessary to prevent this dying man from frustrating his plans for the invasion. He'd expected the oracle's message to be pretentious nonsense. But this . . .

"You've changed, sire," the prince finally said. "And I don't refer to your advancing illness. Always before you treated me like an unruly child, belittling my aspirations, only grudgingly accepting my recommendations in Privy Council even when you knew well enough they were sensible and practicable. You treated me as a gadfly, a bothersome nuisance, never as a future king."

"Bazekoy said I was jealous of you," Olmigon said. He refused to meet Conrig's eye. "Disappointed, rather! What joy have I ever had from my three sons? Stergos, my eldest, is ineligible for kingship because of arcane talent. My second-born, Tancoron, is a sweet-natured mental defective. And you—! Headstrong, insolently superior, aflame with crackbrained ambition, always convinced you're right while I'm wrong."

Conrig could not help but smile. "True enough."

"Yet you were clearly born to some great destiny, as I was not." The words were spat out, like sour bits of unripe fruit. "Jealous? Why shouldn't I be jealous? Look at you—bursting with confidence, young and strong! And me . . . the hunting accident that broke my body when I was scarce four-and-twenty put an end to any hope I had of performing valorous deeds. All I had to look forward to was a legacy of pain. Some men overcome such ill fortune. I . . . couldn't. Instead I chose to rely on the strength of others. Sometimes that was for the best. But there were times when I should have done things another way, even when my advisers opposed me. I know that now. You know it."

"Yes."

"I gave in too often. Wasn't strong. And my choice of councilors . . . hasn't always been sound."

"You've never admitted that before."

The king laughed bitterly. "Emperor Bazekoy considerately pointed it out to me—along with certain other shortcomings of mine. I pondered his words during the long trip home and hated him. Hated him! I told myself over and over that the oracle was a lying fraud. But it wasn't, Con. It told the truth about me . . . and if it did, then we must believe that it also told the truth about the two of us. My kingship is ending and yours will soon begin, but the Sovereignty of Blenholme depends on you *and* me."

Again there was silence, except for the old man's labored breathing. His eyes were misty. "Is it too late to make it up between us? Bazekoy didn't seem to think so." With an effort, the king composed himself. "Can't we decide together what's to be done about the immediate dangers facing our island?"

"Perhaps we can try," Conrig said slowly. He sat in a chair at the king's bedside, large hands resting easily on his black-clad knees, a man both resolute and cold of heart, as both of them knew.

The king said, "You mustn't castigate Odon Falmire for breaking your confidence and informing me about your council of war. The chancellor's a loyal friend to both of us. When he heard that the Tarnian healer had given me only a short time to live, he felt it his duty to let me know what you were up to. It was necessary that Vra-Kilian know of it also, because I needed to have him windspeak you. But I adjured him to secrecy with a solemn oath. No one else on the Privy Council knows that you plan to make war on Didion. But I suppose we must tell them now."

"I've summoned the councilors to an extraordinary session tonight," the prince said. "I intend to tell them that a *defensive* war is in the offing, intended to repulse starving hordes from Didion who might attempt to cross Great Pass before winter snows close it down."

"You summoned my Council!" Olmigon's eyes widened in affronted disbelief. Conrig had usurped a royal prerogative.

"Yes." The prince took from his doublet the writ, signed by the king, forbidding him from taking action against Didion. "You must understand, sire, that any discussion of ours concerning the dangers facing the kingdom will in no way be influenced by this."

At the king's bedside was a nightstand holding a lit candlabrum and a silver tray with vials of medicine and a flagon of water. Conrig cleared the tray, then touched the corner of the vellum document to one of the candleflames.

Olmigon cried out.

The prince held up the burning parchment. "Shall I quench it?"

The king hesitated only for a moment before turning his head away. "No. Let it burn."

Conrig dropped the flaming writ onto the tray, nodding in satisfaction. "If I reveal my plans to you, it must be on condition that you leave to my judgment how much will be told to the Privy Council. I don't intend to debate the matter with them—or with you."

"I understand," the king muttered. "I trust you to do what's best. Only tell me what I must keep secret."

"Everything that I say about the council of war. You must reveal the details to no one—not even to Mother. Swear it on your crown."

"I do," Olmigon whispered. "I do swear." He did not mention that the queen had helped him to draft the writ, and that they had both talked with Princess Maudrayne about the possibility of war with Didion on the return journey from Zeth. He took a linen handkerchief from the sleeve of his nightgown and held it to his mouth. "Take care how you speak. Vra-Kilian may be windwatching us. He lip-reads poorly, I'm told, but no use taking chances."

"Well said." The prince leaned toward the king, his hand hiding the lower part of his face. "The northern peers, including Beorbrook and Vanguard and Ramscrest and the Virago of Marley, are pledged to support an invasion of Didion under my leadership."

"Invasion . . ." The king's eyes widened.

"They're mustering their forces now, some five hundred knights and fighting men, all well-mounted and lightly armored for speed. The underlings believe we'll gather at Great Pass at the end of the Boreal Moon to repel incursions from Didion. In actuality, the army will gather at Castle Vanguard. I intend to attack Holt Mallburn in a lightning thrust over Breakneck Pass."

"Good God—but you can't mean it! Breakneck Pass? The late autumn storms—"

"I have a talented ally who guarantees not only clement weather but also an all-concealing fog that will let us take the enemy by surprise. Princess Ullanoth of Moss is Cathra's secret collaborator in this war. She's promised her arcane help in exchange for my support of her claim to the throne of Moss, First Vassal status in the Sovereignty, plus a sodding great pile of money."

Olmigon gaped in blank astonishment. "A sorceress abetting your army? You'd trust a perfidious Mosslander?"

"She has a bitter rivalry with her younger brother Beynor, who now stands to become Conjure-King as Linndal's favorite. The lady has nothing to gain by dealing with us falsely. Many of the northern lords were aghast at the idea of an alliance with her, as you are. But after thinking the matter over, they saw the plan's wisdom. You must not oppose me in this, sire." Conrig took hold of the king's free hand, and his grip tightened to the point of pain. "I won't be dissuaded. Not by you, nor by any supposed words of Emperor Bazekoy, nor by God himself."

Olmigon stiffened, seeing in his son's eyes a thing that made his soul quake. "My son, I've told you that I trust you. But you must also trust me. I think I know what you intended to do when you came to me tonight, believing I'd oppose you. I *won't* oppose you! But not because I'm afraid."

The prince released the king's hand and the two of them stared wordlessly at one another.

"You should be afraid," Conrig finally said. "But you need not be. Not now. Bazekoy has performed some sort of miracle after all."

The old man gave vent to a sudden bark of laughter, dropping the handkerchief from his mouth and starting up from the pillows with a surge of febrile energy. "Then do it, Con! Crush that viper Achardus Mallburn, undoing my stupidity and my shame!"

"I will . . . Father."

Tension flowed palpably from Olmigon's body, leaving him relaxed. "I bless your enterprise, my son. Only let me know how I can help you. God knows how Bazekoy's oracle will be fulfilled, but if a way presents itself, I swear I'll take it before breathing my last, no matter what the cost."

"There is something you can do now, if you're able." Once again Conrig covered his mouth with his hand. "While I was at Castle Vanguard, I learned that Honigalus and Somarus of Didion had sailed to the Continent along with Prince Beynor of Moss, seeking a strategic alliance with the southern nations. During the past weeks, as I awaited your return, I obtained additional information: The two Didionite princes suspect we intend to invade their homeland, but they don't know when, or the route we plan to take. They have apparently persuaded Stippen and Foraile to strike at Cala from the sea, should I attack their country by land. Andradh has thus far declined to join the alliance, but it may do so in the future."

"My premonition! I knew something dire was in the wind! Is your intelligence reliable?"

"Princess Ullanoth bespoke Stergos three days ago, informing him what she had discovered through her arcane arts. We must recall all of our fighting ships from the blockade immediately and mass them in defense of the capital. I tried to convince Lord Admiral Dundry to abandon the blockade as soon as I learned of the danger, but the fool refused to listen to me. Of course, I could not tell him that my knowledge came from Ullanoth."

"Give me writing materials! The palace alchymists must bespeak every ship's windvoice tonight. We'll issue a joint order. That'll bolster your authority, too, if we're seen to act in concert."

Conrig went to a nearby table for a writing tray, pen, ink, vellum, and the Royal Seal. Everything was at hand, since the ailing king had for months been accustomed to deal with everyday matters of state from within his private chambers.

"Tomorrow," the prince said, after the new writ had been signed and sealed by both of them, "you must confer with naval officers that you trust and decide how the defensive armada might best be arrayed. Unlike yourself, I have little experience in sea warfare."

"Ah, the sea! You can't know me as I was in those early days of my realm, Con." A crooked grin of recollection. "The Battle of the Stormy Isles... my first triumph, so long ago! The Wave-Harriers of Andradh thought they'd take advantage of a callow boy-king, newly crowned, playing at wargames with a small portion of his fleet in the Western Ocean. They would have seized me and held me for a devastating ransom—but I licked the poxy lobscousers and sent them off with burnt rigging and splintered bulwarks! Andradh was a laughing stock for ten years thereafter." He began to chuckle feebly, but the action renewed his pain, and he broke off with a moan.

"You must sleep soon, Father. But something else needs saying. In my opinion, Lord Admiral Dundry is incompetent to command our navy. His blockade tactics have failed miserably, and he's too old and arrogant to accept advice from wiser heads. You must replace him with Elo Copperstrand or Count Woodvale's son, Zednor."

"Dundry has powerful friends among the merchants and commands the loyalty of many captains. But I'll find a way to do as you wish." He considered for a moment. "I think we must also hire a squadron of mercenary frigates from

Tarn. They can get here from Goodfortune Bay in a week or less if the winds are favorable. We have too few speedy warships, and such might be crucial if the Continentals attack. The hirelings can bring us additional stocks of tarnblaze as well. I'll ask the Tarnian shaman, Red Ansel, to windspeak his countrymen. He'll convince them to come."

"Excellent!" Conrig said heartily. "I would never have thought of that." His expression darkened. "There is one more urgent request I must make—concerning the Royal Alchymist." He told the king of his suspicions, and what he felt was now necessary. "It will require another writ, of course."

"I'll do it," the king grumbled, scribbling away, "and trust your judgment on the matter. But it'll put the cat among the pigeons, be sure of it."

"I'll take care of the cat. Don't be concerned." Conrig helped his father with the wax seal, then removed the writing tray and tucked the folded pieces of vellum into his belt-wallet.

Olmigon gave him a tremulous smile. "We'll talk more of these matters tomorrow. But send your mother in now. No others, only she. I must tell her of our reconciliation. It will gladden her heart. And you yourself must give the tidings to Maudrayne. Without the good offices of the Tarnian healer that the dear girl summoned, I think we would not have had this conversation tonight. Certainly, I would never have thought to go to Emperor Bazekoy in time, had Red Ansel not told me that my life was surely drawing to an end."

Conrig leaned down and kissed his father's forehead, saying, "Remember: you must not tell Mother anything about my plans. Kilian would be sure to wangle the information from her somehow."

"Yes, yes. But send her to me now."

"Very well, Father."

The wrinkled eyelids were closing, and the king's lips were slightly open, breathing some final words that Conrig was unable to understand. The prince stood looking down at the helpless old man for a moment.

Could I have done it, he asked himself, if he had forbidden the invasion?

But he knew the answer.

Conrig left the bedchamber. Queen Cataldise was waiting patiently outside, together with the Royal Alchymist, several medical attendants and bodyservants, and four members of the Palace Guard.

"Mother." He bowed to her and smiled. "The King's Grace wishes you to attend him briefly before he sleeps, to share with you the good tidings that he and I have reconciled our differences and are now in loving accord."

"Oh, Con!" Tears sprang to her eyes, and she embraced him. "I'm so very glad."

The Royal Alchymist insinuated himself forward confidently, presuming to take the elbow of Cataldise and guide her toward the bedchamber door. "I would also like to look in on His Grace, to see to his bodily needs."

Conrig blocked the wizard's progress. "I think not." Firmly, he removed Kilian's hand from the queen's arm, ignoring his indignant expostulation. "Go in alone, Mother. It's the king's wish." He then nodded to the four guardsmen, who stepped in front of the door as the queen passed through, unsheathing their swords.

Kilian drew himself up furiously, locking eyes with the prince. It was the selfsame coercive and obdurate glare, fraught with uncanny menace, that had so intimidated Conrig when he was a boy. The wizard exclaimed, "Do you dare to forbid me access to His Grace? Stand aside, you men!"

The guards stood their ground.

Conrig said. "King Olmigon has told me plainly that he no longer requires your services, either as a physician or an adviser. Furthermore, it is the king's command that you accompany me now to an extraordinary meeting of the Privy Council which I have called."

There were gasps from the assembled retainers.

"I don't believe you!" Kilian said.

"Believe it," the prince retorted. His face was like iron and his voice became very soft. "It would be unseemly—and quite useless—for you to use magic to force your way into the royal bedchamber. The king and I now speak with one voice, and I carry his writ to that effect. Come! It's very late, and the other members of the Privy Council are waiting for us." Conrig paused, and a cold smile touched his lips. "Of course, if you're too . . . weary after your long journey to attend the meeting in person, you may retire to your chambers and windwatch the proceedings."

For an instant, black hatred flashed in Kilian's eyes. Then he lowered them and spoke with respectful submissiveness. "Of course I'll come." The two of them strode off together down the corridor.

ten

The long return trip to the capital from Zeth Abbey had been a trying ordeal for Princess Maudrayne. The king had suffered great agitation of mind, clearly the result of the oracle's pronouncement, which he would not discuss. Along with his anxiety, Olmigon's pain intensified and he required more and more of the Tarnian healer's soothing elixir in order to sleep. The two royal women were obliged to care for the king together night and day, since he refused to abide the presence of anyone else—especially the Royal Alchymist. He could no longer control his natural functions and had to be swaddled like an infant; and his appetite, which was already delicate as a result of his malady and the stress of traveling, dwindled to the point where he could take only milksops or broth laced with wine.

By the time the returning cavalcade reached the town of Great Market, some forty leagues from the capital, Olmigon had so weakened that Cataldise and Maudrayne began to fear for his survival. They pleaded with him to break the journey. Why not stop for several days in the mayor's fine mansion, where they were being accommodated? The king could rest and regain his strength.

But he would not. "I have vitally important business to discuss with my son Conrig," he declared. "We'll leave here at dawn, as usual—and tomorrow night I'll sleep again in my own bed."

It was around half-past ten when the royal coach finally entered Cala and rumbled up cobblestoned Blenholme Way to the palace on the hill. The streets of the great city were already cleared of common people by the watch, and a red crescent moon hung low in the western sky above the river ramparts. Advance riders had heralded the party's arrival, and the palace forecourt blazed with torches. A cheering throng of courtiers greeted the ailing king, who was eased from the carriage and installed in a litter that would bear him to his chambers. Servants dashed about in response to the queen's commands and those of Vra-Kilian. The other members of the entourage, famished and exhausted, began to melt away.

Princess Maudrayne was glad that little attention was paid to her, and that her husband was not among those greeting the return of the king. She was able to slip away with Rusgann Moorcock, the sturdy, plainspoken tirewoman who had become her personal maid during the pilgrimage, after Queen Cataldise preempted the services of both ladies-in-waiting.

Unaccountably, the haughty princess and lowborn Rusgann had become friends. Maudrayne's sharpness didn't bother the other woman a bit. When the princess was egregiously rude, Rusgann didn't hesitate to reply in kind, just as independent-minded Tarnian servants were apt to do when provoked. They had many a zestful quarrel, exchanged complaints about the hardships of the trip, and even found things to laugh about.

And in time, Maudrayne had shared her secret . . .

Well ahead of the crowd attending the king and queen, the two women made their way through the palace to the princely apartments. Only the Lord Chamberlain's wife Lady Truary, a dame given to irksome inquisitiveness, made bold to waylay them in the corridor beyond the Hall of Presence, in hopes of learning news of the oracle's reply to the Question.

"Princess, I'm so glad I found you!" Truary cried, dropping a perfunctory curtsey. "Do come with me to the Blue Room, where other Privy Council wives and I have ordered a delicious collation and mulled wine. The whole palace is wild to know what Emperor Bazekoy said! Was there a good omen? You must tell us!"

Doughty Rusgann stepped in front of her mistress. "Now then, my lady. You must contain your curiosity. We've been on the road since sunup, hurrying along because the King's Grace was determined to arrive here tonight. Princess Maudrayne is exhausted and has no time for you now."

The noblewoman pouted. She was dressed in sky-blue satin, ermine-trimmed, and dripped with jewels. "But we've waited for hours and hours! Surely Your Grace can spare us the courtesy of a brief chat. We don't care a bit about your travelworn appearance."

Maudrayne's garments were caked with dust, and her auburn curls had become a sadly bedraggled mop. It was unforgivably tactless for Truary to have made mention of it, but the princess smiled serenely. "I hope I am always courteous, lady. It's my duty to every subject of my royal father-in-law, no matter how low . . . or highborn."

Truary blinked, not certain whether or not she had been insulted.

Neither the Lord Chamberlain's wife nor any of the other peeresses in her set were warm friends of Maudrayne. When she came to Cala to marry Conrig six years earlier, the court ladies had fluttered about her like frivolous butterflies eager to test the nectar of an exotic new flower sprung up in their midst. Soon enough they discovered that the imposing Tarnian bride was indifferent to fashion, flirting, gossip, and party-going—traditional pastimes of the noblewomen of Cala palace.

Instead, the seventeen-year-old Maudrayne read books on philosophy and astronomy. She collected rare seashells on solitary walks along the strand. She had dried and pressed wild plants sent to her from all over Cathra and spent long hours mounting them on parchment sheets, inscribing their names, habit of growth, and any utility they might have to mankind. She played lawn-bowls with the male courtiers and often won. She was an expert shot with a shortbow and hunted gamebirds in season, then prepared strangely spiced sauces for their cooking with her own hands. She brought from her barbaric homeland a sloop-rigged yacht, which she captained without shame, dressed as a common sailor. She could even swim!

As months and years went by without her conceiving an heir to the throne, the princess was both pitied and patronized by the court ladies, who offered charms and nostrums guaranteed to overcome barrenness. Some of them even dared to suggest that a more conventional manner of living would increase her chances of bearing a child. She listened to their comments with ill-concealed scorn and continued doing exactly as she pleased.

Now Maudrayne said to Truary, "Tonight I must disappoint you and the others. King Olmigon has told no living soul what Question he asked of the oracle—much less what answer he received. If you're curious, I'm afraid that you'll have to ask *him* to share your collation and chat. And now I bid you good night."

She swept off down the hall with Rusgann lumbering after. "That's telling the nervy cow!" the tirewoman said, smothering giggles. "So she waited for hours, poor thing. And you've only been traveling and tending a sick man for three perishing weeks!"

"Leave be, Rusgann," the princess said with an irritable gesture. "I'm too tired to be angry."

A sly grin. "You'll soon have sweet revenge on her and the others, if all goes as we hope."

"We can't be certain yet. I've only missed two courses. This has happened to me before, with no good outcome."

"But this time there's a glow about you, my lady, even though you're dead tired. And the morning qualmishness—"

"I intend to wait until there's no possible doubt before telling my husband. You will continue to do my laundry and act as my personal maid as well."

The tirewoman beamed. "It'll be my pleasure."

"I won't need you tonight, however. You're as weary as I am. My other attendants have lazed away while I was gone. Let them earn their salt. Tell Lady Sovanna, my chief lady-in-waiting, to find a nice place for you to live, close to my chambers. Be sure it's to your liking and don't let her fob you off with some airless closet. Take care of yourself, Rusgann, and sleep well. We'll discuss your new duties in the morning."

They came into the elaborate suite of rooms belonging to the Prince Heritor, his wife, and their intimate servants. Lady Sovanna Ironside, the two vapid young noblewomen who assisted her, and a covey of maidservants hastened to attend the princess, and soon Maudrayne was enjoying a long bath before the fire in her own large sitting room.

Like Truary, Sovanna was eager to know what Bazekoy's oracle had said, and was openly annoyed when the princess said she knew nothing about it and curtly refused to discuss details of the journey. The chief lady-in-waiting was a middle-aged woman of great efficiency, appointed by the queen. She pretended a maternal devotion to Maudrayne but had too often borne the brunt of the princess's fiery temper and offhand thoughtlessness to be loyal—much less a confidante.

It's going to be interesting, Maudrayne thought, to see how Sovanna reacts to the promotion of Rusgann. Well—at least I no longer have to worry about the old bitch inspecting my smallclothes and giving the queen monthly fertility reports!

The princess sipped warmed brandywine and ate a bowl of green egg-and-cheese soup, while her women dried and combed her hair, rubbed her swollen feet with rose-scented oil, and dressed her in a cream-colored nightdress of heavy silk and a matching quilted robe edged with swansdown.

Later, made mellow by the spirits and light meal and happy to be clean and comfortable again, Maudrayne began to reconsider her decision not to tell Conrig of her secret. They hadn't seen each other in over two moons, what with the pilgrimage and his own earlier long sojourn at the hunting lodge; and they had parted in a cool humor—she indignant that this year they would not shoot waterfowl and hunt together at Lake Brent, and he adamant that she would not accompany him to the lodge, but refusing to give good reason why.

From a single private conversation with the king during the return journey, Maudrayne now knew something of what Conrig had been up to in the north country. Unlike Olmigon, she had been well aware that her husband intended to pursue the interrupted press for Sovereignty, whether the king gave his consent or not. And if Conrig was headed off to fight against Didion, he deserved to know that she was expecting a child.

"Sovanna, is my lord husband in his bedchamber?" It was not the Cathran custom for married royals to share sleeping quarters.

"I think not, Your Grace," said the lady-in-waiting, refilling the princess's crystal cup with Golden Alembic brandy once again, while giving a grimace of disapproval. Maudrayne, like all Tarnian women, could drink most Cathran men under the table and be none the worse the morning after. "He was occupied with affairs of state all evening before you arrived. I know he hoped to visit the King's Grace as soon as possible to pay his respects, and he's also called for an extraordinary meeting of the Privy Council." She smirked knowingly. "That caused a bit of a stir, I heard. Several of the councilors thought they should wait for the king's approval. But even the reluctant ones finally decided to heed the prince's wish— for fear of missing some juicy bit of news about the oracle."

The other women were gathering up used towels and bathing sundries, while four footmen had come to lift the tub onto a wheeled platform, and were now endeavoring to remove it from the sitting room without spilling water on the fine Incayo carpet.

"Very well," the princess said. "You may all leave me now. Quench the lights save for the hour-marker."

They bowed and did as she bade and trooped out, closing the door. Maudrayne locked it, then went to a writing table where an elaborately carved little casket stood, gleaming in the lone candleflame. It was made of precious sea-unicorn ivory, fashioned by the Tarnian crafters of Havoc Bay in the far north. When one pressed certain prominent parts in the correct manner, its lid sprang open. Inside was Maudrayne's diary.

So many days now to catch up on! But she had not dared to bring the small book along on the pilgrimage. All of her hopes and fears and joys and rages were contained in it, and she intended that no one else should read it until she was dead. She leafed back through the pages, confirming the date of her last womanly course. It was as she'd thought: two moons and more ago. And she had suffered the morning malaise, tender breasts, and swollen feet, and experienced that unaccountable undercurrent of happiness so at odds with the grim tenor of her life of late. Oldwives of Tarn had told her what that meant.

I *will* let Conrig know, she decided, replacing the diary. I'll wait for him in his chamber and tell him this very night.

She sat quietly for some time in the dimness, savoring the rest of the fine brandy. Then she rose from her armchair and went into her dark bedchamber, and thence to the door connecting her apartment with that of her husband. It was locked, and that was unusual; but years ago she had had the key copied, and so she fetched it now, opened the door, and stepped over the threshold.

His sleeping chamber was much larger than her own, with a splendid canopied bed in the middle. Wainscot-faced walls were painted dark crimson above, with touches of white and gold in the moldings. The candle-sconces were also gold, but none of the tapers in them were lit, so that the painted landscapes and tapestries on the walls were engulfed in shadows. The only illumination came from the fireplace, where glowing coals crackled before a backlog, from a slightly open door leading to the prince's sitting room, and from the tall windows. Their draperies had not yet been drawn, so that the lamps on the palace battlements and towers were visible, as well as those in the great city below Cala Hill. Beyond was the black sea, where tiny sparks marked ships at their moorings out in Blenholme Roads.

It was cold in Conrig's room, and an unfamiliar fragrance lingered in the air. Was it vetiver? How odd! He was as fond of perfumes as most Cathran men, but his usual preference was for bergamot, oakmoss, or clary sage.

Maudrayne might have waited for her husband in his bed; but she recalled happier days when they had lain together by the fire in his wide, padded longchair that stood on a hearth-rug of pieced otterskin. Two throws of black mink lay folded neatly on the floor beside the chair to warm the prince when he sat up late, reading or thinking. She shook out both of them to make herself a nest of soft furs.

I'll surprise him, she thought, as she snuggled deeply into the chair. Smiling, she fell asleep watching the embers.

At first Maudrayne thought she was dreaming. There were voices coming from the next room—his, and that of a woman. Conrig spoke angrily and the woman laughed at him, a throaty sound that evoked both derision and sexual enticement.

"Why should I windspeak your boring brother Stergos when it's so much more pleasant to come to you in a Sending and deliver my intelligence reports in person?"

"You should know why—if you had bothered to scry the palace before projecting your Sending. My wife is here and so is the king. Would you destroy me, Ullanoth? I told you not to come here any more!"

"And I told *you* that I go where I please. But lay your fears to rest, my prince. I've secured us against the weak-talented windpeepers dwelling in your palace. Earlier, I watched your touching reunion with your father. I presume that he approved your plan to invade Didion."

"He did. He even acceded to your own role as ally. But you must leave me at once! What if my wife should find us together?"

Maudrayne stifled feelings of amazement and dismay. How could the Conjure-Princess of Moss be here in Cala Palace, speaking to her husband in his private apartment? And what was she saying about an alliance in the invasion of Didion? She strained her ears to learn more.

Ullanoth was laughing again. "Before I came, I scried your beloved Maudrayne taking a bath and drinking a scandalous amount of brandy. Her chamber is dark. She's no doubt dead drunk in her bed, with no thought at all of her wifely duty. What a shame! You'll have to sleep alone . . . unless you mend your manners and beg my pardon for being rude."

"Lady, you go too far—aaah!" He broke off with a cry of pained surprise.

"No," came the scornful retort. "*You* go too far, daring to lay rude hands on a Conjure-Princess of Moss. So there! You've been punished. Now entreat my forgiveness, and I'll say I'm sorry for hurting you with my magic, and we'll make it up between us with a kiss."

Great God of the Arctic Storms! Maudrayne prayed. Grant that this is some nightmare and let me wake! She dares to speak to him like a mistress? And he makes willing answer—

Maudrayne could not doubt the evidence of her own ears. She overheard amorous sighs and murmurings, and the kind of endearments exchanged only by lovers of long standing. Red rage and wounded pride swelled her Tarnian heart, and she would have sprung up and rushed into the next room to confront the guilty pair. But the next words spoken by the sorceress so intrigued her that curiosity overcame anger. She settled back to listen.

"Restrain your ardor, my prince, until I've shared my latest news with you. There is a very serious problem. I have learned that the man killed at Castle Vanguard by your young footman was a high-ranking Mossland sorcerer named Iscannon. He was one of the Glaumerie Guild members who accompanied my brother on the voyage to the Continent. Beyond a doubt he was deeply involved in Beynor's plot to thwart your conquest of Didion."

"But how did he find out about the secret meeting?" Conrig asked. "His joining of Hartrig Skellhaven's train traveling to Castle Vanguard had to be planned well in advance. Surely Beynor could not have windwatched our conferences at Brent Lodge."

"He could have, but he didn't. I took careful precautions against it. That's the problem I spoke of. I believe that you have a traitor among your own people. Beynor had no reason to suspect you were calling a council of war. Furthermore, he and his followers would hardly mount a long-distance surveillance of Cathra on the off-chance of discovering some useful secret. The magic is hellishly difficult, even for Mossland sorcerers. No—my wicked little brother was told of the meeting at Castle Vanguard by some disloyal Cathran."

"A traitor . . . The man who comes immediately to mind is Skellhaven, and yet all my instincts tell me he is loyal."

"In my judgment, your instincts are correct. The pirate lord hates Didion and despises Moss, as does his cousin Holmrangel. And even if one of them was careless and let slip that they were meeting you, they had no advance knowledge of a council of war. So your turncoat must be another."

"He can't be one of the three Heart Companions who accompanied me from Brent Lodge," the prince said. "They didn't know the purpose of the meeting, either. Only two persons were aware in advance of my intention to attack Didion—Duke Tanaby Vanguard, who organized the council of war at my behest, and the Lord Chancellor, Odon Falmire. I can't believe either one would consort with Beynor. What possible motive could they have for doing so? You must investigate further, lady."

"I'll try," Ullanoth said, "but there is little more I can do until I have a long talk with Beynor. He returned to Royal Fenguard a couple of hours ago, quite unexpectedly, in a splendid, brand-new ship hidden beneath a spell of couverture. He went off immediately to speak to our father. I did scry the two princes of Didion at home in Holt Mallburn. They were celebrating their new alliance with Stippen and Foraile. I saw the treaty when they showed it to King Achardus."

"Curse them," Conrig growled.

Ullanoth uttered a soft, wry laugh. "I'll do my best, you may be sure . . . But while I delve into the affairs of my little brother and his cohorts, you must consider who among your own close associates might have a strong reason to betray you."

A long silence.

Conrig said, "There is only one." Another silence. "And he may have been able to find out about the meeting at Castle Vanguard by eavesdropping on my conversations with my brother, or by some other means."

"Who is this person?"

"We'll talk of it later."

"We don't have much time. Less than two weeks remain before your army sets out. And there's something else you should keep in mind. The sorcerer Iscannon was not only a spy. He was also one of Glaumerie's premier assassins."

"God's Blood! Would he have dared to come at me in Castle Vanguard?"

"Beyond a doubt. And now that he's dead, Beynor may send another. You must beware, my prince. Seek magical assistance from your brother Vra-Stergos. There is a certain charm I know that would render you sure protection. Unfortunately, I cannot give it to you via a Sending, nor do I dare share its magic with a Brother of Zeth." She paused, then asked casually, "What did your servant Deveron Austrey do with Iscannon's moonstone amulet? I know that Skellhaven has the golden chain. But the boy took the sigil, didn't he?"

"Why . . . yes. He wanted to hand it over to my brother. But I feared the thing was charged with dangerous magic, so I made him throw it down a necessarium at Castle Vanguard."

"Ah. That was well done. The moonstone might have done great harm in inexperienced hands, and for love of you I would not see your dear brother Stergos imperiled."

"So you love me! You've never said so."

"I say it now. And I prove it thus . . ."

The minutes that followed were broken only by wordless cries. Then the passion of the two in the sitting room grew more intense, until it was evident that neither paid any heed to their surroundings.

With tears of humiliation and fury streaming from her eyes, Princess Maudrayne crept out from beneath the furs, refolded them with shaking hands, and slipped away, locking the door to the prince's bedchamber behind her. When she was safe in her own apartment, she dried her eyes and put on an ermine-lined cloak against the night chill, then lit a candle and went to the elegant small room where her chief lady-in-waiting slept.

"Sovanna! Wake up. I have need of you."

The noblewoman groaned pitiably and emerged from her bedclothes with maddening slowness. "Madam, are you ill?"

"I'm unable to sleep. Every bone in my body aches. You must fetch the shaman Red Ansel Pikan and have him bring me a remedy. I presume he still resides in his usual palace room?"

Sovanna Ironside lurched to her feet and fumbled for her house shoes. Her voice was barely civil. "Well, he should be there. One never knows for sure. Since you left on the king's pilgrimage, the Tarnian leech has prowled the city as he pleases, night and day, doing God knows what. But he usually comes back to the palace for a good meal and strong drink and a warm bed . . . Ah, where's my plaguey cloak? It's freezing in here."

"Fetch Ansel yourself, Sovanna. Don't send a footman. And hurry."

A martyred sigh. "Yes, Your Grace."

When the woman was gone, Maudrayne returned to her sitting room, heaped fuel on the nearly extinct fire, and efficiently poked it back to life. Pouring herself another stiff tot of brandy, she sat brooding by the hearth for over half an hour, until there came a scratching at the hall door.

She opened it to a smiling, rotund man of medium stature. He was clad in a brown leather tunic with matching gartered trews, over which he wore a greatcoat of lustrous sealskin, ornamented at the sleeves and hem with wide bands of gold thread embroidery and ivory beadwork. A massive pectoral of gold paved with Tarnian opals hung on his breast, and he carried a sea-ivory baton ornamented with inlays of precious metal. His hair and bushy beard had the lively tint of tundra fire-lilies, and his eyes were dark, deep set, and kind.

"Can't sleep, Maudie?" he inquired genially. "I've got just the thing." He touched an ornate baldric having numerous pouches closed with ivory toggles.

The sharp-faced lady-in-waiting hovered behind him, carrying a lantern. "Will there be anything else, Your Grace?"

"Thank you, Sovanna," the princess said. "You may retire." She took Red Ansel's arm and drew him inside, locking the door. "I'm sorry to have roused you."

"Oh, I wasn't asleep. There's much ado in the palace tonight. Prince Heritor Conrig summoned me less than half an hour ago, following a wee-hours meeting of the Privy Council. It seems your husband fears an attack on Cala from the Continent. I've been ordered to enlist Tarnian mercenary ships to help defend the city."

She lifted her brows. "And will they come?"

"I'll windspeak the sealords in Goodfortune Bay early tomorrow and we'll see. The prince wanted me to do it at once, but I told him our countrymen would charge him double if they were forced to talk business in the middle of the night."

"Come and sit with me by the fire. Would you like some brandy?"

Ansel chuckled. "Does a Tarnian ever refuse good liquor?" He studied her face as she poured, and his cheerful mien became one of deep concern. "You didn't really summon me for a sleeping potion, did you, lass?"

"No, old friend." She sighed. They took their ease and he waited patiently for her to speak while they both sipped from crystal cups. Her question, when it finally came, made him goggle in astonishment.

"Ansel, what is a Sending?"

"Well, well! So you've got yourself mixed up in sorcery, have you?"

"Not I," she said calmly, "but my lord husband."

A brief look of pity shone in the shaman's eyes. "A Sending is a magical body replica, a double of a highly talented person, sent over a distance to have converse with another who possesses talent. The simulacrum is virtually identical to the Sender's natural form—warm and solid, not a ghost. While a wizard inhabits his Sending, his true body remains alive but totally senseless."

Maudrayne was taken aback. "The—the person receiving the Sending must *also* possess talent?"

"Oh, yes. The receiver helps to solidify the Sending, which may then prowl about anywhere it chooses. But it can only arrive in the near vicinity of an adept."

Her glance fell. When she spoke her voice was desolate. "A Sending came to my husband this night and may still be with him in his chambers. I overheard them but didn't see them together. It was not a wizard who came but a witch: Ullanoth, Conjure-Princess of Moss."

"By the Three Icebound Sisters! Then Prince Conrig is secretly adept! I never got close to him when he returned to the palace, so I had no idea. His talent must be exiguous indeed if no Brother of Zeth has detected it."

"This is a calamity, Ansel. If Conrig's talent were known, he would be barred from the Cathran succession."

"But surely you would not betray your husband's secret, my child. Nor would I."

"I'm not certain what I will do," she said in an ominous tone. "Answer another question for me. Can a Sending become pregnant?"

"Great God of the Boreal Blizzards," Ansel breathed. "The Mossland witch has had sexual congress with your husband?"

Her voice had a preternatural composure. "Yes. This very night—and probably not for the first time. I've told you that Conrig has been cold toward me because he fears I'm barren. Now I think he may intend to put me aside— perhaps taking this Ullanoth to wife." She gave a small, bitter laugh. "But here's a fine jest: I'm virtually certain that I'm two months with child. It was to tell Conrig the wonderful news that I went into his chambers tonight and waited for him. I fell asleep, and when I woke he was in the next room with Ullanoth's Sending. And they—they—" She squeezed her eyes shut. "God help me, Ansel. I heard them! And if she can also give him a child—"

The shaman bent forward, taking the hands of the princess. "Maudie, a Sending *cannot* conceive. Neither can it digest food, or perform any other natural bodily function—or even remain longer than a few hours in the place where it was Sent, for then the genuine body would sicken and die as its energies were drained."

Maudrayne cried, "Say you true?" Tears brimmed in her eyes, and for a moment she was exalted.

"I do, dear girl. I know all about such things, for they are part of the magical heritage of the Far North."

The sudden joy drained from her face, to be replaced with a look of calculation. "Then perhaps there is time to win him back, if my pregnancy goes well. Conrig covets an heir as much as he does the Sovereignty of Blenholme. But I think I shall not tell him yet. No, not until our love is rekindled and I am certain that I have first place in his heart . . . One other thing I must know: What is a sigil?"

The shaman's benign face hardened. "It's a piece of strangely carved moonstone made by the Salka monsters in ages long past, so fraught with peril that no sensible magicker would have anything to do with it—a charm conjured with the dread power of the Coldlight Army. Don't tell me Prince Conrig is meddling with such a thing!"

"I'm not sure. What does a sigil do?"

"They have various purposes, depending upon the spell infused within them. But all have the potential to destroy the soul of the user and do great harm to those around them. You must tell me how you came to know of such a thing. Did the prince and Ullanoth speak of it?"

She told him what she had overheard about Iscannon the wizard-assassin, slain by Conrig's young footman Deveron, and how the Conjure-Princess had inquired offhandedly about what had been done with a sigil taken from his dead body.

"Iscannon," the shaman murmured. "I know of him. A member of Moss's Glaumerie Guild, which has custody of Rothbannon's renowned Seven Stones. So he was killed by a common servant boy! I wonder how that happened?"

"My husband claimed that this sigil was thrown down a latrine in Castle Vanguard by the footman. Ullanoth was happy for its disposal, saying as you do that it was very dangerous. But—I think Conrig may have lied."

"Hmmm! Why don't I search his chambers? One can't scry a sigil, but no locked door can stop *me*. If Prince Conrig has the magical moonstone, perhaps I can find a way to take it away from him and put it in a safe place."

Maudrayne brightened. "Could you do that? I confess that I don't know whether I still love the damned man or hate him at this moment, but I certainly would not have him endangered by evil magic."

"You can trust me, lass. Of course, Conrig may not have the sigil after all. Who is this young footman called Deveron?"

"A furtive lad, always skulking about and turning up in unexpected places. I think Conrig uses him as a sort of domestic spy. He's certainly more than an ordinary servant."

"Does he possess talent?"

"Certainly not."

"Puzzling," mused the shaman. "And to think that such a one killed Iscannon! I think I'll take a discreet look at this interesting young man and find out whether he secretly kept Iscannon's stone—perhaps as a souvenir. If he did, something will have to be done. Don't worry, Maudie. I'll deal with it." He rose to his feet. "You need sleep after your tiring journey." He opened one of the pockets on his baldric and removed a green phial, oddly shaped. "Put three drops of this in water and drink it down. You will fall asleep at once and rest dreamlessly."

She took the tiny bottle. "Thank you, Ansel. Come again to me tomorrow. I'll tell you about the trip to Zeth Abbey, and you can tell me how you've fared for the past three weeks. How is the ambassador's ailing small daughter?"

"Fully recovered and homesick for Tarn."

The princess sighed. "So am I, old friend. Sick and so very, very tired!" She kissed him on the cheek, let him out, and secured the door to the corridor.

At the entrance to her bedchamber she paused. By now, the ceramic bottles of hot water the servants had carefully arranged to warm her sheets would be stone cold. Why not sleep in front of the sitting-room fire? She went for a pillow and a down comforter and settled into an upholstered armchair with a footstool. When she was comfortable, she realized she had forgotten water for the sleeping potion. She studied the gleaming green-glass phial in the firelight. It contained over a dram, enough to bring many nights of sleep.

I don't believe I need this after all, she thought drowsily, tucking it into a pocket of her robe. But it may come in handy later.

eleven

Nightmares had begun to poison Snudge's sleep even before the prince's retinue left Castle Vanguard, and they had persisted during the journey back to Cala Palace and in the weeks since then. The dream was always more or less the same.

First he found himself reliving his encounter with the Mosslander spy, saw that ravaged face materialize out of invisibility and assume an expression of false friendship, stubby teeth exposed in a parody of a smile. Then the hawk-orange eyes turned to orbs of onyx blazing with malignant talent. The boy once again felt a profound cold spreading through his body and steely thumbs throttling the life out of him. At the brink of death, he finally took fumbling hold of his dagger and slammed it deep into the enemy's heart.

And heard the sorcerer's windspoken cry of desperation: *Beynor!*

Snudge never saw the spy die, for that was the signal for the dream to change, for another person to appear, one he had never seen when wide awake.

The man was gauntly attractive and quite tall, perhaps no older than Snudge himself, although there was nothing youthful about his masterful bearing and narrow, pinched countenance. He wore sumptuous clothing edged with fur. His head was bare, and his hair was as pale and glistening as thistledown. At first, the young man in the dream appeared to be standing inside various richly furnished rooms, often backed by a window showing a night sky.

In later dreams, Snudge saw him poised in the bow of a great ship, with his hair blown nearly horizontal in a strong wind, which he seemed not to notice. Sails swelled and crackled above him and spray crashed rail-high as the stem of the vessel split the water at speed. Beyond lay an expanse of dark ocean, incongruously unruffled, a few drifting icebergs, and a sky strewn with brilliant stars.

Whether in strange mansions or on shipboard, the young man always held the same conversation with Snudge. His bloodless lips spoke without audible sound.

Throw it into the sea, Deveron Austrey!

"What?"

Get rid of it as soon as you can. Throw it away!

"What? Throw away what?"

That which is mine. Go down to the docks in Cala Harbor and throw it into the water so that it may return to me. Banish all memory of it, or risk the revenge of the Lights, pain and desolation more terrible than any that a human being can imagine.

"Who are you? What are you talking about?"

You know what I'm talking about. You stole it from my servant Iscannon after you killed him. You keep it well hidden. You search through books taken from the library of the Royal Alchymist, hoping to unlock its secret. You never will. All you'll discover is a horror worse than death.

"Are you the one called Beynor? The Conjure-Prince of Moss?"

I am. And the thing you stole is mine to command—not yours.

"That's not what the arcane books say. Any talented person—"

So you admit you have the sigil! Stupid cullion—how dare you aspire to know the Beaconfolk? Haven't your clumsy researches taught you what you're playing with? The Lights are older than mankind, older than the Salka, older even than the dry land's rising from the sea. The Coldlight Army could destroy us all on a mere whim.

"But they haven't destroyed you, have they? And they didn't protect your spy from my dagger. Perhaps you're lying to me, Prince Beynor . . . I wonder if I should ask your sister Ullanoth about the Beaconfolk. And about the sigil."

Lowborn fool! Whore's kitling! Stinking heap of dogpuke! Do you think you can bandy words with me? Throw the moonstone into the sea! Do it tonight!

"No. And you can't force me to do it, or you would have done so already. Go to hell."

You're the one who will experience hell, Deveron Austrey. Now feel the least punishment the Lights can inflict on ignorant meddlers: BI THO SILSHUA!

Prince Beynor vanished, leaving only a dream-sky with countless stars and that oddly calm northern sea. Snudge felt a gruesome chill again, like the one the sorcerer-spy had inflicted on him, starting at his extremities and flooding slowly toward his body's core, sucking warmth and life from his flesh and entrails and brain. His suffering was appalling—but even worse was the sense of overwhelming fear and foreboding that took hold of him. Somehow, he realized that he had not even begun to experience the fullness of agony. But he would, and very soon, because the torturers were coming for him out of that glittering black sky.

Lights.

Slow-moving blobs of silvery-green, scarlet, and gold, accompanied by a faint hissing crackle, rose up from the horizon. The glowing patches expanded, brightened, became sweeping colored beams and enormous rippling bands and pale bursts of unearthly radiance that finally coalesced into iridescent shapes resembling monstrous living creatures. The Great Lights filled the sky with their brightness and engulfed him, bringing the most atrocious pain he had ever experienced. Whispery laughter mocked him and reveled in his agony as he writhed and tried to scream, and shrank away to a frost-coated nubbin of misery, trapped amidst cracked and shattered bones.

He woke up as always, unable to move, rigid on his palliasse in the chamber where he and the eleven other privileged armigers of the prince's cohort slept. He had flung aside the bedcoverings and lay naked to the cold predawn wind blowing in from Cala Bay, silently cursing the day he had taken the moonstone sigil from the dead sorcerer.

It hung around his neck on a cord. He never took it off and politely refused to let the other boys examine it closely, saying it was a sacred talisman given him by his late grandfather. The bully Mero Elwick had tried to rip it away one day in the washroom, but Snudge had kneed him in the crotch and left him gagging and cursing, and no one had bothered him about it since.

The square of semi-precious gemstone was carved with the circumpolar constellations and odd asymmetrical shapes Snudge could not put a name to. It never glowed or manifested any magic. In the time he had spent in Cala Palace since returning from Castle Vanguard, with Vra-Kilian fortuitously absent on the king's pilgrimage and none of his assistant wizards clever enough to catch him in the act, the boy had rifled the Royal Alchymist's collection of arcane volumes at every opportunity, seeking information about sigils, about the insubstantial beings who empowered them, and about the sorcerers who dared to use such perilous magical instruments. Before retiring each evening, he would report to Prince Conrig the things he had learned—little enough that was useful, but a good deal that scared the wits out of him and made the prince frown with concern.

"I know most of your time is now taken up with learning the knightly arts," Conrig had said, "but keep searching the Alchymical Library whenever you can. I must know more about the Beaconfolk and the royal conjurors of Moss and the sorcerers of the Glaumerie Guild before we invade Didion."

So Snudge obeyed, and each night dreamed the dream, and woke paralyzed in the freezing twilight before sunup.

After a few minutes he would be able to move again. He'd rewind himself tightly in blankets and feather-tick until he stopped shivering. Then—he never told any of this to Prince Conrig—he prowled the wind in search of any hint that Beynor's dream-visitation and awful words were anything but the product of his own imagination. The search for awareness-threads was invariably fruitless. No one ever seemed to be scrying the part of the palace where he lay—not that they would have been able to oversee him! And no one tried to bespeak him from afar.

As Snudge's body warmed, his talented concentration invariably flagged. No matter how hard he tried to stay alert, sleep always claimed him again. Dreamless, he would lie without moving until the rising-bell tolled.

On the morning of the day that the dream changed, the armigers broke their fast with big bowls of oat-and-walnut porridge sweetened with willowherb honey. There were cannikins of small ale to drink, and tasty blobs of yellow cheese-curd and new-crop apples for those who still felt hungry. Snudge usually did.

After the meal, which was all they would get to eat until dinner, the boys trooped off to the palace tiltyard to practice warfare with swords, lance, or morningstar— the latter being a spiked iron ball attached to a wooden handle by a chain, particularly deadly when wielded by a rider against multiple opponents on foot. All of the squires except Snudge believed that they would soon be marching northward to Beorbrook Hold, where they and the Heart Companions they served would join the earl marshal's forces in guarding Great Pass against Didionite incursions.

A few knights were honing their skills in the yard that day. Two Heart Companions, Count Feribor and Count Tayman, fully armored, were tilting in the lists with softwood lances, attended by their squires, Mero and Saundar. But most of the student fighters were armigers—not only of Prince Conrig's cohort but also those who served knights of the royal household. The boys in their short, colored surcoats made a fine display as they charged the quintains on horseback or dueled each other with blunted swords, while trainers looked on and criticized. Only Snudge, the youngest and rawest student, and Vra-Stergos's armiger Gavlok Whitfell—slow-moving, gangling, and cursed with too much intelligence and imagination to enjoy simulated mortal combat—earned serious reprimands from the Palace Master-at-Arms, Sir Hale Brackenfield, who circulated about the yard keeping a close eye on the action.

Easygoing Gavlok saw his own lack of fighting expertise as a great joke. His principal duties were to fetch and carry for the Doctor Arcanorum and serve him when he traveled. Guarding his master against physical attack, while also part of an armiger's responsibility, was a minor charge for Gavlock. In spite of having a rather timid, fussy personality, Vra-Stergos was quite capable of fending off common villains with the protective magic of the Mystic Order of Zeth.

Snudge took his own shortcomings more seriously. Not long after returning to Cala Palace, Prince Conrig had commanded Sir Hale to cram as much martial training as possible into his young protégé during the few weeks available to them, even if it left Snudge temporarily lame.

"You'll recover on the march to the north country," Conrig had told the boy with a heartless laugh. "Do us both proud! Remember you're a prince's man now, with a new blazon and honor all your own."

In a stretch of the Cathran custom of battlefield dubbing of commoners who performed deeds of great prowess, the footman Deveron Austry had been declared worthy of knighthood for signal service rendered to the Prince Heritor. (Details were not forthcoming.) The ceremony was brief, attended only by Vra-Stergos, the Heart Companions, and their squires. Snudge swore fealty to Conrig as his liege lord, and the prince gifted him with a sword, a handsome suit of light armor, a silver drinking cup, and enough money to kit him out decently for his new duties. The knight's belt and the associated grant of lands in fee would not be bestowed until Snudge reached the age of twenty and was legally adult, but he was now an armiger, entitled to be invested with personal armorial bearings. The choice was Snudge's own.

After much thought, he chose a silver owl gardant on a sable field for his coat-of-arms. As a result, he'd had to put up with jeering hoots from the other boys, endless jokes about mouse-catching, and a plump rat, cooked to a turn, served up with a flourish at breakfast one morn by a solemn-faced kitchen lad, while the other armigers fell about laughing.

Snudge had done his utmost to absorb the crash course of knightly training. His performance at quintain was respectable enough, because he could influence horses with his talent. He'd gallop at full tilt toward the pivoting dummy on its post and usually managed to hit it squarely with lance or morningstar. Even if he was off center, his control of his mount was so adroit that the treacherous back-swing of the dummy never knocked him out of the saddle.

But swordplay was another kettle of fish. Sir Hale let him learn the basic longsword moves practicing with amiable Gavlok; but after two weeks of slow-motion thrust and parry, Snudge had been passed on to stocky, blackhaired Belamil Langsands, the best swordsman among the armigers, to learn use of the curved varg sword that had been bestowed upon him at his dubbing. The lighter blade was more deadly against skilled warriors when fighting afoot.

Belamil's varg could whirl like a silver windmill and change direction faster than a spooked trout. Even worse, he sang lustily as he fought—for Snudge's benefit the ditty of choice was "The Wise Old Owl"—and rewarded the boy's mistakes by whacking him stoutly with the flat of his varg while caroling the refrain: *"To-whit to-whooo!"* Even wearing chain mail and a padded jerkin, Snudge ended up bruised from neck to knee after a week of this tutelage. His ego was even more seriously damaged by the universal applause that accompanied Belamil's punishments.

"I'll never be any good with swords," Snudge moaned to Gavlok, as the young fighters paused to rest and quench their thirst with deep drafts of cider.

"It takes time," the lanky squire said, smiling. "At least you've got a certain natural flair. I don't! I'll never be anything better than a bumbling hacker. I plan to ask Lord Stergos for a protective charm before we start out for the north."

"Who says I've got a natural flair?" Snudge asked in disbelief.

"Belamil. He's actually quite pleased at the way you're coming along with the varg."

"You're joking! He laughs at me. He's never given me the least word of encouragement or praise."

"That's the way it works, young Deveron. Now don't get all puffed up, or tell Belamil that I spoke out of turn."

"I won't," said Snudge humbly. "But thank you for telling me. I've been feeling pretty rotten about letting Prince Conrig down. I know the rest of the armigers think I'm just a jumped-up servant—"

"Some do. Most of us don't know what to make of you." Gavlok grinned. "You're a strange one. You keep to yourself too much. You creep away, going God knows where after dinner instead of joining the rest of us for games and other fun."

Snudge hesitated. "I have certain tasks to do for the prince."

"Snooping and sneaking?" The other boy's eyes sparkled, taking some of the sting out of his words. But he was in earnest.

"I can't talk about it, Gavlok. I'm sorry." Snudge looked away. Some sort of commotion was going on at the far end of the tilting yard, near the passageway leading into the main block of the palace.

"Did you really save Prince Conrig's life?" The question was offhand. "They say an assassin got into Castle Vanguard and you found him out. But I know you never strayed from the repository tower until the day after the great secret meeting, any more than Belamil and Saundar and Mero and I did. We were always together."

"No, we weren't. The lot of you slept too much." Snudge's attention was on the increasing activity across the yard. Even Feribor and Tayman had abandoned their jousting to join the crowd.

"You left the tower when the rest of us were asleep? But there were guards . . ."

"And secret passages," said Snudge absently. "What d'you suppose is going on over there? Maybe we'd better go and see."

"So you skulked about Castle Vanguard stealthily," Gavlok prompted, "and discovered the assassin, and alerted the guard."

"No." Snudge turned and fixed the older boy with a calm look. "I stabbed the bastard in the heart."

"God's Teeth!" Gavlok blurted.

"And that's all I'm going to say about it. Tell the other armigers if you like. I don't suppose it matters now. But warn them that I don't want to discuss the matter. It was the most awful moment of my life . . . And now please excuse me. I've got to find out what the excitement is about."

Most of the squires and their trainers were gathered around a small figure wearing rich court dress, who was jumping up and down in manic glee and exclaiming, "Tonight! Tonight! Papa and Mummy are coming back tonight!"

He was Prince Tancoron the Simple, second-born son of King Olmigon, seven-and-twenty years of age, but having the stature and mentality of a ten-year-old. He had bright blue eyes that were too wide set and oddly slanted, a button nose, and beardless cheeks. His sunny, unspoiled nature had made him a favorite of almost everyone in Cala Palace.

"Tonight! They're coming tonight! I heard Con say so. An outrider brought the news. Maybe we'll have a party!" Beaming, he looked up at the Master-at-Arms. "Will we have a party, Sir Hale?"

"I think not, Your Grace," Brackenfield said in a patient voice. "Your royal father the king is not well. When he comes home, he'll have to rest. But we can gather in the forecourt to welcome him, and perhaps there will be a party later."

The simpleton's face fell. "But I thought Papa went away to get better. He told me he'd ask the emperor's ghost to help him."

Count Feribor's laugh was full of cruel condescension. "Ghosts are not very good doctors, Prince Tanny. Actually, they're rather frightful things! The king didn't really expect Emperor Bazekoy's spirit to make him well. He wanted the emperor to give him uncanny advice. Advice about the kingdom. Every king of Cathra may ask the emperor's spirit one important Question."

Tancoron nodded gravely. "What if the Question is, 'How can I get well?'"

Mero, Count Feribor's squire, gave a snort of contempt. Others in the crowd murmured uneasily, afraid of what might be coming. Count Tayman said, "Feri, I don't think you should—"

"Oh, your father the king would never ask a silly thing like that, Prince Tanny." Feribor was still in full armor, except for the tilting helm, which was held by Mero. His saturnine face was streaked with sweat and his dark eyes held a gleam of expectant mirth. But his next words were spoken with great gentleness. "You see, only a dying king may ask Emperor Bazekoy a Question."

There were gasps from the armigers. The prince uttered a forlorn little wail. "Papa is dying?"

"Didn't they tell you?" Feribor Blackhorse was all solicitude. "Well, maybe they were afraid it would make you cry. And princes should never be crybabies."

"Damn you, Feri!" muttered Count Tayman. But no one else dared say a word against the queen's nephew, who only played his little games when Conrig or other members of the royal family were not present.

"I—I don't want to be a crybaby." Tancoron's face was dark with woe. Tears brimmed in his blue eyes. "But I don't want my papa to die. Papa! Papa!" With desperate strength, the small man pushed his way through the crowd of appalled fighters and dashed away into the passage leading to the palace.

"Poor lackwit," said Feribor cheerfully. "Well, he brought good news, at any rate, didn't he, lads? With the king back and giving his royal permission, we'll be off to fight the starving Diddlies in no time at all! . . . Come on, Tayman. Let's have one more joust before we call it a day."

After the evening meal, at about the eighth hour, Snudge hastened to the tower where the Royal Alchymist had his quarters. If the king's cavalcade was due before midnight, as Prince Conrig had announced during dinner, then this would be the last safe opportunity get at Vra-Kilian's books before his return.

Two young novice wizards had guard duty outside the door of the Alchymical Library, which connected to Kilian's private chambers. They sat at flanking desks equipped with oil lamps, copying out manuscripts. The library door was slightly ajar, as was usual during the daylight and evening hours, when Kilian's many assistants might need to consult the volumes of arcana or collections of magical paraphernalia in their master's outer offices. Above the doorframe hung a brass bell of peculiar form, with a clapper attached to a cord. If it was rung, every alchymist and windvoice in the palace would come running.

Snudge took off his house shoes and left them in a dark alcove, then cast his windsight about to make sure no one else was working in the library or approaching. The coast was clear, and the guardian novices hadn't noticed him. It was time to hide. Taking a deep breath, he concentrated his talent upon the two heads bent over leaves of parchment, commanding them not to look up. Quill pens continued to scratch industriously. The boy left the alcove and walked boldly up to the novices in his stocking feet, went through the door, and closed it without a sound. Neither of the men paid any attention to him.

Strictly speaking, Snudge's method of "hiding" had nothing to do with genuine invisibility. It was rather a way of distracting the minds of others, so that people had no desire to look at him and never noticed his presence. The trick didn't always work, especially with the adept, who were sensitive to mental meddling. Even ordinary folk might penetrate his spell if he made noise or tried the trick when there were more than two or three persons about in broad daylight.

Tonight he was home free again! So—one last chance to search out the sigil's secret, and better be quick about it. He'd long since examined the books on the open shelves and knew they contained nothing very useful. The volumes that remained to be investigated were inside the Royal Alchymist's private rooms, located at the far end of the library. He'd been in there before, taking advantage of Vra-Kilian's absence.

It was laughably easy to pick the lock, slip inside, and refasten the door behind him. His talent ignited the tapers of a silver candelabrum standing on a table, which he took up to illuminate his way.

The alchymist's sitting room gave onto his bedchamber and the inner sanctum, the latter being secured with two complex locks, which Snudge spent some time opening. That small room, where the most important books and magical apparatus were kept, was a windowless place having a single worktable and a tier of shelves holding curious contraptions, some protected by glass covers. Against the wall on the right stood four magnificently carved oaken cabinets equipped with elaborate locks—and indwelling magical spells to prevent windsnoopers from discerning their contents. Snudge had already opened and scrutinized the contents of two of them. Several of the ancient volumes inside had provided him with general information on the Beaconfolk and the Glaumerie Guild of Moss, facts that he had dutifully shared with Prince Conrig; but there had been no details about the sigils' function, only emphatic warnings against using them.

It took Snudge nearly half an hour to open the third enchanted cabinet, using his most delicate picks. The thing turned out to be packed with sacks of gold coins, bejeweled rings, and other portable riches that the austere Brothers of Zeth weren't supposed to concern themselves with. Snudge grunted in disgust, wondering whether the prince would be interested to know about his uncle's inappropriate cache of valuables. He never thought of taking any of it for himself.

The fourth cabinet was smaller than the others and bound about sturdily with heavy iron bands. It was not secured by a mortise lockset, as the other three had been, but had a steel escutcheon with a type of locking device that Snudge had never seen before. It had no keyhole and thus was immune to his picks. Four tiny revolving ring-cylinders were set into the plate beside the handle, and each was etched with a succession of odd characters, like letters of an alien alphabet. The boy quickly decided that opening the lock would require aligning the appropriate characters, and there seemed to be a dozen or more on each cylinder.

Snudge's knowledge of mathematics was only rudimentary, but he realized that the potential number of character-combinations was very large.

Hopeless! Unless . . .

Was Vra-Kilian as lazy as ordinary mortals? Would he bother spinning the four rings each time he locked the cabinet, or was he so confident of his magisterial authority over his underlings that he used a shortcut?

Snudge turned the lowest cylinder clockwise a single notch to a new character. Nothing. He turned it counter-clockwise—

Click.

Yes!

Easing open the cabinet's weighty door, he choked back a blasphemous exclamation. Most of the shelves were empty. But the middle one held two wicker baskets full of sigils.

They were of various shapes and sizes, thick and thin, densely carved or nearly plain. Many were perforated and strung on rotting cords, or on golden chains like the one worn by the dead sorcerer Iscannon. All were carved from blue-white, translucent mineral. None of them possessed the uncanny foxfire glow of magical life, but Snudge was still afraid to touch them.

Three volumes bound in stained, crumbling, pearl-colored leather lay beside the baskets. Each had a round wafer of moonstone in a golden setting fastened firmly to its cover. There was no lettering stamped on the books to hint at the subject matter within. He picked one up and felt the fragile pages shift, as if they were separating from the binding.

How old *was* this collection? Had Vra-Kilian inherited these things from some long-dead predecessor, and had he kept them hidden, too prudent (or fearful) to invoke the magic of the Beaconfolk himself?

But if that was so, why had he left the strange lock ready to open? Had he anticipated that he might sometime need the cabinet's contents in a hurry?

Snudge removed the three books and sat on the floor to study them by candlelight. The two larger ones were in an unknown language, and he set them aside. The third volume, smaller and more slender than the others, seemed to be written in some variant of the Cathran tongue; but the inscribed letters were faded and oddly shaped, and the spelling was strange. Many of the words were incomprehensible, and he realized that it would take some effort to decipher the book's contents.

He turned the brittle pages cautiously. There were five short chapters with titles he could read fairly easily: *A [Brief?] Thaumaturgia of the Cold Light Host; A Catalogus of Sigils; Conjuration and Abolition of the Sigil; Commanding the Sigil;* and, last and most ominously, *Vital Precautions for the Thaumaturgist.*

"Futter me!" he whispered, stricken with awe and delight. "Bull's-eye at last!" Now what?

He didn't dare take any of the stones. Having one of them in his possession was hard enough to explain to his overcurious peers. But the smallest book could be concealed easily enough, and perhaps Vra-Kilian wouldn't notice that it was missing. Snudge reckoned it must hold the secret to activating his own sigil, if he could only puzzle it out.

Time had flown, and he had to cover his traces and get out quickly. It had to be nearly ten, the hour when the guardian novices secured the main library for the night. He couldn't risk being locked in. Snudge knew well enough that none of the picks he carried were large enough to open the massive lock on the outer door. And, of course, the Royal Alchymist himself would be returning to his rooms shortly after the king's train arrived . . .

Hastily, the boy scooped up the two foreign-language books and replaced them on the shelf. He shut the cabinet and reset the lock combination as he had found it.

Now, how to carry the other book safely? If he hid it in his clothes or crammed it into his wallet, the old thing might fall to pieces.

Snudge sighed. The lining of his brand-new armiger's doublet would have to be sacrificed. He used his knife to slice out a strip of silk, wrapped the book, and thrust it under his shirt, where it nestled against the sigil on its long cord. What next? A few crumbs of pale bookbinding had fallen to the floor. He moistened a finger, picked them up, and tapped them down his neck.

The burnt-down candles would have to be replaced. Snudge had found unused ones in the sitting room's candelabrum when he first broke in. He wasted frantic minutes searching tabourets and presses until he discovered a box of fresh candles. The stubs and fallen blobs of beeswax went into his wallet. He scried the main library to be sure it was unoccupied and went out, locking the door to the private rooms behind him.

Another quick windscan showed him the two novices nodding over their work. He heard the castle chimes begin to strike the tenth hour. The young wizards sighed, stretched, and grinned at each other as they began putting their work away inside their desks.

Snudge concentrated his talent and slipped through the outer door. Neither robed figure looked up as he moved down the gloomy corridor, retrieved his shoes, and went away quietly. Behind him, the sound of an enormous iron key grated in its lock. He hurried toward the wing of the palace where the Prince Heritor's apartments were, intending to show his master what he'd discovered; but when he arrived, the lord-in-waiting on duty, whose name was Telifar, turned him away.

"His Grace is preparing for the arrival of the king," the man said, "as well as an extraordinary meeting of the Privy Council. You won't be giving him your usual report tonight, young Deveron. He says to come tomorrow after breakfast if you've anything important to tell him."

"Very well, my lord," said Snudge, disappointed. But as he walked toward the armigers' quarters in the Square Tower of the palace, he decided that the delay was all for the best. If he had time to explore the book's contents, he might have something really useful to tell Prince Conrig.

His hand stole inside his jerkin, then beneath the shirt where the book was hidden. He felt the slippery silk wound around it starting to come loose. Codders! Better stop and wrap it up tightly again lest the book be damaged. He ducked behind a heavy window-drape and began to unfasten his clothes, then stopped abruptly as a faint aching pain spread across his chest.

A greenish light had ignited beneath the white linen of his shirt.

"Oh, God!" he moaned, tearing open the rest of the buttons. The silk had fallen away from the book, and the moonstone disk attached to its cover was pressed against the sigil that hung about his neck. Both pieces of stone were aglow. Carefully, he lifted the book away, holding it through the silk.

The disk's light winked out, but that of the sigil continued to shine. The dull ache persisted as well, and out of the corner of his eye he thought he spied a quick movement. But he was almost completely enveloped in the drape, concealed between it and the window, with dark night beyond the panes of thick glass. When he looked about the constricted space he saw nothing—no fluttering moth, no drifting bit of lint, no disturbed spiderling creeping on the dusty cloth.

Once again he detected that elusive movement just beyond his field of vision. And there was a harsh deep voice, asking a question.

CADAY AN RUDAY?

Snudge gave a great start and almost yelped in terror. Then he realized that the words were being spoken on the wind. But it was no human voice asking the question. The words meant nothing to him.

CADAY AN RUDAY?!

The pain! It was sharper, and the windvoice was louder as well, an invisible giant bellowing out of an echoing cavern. Getting impatient, too.

CADAY AN RUDAY?!!!

The voice was like rolling thunder in his mind. A sudden piercing chest-thrust from the moonstone, like an icicle's stab, bent him over double. His vision was beginning to dim and he choked back a scream. The sigil swung on its cord away from his flesh and the pain ceased abruptly. He clawed at the cord and pulled the amulet off. It fell to the floor, where it lay with its glow extinguished.

In his mind, there was only silence.

twelve

Louring clouds hid the sky over Moss, and decrepit old Fenguard Castle seemed more dank and uncomfortable than usual to Ullanoth when she returned from her windflight.

Earlier, before she had Sent herself to Prince Conrig in Cala, she had her trusted slave Wix build a goodly fire in her sitting room and batten up the shutters on all the windows. Now she went to the hearth to savor the warmth of the glowing peat. A pot of heated wine with cinnamon and darnel hung waiting on a crane, and she helped herself to a soothing cupful. She had suffered from an unquiet mind often of late—and no wonder, with all her plots and stratagems to keep in order, like a juggler with too many duck-eggs in the air.

Beynor's unexpected return to the castle that evening had been a most unwelcome development. His magnificent new barque, a gift from the two princes of Didion, had appeared in the estuary without warning, masked by Fortress sorcery until the last moment. He had rebuffed her invitation to supper and gone immediately to see Conjure-King Linndal, doubtless to crow about his diplomatic coup on the Continent.

She had hoped her brother's voyage home would take a few days longer so that she might sort out the spunkies without risking his interference. Well, there was no helping it now. With Beynor here, even though he was still closeted with their father inside the spell of his Fortress sigil, it wasn't safe to summon the little creatures to the castle. Since they refused to engage in long windspeech conversations for fear of attracting their Salka enemies, she'd have to endure an uncomfortable journey into the fens in the middle of the night.

Ullanoth finished off the cup of hot wine, enjoying the way the spicy fumes went to her head and eased both anxiety and the perpetual minor discomfort of the guardian moonstone. She let her mind dwell briefly on her hopes for the future. They *would* succeed, she and Conrig. In a short time the Sovereignty would control the island. And she would control the Sovereign . . .

She went to her bedchamber for outdoor clothing. On a stand beside the bed was a little ever-burning lamp that she kept filled with the finest scented oil. It illuminated a portrait painted on precious narwhal ivory and framed in solid gold, a crowned woman with fair hair drawn tightly back. Her face was thin to the point of gauntness, and her black eyes enormous and bright with dangerous talent. Only her smile was beautiful, sweetly tender, as if about to kiss a beloved child.

Ullanoth inclined her head to her mother's portrait, then found and put on waterproof boots and took from her wardrobe a hooded sheared-seal robe that was both warm and light of weight. Back in her workroom, she removed Concealer and Interpenetrator from the gold-mesh purse where she kept all of her moonstones save Fortress and carefully conjured them into readiness. As commanded, they glowed brightly and were active only when in contact with her bare hands—and hurt her only then, as the Lights had decreed. She wrapped the amulets separately in black satin squares, put them back into her belt-purse, and donned sturdy leather gloves.

She glanced about the capacious chamber, reluctant to leave now that her brother was back in residence, even though the place would be safe enough. Her Sending couch was here, her books, the sheets of parchment with her maps and battle-plans, and benches and shelves crowded with arcane equipment. In the center of the workroom stood an iron candlestick nearly two ells in height, holding a waxen blob. Affixed in it was the green-glowing plaque of moonstone called Fortress, which shielded all rooms on this top floor of the South Tower from windwatching, and interdicted any person other than herself from entering or leaving without her freely spoken permission. Only a Sender sigil could penetrate the spell of couverture—and no one possessed such a sigil save herself.

She left without locking her door. There was no need. Then she unwrapped Concealer, slipped it into her glove, and spoke its spell. Immediately, she vanished from sight.

A spiral staircase of rusting ironwork led from her tower rooms to the second floor of the keep, where the regal apartments, presence chamber, and cavernous throne room were situated. She descended the once-grandiose flight of broad steps giving access to the great hall, meeting no one on the way.

Fenguard Castle was a rather small place but massively fortified. The mighty sorcerer Rothbannon, first Conjure-King of Moss, had furnished it richly using gold wrested from Didion; but over the years his successors shrank away from using his powerful Seven Stones because of the concomitant penalties demanded by the Beaconfolk. For all their expertise in glamour, scrying, and other conventional magic, the rulers of the isolated little kingdom had been poor for many generations, and the royal seat had sadly deteriorated. Fenguard's tapestries and insulating arras had succumbed to moth and mildew, brightwork had tarnished, and the thick carpets had worn to shreds and were replaced—at least in the common rooms—by lowly rush matting. Firewood had always been scarce in Moss, where most trees were small and gnarled by the soggy soil and northerly climate, and charcoal was too dear for any use save forging. In these straitened times, even the king's household burned mostly peat blocks for warmth and cooking, and used rushlights, fagot-torches, or smelly seal-oil lanterns for light rather than expensive wax candles.

When I am Conjure-Queen, Ullanoth promised herself, all that will change.

She hurried through the gloomy great hall, where the freeborn servants were long since asleep on their pallets, down the staircase to the forebuilding, which was guarded but not locked, and out into the torchlit inner ward. Rothbannon's Marvel, a spectacular mechanical clock mounted above the massive gatehouse, showed a quarter past three in the morning.

She looked back toward the keep and saw lights shining in the royal chambers above. The occupants were shielded by Beynor's own Fortress sigil. For a moment she contemplated Sending herself to them and forcing a confrontation. Her Great Stone had the power to penetrate Fortress's guardian spell, and Interpenetrator would make the strongest door as easy to pierce as smoke. But she discarded the notion at once. She was not yet ready to reveal her own powerful weaponry to the enemy. Beynor believed that her sigils were only capable of defending her and performing minor sorcery. She'd taken care not to contradict his misapprehension, and now was not the time to disabuse him.

No one was about as she hurried past the quiet cookhouse, bakery, and stables and approached the guardhouse beside the inner gate, where special caution would be needed to avoid detection. She paused in the heavy shadows and slipped Interpenetrator into the palm of her other glove. Mentally, she spoke its enabling spell, gritting her teeth. Fortunately, the pain associated with the magic of the two minor sigils was not too severe.

Concealer had enabled her to vanish completely, except for a faint shadow cast by the light of the guards' peat brazier. Three armed men were gathered around it, warming themselves and gossiping in low voices. They never noticed the shadow drift past. Another pair of sentries stood on either side of the lowered inner portcullis next to the ropes of the alarm bells. They seemed half-asleep and ignored the almost inaudible sound of footsteps approaching the black iron grating . . . and the shadow that melted through the heavy metal without hindrance, then conquered the outer portcullis with equal ease.

She continued through the barbican, seeped past its barred oaken door, and traversed the outer ward, which was deserted except for sentries at the torchlit towngate and watergate. She approached the latter, keeping close to the wall to obscure her shadow, and used magic to make the four men on duty sneeze. As they were distracted, she drifted through the closed gate like a wraith, went cautiously down the long flight of stairs that wound through the rocks, and came finally onto the landing stage along the Darkling River.

She deactivated Interpenetrator and tucked it away. The shield of invisibility hurt hardly at all. A number of skiffs were chained at the far end of the landing. She unlocked the cleanest-looking one with a tap of her finger, climbed into it, and caused it to move rapidly upstream.

With the moon down and the sky mostly cloudy, it was very dark. Quick flicks of her windsight reassured her that no one was watching the "empty" boat mysteriously breasting the sluggish current. Mosslanders didn't often go abroad at night, for fear of the Salka cannibals and other nocturnal horrors. Rothbannon's clock tolled the half-hour, and she heard sentinels on the battlements of the castle faintly calling "All's well." From overhead came the mellow, hornlike calls of migrating swans, abandoning the fens for their winter refuges on the Southern Continent even though the first frost had yet to touch Moss. The only other sound was the chuckling of the river against the driving hull of the rickety boat. Patches of mist hung over the water.

When she was beyond the small capital city of Royal Fenguard, in the marshes of the Little Fen that extended between it and the broad expanse of Moss Lake, she guided the skiff out of the main channel and made it go up one of the innumerable small creeks that led back into the bulrushes. Soon she arrived at a small area of open water, dark as ink beneath the faint luminosity of the sky. It was a suitable spot, and she brought the boat to a halt.

Ullanoth stood up, threw back her fur hood, and called out on the wind.

Shanakin! Tyarn na tean gelain! Bi isti!

She waited impatiently. A light breeze, freighted with chill, began to blow out of the north, parting the wisps of mist, rustling the leaves of the marsh plants, and hinting of the arctic cold that would eventually spread down from the Great Fen, locking the land in winter fastness. Even with the weather changes brought about by the Wolf's Breath, the snows would start in Moss at the beginning of the Ice Moon. Dilapidated old Royal Fenguard would be swathed in white crystalline hoarfrost, even more beautiful than it had been in the day of the first Conjure-King—at least until the spring thaw unclothed its shabbiness.

Before then I'll rule, she told herself. Father couldn't deny her the succession if she confronted him with the power and wealth of the Sovereignty . . . and her own collection of activated sigils, which she was confident would overwhelm those now controlled by Beynor, that vainglorious little maggot!

Her detestable (but hugely talented) younger brother had been the first sorcerer since Rothbannon to successfully dare the Great Lights, and in doing so he had deprived Ullanoth of her royal birthright. Undaunted by the appalling fate of their mother, and with King Linndal distracted by periodic attacks of insanity, the youth had delved recklessly into Beaconfolk magic without hesitation or hindrance. By the time he was fourteen, he had activated five of the Seven Stones of Rothbannon kept in the custody of the Glaumerie Guild, in spite of the horrified wizards' best efforts to restrain him. His success emboldened him to demand the throne that was rightfully Ullanoth's. Their father, in his lucid moments, was not only delighted with Beynor's prowess at high sorcery, but also approved the boy's plot to subvert Didion and restore Moss's lost glory.

Ullanoth had at first despaired of equalling her brother's accomplishments and regaining what she felt was her birthright. The ruler of Moss had traditionally nominated his or her successor, although the eldest child had almost always ascended to the throne in the past. But how could she hope to oppose Beynor, who could command the Coldlight Army? He had brought four minor sigils and one Great Stone—Weathermaker—to life, while she was capable only of conventional magic. He felt free to insult her openly, invade her dreams, and torment her with ugly hints of what he would do to her when he became king. Ullanoth had sunk into despondency and even considered ending her life before she fell completely into her brother's power.

Then fate, or perhaps the benevolent Lady Moon, intervened on her behalf. One spring night, just after Beynor had miraculously deflected the Wolf's Breath away from Moss with the newly empowered Weathermaker (nearly killing himself at the same time that he earned the rapturous approbation of the mad king and the Guild), Ullanoth dreamed of her late mother, Taspiroth. It was as if the beloved ivory portrait had come to life and roused the sleeping princess by taking hold of her hand.

"Mother!" Ullanoth had cried joyfully, sitting up in bed. "You're alive!"

"Not in your world, dear child. You're dreaming—and when you wake I will be gone. Nevertheless, what I'm about to tell you is true, and you must do as I say."

Stricken with sorrow and fear, Ullanoth could only nod her head.

"Your brother has a heart dedicated only to himself," Conjure-Queen Taspiroth continued, "and he must not be allowed to prevail. You, my dear Ulla, are to rule Moss, and to do so you will have to conquer Beynor. However, I adjure you under pain of damnation not to kill him, nor even to harm a single hair of his head. Your brother will encompass his own doom after fulfilling the role he is destined to play in the history of our magical island of High Blenholme."

In the dream, Ullanoth gave protest. "But, Mother, how can I conquer Beynor without harming him? In fact, how can I manage the task at all, since he conjures the Lights and I'm helpless before their power?"

"I have a gift for you. Use it with the greatest of care, only when absolutely necessary, and all will come about as I have said."

The queen told her what she must do to find the gift and then kissed her on the brow, whereupon Ullanoth woke to the sound of spring birdsong. Most of the dream was still vivid in her mind; the only part she would forget was the implication that Beynor would rule Moss before her.

The next day, dressing herself in fusty old garments and concealing her bright hair, the princess had crept from the castle, stolen a small boat, and gone alone into the trackless swamp called the Little Fen, west of the castle. There, on a tiny rocky islet, she found the lightning-blasted skeleton of a dead willow, exactly as Queen Taspiroth had said.

Hidden among its roots was a rotting chest containing seven inactive sigils.

From her arcane studies, she realized that each one was capable of being conjured in a different mode of enchantment. Like the sigils owned by Beynor, four were minor and three were Great Stones capable of formidable sorcery. Furthermore, the means of activating them was contained in books within the Guild archives, freely accessible to all members of Moss's royal family.

Remembering how her poor mother had been destroyed by the Lights after bungling the empowerment of one of Rothbannon's Great Stones, Ullanoth had decided then and there against activating any of these new-found sigils out of mere curiosity. She would bring them to life only as needed, as the Conjure-Queen had advised.

She would certainly rule Moss. But why stop there?

In the years that followed, Ullanoth plotted her own strategy well. Studies of island history had taught her that magic alone was not enough to found an enduring empire, and neither were military leadership nor political astuteness, taken by themselves. At least two of those factors were necessary for any chance of success; and the odds would shoot up vastly if one possessed all three.

She had looked beyond her younger brother's puny scheme to gain the allegiance of Didion's princelings. With the Great Stone called Sender, she possessed a way to enlist Conrig Wincantor himself in her great enterprise. The heir to the throne of Cathra was a brilliant and dangerous man, and one not to be trusted. But she was confident that she could manipulate him, at least for the time being. And later—

What was that?

Shanakin? Is it you?

A swarm of fuzzy yellow sparks came meandering through the misty rushes, taking its own sweet time reaching her. One of the sparks was considerably brighter than the others and had a blue-white, starlike center. She deactivated Concealer and became visible. After a few minutes the bright spark separated itself from the swarm, bobbed over the open water, and hovered in mid-air beside the boat, greeting her in her own language:

"Princess Ulla. It's been many a moon. May I presume that the time has come for taking action?"

"You may," she replied. "Mounted warriors are on the move in small groups down in northeastern Cathra, heading for Castle Vanguard in the foothills of the

Dextral Mountains. Command your subjects to conceal the travelers in warm mist, harmless and natural-appearing, until they reach their destination. Take care that none of the humans lose their way, but hide them well from my brother's windwatchers."

"What about befogging the mountain passes and the road to Holt Mallburn in Didion? Do you still want that done?"

"Later, Shanakin, in less than two weeks. I'll give you plenty of notice, but your people should be ready."

"The weather remains unseasonably warm in the south because of the winds protecting Moss from the Wolf's Breath. But the volcanic eruptions are diminishing. As they do this, the magical winds called up by your brother will die away and arctic air will sweep down from the Barren Lands, freezing our misty cover."

"If this seems likely to happen, I will use my own strong magic to hold the winter cold at bay. Just do your job as we agreed, and leave the rest to me."

"And our reward, Princess?" The spark flared greedily.

"As I promised, it will be given you within the Didionite capital city. There will be plenty for all to share."

"There'd better be!" said the spark, with a wicked little laugh. "Don't even think of cheating us of our due. Remember what happened to Conjure-King Lisfallon, your grandsire, who thought he could trifle with us. Many Mosslanders now thoughtlessly consider my people to be impotent and of no account. Beware! We may be only Small Lights, but we have our ways."

"Of course you do," she said smoothly, "and excellent they are. Farewell for now, my friend."

"Farewell yourself, Princess. May the Salka monsters trip and break their tusks as they pursue you, and the Beacons fail to find your shadow!"

The spark zipped away to join its fellows, and the swarm of them faded into the night.

Ullanoth sighed and sat down again in the skiff. Insolent little hellspawn! She hoped there'd be enough prey left alive in famine-ridden Mallburn Town to satisfy them.

Well. Time she went back to the castle and to bed. It was devilishly damp and chilly out here. Another cup of hot spiced wine would be welcome, and then she'd have to find out what Beynor had been up to with the king. The two of them had spent an unusually long time together.

Ullanoth glanced in the direction of home and gave a soft gasp of surprise. Fenguard Castle, situated among crags above the river, had its keep ablaze with light. "Moon Mother mine!" she cried. "What can have happened?"

She sent her windsight soaring and found that the entire place seemed to be awake. People were rushing about, some frightened and others grim-faced as they streamed out of their various sleeping quarters and hurried toward the great hall, which was thronged. Many of the people bore rushlights or torches, since the usual oil lamps had been extinguished for the night. There was no special magic shielding the area, but her windsight was frustrated by the sheer numbers of servants, courtiers, guards, and half-dressed magickers crowded around the base of the grand staircase.

Beynor was standing there, a few steps up so he had a good view of whatever was happening almost at his feet. Warlock-knights with drawn swords flaming prevented any ordinary folk from ascending and made a bright protective semi-circle around those at the very bottom of the stairs. She could not read anyone's lips, but it was evident that the place was a bedlam of noise. After a few minutes, one of the kneeling figures arose and climbed the steps to stand beside Beynor. It was Ridcanndal, Grand Master of the Glaumerie Guild, the king's principal adviser. He made a brief announcement. His face, disfigured by a bulbous nose and unfortunately prominent front teeth, was grave.

The people assembled in the hall seemed to crumple in response to his words. Mouths gaped as they cried out. The huddled Guildsmen behind the war-locks at the foot of the stairs finally stepped away, and the light of their flaming swords revealed a collapsed figure dressed in a purple brocade robe trimmed in white fox. Beside it knelt Akossanor, the diminutive Royal Physician, and Lady Zimroth, the High Thaumaturge. Both were weeping.

Ullanoth saw her father, Conjure-King Linndal, lying motionless on his back, his balding head turned at an impossible angle. He was only five-and-forty, but he looked twenty years older. His hawk-yellow eyes, once smoldering with lunacy, were wide open and calm—until the physician closed the lids with a gentle hand.

"Where were you, Sister? We pounded on your door to give you the sad tidings, but there was no response. And of course your Fortress spell prevented entry."

Beynor's face bore no trace of tears, and he spoke to Ullanoth in his usual insolent tone.

After speeding back to Fenguard and entering the keep unseen, she had located her brother in the throne room, perched nonchalantly on the royal footstool while Guild members worked behind a wall of folding screens some distance away, preparing Linndal's body. It was a Mossland custom for the deceased ruler to sit for one final day upon his throne and be viewed by his more important subjects. Because of unfortunate incidents in the past, the Guild and the nobility needed to be certain that the late monarch was well and truly dead before consigning his body to its funeral pyre.

Ullanoth had come in through a secret corridor, via the royal wardrobe, rather than reveal to Beynor her ability to interpenetrate the walls and become invisible. The throne room was stone cold and thick with shadows, except for the lights used by the ministering wizards and a single silver-gilt oil lamp that hung above the throne itself. Four armed warlock-knights stood before the main entrance, at the far end of the chamber. Their swords were mercifully sheathed, so there was no stink of burning brimstone. The unguents and spices being used to embalm the body filled the air with pungent perfume.

"I was inside my sanctum," Ullanoth replied evenly, "distracted by a complex magical procedure. I would have heard nothing if the heavens had fallen. Then I finished my work and saw fire-kettles being lighted on the keep battlements, and came out to see what had happened. They say our father fell down the staircase and perished of a broken neck."

Beynor's pale hair seemed almost opalescent in the gloom, and his eyes were narrowed, as if in secret amusement, so that their blackness was minimized. He wore a fine houserobe of quilted spruce-green velvet, embroidered with golden stars and edged about the sleeves and neck with sable. The heavy royal sword in its jeweled scabbard was girded incongruously about his narrow loins.

Ah, thought Ullanoth. So the little toad thinks he's won at last! But without a royal proclamation to the contrary, the firstborn will inherit the throne.

He said, "Father and I were talking in the gallery at the head of the stairs when suddenly he seemed stricken within his body. He cried out and clutched at his breast, then staggered away from me. Before I could go to his aid, he tumbled the full length of the steps."

"How awful!"

"When I reached him, it was evident that the king's life had fled. His neck was plainly broken—but Doctor Akossanor believes that he may have suffered a mortal heart seizure. He might have died before he ever reached the floor of the great hall."

"What a terrible tragedy," Ullanoth said, casting her eyes down. "Who would have thought Father's heart was weak? Except for his poor wandering mind, he seemed in good health . . . May the Moon Mother lead him to the abode of eternal peace." She paused for a significant moment before looking straight at her brother. "How strange that Father should have accompanied you to the gallery overlooking the great hall, rather than remaining in his chambers, where you had been conferring. It was so very late."

Beynor shrugged.

"Was anyone else present at the time of the king's fall?"

"The hall was full of sleepers, of course, who woke as I sounded the alarm. The physician, Ridcanndal, and Lady Zimroth came almost immediately to render what assistance they could. It was futile."

"But no one was with you while you and Father conversed at the top of the staircase?"

"Unfortunately not. If others had been there, then perhaps the king would not have fallen down. As it was . . . " He gave a deep sigh. "And Father was so happy moments before."

"Why so?" she asked suspiciously.

"We'd spent long hours talking. The king's mental state was excellent. I told him about my satisfactory journey to the Continent, of course, and the bargain I'd struck with Honigalus and Somarus of Didion. Sensible men—even if it took them too long a time to take me seriously." He gave her a winning smile. "One of the disadvantages of youth."

"What is this great bargain?"

"I have promised to abolish the Wolf's Breath, and to render them powerful magical assistance should Cathra attempt to annex their country by force. In turn, they'll pay Moss a generous annual tribute when their fortunes are mended."

She kept her face stony. "How in the world did you convince the Didionite princes you could shut down the volcanos? Not even the Destroyer sigil could accomplish that—presuming you dared to activate it."

"The Diddlies are barbarians!" he said, with a scornful laugh. "Ignorant louts. What do they know of sigils? My demonstrations of high sorcery impressed them no end—especially Weathermaker's fair winds that sped our ship all the way to Stippen and back, contrary to the season, and Moss's ash-free skies. If I could deflect the Wolf's Breath from our country and blow a three-tier barque along at twelve knots, why should they doubt I could stop the ashfall altogether?"

"When it doesn't happen—" she began to say.

But he broke in with a triumphant grin. "Father told me before I left for the Continent that the volcanos are calming down. By spring, the Wolf will be dead. Father has been been bespeaking our dear auntie, Thalassa Dru, in her Tarn eyrie. She knows all about such things."

"That's impossible!" Ullanoth cried. "He'd never consult her!"

"Lower your voice," Beynor hissed, nodding toward the screens that hid the mortuary workers.

"Father would never take counsel with his sister—nor would she bespeak him," she whispered. "Not after he banished her so cruelly and blackened her name."

Beynor spoke matter-of-factly. "I think Father and Thalassa mended their quarrel. What's more, he confided to me some weeks ago that he was thinking of sending *you* to her when the unrest in Didion simmers down and the Wold Road reopens. Father thought you'd benefit from a long course of arcane instruction. You see, he knew you'd been playing dangerous little games with sigils. In his more rational moments he was afraid—and I quite agreed with him—that you'd endanger the stability of the realm with your girlish dabbling." He drew a rolled parchment out of his robe and flourished it. "We spoke of that tonight at some length. It helped convince him to sign this decree."

"Damn you, Beynor! Damn you! What have you done?" She rushed at him in a rage and would have torn the document from his hand, but a shimmering veil of air sprang into being between them, and when she met it, she recoiled with a scream of pain. "Aaah! You demon dog-scat!"

The shield winked out and his pale face was suddenly a mask of odious exultation. He pulled a shining sigil from the collar of his robe. It was the one named Subtle Armor. "Watch how you speak to me, Sister. I'm the new Conjure-King of Moss."

"No . . ."

He loosed the red ribbon that held the vellum. "Here's the decree, witnessed earlier this evening by Master Ridcanndal and Lady Zimroth." The document dangled before her eyes, a thing finely illuminated with red and blue and gold leaf, stamped with Linndal's bloody thumbprint and those of the witnesses. "You, the eldest child of his body, are explicitly debarred from the succession, and I am created heir to the throne. Should I die without issue, the crown will pass to our young cousin Habenor or his siblings, with Ridcanndal and Zimroth acting as co-regents until their majority."

"I see," she said in a flat voice.

"There are two duplicates of the decree, held for safekeeping by the Guild. You may keep this copy if you wish. It's quite legal." He beamed at her. "My death would gain you nothing, so forget about poison in the soup or cruder forms of assassination. You've lost, Ulla."

"Poor Father!" She looked away without touching the document. "He loved neither of us. I think all the love that was in him turned to dust when our mother was slain so hideously by the Lights."

When she made no move to accept the parchment, he rolled it up and retied the ribbon. "It will do you no good to accuse me publicly of causing Father's death. The Glaumerie Guild is relieved that he's gone, and so are most of the rest of the court. They're bound to approve my lucrative new alliance with Didion, and I have long-range plans for Cathra, too! Your sweetheart Conrig won't catch the Didion-ite garrisons at Castlemont and Boarsden by surprise. Advise your prince to hang up his spurs and forget about launching that invasion through Great Pass."

"Better perhaps that I tell him to prepare to defend Cala city against a sur-prise attack from the mainland—instigated by you!"

"Say whatever you please," Beynor said indifferently. "You are to be confined to the dungeon until I make arrangements to ship you off to Thalassa Dru in Tarn . . . Knights! Arrest the Conjure-Princess!"

The armed warlocks standing at the door came toward her with condescend-ing smiles. They did not even bother to draw their magical weapons.

"So you think you can exile me," she said to Beynor. "Have you forgotten that I am also able to command sigils?"

"To do what?" he scoffed. "Defend your rooms against intruders while you mess about in deep matters weakminded women can never understand? You're not safe in your sanctum now, Ulla—you're here, in my power."

Beynor gestured, and suddenly he stood four ells tall with his head grazing the vaulted ceiling and huge arms resting akimbo. He had activated Shapechanger in a childish attempt to intimidate her. She was unafraid, but the warlocks who took hold of her were strong men she could not shake off. One of them had a thick silken cord, which he used to bind her gloved wrists behind her. Another knelt, chuckling insolently, and began to tie her ankles. They intended to carry her off like a trussed calf.

Beynor's gigantic apparition howled a peal of scornful laughter. "Not so high and mighty now, are you, Sister?"

"Imbecile," she said. The sigils Interpenetrator and Concealer were still within her gloves, resting painfully in the palms of her hands. She whispered the spells commanding them and vanished from the confining arms of the warlocks like a puff of vapor, leaving the knotted silk cords behind in a heap on the scuffed rush matting of the throne room floor.

thirteen

Iscannon's sigil lay on the stone floor of the corridor, its glow and pain-giving potential temporarily in abeyance.

Without touching the thing with his bare hand, Snudge maneuvered it by its thong into his belt-wallet. The book seemed harmless enough when he gave it a fearful tap with his finger, so he rewrapped it and hid it again inside his shirt.

He hurried to the armigers' quarters, arriving as the half-tenth-hour chime sounded. It was the usual bedtime for squires of the prince's cohort, but none of the other boys were there. A quick overview of the palace showed him that they were part of the throng of courtiers waiting to welcome King Olmigon home from his pilgrimage. No one would miss Snudge. People were used to his odd comings and goings.

He hid the wallet with the sigil under his palliasse, which was closest to the outer door so he could sneak out easily at night, then went down the corridor to the necessarium. After entering and fastening the latch, he ignited the candle with his talent, unwrapped the book, and sat down on the covered stool to study.

The chapter that claimed his immediate attention was the one entitled *Vital Precautions for the Thaumaturgist.*

Nearly an hour later, hearing the sound of distant cheers through the latrine's loophole, he closed the small volume with a sigh and returned to the dormitorium. The other boys wouldn't tarry long in the forecourt once the royals arrived. The Palace Steward would shoo them off to bed.

He undressed, tucked the wrapped book under his pillow, and lay beneath his covers, watching the smoky flames in the oil sconce hanging on the wall, thinking about what he had discovered.

Parts of the book were straightforward enough. Empowering a sigil—bringing it to life—always inflicted great pain upon the conjurer. Invoking the magic of the moonstones caused more or less suffering, depending upon the strength of the spell required. Also, certain sigils affecting the human body would only work when in contact with the owner's skin. The invisibility charm he'd taken from the spy was of that type.

When the owner died, a sigil's efficacy was cancelled. Ordinarily, someone else wishing to conjure a "dead" sigil into fresh activity would intone a rather lengthy incantation laying claim to it. The formula was in the book, but unfortunately written in that same unknown language used in the two larger books he'd left behind in Kilian's sanctum. As written, the strange words had far too many consonants and odd diphthongs for Snudge to guess at their correct pronunciation. Saying them wrong, he had learned from the *Vital Precautions* led to horrible penalties.

By chance, using the moonstone disk on the book's cover, he had stumbled upon a hazardous shortcut that invoked the Beaconfolk directly without the appropriate ceremonial overtures. This constituted a breach of magical etiquette that the book strongly cautioned against. As he had suspected, the cranky wind-voice he'd heard had been one of the Beaconfolk (a low-ranking one, in charge of less-important sigils), asking him what the bloody hell he wanted. According to the book, his failure to answer the query properly might well have resulted in his annihilation. Only lucky happenstance had saved him.

The appropriate response to the affronted Light was right there in the book—also given in the foreign tongue, and thus quite useless to Snudge.

The *Vital Precautions* chapter had a long list of magical missteps with consequences that were mortal—or worse. Reading them with a sinking heart, he had almost dropped the terrible book down the dunghole right then and there.

I can't do this! he'd said to himself. I want to be Prince Conrig's intelligencer—not risk my life mucking about with sky-monsters that can squash me like a gnat.

But niggling curiosity, and a feeling that he would be nothing more than a craven child if he gave up so easily, had compelled him to turn back to the beginning of the little volume and skim through it as best he could. The unfamiliar spelling and peculiarly shaped letters bothered him less and less as he read the short chapters; but there were still certain explanatory sections he could make no sense of, as well as the all-important spells written in the foreign tongue.

The much longer chapter with the catalogue of sigils included a precise drawing of Iscannon's piece of moonstone and its proper name, Concealer, together with its uses and its activating incantation. The thing was a futtering miracle! Not only was it capable of making its wearer invisible, it could also hide other specified living or inanimate things within a radius of "four armes longthes" if given the proper command. With that feature, he learned, a sorcerer might conceal the horse he was riding on or even a small boat, or shield a group of people huddling within about four ells of him.

But only if he pronounced the alien spell properly. If he said the words wrong, the sigil might kill him in various hideous ways, or the annoyed Beaconfolk might play one of their capricious jokes—such as casting him into an abominable arctic netherworld minus his skin, where he'd spend eternity in frozen agony.

I'm stumped, Snudge admitted miserably, as he lay in bed. He might as well throw both the sigil and the book into the sea, as Conjure-Prince Beynor had commanded. There was no way he'd ever be able to use this magic safely.

By now he had read or paged through virtually every volume in Vra-Kilian's main Alchymical Library. He knew for certain that none of them had been a pronouncing dictionary of that distinctive weird language. Neither had there been such a book in the locked cases in the inner sanctum. Perhaps the inability to pronounce the spells was the fatal flaw that had deterred the villainous Royal Alchymist from utilizing his own large collection of sigils.

Shite . . .

By rights, Snudge concluded, I should speak to Prince Conrig before getting rid of Iscannon's sigil and the book. His master might want to confer with Princess Ullanoth, who doubtless was familiar with such dangerous sorcery. Perhaps she'd tell the prince how to pronounce the spell of invisibility.

But all the boy's instincts rebelled against that course of action. Ullanoth had warned Conrig that the sigil was too dangerous to keep. Rather than share its spell with him, she'd more likely demand that he turn the moonstone over to her immediately, or throw it away.

Snudge heard young voices in the corridor outside. The armigers were return- ing. As they trooped into the room, some of the boys giggled and gave owl hoots

when they saw Snudge already abed, but he cursed them good-naturedly and drew
his feather-tick over his head. After the usual noisy scrambling about subsided,
Belamil snuffed the light and commanded silence. Everyone settled down just as
the castle chimes struck the first hour of morning.

I'll decide what to do tomorrow, Snudge thought.

But he'd reckoned without his nightmare, which was about to change.

In it, he fought Iscannon as usual, and felt himself succumbing to the icy
enchantment. But when he stabbed the spy to the heart and heard the windvoice
cry out desperately for Beynor, the Conjure-Prince entered Snudge's dream in
a completely different aspect.

No longer at sea, the Mosslander was sitting at a table in a darkened room,
wearing a quilted robe decorated with rather silly little stars. His expression was
different; the erstwhile haughty self-confidence was gone and he looked both
angry and diminished, as though he had experienced some great defeat or
humiliation.

I know what you've done, Deveron Austrey.

"Oh, really?"

The question is, what am I going to do about it?

"I hope you don't intend to bore me with your usual threats and insults—
or bring me more painful nightmares. They're a nuisance, nothing more. If you
could have harmed me seriously, you'd have done it already. You're all piss and
wind, Prince Beynor."

*Not quite! But in light of recent events, I'm reconsidering our adversarial
relationship, and I suggest you do so as well. It would be mutually profitable if we
were allies instead of enemies.*

"I doubt it."

Let me explain. I know about the book you stole.

"I didn't steal any book."

*You're the only one who could have taken it. No one else would have dared enter
the Royal Alchymist's sanctum. No one else in Cala Palace has a use for the ancient
book he kept hidden there.*

"Hah! So you admit you aren't certain I have it! You weren't windwatching me."

*No one can windwatch you, Deveron Austrey. This is why you're such a danger—
and such a potential asset. I knew someone must have taken Iscannon's sigil. No sigil,*

alive or dead, can be perceived by a windwatcher, but persons possessing them usually give themselves away by their actions. Since neither the prince nor his brother Stergos seemed to have Iscannon's stone, that left you—the strangely unwatchable servant boy. A sight of you was flashed to me by Iscannon even as he died.

"And you snuck into my dreams."

I have that ability. It was a source of great distress to my dear sister until she learned how to shut me out. I even used it on my father, to sway his poor mad mind.

"Will you stop beating about the bush and tell me what you want?"

All in good time. Would it surprise you to know that Vra-Kilian, the Royal Alchymist of Cathra, is my creature? He discovered that the small magical book was gone almost as soon as he returned to Cala Palace. He had no notion of who might have taken it while he was away on the pilgrimage.

"So Kilian's the traitor! Thanks for the information. I'll tell Prince Conrig right away. He's suspected the alchymist for some time."

Don't talk like a fool. There's no way Conrig can prove his uncle's treachery. Your word on the matter is worth less than a fart in a beermug.

"Elegantly put, my prince."

I'm not a prince any more. My father Linndal died—may the Moon shine kindly on his spirit—and he named me his successor and debarred my sister Ullanoth from the throne. I'm Conjure-King Beynor now! The news will be windspoken all over High Blenholme by tomorrow.

"Congratulations. But why bother telling me?"

You can be very valuable to me, and vice versa. My sigil and the book that you stole from the Royal Alchymist—

"How many times must I say that I don't have anything that belongs to you. And nothing that Kilian has a true claim on, either."

He believes otherwise . . . and he knows that you're the thief. I told him so. He'll be coming for you unless you agree to serve me. He'll slice off your body's flesh by inches, you upstart horse-lackey, and toast the bloody collops and force-feed them to you, unless I call him off.

"Do you know what I think? I think you're lying again. If you'd told Vra-Kilian that I have his book, he'd be here in the dormitorium with his henchmen trying to drag me out of bed. And I'd be screaming for my master, Prince Conrig, and eleven hopping-mad armigers would be whacking at wizards and raising a ruckus that'd lift off the palace roof."

You think you're clever, Deveron Austrey, but—

"Stop trying to bluff! You're not absolutely certain that I have the book and the sigil, and you don't know where I might have hidden them. Vra-Kilian and his magickers will never find the things . . . and they'll never find me if I decide to hide. Cala Palace is enormous! I can windwatch Kilian, but he and his windbags can't scry me, any more than you can. If necessary, I'll stay out of reach in Conrig's apartments until his force leaves for—for the north country. I'm the Prince Heritor's liege man, damn your eyes, not a paltry servant!"

Very well. You win.

". . . What's that supposed to mean?"

I have no intention of setting the Royal Alchymist on you. I'm actually extremely disappointed in him. I've decided to offer you his job—together with the rewards that go with it.

"What!"

Become my secret retainer, Deveron Austrey. Conrig Wincantor gave you a sword and a suit of armor and some flimsy promises of manorlands when you're twenty. I'll give you power and riches beyond imagining, and do it right now.

"Until I 'disappoint' you, Conjure-King! Then you'll toss me to the monsters."

Your skepticism is understandable. So I'll give you a demonstration of my good faith and regal generosity. I'll instruct you how to activate your sigil of invisibility, with no strings attached. As a free gift.

"I don't believe you. You'll trick me. Destroy me!"

Why should I bother? I'm trying to make friends. To win you over. You can find the proper words right there in your stolen book, under the picture of Concealer, but they're useless because you can't say them correctly.

"If I had the book, that'd be true."

Don't be tedious. Now: you must always keep this kind of sigil against your flesh for it to work. To be unseen, say or whisper: BI DO FYSINEK. To be visible again, say: BI FYSINEK. If you want the magical cover to extend about four ells around you—to shield other people, for instance—say: FASH AH. To make the cover shrink again: KRUF AH. It's all quite simple. Say the words, Deveron.

"Bi do fysinek. Bi fysinek. Fash ah. Kruf ah."

No no no! Don't use your disgusting Cathran drawl. Roar the words! Speak deeply as I did, breathing roughly.

"BI DO FYSINEK. BI FYSINEK. FASH AH. KRUF AH."

Perfect. What a great memory you have! Now there's a bit more to learn, and I'll admit that this is the rather sticky part. Concealer is dead, because it was conjured to Iscannon, and he's dead. To make it live again, you must—um—introduce yourself to the Lights as the new owner. The safest way to do this is with a long incantation written there in your book, but you'd never remember how to say it all, so you'll have to do things another way.

"I know. By wearing the sigil, then touching it to the moonstone disk on the cover of the book. Then the monster howls: CADAY AN RUDAY? and I start to die."

Hah! So you've already tried it.

"And not about to do it again—not for a peck of rubies."

No, listen. The Light was only asking what you wanted. They do get a bit testy if one doesn't answer properly. The correct reply is: GO TUGA LUVKRO AN AY COMASH DOM. It means, "May the Cold Light grant me power." Then the Light asks you your name, and you say it in the same gruff accent. That's all there is to it.

"If the magic was as simple as that, sigils wouldn't have such an evil reputation. Neither would the Lights."

Well, activating a lesser sigil does hurt a bit, but not more than a strong lad like you can easily bear. And there are things that can get you into serious trouble, but that happens mostly with the more complicated and powerful stones. An invisibility charm is about as simple and foolproof as Beaconfolk magic can be. That's why I let my late associate Iscannon borrow and empower Concealer, and why I'm offering it to you.

"Many a spy would sell his soul for such a thing . . ."

I want you to be my spy—and I have no interest at all in your soul, provided that it doesn't get in the way of your loyalty to me. What do you say, Deveron? Prince Conrig's scheme to conquer Didion will never succeed. I know all about his plans. He'll get himself killed by sorcery or Didionite battle-axes up on Great Pass, and take a lot of fine warriors along with him to hell. And you, too, unless you re-enlist on the winning side.

"How old are you, Conjure-King?"

Sixteen, as you are, Deveron Austrey. And in my kingdom, an adult man by law.

"Interesting. Thank you for the offer, but I don't want to be your minion. I'm already pledged to Prince Conrig, and my word is good."

You're a shortsighted fool.

"Perhaps. But now I know how to make the sigil work—so what does that make you?"

A brand-new king who made a sad misjudgment. We live and learn! Well, other pressing matters demand my attention. I assure you that I won't be troubling your dreams anymore. Think of me as you make use of Concealer. I might even suggest that you avail yourself of it this very night to raid Vra-Kilian's treasure trove of sigils. He'll certainly hide it somewhere else tomorrow, now that he knows an intruder has access to his sanctum, and you'll never find them with a windsearch. Good-bye, Deveron Austrey. I don't think we'll meet again.

Snudge woke, adequately warm and unparalyzed beneath his covers. The sky outside the window was black, with a few stars, and it felt as though it was still fast night. His surmise was confirmed a few moments later when the chimes struck the fifth hour of the morning. At this time of year, the sun didn't come up until nearly seven.

He remembered every word of his conversation with Beynor and knew beyond any doubt that it had not been a figment of his imagination. It was real.

And so was the imminent danger.

Steal the Royal Alchymist's collection of sigils right now, after activating Concealer? Did Beynor really think he was so asinine?

I don't think we'll meet again . . .

Right. And Snudge had a good notion why! He had no intention of playing into whatever booby trap the Mosslander had prepared for him, but something had to be done, and he didn't dare wait until morning to do it. He felt beneath his palliasse, finding the wrapped book and the sigil inside his wallet just as he had left them. He couldn't possibly keep them now, even if Beynor had told the truth about the activation spell. There was Vra-Kilian to consider.

In the dream-conversation, Snudge had boasted that he wasn't afraid of the wizard. Now that he was awake, he sensibly reconsidered.

It did seem all too likely that Kilian had discovered that the book was gone, and he was probably searching for it this very minute. Like all Brothers of Zeth, he possessed powerful magic of his own that he could use to hunt for lost items. Stergos had once explained to Snudge that the windsearch was a faculty closely related to scrying. It could be focused intensely over nearby areas, "calling out" to the object of the search. Its effectiveness varied according to the power of the individual adept, but not even the sprawling expanse of Cala Palace would faze the Royal Alchymist. Beynor had said that sigils couldn't be scried. But the book might not fall under that exemption, even if the moonstone on its cover did.

Perhaps Snudge's personal immunity from windwatching would keep him and a book in close proximity to him safe from the wizard's scrutiny—but maybe it wouldn't. He wasn't going to take chances, especially now that he had firmly decided to eschew Beaconfolk magic.

Both the book and the sigil named Concealer were going down down down—to the bottom of Cala Bay, before another hour struck on the palace chimes.

The other armigers were still snoring merrily. Snudge crept out from the covers, cautiously opened his trussing coffer, and found a stout winter jerkin, a wool tunic, and leather trews. After he finished dressing, except for his boots, he stowed the book and sigil and retrieved his new heavy cloak and sword-belt from their wall-pegs. Then he picked up his boots and slipped out of the chamber.

The bare flagstones of the corridor were like ice beneath his stockinged feet, even though Cathra had yet to experience its first frost. He pulled on his footgear quickly. There were no rush-mats or other frivolous luxuries in the Square Tower where the household knights, squires, and palace guardsmen lived. The tower also housed the armory and the cells for high-ranking prisoners. It was a comfortless place where the walls had no tapestries and the leaded windows no drapes, only strong oak shutters that would be closed when the terrible Hammer and Anvil storms of winter finally returned and smashed the lands around Cala Bay between them. A single hanging oil-lamp at the far end of the passage lit the juncture with another corridor, as well as the stairs leading down to the warriors' common rooms.

Two guardsmen were on nightwatch there. Snudge hid from them with the ease of long practice and continued down the stairs to the first storey, where signs of opulence became evident. There were fine brass standard-lamps every dozen feet, having only a single flame burning at this hour. Polished wood overlay the stone flooring of an enclosed arcade, where there were beautifully carved marble pillars and ornamental pots holding living shrubs. The arcade led to the main block of the palace and the apartments of the royals and the high nobility. There were more guards, splendidly accoutered, stationed at the entrance, but he crept past them unseen.

To reach Vra-Kilian's rooms, Snudge would have had to turn right at the arcade's end. He only paused for a moment, concealed in heavy shadows behind a statue, before turning left. After descending a handsome flight of banistered stairs and slipping through an unbarred but guarded door, he arrived in the royal mounting-yard. Beyond lay the stables sheltering the king's horses, which numbered nearly two hundred, and behind them were buildings devoted to the care of the pampered animals and their tack. When he was young, Snudge had worked there with his grandfather. He knew every inch of the area, and was familiar with its special-purpose gate.

Even in the dark of night, there were plenty of people moving about. Some were unloading firewood or other bulk goods from the wagons of tradesmen. But most were bent on shoveling muck, befouled straw, and kitchen garbage from a big pile near the curtain wall and loading it into stout carts that would haul it away. This homely task was attended to every other night in the late autumn and winter, when the stench from the accumulated refuse was only moderate. In warm weather, the carts rolled in and out of the palace every night, using the appropriately named Dung Gate. They were forbidden to travel the city streets after sunrise.

The Dung Gate guard detail was not drawn from the cream of the palace's men-at-arms. Its roster was composed of unfortunates who had been found drunk on duty or were guilty of brawling, petty theft, or other derelictions. The guards were notoriously susceptible to bribery, and denizens of the palace who wished to slip out anonymously into the town on clandestine errands invariably went by way of the Dung Gate.

Snudge didn't even bother to hide as he approached the wide-open portcullises. He simply gave one of the men-at-arms a silver quarter-mark, said, "Back before sunup," and strode out in the wake of a creaking load of ordure.

"And a good morn to you, messire!" the soldier said, with a sloppy salute. "Watch where you tread."

Snudge made his way to the docks by means of familiar byways, easily eluding the circulating squads of night-watchmen. Cala was quiet, and the moon had gone down so that the alleys were exceptionally dark. There were no beggars in Olmigon's beautiful capital city, and very few footpads, since the citizenry was obliged to observe the tenth-hour curfew. The only area where the law was winked at was the waterfront. Ships might arrive or depart at any hour, according to the tide, so dockworkers and sailors were abroad around the clock. Many of the taverns, cheap inns, and bawdy houses that catered to them never closed.

Water Street was only moderately crowded when Snudge reached it. The

Wolf's Breath had put a severe dent in commercial traffic, and most of the sailors still carousing belonged to Cathran warships at anchor out in the Roads, come into port after a tour of blockade duty. Some of the noisy, reeling seamen were heading for Red Gull Pier, where small craft could be cheaply hired to ferry them out to vessels moored in deep water. Snudge followed a gang of them, keeping his head down and his hand on his sword hilt.

The sky was going grey now, and not many boats were manned and available. The returning sailors piled into the last pair of them, and the boatmen promptly cast off and rowed away over the oily-calm water, leaving the boy standing on the dock cursing through clenched teeth.

"May I be of service, messire?" said a voice behind Snudge.

He turned and the light of a nearly spent torch mounted on a pole showed him a smiling, rather portly man of medium stature. He wore a brown leather tunic with gartered trews and a hooded cloak of raggedy fur that muffled his hair and beard. His eyes were kindly.

"Do you have a boat?" Snudge asked, after a moment's hesitation.

"If you have the hire of it, young lord. Three silver pennies, no matter how many are carried." The boatman had a slight foreign accent and his voice was unexpectedly cultured.

"Good," said Snudge. "There's only me."

"Which ship are you bound for?"

He had a story ready: The Wronged Lover. "No ship, goodman." He touched his breast. "I carry some tokens—of value only to a poor scorned and wounded heart—that I wish to cast into the sea so that I may forget ever having met . . . a certain lady. I will pay your fee gladly, twice over, if you'll take me to some deep spot in the bay where I can be certain that no current or tidal flux will ever bring these forlorn objects to the surface again."

The boatman nodded. "I know such a spot. But you must swear to me that it's not your own self you intend to cast overboard. I won't be a party to suicide."

"I swear by Bazekoy's Bones that I won't jump. I just have to get rid of these damned things."

The boatman cocked his head, and his eyes caught the gleam of the torch guttering above the quay. Or did they?

"Are you certain you won't regret throwing the tokens away?" he inquired.

"Absolutely," said Snudge. "Let's go. I want to get this over with."

The boat was a sturdy sailing dinghy with a raked mast, such as was favored as a tender or auxiliary craft by the big trading schooners of Tarn. It was by no means the usual sort of nondescript puddle-skimmer engaged in the Cala Bay ferry trade. Snudge expected her skipper to row, but no sooner had they settled in than a fair breeze sprang up. The boatman hoisted a striped sail and they moved off swiftly, giving a wide berth to the men o' war riding at anchor.

"You are not a native of Cathra," Snudge said to the skipper.

"You're very observant, young lord. Nay—I'm of Wave-Harrier stock, but living in Cala now, and eking out a living as best I can. You were fortunate to find me at Red Gull Pier. I've been doing other work of late, hardly taking to the water at all."

"Are . . . your people back in Tarn suffering because of the ashfall?"

"There's always the sea to feed us Harriers, but folk who work the gold and opal mines will just scrape by this third bad winter. Thanks be to the God of the Depths, the Wolf's Breath is belching its last. By the time the Boreal Moon wanes, the skies of my homeland will be clear again."

"You're certain?" Snudge was both astounded and skeptical.

"Oh, yes," said the rotund skipper with supreme confidence, and for some reason the boy didn't press him further about the matter, nor did he feel like asking him any more casual questions. It was getting very cold now that they were farther from land, and the sky was lightening, beginning to dim the stars.

"Are we almost there?" he finally asked. "I really don't have much time left."

"This is the place." The Tarnian came about, spilled wind from the sail, and then lowered it. "I can't anchor here. Better do what you came for." The dinghy rocked in the light chop. The wind had gone dead.

Snudge opened his belt-wallet and gingerly fished out Concealer by its thong. The pendant moonstone dangled from his fingers, and for an instant he thought he saw a faint greenish glow. Averting his eyes, he held the sigil over the gunwale.

"Are you sure you want to do that?" the boatman said softly. "Look out there. They're waiting to take it."

Snudge lifted his gaze and gasped. Three forms were rising from the dark wavelets not a stone's throw away. They were almost man-shaped but considerably more bulky than humankind, with enormous shoulders, peculiarly shaped heads, and wideset bulging eyes that shone scarlet-gold, like coals in a blacksmith's forge. As the boy stared at them, struck rigid with terror, the creature in the center began approaching the boat, extending a tentacular limb with a four-fingered hand at the end of it.

Hanging from a cord around its wide neck was a glowing sigil.

"Stop," the Tarnian skipper commanded in a loud voice. He held high an object like a short club, fashioned of ivory and gold. "Do you know me?"

The thing paused. For a moment it was still. Then it reared up, boneless arms flung violently toward the sky and fanged mouth wide open. It roared, shocking Snudge to quivering life, then fell back into the sea with a tremendous splash. The rocking boat was drenched with icy spray.

"You are Red Ansel," it cried in a rasping bellow, like storm-surf on a rocky shore. Its teeth gleamed in the halflight as its grotesque mouth formed the Cathran words with difficulty. "Give the thief to us. Give back our sacred Coldlight Stones."

"Go below and wait until I summon you," said the shaman.

The monster uttered another frustrated roar. It subsided slowly, its baleful gaze lingering above the surface before finally submerging. The other two creatures also disappeared.

Ansel turned a mild face to Snudge. In his eyes, the glow of talent was more powerful than the boy had ever known before. "They are Salka. The sigils were created by their wise ones in an era long gone to conjure the power of the Beaconfolk. Their language is still used to empower the stones. Once, there were countless thousands of Salka and they ruled the island of High Blenholme. Human invaders killed off many of them because they're slow-moving and awkward on land, and drove the rest away. A few Salka still live in the Great Fen of Moss, but most of them have retreated to the Dawntide Isles, far away to the east."

"I—I've heard the legends." Snudge had jerked Concealer back into the boat. It lay on the thwart beside him.

"Beynor sent these three. If you'd gone out in an ordinary boat, you and its skipper would have been eaten alive, and the sigil and the book would have been taken back to the Conjure-King."

"He knew just what I'd do," Snudge said bitterly. "The Mossbelly bastard! He played me like a farthing flute!"

Ansel smiled. "I think he's rather afraid of you. Wild talents are messy to deal with. Especially one pledged to serve a pivotal figure such as Conrig Wincantor, who has Bazekoy's eye watching him. And mine."

"I don't understand."

"Why did you take the sigil from Iscannon? And why did you take the book from Vra-Kilian?"

"I thought they'd help me be a better snudge," the boy said tiredly. "I'm Prince Conrig's man. His intelligencer. But I didn't have the courage to activate the sigil even though Beynor told me how. I was afraid he'd trick me—but I suppose it was a bluff."

"Not at all. If you'd followed Beynor's instructions, the Beaconfolk would have slain you in a particularly ghastly fashion. You see, he left out one important part of the activation formula. After asking you your name, the Lights would say: 'THASHIN AH GAV,' which means 'We accept.' And that would be your signal to say 'Thank you,' which is 'MO TENGALAH SHERUV.' If you neglected that final courtesy . . ."

Snudge uttered a hollow laugh. "I'd be dead, just as Beynor planned it. Why are you telling me this? Who are you, Red Ansel?"

"I'm the High Shaman of Tarn, and I was summoned from that country by Princess Maudrayne to ease King Olmigon's suffering. I stayed in Cala when the king went journeying to Zeth Abbey, and I was most intrigued when you arrived with Prince Conrig's party, carrying a sigil. Wild talents aren't common, not even in my country, and one possessed of a dead moonstone who received dream visitations from Beynor of Moss was something extraordinary. I windwatched you as you rifled Kilian's library—"

"But that's impossible!"

The shaman shook his head benignly. "Not for me. I watched you and I consulted my Source to discover where my duty lay. Was it proper for me to let you die, one way or another, or was I obligated to save you to serve a higher purpose?"

Snudge gawped at him, unable to speak.

"Imagine my surprise when I was instructed not only to save your foolhardy young life, but also to help you to empower the sigil called Concealer."

"What!"

"Do you remember Beynor's instructions?"

Snudge nodded fearfully, casting an oblique glance at the moonstone beside him.

"And do you recall the words for 'thank you' in the Salkan tongue?"

"MO TENGALAH SHERUV."

"Well said. Now take out the book you have concealed beneath your shirt and hang Concealer around your neck. Perform the Light Summoning as you did before, using the proper words—but with one difference only: When asked for your name, reply 'Snudge.' It is, and is not, your true name, and the ambiguity will protect you from the more deadly jests of the Beaconfolk."

Snudge said, "Ansel, I'm afraid."

"Of course you are, and rightly so. You will suffer pain in the sigil's empowering. But your royal master, Conrig, will have great need of this stone's magic one day soon, and it is your duty to provide it. You can refuse, of course, and I'll take charge of the thing myself and safely dispose of it. But think, lad! Will you let timidity and fear deprive your master of a great boon?"

"I—I am no coward. But I fear that Beynor will tell Kilian that I have his book and a sigil. Even if that doesn't happen, the Royal Alchymist may deduce that I'm talented because I can't be windwatched. He'll betray me to the Brethren—if he doesn't kill me out of hand. Either way, I'll no longer be able serve my prince."

"Beynor can't be sure you have his sigil. As for the book, you'll have no need of it after the Light Summoning. I'll take care of it."

The boy hesitated as he considered what to do, then remembered something else the Conjure-King had said. "Do you know that Vra-Kilian has two baskets of sigils hidden within a strongbox in his sanctum? There must be scores of the things! Beynor suggested that I steal them."

The shaman rose from his seat in the stern and was silhouetted against the twilit sky. The dinghy remained rock-solid in the water. "I suggest you do no such thing," Ansel said softly, "not if you value your soul. Come now, Deveron Austrey! Make your choice. Either give me sigil and book, or else dare the Lights."

Snudge took a great breath. "I'll do it."

When the Summoning was successfully accomplished and Concealer hung harmlessly around his neck, faintly aglow with life, Snudge sank back onto the thwart trembling in every limb like a beaten dog. Tears coursed down his cheeks. "I'm still alive," he whispered in wonder.

"Of course you are," Ansel said.

"The sigil doesn't hurt now." He wiped his face with his sleeve.

"There is pain only when you use it, and then nothing like so much as when the stone was first empowered. Concealer is a lesser stone. Nevertheless, I strongly advise you not to conjure it except under the most grave circumstances. Even though the Lights don't know your true name, there's still a certain danger of their interfering." He handed the boy a small wash-leather sack. "Cover the stone with this as you wear it. Your comrades would be disconcerted by its pale glow, and if one of them touched it he might be badly hurt—especially if he tried to take it from you. Keep the stone out of sight always."

Snudge complied, then tucked the bagged moonstone under his shirt. "Am I to tell Prince Conrig that now I can command Iscannon's sigil?"

"Better not. Let him know you still have it, if you must. Say you're keeping it just in case you discover how to make it work someday. It wouldn't do if he were to think the sigil could be used with impunity for commonplace spying. When circumstances dictate, you'll have to reveal its empowerment to him. But better later than sooner."

"I understand." I think . . .

"Give me the book now. It's time we were out of here."

Snudge handed the small volume over and the shaman held it high.

"SHALKYE, GRAYD KALEET!" he intoned.

The moonstone disk on the book's cover blazed a blinding green. A dozen ells away, three monstrous shapes vaulted out of the water, booming louder than harpooned bull sea lions. One of them had a coruscating emerald star at its neck. They fell back with splashes that tossed the boat and vanished again.

"Codders!" said Snudge. "Are they gone for good?"

"I don't recommend you take any sea voyages soon," said Red Ansel of Tarn, with a short laugh.

He hoisted the sail, and a smart breeze sprang up obediently, carrying them back to the shore as the eastern sky warmed in the dawn.

fourteen

Vra-stergos came to bring Conrig the morning wind tidings and found him being ministered to by the Royal Barber, Hindel, who made finicky darts at the princely beard with flickering shears, snipping off a few golden hairs at each pass and muttering, "Not quite! Not quite right." Telifar Bankstead, the prince's most trusted lord-in-waiting, was supervising the setup of the breakfast table, while the secretary, Lord Mullan Overgard, stood at the desk unpacking a portfolio of documents. There was no sign of Princess Maudrayne.

"Leave be, Hindel," Conrig said, taking note of his brother's agitated expression. Something noteworthy must have happened.

"But, Your Grace!" the barber protested. "A bit more trimming, and you'll be perfect!"

Conrig pulled the cloth away from his neck and rose from his chair with a grimace. "I doubt that. At any rate, I'll not require your services any more today."

"I have a marvelous new musk-scented pomade—"

"Go!" the prince commanded, and the barber gathered up his equipment and fairly ran out of the room. To Telifar: "You and Mullan may also withdraw until I send for you."

The secretary said, "We must present these signed letters of appeal to the grain merchants and shipowners as soon as possible. The King's Grace has already endorsed them."

"Oh, very well. Give me a pen." He scrawled his name and thrust the pages back into Overgard's hands. "Close the door after you and see that I'm not disturbed."

The two men bowed and left the room, leaving the brothers alone.

"Well, what is it, Gossy?" Conrig inquired. "You look a bit white about the gills. Was there bad news flying on the wind? Out with it—unless you think we might be overseen."

"No one watches us," Stergos assured him. "Even the Royal Alchymist is sequestered in his sanctum, so completely shielded in a spell of couverture that he can no more see out than any other adept can see in."

"Then tell me what's happened."

Stergos stated it baldly. "Linndal of Moss is dead, and he named young Beynor his successor."

"Bazekoy's Ballocks!" the prince exclaimed in dismay. "That'll put a cold breeze up Ullanoth's skirts. Was anything said of her?"

"Only that she's permanently removed from succession to the Mossland throne. Some cousins are next in line now. I tried to bespeak the Conjure-Princess immediately, but she gave no reply. I hope—" He trailed off, seeing the look on Conrig's face.

"If Beynor's killed her," the prince said quietly, "or managed to imprison her inside some enchantment so she can't talk to us, our invasion of Didion may be futtered to a fare-thee-well."

The Doctor Arcanorum nodded unhappily. "The windcrier gave only a few more details. Linndal perished of a broken neck after falling down a flight of stairs. The new young king has been acclaimed by the Glaumerie Guild. His coronation is set for next week, and King Achardus of Didion will attend and offer his personal felicitations."

The prince uttered a more eloquent curse. "We've got to find out what's happened to Ulla. I know you can't windsearch for her at such a long distance, but perhaps Snudge can manage it."

"Perhaps." The alchymist sighed. "I'll find him and ask him."

"Have you had breakfast?" Conrig asked. When Stergos shook his head, the two of them went to the table that had been prepared near the windows of the sitting room. "I don't think Maudrayne will be joining me. Sovanna told Telifar that my lady intended to sleep in to recover from the long journey. You can have her share."

Covered dishes held smoking grilled trout with pepper and verjuice, cold roast quail and their hard-boiled eggs in mustard sauce, golden toast with gooseberry jam, and sweet cheese pastries. The beverages were clover wine, honeysuckle tea kept hot by a tiny brazier, and a crystal pitcher of unhopped wheat beer, especially favored by Conrig as an eye-opener.

The two of them fell to, Stergos concentrating on the succulent fish, the pastries, and the tea. Conrig was preoccupied. He recalled his last tryst with Ullanoth, and her warning that Beynor might attempt to kill him.

"The Conjure-Princess bespoke me yesterday," said the prince, popping two of the little eggs into his mouth and speaking while he chewed. "She said that Beynor might send an assassin after me. I know you've got remedies against poison, but can you give me something magical to fend off physical attack?"

"Alas—there's no general shield of invulnerability contained in the Zeth Codex. Some authorities say that the Glaumerie Guild of Moss owns an amulet of the Beaconfolk that subtly armors one's body, but such high sorcery is beyond our Order. Perhaps I can devise a warning charm of some sort. I could consult Vra-Kilian—"

Conrig gave a negative grunt, nibbling quail meat. "Don't. It's likely he'd be the designated murderer."

"Oh, no!" Stergos nearly dropped his cup of tea.

"I dismissed him from the Privy Council last night. From now on, he has nothing to do with affairs of state—only arcana."

"Dear God. He'll be in a terrible rage!"

"Not if he knows what's good for him." Conrig smiled with grim satisfaction. "However, I certainly don't intend to be alone with him—and that goes for those three muckmates of his, as well. You know the ones I mean—Brothers Butterball, Squinty, and Vinegar-Face. I think you better watch your back around them, too, Gossy."

"I can't believe they'd try to harm either of us." But Stergos's eyes shifted nervously.

The trio, whose actual names were Raldo, Niavar, and Cleaton, had a dubious reputation among the Brethren resident in the palace. Even though their magical talents were only modest, they were Vra-Kilian's closest associates, holding the positions of Novice Master, Keeper of Arcana, and Hebdomader, or chief disciplinarian of the Brothers.

"We already know why Kilian's loyalty to me is suspect," Conrig continued. "One of the oldest motives of all: familial ambition. What I still can't understand is what threat or bribe Beynor might have used to turn his coat. And trusting a boy-wizard to kill me off isn't particularly efficient. Kilian could do a better job of it using his own people—if he dared. But we know he *wouldn't* dare—at least, not until the king is dead. Father could appoint another heir, cutting off Duke Shi-Shi or Feribor, if he chose to."

"Beynor could never bribe Vra-Kilian with money," Stergos observed. "Moss has none to spare, and the Blackhorse family's wallowing in it. Beynor might be holding some threat over Kilian, but I can't imagine what it might be. Perhaps we're misjudging the Royal Alchymist after all, letting our personal dislike of him cloud our reasoning."

They ate in silence for a time, and then there was a scratching at the door. Lord Telifar's apologetic face appeared. "Your Grace, the armiger Deveron Austrey prays leave to speak with you. He says it's most urgent."

"Send him in." Conrig wiped his greasy lips on a napkin and took a pull of the sparkling pale beer. He greeted Snudge warmly. "So you've learned something important?"

The boy's gaze went momentarily to the Doctor Arcanorum. "Very important, Your Grace."

"You may speak before Brother Stergos."

The tale poured forth in a rush. "Last night I went secretly to the inner sanctum of the Royal Alchymist, as I've been doing for more than a week. In a locked cabinet secured against windwatching I found two sizable baskets full of moonstone sigils and a book explaining their use. I dared not take the sigils, but I did make off with the book, which had a disk of moonstone fastened to it. As I was going back to my room, the disk on the book cover accidentally touched the sigil hanging around my neck—"

"What sigil?" Stergos cried in horror.

"Tell him," Conrig commanded Snudge.

"The one I took from the sorcerer Iscannon when I killed him in Castle Vanguard. It rendered him invisible—both to the naked eye and to windsight. When I took the thing, it was as dead as its master, but I kept it with Prince Conrig's permission and searched for information about it in the libraries of the Royal Alchymist."

Stergos groaned. "Oh, Blessed Zeth. You don't understand the horrible peril—"

Conrig said, "Continue, lad."

"When the two pieces of moonstone touched," Snudge said, "they glowed. And right there in the south-wing corridor of the palace, I was bespoken by one of the Beaconfolk."

"God save us!" said Stergos. "What did it look like?"

"The creature wasn't visible, but it seemed very angry and inflicted great pain on me, so that I bent forward and caused the moonstone to fall away from my flesh. The pain vanished and the monstrous voice was stilled. I snatched the sigil off my neck and put it into my wallet so it couldn't touch the book again, then went to my room. I was alone, so I studied the contents of the book for a time. Parts were in a foreign language. I concluded that there was no way I could safely make use of the invisibility sigil—"

"I should hope not!" Stergos exclaimed.

"—so I decided that, in the morning, I'd throw both sigil and book into the sea. I went to sleep, and dreamed of Prince Beynor." The boy paused, and looked with longing at the pitcher of beer. Without a word, Conrig filled a crystal cup and handed it over. "Thank you, Your Grace . . . The dream was more than a dream. I'm convinced Beynor actually bespoke me. He wanted me to become his follower, because he said he'd fallen out with an accomplice already living in the palace: Vra-Kilian, the Royal Alchymist."

"I knew it!" Conrig cried. "Oh, the poxy shite-weasel! I'll slice out his guts and flog him to death with them!"

Stergos's normally ruddy face had gone the color of chalk. He managed to say, "Is there more, Deveron?"

"Yes, my lord. Beynor told me that his father Linndal had died, and that he was now Conjure-King of Moss. He claimed to know all about the plan to invade Didion—but I think he believes we intend to strike through Great Pass. He offered to show me freely, without obligation, how to conjure Iscannon's sigil into usability. This was to be proof of his goodwill. Then he gave me the necessary spells."

"Good God!" Conrig whispered. "So now you can make the thing work? You can go about invisible?"

Snudge shook his head. "Hear me out, Your Grace. Even though Beynor had told me the magical words, I still declined to serve him. I had already sworn to be your liege man and told him so. He professed to be very disappointed in me and called me a fool. Then he left my dream and I woke. It was still night, a couple of hours before dawn. I was consumed with dread. Only a simpleton would have believed that Beynor had given me the correct spell to activate the sigil. I was certain that if I tried to use it, some terrible calamity would occur. So I dressed, made my way from the palace to the waterfront, hired a small boat, and threw both sigil and book into Cala Bay."

He gulped beer, keeping his eyes downcast. When neither Conrig nor Stergos spoke, he added, "The sentry at the Dung Gate can confirm my coming and going. Perhaps we can find the boatman, too."

"We don't doubt your story," Conrig said. "Even your dream of Beynor is plausible. My brother was informed on the wind this morning that the young scoundrel is now Conjure-King, and Princess Ullanoth has been removed from the line of succession. We don't know what has become of her, Snudge. Can you do a windsearch?"

The boy looked up, troubled. "I can try, Your Grace. May I withdraw to your bedchamber? It'd be best if I was alone."

"Go."

When the door closed behind Snudge, Conrig said, "I'll tell the king about Kilian at once. We must lock this traitor in the deepest dungeon, under the strongest magical constraints possible. It's clear enough now how young Beynor won his loyalty. The knave told our dear uncle he'd give him the spells to activate those baskets of sigils he has hidden away. Or perhaps the two of them intended to share out the magical moonstones and use them to rule the world!"

"Con, we must get hold of those cursèd things and destroy them. Deveron did right throwing his into Cala Bay."

The prince frowned, picked up a piece of golden toast, and took a bite. "Perhaps, Gossy. But what a pity the explanatory book is gone. You might have deciphered the spells where the boy Snudge could not."

"Don't even think such a thing, Brother." Stergos was beyond indignation. His mild face was as adamant as Conrig had ever seen it. "I would never assist you in such an abomination, nor would any other faithful member of my Mystic Order. That Vra-Kilian dared to keep sigils of the Beaconfolk hidden in his sanctum shows the depth of his depravity. He deserves to be executed—for committing treason and for betraying his solemn vows as a Doctor Arcanorum of Zeth."

"Hmmm. Would that I could dispose of him so easily! But he is our mother's brother. Even if we could prove treason—and I doubt that would be easy—she'd prevail on the king, and he'd never sign Kilian's death warrant.

Besides, the Blackhorse family is too powerful to antagonize, especially now that Sovereignty is within our grasp. No, we'll give Kilian a quick trial on trumped-up charges and find him guilty, then lock him up in a cell reinforced by the strongest alchymical magic. As for his moonstones . . . we'll see."

He finished the last of his breakfast, pushed away from the table, and began to don his black-and-silver brocade doublet and a swordbelt ornamented with white gold. "I'd best lead the arresting party myself. We'll take the miscreant in charge before he tries to escape. Gossy, how can we fend off any magical mayhem Kilian might attempt? And you did say he's locked inside his sanctum. We'll need to neutralize whatever protective enchantments he's set up."

"Oh, my, yes. I'll have to consult Abbas Noachil on the wind." Stergos's former air of resolution had evaporated and he was dithering with anxiety. "There are incantations to bind renegade wizards, of course, but we'll probably need all of the loyal Brethren in the palace, working together, to manage Vra-Kilian. He's so very strong! And shut up in his sanctum, he has access to significant magical equipment . . . I'll make preparations immediately. Shall I assemble the other Brethren in the Blue Foyer when we're ready? It's close to the Alchymical Library and will make a good rallying point."

"An excellent idea. Summon my ten Heart Companions also, and bid them come armed in full panoply. Go now. I'll remain here a few minutes more, in case Snudge has found Princess Ullanoth. Then I must share this information with our father the king, and draw up a warrant for Kilian's arrest."

Stergos left the room, and the prince strode back and forth before the fire, chewing his lip, wondering how his press for Sovereignty might be salvaged if he had to abandon the invasion of Didion. But that might be the least of his worries if young Beynor instigated a sea-attack on Cathra from the Continent—

Snudge came into the sitting room. "Your Grace?"

The prince spun about. "You've seen her?"

"No. But then, I didn't think I would. However, Princess Ullanoth's tower rooms in Royal Fenguard are enveloped in their usual covering spell. She's very likely inside."

The prince brightened. "Yes! That's sure to be it. Mourning her father, perhaps, or thinking how to take vengeance on her crafty little brother."

"Beynor's hidden himself, too, in his own apartments. King Lindall's body is propped up on the throne, dressed in regal robes. A great crowd of his subjects

are parading before it. Some of them kiss his golden slippers for good luck as they
pay their last respects."

"Ugh!" said the prince. "Superstitious swamp-stompers!"

"Do you require anything more of me, Your Grace?" The boy looked listless
and drained after his arcane effort.

Conrig's eyes narrowed. "Snudge, my own talent is small, but nevertheless it
often guides me in sniffing out falsehood. Did you tell me the whole truth about
that book you stole from Kilian? I thought I sensed you were withholding something from me."

The boy considered for a moment, then said in a level voice, "I'm your man till
my death, Your Grace. I told you what you should know. You must trust me to do
what's best in matters concerning my own talent and other sorcery. I'll never do
you harm, but sometimes I must protect you from things you might misunderstand,
that could put both of us in terrible danger. If you can't accept this, then dismiss me
from your service."

The prince drew in his breath sharply in outrage and opened his mouth. But
the cutting words of reprimand died in his throat when he saw the look in
Snudge's eyes—the same stubborn integrity possessed by Stergos. The boy's loyalty was not blind, and he, the master, could take it or leave it.

"I won't dismiss you," Conrig said, sighing. "And I will trust you." For
now . . .

"Thank you, Your Grace."

"Do one final thing for me. Oversee Kilian's chambers and see if you detect
any specific threats to me and my men. We're going to arrest him with the help of
Stergos and the faithful Brothers."

The short-range scry was easy enough. Snudge closed his eyes and let the
wind carry him. The outer rooms of the Royal Alchymist were open, guarded by
a pair of novices as usual. Three red-robed adepts were seated at carrels in the
library, consulting magical volumes, making notes, and whispering to one
another; they were the infamous Brothers Raldo, Niavar, and Cleaton. Kilian's
door was locked, and his chambers were enveloped in couverture.

Snudge described what he had windwatched. "Is there anything else, Your
Grace?"

"No. Go practice your knightly arts as usual, but from time to time during
the day, go apart and windsearch for the Princess Ullanoth again. If she's dead,

and her mysterious allies unable or unwilling to assist us during the invasion, we may be forced to rethink our attempt to conquer Didion."

"I'll do my utmost to find her. But if she lives, I think it likely that she'll tell you herself, at a time of her own choosing."

He bowed and left the room, leaving Conrig frowning thoughtfully.

Had the boy really cast book and sigil into the sea? The prince knew he'd have to find out the truth.

fifteen

Vra-Kilian Blackhorse, Royal Alchymist of Cathra, had gone briefly to his rooms after the king's cavalcade returned home from the pilgrimage, intending to change his dusty garments, refresh himself, and then attend upon the ailing Olmigon, making yet another attempt to learn the oracle's response to the Question.

Almost immediately he discovered that someone had been inside his inner sanctum—not once, but *nine times* during the three weeks he was away. A simple mechanical device concealed in the doorframe tripped each time the door was opened, making a small mark on a black wax tablet; the device reset itself each time the door closed. Its operation was so unobtrusive that it was beneath the notice of any thief—whether or not he possessed arcane ability.

With a sinking heart, Vra-Kilian had hastened to open his four windsight-secure cabinets to see whether anything had been taken. Nothing appeared to be missing except the small book that gave a condensed description of sigils and their operation. He took the baskets of moonstones to his worktable and counted them twice, but all of them were there, as were the large volumes dealing with Beaconfolk magic, written in the Salkan tongue.

Kilian muttered a curse as he left his sanctum, poured a goblet of wine to ease his nerves, and settled into a cushioned armchair to think. Could an agent of Prince Beynor have insinuated himself into the palace during his absence? It hardly seemed likely. Why would a Mosslander thief have taken only the small book—the one written mostly in the Cathran language—and left the more valuable Salkan volumes and the priceless sigils themselves behind?

Beynor did covet those sigils desperately, but he had no notion of where they were hidden, nor did he know precisely how many moonstones Kilian possessed. The alchymist had hinted to the boy-wizard that there were fifty in the collection, while the trove actually included more than twice that number. They had originally come from a prehistoric Salkan grave, discovered by another Royal Alchymist of Cathra, a certain Vra-Darasilo Lednok, over seven hundred years ago. That long-dead Brother of Zeth had compromised his vows by preserving artifacts of Beacon-folk magic; but Darasilo, who was both a scholar and a devotee of magical history, simply could not bring himself to destroy such a treasure. Instead he had hidden them away. What was the real harm, when both sigils and spells could never be used? Darasilo bequeathed his hoard to his successor, advising him to destroy the books and the moonstones if he deemed it necessary.

The successor did not. Neither did the Royal Alchymists who followed him in office. Instead, Darasilo's collection was passed along under a strict oath of secrecy. Venerated as relics of ancient, unattainable magic, they were marveled at and morbidly speculated about, but were never objects of temptation. To empower those sigils would require the cooperation of the few remaining Salka, hideous man-eaters whose hatred of humans was legendary. What Brother of Zeth would risk both his life and his immortal soul to acquire magic so perilous?

None . . . until Vra-Kilian Blackhorse.

He'd only conceived the great notion a little over a year ago, when the political situation on the island had come to a boil because of the continuing curse of the Wolf's Breath. Kilian's influence in the Privy Council was clearly waning as the Prince Heritor championed the push for Sovereignty. Conrig's animosity towards Kilian was immutable, and the alchymist realized that he had no chance of retaining his high office if Conrig became king.

One winter evening, as the wizard brooded over the dead sigils in his sanctum, knowing that even one of them, conjured into life, might give him the power to reverse his fortunes, the brilliant idea came to him. It was so simple that he could hardly believe that none of his predecessors had considered it. Or perhaps they had, but lacked the ingenuity or courage to follow through . . .

Unlike the people of the southern part of the island, who had long since lost any contact with the uncanny amphibian beings conquered by Emperor Bazekoy, the folk of Moss still shared territory with the Salka. The Glaumerie Guild knew the Salkan language, and so did the royal family. Rothbannon, the first Conjure-King, had taken particular pains to ingratiate himself with Salka shamans. How the fearless sorcerer had acquired the Seven Stones from the monsters and used them to found a kingdom was a cornerstone of Moss's brief history.

The rulers who succeeded Rothbannon over the next century proved less expert in dealing with the dreaded Beaconfolk and the marvelous sigils they empowered. After several appalling mishaps, the Seven Stones were locked away by the Guild wizards, to be used only in case of some overwhelming national emergency—which fortunately never occurred, Moss being such an insignificant backwater of the otherwise lively island.

The ultracautious tradition had finally been broken by Linndal and his wife Taspiroth, formidable magickers both, who once again made use of the Stones. But the Conjure-Queen miscalculated and died atrociously on a whim of the Coldlight Army, and her husband's mind foundered as he witnessed her fate. He deactivated the sigils and locked them away.

Which left their children.

Beynor and Ullanoth, like their parents before them, had been taught the Salkan language as part of their thaumaturgical education, so that they would be able to command the Seven Stones, should the need arise. Kilian was aware that the brother and sister were implacable rivals, Beynor favored to inherit the throne and already experimenting with the Stones as his parents had done, Ullanoth choked with bitter resentment until—as rumor had it—the spirit of her mother had gifted her with a few minor sigils of her own.

How that must have dismayed the Conjure-Prince! In his own callow way, he was as politically ambitious as Conrig Wincantor. Kilian knew for a fact that it was Beynor who had convinced King Achardus of Didion to sell warships to Stippen, Foraile, and Andradh, worming his way into the barbarian ruler's confidence. The boy-wizard hadn't caused the Wolf's Breath, but he'd known how to take advantage of it by lying to his gullible neighbors and pretending to powers he didn't possess.

In short, Beynor of Moss was the very person Vra-Kilian needed.

He had bespoken the aspiring young man, offering him twenty-five precious sigils—"half the number I inherited from my predecessor"—in exchange for Salkan language lessons.

Dumfounded, Beynor had tentatively agreed. But he'd proved shrewder in negotiation than Kilian had anticipated, postponing the actual fulfillment of the bargain again and again. He refused to meet Kilian in person for fear the older man would take magical advantage of him.

And so a temporary impasse was reached. Neither Royal Alchymist nor Conjure-Prince trusted the other, with good reason; but by unspoken agreement, they became co-conspirators, seeking mutual advantage in the increasingly chaotic politics of the island, and hoping that fate would show them the way to achieve their separate goals.

Kilian's manipulation of King Olmigon eventually culminated in the Edict of Sovereignty massacre; while Beynor (unbeknownst to Kilian) pressed Didion to form an alliance with the Continental nations. The odd bedfellows had been drawn closer by Prince Conrig's unexpected teaming up with Ullanoth and his decision to invade Didion.

When Kilian learned of the secret council of war to be held at Castle Vanguard, he had informed Beynor, who suggested sending one of his wizards to spy on the meeting, hidden by the Concealer. If the opportunity arose, Iscannon was also instructed to inflict serious injury on Conrig—but not kill him, lest Olmigon appoint a new heir—effectively ending the threat of an invasion.

Iscannon's death and the theft of his sigil had thrown the plans awry. The alchymist feared that Conrig had learned of Beynor's complicity from Princess Ullanoth. Perhaps the prince also suspected *him* of treason . . .

"And now this mysterious intruder!" the Royal Alchymist exclaimed aloud.

Could he have been sent by Conrig? Had the Prince Heritor ordered his brother Stergos to pry into Kilian's things, hoping to incriminate him? The little book of Beaconfolk magic was a thing forbidden to the Brethren. Perhaps it alone had been taken in hopes that Kilian would not notice its loss. Conrig might have planned to use the thing to discredit Kilian in the eyes of his Order, paving the way for the alchymist's disgrace and banishment from court.

There was a way to find out.

Kilian resumed his seat, closed his eyes, and began a windsearch—first of the Doctor Arcanorum's chambers, and then of the prince's. The purloined book was not there. Clenching his teeth, he began to search the rest of the palace. But even a superficial overview of the sprawling edifice took over an hour to perform and proved to be fruitless and doubly frustrating. Searching beyond the palace was not within his powers.

While Kilian wasted time hunting for the book, Prince Conrig managed to reach the king's bedside before him and leave orders forbidding him entrance.

I've probably lost the game, the Royal Alchymist told himself, as he waited outside the royal bedchamber. All I can do now is brazen it out and salvage what I can from the wreckage.

Later, after King Olmigon and the prince had conferred and reconciled, Kilian had been forced to accompany Conrig to a meeting of the Privy Council, attended only by the principal members. There Conrig had displayed the writ affirming that he was now the only one who addressed the Council with King Olmigon's authority. The Royal Alchymist would no longer have a seat after tonight. Henceforth, he would only administer arcane affairs, as his predecessors had.

In a state of eerie tranquillity, Vra-Kilian had returned to his rooms. He tried to bespeak Beynor of Moss and tell him of his abrupt demotion and the book's theft, but the young wizard was not disposed to answer. All Kilian could do was have wind-converse with Ridcanndal, Grand Master of the Glaumerie Guild, and request that the Conjure-Prince contact him as soon as possible. Then Kilian stripped off his garments, downed a sleeping potion, and threw himself wearily into bed. He fell asleep almost at once.

The windspoken voice of Beynor did not wake him until nearly six in the morning, and its tone was ominous.

Vra-Kilian, my friend, you are in very serious trouble. But perhaps you already realize that.

Yes, but he still had to put a good face on it!

"I know I've been dismissed from the Privy Council by Prince Conrig, but this may be only a temporary setback. I also know that a clever thief has stolen one of my books of Beaconfolk magic. The other two volumes are safe, as are the sigils and all the rest of my things. There's no trace of the missing book within Cala Palace. I did a windsearch. So the thief is probably long gone away. The book's loss is unfortunate, but hardly a catastrophe."

You're wrong. The book was taken by Deveron Austrey, Prince Conrig's personal agent, a boy of sixteen years. He knows now that you have large numbers of sigils in your possession and will certainly report this to his royal master.

"But—that's unbelievable! I remember this Deveron now. He's only the prince's footman. How could a mere housecarl get past my guardian novices and intricate locks? Did you windwatch him in the act?"

No. Deveron is a powerful wild talent, which is why he serves Conrig. His arcane abilities cannot be detected by an adept examiner, and it's impossible to windwatch him. I'm now certain that he was the one who discovered my spy Iscannon at work in Castle Vanguard and slew him. For this service Conrig created the boy an armiger while you were away on the king's pilgrimage.

"Blessed Zeth . . ."

Even worse, I'm certain Deveron took Iscannon's invisibility sigil. His motive for stealing your book was to discover how to use the moonstone himself.

"The boy's not in the palace now, because the book's not here and he'd surely keep it with him. As I said, I windsearched for the book hours ago and found no trace of it. Tomorrow my loyal followers will track down the damned brat, wherever he's hidden himself in the city, using ordinary means. They'll slit his throat and retrieve both the book and the sigil. Conrig will be none the wiser if we dispose of the body—"

You don't know that Deveron's left the palace. I told you that he can't be windwatched! If his innate body-shielding talent is strong enough, you may not be able to descry the book as he carries it about. You're in great danger, Vra-Kilian, and you must flee at once.

"Not so fast! If the boy had already betrayed me, Conrig's Heart Companions would have been battering my chamber door with the hilts of their swords, rousting me out of bed. Nothing of the sort has happened. No doubt the young knave didn't want to disturb his royal master's sleep and decided to wait until morning to give his report. Before he can betray me, I'll have my men seize him. He'll vanish as though he'd never existed."

You're a shortsighted clodpate, Kilian! I told you that Conrig himself authorized the boy to invade your sanctum. The prince already suspects you of betraying his council of war to me. He's on to you. This is why he removed you from the Privy Council. Escape while you can. Make your way to Moss by ship. My Glaumerie Guild and I will welcome your great talent.

"But I can't leave without my things—my magical apparatus and reference volumes. They're beyond price!"

So is your neck, my friend. Find a way to take the sigils and the Salkan magical books with you, but forget the rest. Slip away from the palace immediately. Conrig and his cohorts may not act against you at once because of your high position and august lineage—but act they will. Be assured of it.

"You—you are able to visualize this dire outcome through your sorcery?"

Silly old fool! I don't need magic to read your future. Do as I tell you, or go to hell!

"Prince Beynor, I must protest. I'm willing to make allowances for your youth and impatience, but you have no call to speak to me so disrespectfully. I demand an apology."

I am not a prince any longer, Vra-Kilian, but Conjure-King of Moss according to the decree of my late father. And kings apologize to no one. Farewell.

Kilian listened, but the windthread had been severed.

"Damnation," he said. "So it all comes tumbling down. I thought I might have a bit more time."

He felt anger and he felt fear, but both of these useless emotions were readily quashed by his invincible will. He was Kilian Blackhorse, the most powerful member of a great family, archwizard of the realm, the royal counselor who had controlled a king like a doll on a string. He had faced challenges before and conquered them. He'd find a way to prevail this time as well.

He realized that it was too late for him to flee. His betrayal by the boy Deveron would soon be an accomplished fact. If he, Kilian, disappeared, the palace guard would simply raise a hue and cry throughout the city. Even if he did manage to coerce or bribe some ocean-going skipper to carry him to Moss, there was nothing to prevent Prince Conrig from sending a fast naval frigate after him. A pursuing warship could easily stay out of range of his defensive magic and bombard his own vessel with tarnblaze. And *that* diabolical stuff could not be deflected with ordinary magic.

Why hadn't Beynor windspoken the bad tidings earlier, when escape might have been possible? The question had no answer, but Kilian was sure that the last thing the newly minted Conjure-King would want was for the secret trove of moonstones to fall into Conrig's hands. Conrig: in league with the sister Beynor hated more than anyone alive! No, the young sorcerer was still Kilian's ally, at least until he got his hands on Darasilo's moonstones.

What to do? The sigils had to be hidden at once, in a place where no adept—especially one loyal to Beynor—could ever find them.

. . . Yes, of course!

Shivering in the chill, Vra-Kilian left his bed, put on fur-lined house shoes and a heavy robe, threw billets of wood on the dead ashes in the fireplace, and conjured a brisk blaze with his talent. Outside the windows of his bedchamber, dawn already brightened the sky, and he could see lamps moving in the corridors of the opposite wing of the palace. Servants were up and about, carrying cans of hot water for morning ablutions, bringing baskets of fuel to be left outside the chambers of the nobles, lighting braziers and lamps in the common rooms. Before long kitchen boys would tote trays of breakfast to the fortunate. Valets, ladies' maids, messengers, and courtiers of every stripe would be bustling in all directions as Cala Palace came fully awake with the rising sun.

I know what must be done, Vra-Kilian told himself, as he made his way to his sitting room. But first, the safety measures. It would be a disaster if Prince Conrig's men burst in before he was ready.

He checked the tripod and the carved malachite charm that generated the spell of couverture around his private chambers. He had installed it before going to sleep, and it was still functioning properly. No ordinary adept could possibly windwatch him through its shield. Please, God—that included the accursèd Deveron Austrey!

So that left the barricade against physical incursion to be erected. He fetched a certain flask from a locked cabinet, let five drops of sizzling liquid fall into a stoneware dish where they formed an evil-smelling puddle, and pronounced a complex incantation.

Foom!

The flash was dazzling, and the smoke cleared in a moment. Now the walls and doors of his private rooms were sealed, impervious to all but the most advanced sorcery or superior siege engines. He'd left the chimney flues unconjured for obvious reasons, as well as the drafty windows. Many an incautious wizard had smothered himself by neglecting the elementary laws of natural science! The flooring was also left unprotected by magic, but for a very different reason.

I'm hungry, he realized. Well, there was probably enough time to eat, and who knew when he'd get his next meal?

He kindled a larger fire in the sitting room and sat down at the table in front of it, where the food he'd had no appetite for last night still waited: spicy finger sausages, two kinds of fine cheese, bread rolls, crocks of bilberry conserve and butter, a silver ewer of mead. As he ate and considered the situation, he felt confident that his life was in no immediate danger—at least, not from the King's Justice. Young Beynor didn't understand how Cathran law worked. No one could prove treason against him. Banishment at the royal pleasure, however, was a very real possibility. He would suffer a galling comedown after having been the shadow-ruler of Cathra for nearly twenty years, but at least his life and dignity would remain intact. And the future always beckoned.

However, mending his devastated fortunes would be impossible without the moonstones and the books. Lacking them, he might as well be dead. With them—and with the grudging assistance of the Conjure-King of Moss—he would eventually recover all that was about to be lost. And much more.

Vra-Kilian finished his meal and assembled the necessary tools, then unlocked and entered his violated inner sanctum. The room was very dark and he lit a candelabrum. The iron-bound small cabinet still stood with its door open, as he'd left it, and the sigils were on the worktable. For a lingering moment he fingered the cool stones in their baskets—so wonder-working, if only they were alive! And the books, the other secret legacy of the imprudent Darasilo—once tantalizing Kilian with their inaccessible learning, but perhaps soon susceptible to decryption.

He put the things away, closed and locked the cabinet, then took four small quartz crystals from a blue velvet bag and placed them in a precise square on the container's top. The bag also yielded a larger prism of quartz, longer than his index finger. He pointed it at the cabinet and said, "Rise!"

The heavy oaken safe-box lifted from the floor and hovered a few inches above it.

"Follow," Vra-Kilian commanded, gesturing with the long prism. He left the sanctum and went to his bedroom, with the ensorcelled cabinet floating obediently behind. Once there he attacked his bed, tossing pillows aside, tearing off coverlets, feather-tick, and linen, finally hauling the mattress off the undernet and shoving it out of the way. He knelt and swiftly began to untie each leather thong from its hole in the massive bedframe, muttering knot-abolishing spells as he worked. When three sides were free, he lifted the netting and laid it carefully to one side.

The space beneath the bed was clean; his manservant knew better than to let dust accumulate on the floor. Vra-Kilian knelt, peered closely at the wooden parquet-blocks for a moment, extended his arms, and simultaneously pressed two blocks spaced almost four feet apart. The bits of wood seemed identical to the others except for two minute protuberances, but as the wizard depressed them there was a loud *clack*. A section of the floor began to sink, hinged like a trapdoor, revealing an opening and a flight of stone steps.

They led to a musty crypt that held two roughly hewn tombs—one containing the skeleton of a woman, the other the remains of a small child. The names

JOVALA and *CHALLO* were chiseled crudely on the lids, and on the wall above them was the date C.Y. 413. Vra-Kilian suspected that the long-dead Darasilo had something to do with the tomb occupants. After all, they had been interred beneath chambers that had traditionally belonged to the Royal Alchymists of Cathra since a century after Bazekoy's conquest. The existence of the crypt was another of the secrets passed on to him by his late predecessor. Kilian had never thought to make use of it before, but now it seemed predestined by some higher power to be the perfect hiding place for the sigils and books, until he should find a way to retrieve them.

He pointed the quartz prism at the cabinet and said, "Follow."

It hopped the bedframe and wafted down into the hole in the floor, dogging his footsteps. He led it behind the tombs, retrieved the four small quartz crystals from its top, then went up and closed the crypt's trapdoor.

By the time he had restored his bed to its former state, he felt exhausted and irritated. There was brandy in the sitting room, so he decided to return there and sit by the fire to await the inevitable. But first he abolished the enchantment that protected his rooms from assault. He kept the windwatching shield in place. They'd think it odd if he left himself completely vulnerable.

He settled back in the soft chair. Outside, the palace chimes sounded the seventh hour of morning.

There'd be a trial, of course. But what could Conrig really prove? The sigils and the forbidden tomes were safely hidden now, impossible to windwatch. It was Kilian's word against that of an upstart former servant-boy that the things existed at all, and the little book could be explained away.

For treason, the evidence was even flimsier. No one could prove he'd intercepted and read the letter from Conrig to Duke Tanaby that convened the council of war. No one—save possibly the wretched Deveron—could connect him to Beynor of Moss and the sorcerer-spy slain at Castle Vanguard. Would a tribunal of Royal Justices deign to accept the hearsay evidence of a wild talent, even one employed by Prince Conrig? Would Conrig even permit his secret snudge to testify, knowing that thereby his anonymity would be lost and his value forfeit?

No.

But there was another peril Kilian might not be able to evade. False witnesses, alas, were always procurable. Kilian had used them himself to dispose of certain enemies. But even if he were found guilty, his loving sister, Queen Cataldise, would never permit the Royal Executioner to lop off his head. He would whisper to her the penalty he had decided would best suit his purpose: confinement in Zeth Abbey at the king's pleasure.

Zeth Abbey, so close to the Didionite frontier.

Zeth Abbey, whose ruler, Abbas Noachil, was in his ninety-first year of life.

Zeth Abbey, where so many of his loyal old comrades still lived and worked, numbers of them the beneficiaries of his personal generosity.

For the first time on that disastrous morning, Vra-Kilian smiled. His eyes closed and in another moment he was fast asleep, and remained so until he heard a loud pounding on his door.

He rose, unlocked it, and pulled it wide open. Vra-Stergos stood there white-faced, holding high a golden reliquary that held one of Emperor Bazekoy's blue pearls. Behind him knelt three ranks of red-robed Brethren with arms folded on their breasts.

Stergos intoned: "All harmful spells avaunt!"

There was a bright flash and a sound of clumping mailed feet. When Kilian's bedazzled vision cleared, he saw that Conrig's ten Heart Companions had taken a stand in front of the magickers. They wore full armor, and their two-handed broadswords were pointed straight at him.

"Good morning," said the Royal Alchymist, nodding austerely. He was now helpless to attack the others with magic.

Prince Conrig stepped forward, unarmored, hatless, and wearing his usual black clothing. His sword was sheathed. "Vra-Kilian Blackhorse, you are under arrest. The charge—for the moment—is disrupting the King's Peace." He proffered the warrant.

The wizard began to laugh. "Well, that'll serve your purpose tidily enough! Do you intend to lock me in fetters?"

"No," said Conrig, beckoning to one of the Brothers, who held a small wooden box. He opened it and took out a perforated piece of iron, like a bit of unsharpened knife-blade hung on a string. The voided cross of Saint Zeth's gammadion had been scratched on it. It was a crude replica of the gold amulet worn by every member of the Mystical Order, including Vra-Kilian. At the sight of the thing, the Royal Alchymist tensed.

"You know what this is," Conrig said, holding it out. "Take off your own gammadion and replace it with this, or we will slay you as you stand there."

Kilian obeyed. As the iron touched his breast, a red radiance flared from it. He groaned, staggered, and would have collapsed if Count Sividian and Count Feribor had not stepped forward to support him.

"You are now bound to your Order's will," Conrig said, "and your talent quenched until it pleases Abbas Noachil to restore it. We take you into custody with his permission. Now give me the keys to your chambers."

With some difficulty, Kilian detached them from his belt and handed them over. "These . . . will open everything within. Search without fear. I have prepared no magical man-traps."

"We'll make certain of that." Conrig turned to the knights. "Bring the former Royal Alchymist to the council chamber, and his three cronies as well. I'll follow as soon as Vra-Stergos and I perform a quick search of his rooms."

Sividian and Feribor still held Kilian's arms. He suffered them to lead him through the library, flanked by the other Companions, past the ranks of wide-eyed Brethren. Kilian noted that poor Butterball, Squinty, and Vinegar-Face were already in the custody of the Palace Guard. Well, he'd see that they joined him in exile.

Count Sividian stepped ahead to unlock and inspect the room where the three of them would wait until summoned, leaving Feribor alone at Kilian's side. He asked softly, "Nephew, am I to be put on trial at once?"

A sardonic smile. "I believe so, Uncle. The King's Grace has himself summoned the tribunal, and he will preside. You will be allowed a single advocate to help plead your case. Perhaps you might think on whom we might summon, as we await our summons to the council chamber."

Vra-Kilian smiled. "Oh, I've decided that already." He regarded Feribor Blackhorse with new interest. Unlike his indolent elder brother, he was a valiant warrior and a man of action. He was as yet unmarried; too many potential brides knew his reputation. He was not a man to be easily beguiled, but one who was reputedly ambitious and single-minded.

He might just do.

"Nephew," the alchymist said in a low voice, "after many years of wielding power, I am about to go into eclipse. These things happen to the best of us. But the day will come when my sun shines again, and when it does, I'll be in a position to reward those who are my friends. Reward them most generously."

Feribor said, "I'll not help you escape. Such is impossible."

"I'm aware of that. I intend to call upon my friends some time in the future. Perhaps several years from now. Maybe I count upon you?"

The young man shrugged in disdain. "Probably not. I don't need gold, Uncle."

"Neither do I offer it," said Vra-Kilian. "But what would you say to the throne of Cathra?"

Feribor stared at him, his face without expression. He said nothing.

"In time, it may be yours," said the wizard. "Listen carefully, for we have little time. The first thing you should know is that Conrig's new armiger, Deveron Austrey, is a strong wild talent . . ."

sixteen

When the tumultuous day ended, and Kilian and his henchmen had been sent on their way to Zeth Abbey in a prison-coach guarded by a detachment of the Palace Guard and three highly talented Brethren vouched for by Stergos, Conrig sequestered himself in his own apartment. Attended only by Lord Telifar, the prince ate a small supper then dismissed the lord-in-waiting and occupied himself reading the replies to the urgent letters sent out that morning. Earlier, Red Ansel had reported that Tarnian mercenary sealords would come to Cathra's defense only if they were paid in corn, not gold, so Conrig had had the royal scribes draft appeals to Cala's grain merchants and shipowners.

The responses were predictably bleak.

With profound regret, the merchants informed the Crown that they were unable to donate wheat and barley from their reserve stores. What little grain they had was already promised to certain high-ranking lords of Cathra (at a pretty price, quoted in the letters), and surely the prospects of an imminent attack from the south were vanishingly small and no mercenaries were needed. Why, Lord Admiral Dundry had said so himself!

In a similarly apologetic fashion, the shipowners told the Crown that even though they would gladly cooperate, no Cathran master mariner would be willing to set sail for Tarn at the present time, since the season of storms was due to strike the Western Ocean any day now. Several of the letters gave assurance that the weather would certainly keep Continental invaders in port as well. Besides, Lord Admiral Dundry had declared that there was no evidence that the southern nations were contemplating a sea war.

Conrig muttered imprecations under his breath. The damned trader-lords were confident they could ignore his appeals to patriotism with impunity. There was no helping it: he'd have to pay the inflated reserve price for the grain and do whatever was necessary to hire ships to carry it.

He worked for nearly an hour, drafting responses to the least venal-appearing of the prospects, inviting them to confer with him at the palace. Then there came a scratching at his door. He hastened to throw it open, expecting Snudge. But it was his wife, Princess Maudrayne.

"My lord husband," she said by way of greeting, and sailed into the room as boldly as always. He had not yet bade her welcome home, since she had kept to her chambers during the day's commotion.

Conrig nodded graciously to her. "My lady, I trust you've begun to recover from the rigors of the pilgrimage. I apologize for not presenting myself to you earlier. As you probably know, there's been hell to pay. This morning I received evidence that Vra-Kilian was guilty of treason—"

"The Queen's Grace told me everything. Including the fact that suborned witnesses testified against the Royal Alchymist and his associates. She also said that it was only through her personal plea for clemency that Kilian was banished rather than having his head chopped off. The poor woman was beside herself when she told me the story, but I have the impression that she bore up rather stoutly while bargaining for her brother's life."

Conrig smiled. "She did indeed. Please be seated. May I offer you refreshment? I was going to have some malt myself." He gestured at the table covered with papers. "I'm still hard at work, you see."

"My poor beleaguered love. Yes, I'll have a drink. Don't be stingy pouring."

She took the chair at the table opposite his, arranging her loose robe of tawny velvet trimmed with dark mink. Conrig handed her a crystal goblet, which she drank from liberally and then set down. He resumed his seat and sipped his own drink, keeping his eyes on her. She was two-and-twenty years of age and looked more beautiful than ever, her unbound auburn hair flowing down her back like liquid fire and her fair skin luminous in the candlelight. Bazekoy's Brisket! If only she'd given him an heir . . .

"It's true enough," he said offhandedly, "that Kilian was convicted of treason through perjury. It's also true that he was guilty as the devil himself. The evidence came to me through one of my most trusted men, who gathers intelligence for me secretly. I couldn't possibly have let him testify before the tribunal and reveal himself, so the dissembling was necessary."

She took up her cup again and stared into the amber depths. "You needn't justify yourself to me, Con. I'm no friend of the Royal Alchymist. His evil influence on King Olmigon was deplorable. I'm quite sure Kilian got what he deserved."

"No," the prince said starkly. "Not yet. But one day he will, when I'm king. You see, we're going to war against Didion. Kilian found out and informed Beynor of Moss, who has allied himself with the Didionite princes. The gang of them hatched a plot to foil our military operation and assassinate me after Father passed away. With that pudding-head Shiantil Blackhorse on the throne of Cathra, Kilian would rule the realm absolutely." He gave a vulpine grin. "Until Beynor's confederates in Stippen and Foraile launched an attack on our southern seaboard and Didion hammered us in the north. Presumably, Cathra was to be carved up like a roast ox, and I doubt Kilian would have been invited to the feast. Plots within plots, my lady! I've been hard put to keep up with them, but all's well for the moment."

She inclined her head without comment. Then: "Tell me about Ullanoth of Moss."

Conrig's eyes narrowed. For a moment, he kept silent, wondering how much she knew. Finally, he said, "She's our secret ally in the war against Didion—the press for Sovereignty. Months ago, she came to Stergos and me at Brent Lodge and told us of a scheme by which we might invade Didion over Breakneck Pass at the end of the Boreal Moon."

"Ah!"

"I must ask you to swear to keep this information secret."

She said, "Do you really think I'd betray Cathra and send you to your death?"

He only stared at her evenly.

"Of course I swear." Her tone was clipped.

He continued as though there had been no interruption. "Ullanoth pledged magical assistance that would enable us to enter Holt Mallburn without detection and seize King Achardus, his sons, and his high officials. I intend to implement this plan within less than two weeks. The announcement that my Heart Companions and I would go to Beorbrook Hold to help the earl marshal repel incursions over Great Pass is only a ruse. We'll go to Castle Vanguard, where an invasion force led by the Lords of the North is gathering, even as we speak, and enter Didion through Breakneck Pass."

"What reward did Princess Ullanoth ask of you for her assistance?"

"Money," Conrig said. "A lot of it. And my solemn promise to set her on the throne of Moss when the Sovereignty is established, and declare her First Vassal—which means low taxation, among other things."

Maudrayne swirled her liquor in the faceted cup. Her expression was unreadable. "That may not be easy, now that her brother is king and she's barred from the succession."

"When Moss is part of the Sovereignty of High Blenholme, its laws of succession will be as I decree. The princess is also a powerful sorceress, with her own ways of countering her brother's claim to the throne. She's a very formidable young woman."

"Oh, I don't doubt that," said Maudrayne. She was silent for a time, then downed the last of her drink and said, "Con, I wish to spend this winter in Tarn, with my suffering people. Red Ansel says that you plan to send grain ships to Goodfortune Bay, as payment for mercenary sealords to defend Cala. Let me go on one of the ships—and Ansel, too. I can return in the spring."

"I'm sorry, my lady. Your place is here."

"But I have set my heart on going! I've nursed King Olmigon devotedly for months. Now he's at ease as he approaches his end, but I'm dog-weary. I must find some way to refresh my battered spirits. Let me see my own country again! If you wish, I can even speak to my uncle, the High Sealord Sernin, of your plan for Sovereignty—"

"No. That would be . . . premature and contrary to my wishes. And a voyage could be perilous, with the season of storms nearly upon us. No, you must remain here, Maude. If all goes well with the war, you shall visit your homeland next year, as consort to the Sovereign of High Blenholme and its Lady Ambassador to Tarn."

She leapt to her feet, sea-blue eyes blazing. "But I want to go now! How can you object to my absence? You're never here! And now you talk of going off to conquer Didion, leaving me once again. Do you have any idea of what my life is like? I'm nothing but an object of pity and derision to these noble Cathran snobs! Conrig's barren, oh-so-unsuitable wife! They whisper about me and snicker when they think I don't notice. I have not a single friend at court! My chief lady-in-waiting reports my every action to Queen Cataldise—and *she* patronizes me and invents things to quarrel about when she's not ignoring me altogether. Only your father treats me like an intelligent human being, and he's dying. I'm suffocating here, Conrig! Let me go!"

"I cannot," he said, rising and taking her hand. "The times are too critical. You must remain in the palace and perform your duties cheerfully—or at least willingly. As your loving husband and lord, I command it."

"Faithless cock-hound!" She tore her hand from his, seized her empty crystal goblet, and dashed it onto the hearthstone where the shards scattered like fiery sparks. "You dare speak to me of your love?" she screamed. "Liar! I know you've betrayed me with that Mossland slut. I know everything about you! *Everything,* Conrig Wincantor." A ferocious triumph shone in her eyes. "Remember that, when you meet again with the witch Ullanoth."

She whirled about and stormed out of the room, slamming the door behind her.

"Futter me," said the prince wearily, slumping back into his seat.

My dearest one. If I were only there to console you.

He started up from the table, nearly upsetting the decanter of liquor over the papers. "Is it you, Ulla? Were you watching?"

Yes, and waiting. This is the first opportunity I've had to bespeak you. And what do I descry? A wife threatening her husband—and king-to-be—with revelation of his deepest, most perilous secret. Even though my lip-reading ability is minimal, that part of her tirade was plain enough.

"Ah, God, no!" Conrig let his brow fall onto his knuckles. "She can't have meant that. She knows nothing of high magic and the indicators of talent. And she'd not tear the crown away from me, knowing it would go to one so unworthy as Duke Shiantil . . . would she?"

It's evident that she eavesdropped upon our meeting last night. I think she hoped to return to Tarn and there divorce you without fault. But now—who knows? You must do something about her, Conrig. Before you go off to war.

He sat bolt upright, addressing the empty space that Ullanoth seemed to inhabit. "I will not harm her," he said. "Never!"

So. You still love your wife.

"No!" he cried. "It's over between us. But now is not the time to publish the breakdown of our marriage. It would alienate Tarn and put the entire scheme of Sovereignty at risk."

She might violate her oath and betray your invasion. Her silence must be assured.

"I can manage that. Stergos can supply the proper potion. It'll be no surprise that she falls slightly ill, after such an arduous journey. Later . . . everything can be resolved."

My dearest prince. Maudrayne will run away. And the Tarnian shaman Ansel will help her.

He thought furiously. "I'll have her sailboat disabled. Send Ansel off with the grain ships—if I ever get the cursèd things organized. Take my mother and Lady Sovanna into my confidence and leave them to deal with Maude while I'm away in Didion. It can all be worked out."

What's this about sending grain to Tarn?

"We need mercenaries to help defend Cala, in case Beynor incites the Continentals to launch an attack. The sealords agreed to send twenty double-tier frigates, but they demand to be paid in food, not gold, and won't set sail for Cathra until grain-ships arrive in Goodfortune Bay. I'll arrange it, even if I have to empty the treasury." He paused. "But tell me how you are faring, lady. I know of your father Linndal's accidental death—"

No accident! It happened as soon as he signed the decree granting Beynor the right of succession. The little pismire tried to have me arrested and confined, but I escaped him using two of my sigils. I'm still secure in my tower, but I won't remain here for long. As soon as I've conjured the appropriate enchantments, I'll leave for Didion, where I'll assist you to enter Holt Mallburn Palace and seize the king. We'll drink a victory cup together, my prince.

Conrig felt himself going boneless with relief. The invasion would not have to be postponed after all.

He found his goblet, refilled it, and swallowed half its contents, ignoring the flames in his gullet. "Thank heaven you're safe, Ulla! I feared for your life."

It's about time you thought to mention it.

He groaned, putting his heart and soul into it. "Ah, lady, this day I've been tried like a blade in a forge. Forgive me my distraction. The good news is, I've disposed of my old enemy Vra-Kilian. He's convicted of high treason, his talent is extinguished, and I've sent him off to lifelong exile in the Abbey of Zeth."

Well done. And I also have news to cheer you. Your northern allies have begun to send groups of fighters toward Castle Vanguard, according to your plan. So I've instructed my magical partners to bring down the first of the fog.

To hide the troop movements?

Exactly. At the appropriate time, I'll blanket all of northeastern Cathra, from Beorbrook Hold and the Great North Road to the eastern shore, and as far south as Swan Lake and Lake Brent. For now, there'll be small areas of mist—just enough to confuse Beynor or other hostile windwatchers of the Glaumerie Guild. If they spy warriors on the move, they'll assume they're converging on Great Pass. Incidentally, my brother seems thus far to have accepted the fiction that you intend to invade via that route.

"Thank God."

I have a sigil able to spy through any enchantment Beynor may try to hide behind, vouchsafed me by the dead hand of my mother. It is not yet empowered, because it is one of the Great Stones that afflicts its owner with considerable suffering. But I will bring it to life when the proper time comes and use it to remove my brother from the throne he stole.

Conrig caught his breath. "But—you told me you would not resort to Beaconfolk magic, save to conceal and protect yourself, and visit me!"

I do what I must do. I have seven stones, just as Beynor does. Two of my Great Stones are not yet alive, because the thaumaturgical debt to the Lights increases with each sigil made active. And so does the danger of having the creatures . . . intervene in the magic, as my poor mother discovered.

"What happened to her, Ulla?"

We won't talk of it now. Be assured that I intend to be far more cautious than she. The stones are perilous, but so is a sharp sword in the hands of a child. I'm no child, my love. I know how to control the power of the Coldlight Army, and so does my damned little brother. He only has six stones left now, after losing Concealer, but three of them are capable of tremendous magic. Our war is against Beynor as much as against Achardus of Didion.

"And . . . you also possess sigils capable of tremendous magic."

What if I do? I won't be hamstrung by your ignorance or fear, Conrig. If you aren't willing to trust me, then tell me to be gone.

"Ah, lady! What else can I do but trust you?"

You do have other options, of course. Call off your invasion! Command your brother Stergos to bespeak the windvoices of your allies and recall the troops. Try to make peace with Didion by freely sending them food to ease their famine. Perhaps sweet charity will accomplish what your high-handed Edict failed to do! Or else abandon your dream of the Soverignty of Blenholme until you conceive another scheme more likely to succeed than this one I gave to you—along with my love.

"Ullanoth, don't be angry with me. I must trust you and continue as we've planned. I can do nothing else, God help me!"

I will help you, Conrig. I! Hold fast to that certainty and lead your Heart Companions from Cala Palace on the appointed day. You'll triumph in Didion, and in time you'll unite all Blenholme.

He uttered a harsh laugh. "If my royal father rises from his deathbed."

What? Are you making mock of me?

"Hardly. That's the answer Emperor Bazekoy's oracle gave to King Olmigon's Question. Father asked if I would succeed in unifying the island. The oracle told him: 'Only if you rise from your deathbed to assist him.'"

I—I knew nothing of this. Why didn't you tell me?

"I presumed you learned of it already through your occult arts, Conjure-Princess."

No. This is . . . a very interesting thing. I must think about it and consult my books of prophecy. No king of Cathra has Questioned the emperor for nigh unto three hundred years. I presumed the oracle was extinct.

"The king was convinced it was quite real. The Question's answer can be interpreted several ways, of course—including the ruin of all my hopes! But Bazekoy did accomplish the unlikely reconciliation of my father and me, so I'm inclined to keep an open mind."

Quite right, my prince. And so will I. Now rest and dream of the great triumph to come. I must be about my work.

"Calling on the Beaconfolk to make fog?" he suggested cynically.

Not at all. A simpler enchantment will accomplish that. Good night, dearest love.

He hesitated only a moment before responding, "And good night to you, princess of my heart."

Since it was not yet the tenth hour of evening, Conrig went to the apartments of Queen Cataldise to make his peace with her and ask her assistance in dealing with Maudrayne. There was no time to waste, given the famous impulsiveness of the princess.

The queen's principal lady-in-waiting, a battle-axe named Vandaya Gullmont, who had changed Conrig's swaddling clouts when he was an infant, greeted him with a forbidding frown.

"Look here, my prince! I can't let you in. The Queen's Grace is most distressed by the events of the day and none too pleased with you. Come back tomorrow."

"Vandaya, has Mother gone to bed yet?" Conrig demanded.

"No, but—"

"Then I'll see her, by God."

He pushed past the spluttering woman and went into the queen's sitting room. Cataldise, wearing a nightrobe, sat on a footstool in front of her favorite fireside armchair. The chair itself was occupied by a long-haired white mother cat and four nursing kittens, which the queen stroked gently. Her eyes were puffy from weeping, but she looked up with a calm expression as Conrig came and knelt beside her.

"See how beautiful Syla's babies are," she said abstractedly. "Three snowy little girls and one coal-black boy. They'll be wonderful fun now that their eyes are finally open."

"Mother—" Conrig took her plump hand and kissed it. "I'm sorry for what you've had to suffer this day. So very sorry."

A fresh tear appeared and trickled down the queen's cheek. "Your father will be gone soon. And now my dear brother as well. Not dead, but banished so far away that I'll never see him again. And if I hadn't been there to plead for him, poor Kilian might have gone to the block."

Conrig was gentle but firm. "All of the charges laid against him were true. And you may as well know his motive, even though it wasn't spoken of before the tribunal: He intended to put your silly nephew Shiantil on the throne after assassins had disposed of me, and rule Cathra through him."

"Yes," the queen conceded, her tears falling faster. "Kilian would do that. He hates you, my dear, because he knows he can never control you. I'm ashamed of him and regret with all my heart that he gave in to the base lure of illicit power. But I can't help but love him still."

He folded her in his arms. "I know. And thanks to you, he'll live and do penance for his treason and perhaps experience remorse. If you wish, you shall visit him regularly. He won't be imprisoned—only confined to the abbey grounds. His magical powers are abrogated, but he may still enjoy use of the library and socialize with certain of the Brethren, including his three close friends who were convicted with him. Their punishment is actually very lenient."

She nodded, took a lace-edged handkerchief from her sleeve, and wiped her eyes. "I know, dear."

"So you aren't embittered toward me?" He held her at arm's length, entreaty in his gaze.

"No, of course not. I understand what you had to do. You're the Prince Heritor and soon you'll be my king, and I'll be your loyal subject until I die. But even more, I'll love you because you're my dear son. Whatever you do."

He took a breath. "Mother, I need your help in a very delicate matter."

"Only ask." She had regained her composure and once again began to stroke the nursing cat.

"It's a sad thing, regarding my lady Maudrayne. She begged me to let her travel to Tarn this winter with the shaman Ansel. But I can't permit her to leave. Not while there's danger of war with Didion. Maude was wildly angry when I refused her. She accused me of ridiculous acts of infidelity with Princess Ullanoth of Moss and threatened to run off on her own."

"She's very unhappy." The queen's voice held little sympathy for her daughter-in-law. "You know why."

"Maude has her duty. And I would beseech you to help her know and appreciate it. And if she will not, then I ask your assistance in making certain that she does nothing foolish. I must go north very soon to help Beorbrook guard the frontier. When the snows fall and Great Pass closes, I'll come back to Cala and devote the entire winter to mending our marriage. But Maude *must* be here when I return."

The queen was thoughtful. "She's a headstrong woman. Stern measures may be needed, but I'll do my best to combine them with compassion. Rely on me."

The prince said, with evident relief, "Tomorrow, Stergos will provide you with remedies against melancholia, if the princess's health should require them. He'll also make suggestions for her care, and Lady Sovanna will doubtless be eager so assist. I'm so glad I can depend on you, Mother."

"Always," Cataldise replied. She rose from her stool and took his hand. "And now you must be off. Tomorrow I'll make arrangements for Maudrayne's . . . well-being."

They kissed, and Conrig left the sitting room. Lady Vandaya asked the queen whether she needed anything further, then retired when Cataldise shook her head. When the woman was gone, the queen went about the room snuffing candles before returning to gaze fondly at her cats. The three white kittens were nestled against their dam, fast asleep, but the venturesome little black male had tumbled out of the chair onto the carpet and was creeping feebly about.

She picked him up and held the soft, warm little body to her cheek. But he would not be caressed, and squirmed and squealed and scratched her hand with minute claws.

"Naughty boy!" the queen chided, and fetched him a smart tap on the head with her finger before giving him back to his mother.

seventeen

The knobby ring of moonstone named Weathermaker blazed green for five interminable heartbeats, and Beynor gritted his teeth to stifle his outcry as every nerve in his body reacted to its sorcery by bursting into searing flame. He endured it, tears pouring down his beardless face from eyes wide open, until the Great Stone paled and the agony receded and he let his breath escape in a long, broken sob.

Done. And the Diddlies damn well better be impressed!

It was mid-afternoon on the eve of his coronation. Low clouds the color of lead had hung over Royal Fenguard for the past four days, pissing oddly warm rain as though the Sky Father himself were registering his contempt for the patricidal new Conjure-King. Beynor stood looking out one of the windows of his bedchamber in the refurbished apartment that had once belonged to Linndal, dressed only in his undergarments and a light dressing gown. As he waited expectantly, his view of the Darkling Estuary cleared. The rain ceased, the clouds ripped apart, and the low-riding sun of subarctic Moss appeared over the Little Fen on the other side of the river. Although he was not in a position to see it, he had no doubt at all that the triple rainbow he'd requested now haloed Fenguard Castle, edifying those aboard the Didionite royal flagship and its escort of four fighting barques that were now creeping up the treacherous channel in the wake of the pilot-vessel.

"So let the theatricals commence," the boy-king muttered, turning away. There was a more crucial matter to consider once again before he put on his fine clothes and went down to the throne room to welcome the arriving guests.

He went to a magnificent small table, cleverly fashioned of leviathan bones and slabs of amber, and sat down. On the table was the flat, velvet-lined platinum case that Rothbannon had made to hold his Seven Stones. Beynor carried it with him always. Only Fortress was not kept inside it, resting instead in a golden monstrance as it guarded his chambers. The Conjure-King opened the case, fitted Weathermaker into its nest, and spent some minutes considering the sigils, as he had done each day for the past week.

There were only six of the original moonstones left now. Concealer was gone for good. The Southwater Salka delegated by his monstrous friends to retrieve Iscannon's stolen sigil had windspoken him a vivid description of the fiasco in Cala Bay. It had shaken Beynor's mercurial self-confidence almost as much as Ullanoth's effortless escape from his trap.

So the High Shaman of Tarn and a wild-talented stable lad, sworn to the Cathran prince, had worked together to foil him . . . How could such a catastrophe have happened?

Even worse, thanks to the meddling Tarnian magicker, that bloody boy now owned a living sigil! The preternatural sensibilities of Gawnn the Salka had clearly perceived the empowered Concealer hanging about the young wight's neck, covered by a bag of thin leather. As for the magical book, is seemed all too likely that the shaman had taken it.

What was he to do?

Or was doing nothing the safest option?

Damn Ullanoth! And damn Ansel and the boy Deveron!

"I'll get back what's mine," Beynor vowed, "and send Deveron Austrey and Red Ansel Pikan to the Hell of Lights if it's my last living act! And Ulla as well— but only after I've inflicted my own particular revenge upon her."

But there was no time for plotting retaliation now. The ship carrying the royal family of Didion and its entourage of high-ranking nobles was due to drop anchor in less than an hour, having been borne 450 leagues northward from Holt Mallburn in less than two days by Weathermaker's uncanny winds. Inviting the barbarians to his coronation had been a grandiose (and perhaps incautious) gesture. However, it was one Beynor felt was necessary in order to validate his authority as Conjure-King and a man fully mature, worthy to treat with other monarchs as an equal.

Putting tumbledown Royal Fenguard in shape to receive important guests in just a week had proved to be a daunting proposition, but most of the work had been accomplished with fair success. Grand Master Ridcanndal and Lady Zimroth were still hard at work marshaling the resources of the Glaumerie Guild down by the waterfront and along the parade route leading to the castle's towngate. The type of illusory magic the Guild excelled in would readily deceive the eyes of the visitors, making the unprepossessing little city seem in good repair and smartening up the appearance of its shabby inhabitants.

The Guild's sleight-of-mind was also capable of restoring Castle Fenguard's exterior, public rooms, and furnishings to a semblance of their ancient splendor. But sleeping accommodations for the Didionites had to be authentically magnificent and comfortable, and their food and drink as well. It was devilishly difficult to conjure a good night's rest for guests using musty old beds that were actually lumpy, hard, and home to the occasional bloodsucking bug, and counting upon glamour to satisfy the appetite and thirst of high-born diners was an even more dubious proposition. The Mossland national dish of swamp-fitch stew flavored with mat-fungus and wild leeks, while nourishing, could hardly be transmogrified into a lavish banquet, nor would the castle's stock of spruce beer, sour bilberry wine, and bulrush-tuber spirits impress hard-drinking King Achardus and his tosspot sons.

So Beynor had commanded his wealthier subjects to loan him swansdown comforters, plump pillows, and linen that was clean and flea-free, along with bedroom rugs and fine tester hangings. Those who possessed elegant dinnerware and napery had to contribute it to the castle for the duration of the royal visit. The Conjure-King also insisted, under pain of hexing, that the local aristocracy present him with their stocks of wax candles, sugar, wheat flour, butter, and imported liquor. The lords and ladies themselves were instructed to come to court in their richest apparel; and their older children, suitably attired, were recruited to take the place of the slovenly servitors who usually waited upon the castle-dwellers. The Conjure-Duke of Salkbane, who employed a famous cook, had been ordered to bring him along to Fenguard, together with all his kitchen staff and his store of rare spices. The Countess of Sandport lent her cherished portative wind-organ and an ensemble of musicians to enhance the dignity of the feast of welcome and the coronation ceremony itself, while the gleemen of Lord Mosstor would provide earthier entertainment during the reception and grand banquet scheduled to wind up the celebration tomorrow.

The common folk of the city and its environs had also been coerced into doing their share. Each merchant had a quota of foodstuffs or other needful commodities, to be donated gratis to the Crown. Every family was tithed a quantity of seal oil for the festive illumination of Fenguard's exterior, along with a barrow of peat for its fireplaces. Girls gathered sweet-smelling bog herbs and made posies to freshen the castle's stale air. They picked bouquets of late wildflowers to decorate the feasting boards and wove green garlands to drape the coaches that would carry the guests from the waterfront to the castle. Boys were put to work sweeping the streets, pulling weeds, and covering the worst of the midden-heaps with sand. Each townswoman had to relinquish a single shift or its equivalent in decent thin cloth, this to be dyed green or gold, then cut up and stitched into banners to adorn the parade route and the castle's gates and battlements. Their menfolk went into the marshes to hunt late-season wildfowl and venison. Well-to-do householders were assessed two stone of cheese, sausage, smoked salmon, jerked meat, or pickled fish. Those who skimped or shirked could expect a punitive visit from the king's warlocks, who had orders to empty the guilty family's larder.

Now the preparations were all but complete, and only two problems remained for Beynor to solve. The most pressing one was Ullanoth.

Since her escape from his warlock-knights in the throne room, she had apparently barricaded herself in her apartments, secure behind the spell of her guardian sigil. He might have concluded that his sister had fled, abandoning her Fortress to put him off—except that for the past two evenings, just as he and his coterie sat down to dine, a portion of the best food and drink vanished from the high table. The trick might also be only a parting jest of Ulla's, designed to infuriate him long after she'd left the castle; but such a tame piece of mischief hardly seemed appropriate to the enormity of her humiliation at his hands. She was still here. He was convinced of it. And somehow, he had to find a way to make certain she did not make a shambles of his great day tomorrow—to say nothing of the days that followed. Ullanoth and her sigils were a mortal menace to his reign, one that must be dealt with immediately.

He had no idea how many stones she possessed nor what their capabilities were. Sigils, whether dead or alive, could not be scried. Ridcanndal and Zimroth had scoffed at the rumor that Queen Taspiroth's spirit had gifted Ullanoth with a full dozen of the things. The notion was ridiculous, they said. If the princess owned powerful sigils, would she not have used them already? Perhaps she had found a few lesser stones left by Salka in some forgotten place, but such things were capable only of minor magic, as were the moonstone amulets worn by some of the Salka leaders. Hadn't Conjure-King Linndal himself been assured by the shamans of the Dawntide Isles that all of their Great Stones save the three given to Rothbannon had been carried away from the lands ceded to humanity? The two Glaumerie Guild officials told the young king that it was virtually impossible for Ullanoth to have sigils capable of high sorcery.

But Beynor wasn't so sure. The Dawntide Salka had been ignorant of Darasilo's trove of ancient stones, hidden away for centuries by the Royal Alchymists of Cathra, so the monsters were hardly all-knowing. And even though his sister was a clever bitch, she could not have made an ally of a man such as Conrig Wincantor by going to him empty-handed. Chances were that at least one of her sigils was a Great Stone, capable of doing him considerable harm.

A secondary but still vexing dilemma confronting the young king involved an appropriate demonstration of thaumaturgical power to impress the barbarian visitors. No mere conjuration of rainbows, fabulous beasts, costumed dancers, or phantom jousters would do. Only a truly unforgettable spectacle would overawe the notoriously cynical Didionites.

There was one sure way to solve both problems: by empowering one of his two remaining Great Stones, even if it meant enduring atrocious pain throughout his coronation, which should have been the most joyous moment of his life, and on many days thereafter. If the activation of Weathermaker was any criterion, he could expect the worst suffering while he slept, and the Coldlight Army invaded his dreams to extract the price for their favors. Awake, he would be physically debilitated but the pain would be less severe. He could do it. He'd already done it once . . .

Using Weathermaker for the first time, he had created a mighty stream of wind that had permanently diverted the Wolf's Breath away from the southern, settled part of Moss. His father and the Glaumerie Guild had been mightily impressed; but the activation of the stone and the subsequent conjuration of the wind had left Beynor half-dead for eight days. He had no intention of ever again attempting weather-sorcery on such a grand scale—not even to fulfill his boast to Didion.

The two Great Stones yet to be empowered rested in the case next to Weathermaker. Their names were Destroyer and Unknown Potency. No Guild wizard had ever fathomed the capabilities of the Unknown, which not even Rothbannon had dared to use. Salka legend called it the mightiest tool of sorcery ever vouchsafed by the Lights to lowlier beings. Only one sigil of that name had ever been fashioned by the monsters. The Salka still reviled the shaman who had cravenly turned it over to a human because none of their own wizards possessed the audacity to empower it.

Beynor had expected Vra-Kilian's ancient treatises to provide the key to the Unknown's mysteries, as well as more information on the powers of the other Great Stones; but that hope had been dashed, at least for the foreseeable future, by the Royal Alchymist's downfall.

The boy-king had also abandoned any notion that the exiled Cathran magicker might be compelled to share Darasilo's trove of sigils with him. He now prayed with all his heart and soul that Kilian had managed to hide the stones in a secure place before being captured and windsilenced. If Prince Conrig got his hands on the sigils and somehow empowered them, he'd become the true Emperor of the World.

And tiny Moss's saucy young ruler would be lucky to escape into the fens with a whole skin, to seek sanctuary among his Salka friends . . .

Reverently, Beynor lifted the inactive sigils from their velvet nests and set them on the table. Destroyer was rod-shaped, almost like a stubby wand with a drilled perforation at one end; it was incised with the phases of the changeable Moon. The Unknown Potency had the strangest form of all the collection, a kind of twisted ribbon of thin, delicately wrought stone that resembled a figure eight. The symbols engraved on it were so minuscule that they were almost imperceptible to the strongest magnifying glass, and their meaning was a mystery. As he had often done before, Beynor ran one of his slender fingers along the ribbon's cool surface. In some miraculous way, he was able to caress both sides continuously without let or hindrance, as though the thing had only one surface with no beginning or end. The ribbon had but a single edge as well.

Destroyer and the Unknown Potency. Either one of them could be the key to solving his dilemma . . . or the instrument of his destruction.

Earlier, when the seriousness of Ulla's threat to him had finally sunk in, he had sought counsel from those aloof Salka shamans in the Dawntide Isles who had been cronies of his crackbrained father. After all, their ancestors had created the stones, and some of the monsters were even old enough to remember dealing with Rothbannon. But Kalawnn, the Master Shaman, had only laughed at Beynor's plea for advice and told him to grow up a bit before messing about with high sorcery.

Arrogant troll!

The Salka of the Darkling Sands, who had so fortuitously befriended him when he was a foolish child in imminent danger of drowning in a flood tide, and had even encouraged him to empower Rothbannon's lesser sigils, could tell Beynor nothing about the nature of the two inactive Great Stones. Such important matters were beyond their simple ken, and they feared even to discuss them.

Beynor had even considered seeking help from his paternal aunt, the sorceress Thalassa Dru, who dwelt far to the west in the high mountains along the disputed borderlands of Didion and Tarn. She had a reputation for great wisdom, and Conjure-King Linndal had lately claimed that the long estrangement between the two of them had been mended. Thalassa had even agreed to take charge of troublesome Ullanoth and see that the girl never returned to Moss again.

But what if the sly old witch had only feigned a reconciliation with the king in order to rescue her niece from an increasingly difficult home situation? Would Thalassa be sympathetic to Beynor's quandary concerning the Great Stones, or would she side with Ullanoth for reasons of her own and play some perfidious trick on him?

In the end, he'd decided not to windspeak his problematical aunt, going instead to the two high officials of the Glaumerie Guild who had tacitly approved his magical experiments from the first, Master Ridcanndal and Lady Zimroth. They had advised him as best they could.

He stared now at the inactive sigils before him, milky-translucent and compelling. Which one would enable him to dispose of his sister once and for all, no matter how many stones of her own she had squirreled away? (The astonishment and intimidation of Didion by the new stone's sorcery would be a mere bonus.)

He picked up the wand called Destroyer.

When he had discussed his problem with Ridcanndal and Zimroth, they had both urged him to activate this sigil. Rothbannon had utilized it to secure his new kingdom, and by itself, it might very well enable Moss to conquer all of High Blenholme. But the first Conjure-King had been extremely circumspect in wielding this particular stone; and when he brought it to life he was a profoundly experienced sorcerer who had dealt successfully with the Beaconfolk for many years.

Beynor knew *he* was nothing of the sort.

Furthermore, Guild Master Ridcanndal and High Thaumaturge Zimroth were not the ones who would have to endure the mind-draining agony that Destroyer inflicted on its conjurer. King Linndal had confided to Beynor that the stone had wreaked terrible physical and spiritual damage upon Queen Taspiroth when she botched its use eleven years earlier. The king blamed the sigil for sending his wife to the Hell of Lights after two weeks of unspeakable torture. She had been only three-and-twenty years old.

Beynor had been a child of five when it happened. He only remembered his mother as a remote and beautiful woman with burning eyes and a braid of fair hair coiled at the base of her neck, who never had time to cuddle him or play magical games as dear old Lady Zimroth did. The death of the Conjure-Queen hadn't saddened the little prince much. He'd been rather glad that his big sister Ullanoth was so prostrate with grief that she forgot about tormenting him during the months that followed.

Father, on the other hand, during his interludes of sanity, seemed to discover for the first time that he had a son . . .

Beynor replaced Destroyer and picked up the Unknown Potency, the sigil neither the Salka nor Rothbannon had dared to empower.

Might it combine the powers of all the other sigils into one? Would it convert dross into gold? Would it make its owner supremely intelligent? Might it change the dreary clime of Moss into paradise, or cause all enemies to bend servile necks to the wielder's foot? Could it grant any wish—transforming that she-demon Ullanoth into a tiny swamp vole he might drown in a slop bucket? Or was its magical action so rarefied and esoteric that only some scholarly armchair-thaumaturge would find any use for it?

The only way one could find out was to activate the Unknown Potency and beg the Great Lights to explain how it worked. After enduring the terrible pain of the empowerment, he'd have to risk his life and mind questioning the capricious sky-beings, who might only respond with riddles, or even torture him to death because of some fancied insult.

He put the Unknown back into its place.

In his frustration, Beynor cursed Deveron Austrey for depriving him of the small magical book that might have helped with the difficult decision. The Guild's library had plenty of information about the lesser sigils, but almost nothing concerning the safe operation of the Great Stones. Sweat trickled from his scalp as his hand hovered again over the small, deceptively simple-looking wand named Destroyer. It was the undeniable instrument of triumph, but one that might also provoke the wrath of the Beaconfolk in some unimaginably horrible fashion.

"What shall I do?" he whispered. "Activate Destroyer and risk my mother's fate? Or defy logic and common sense and empower the Unknown Potency itself?"

With time running out before he must greet his royal guests, he knew at last that he was going to do nothing. Along with the realization, a vast sense of relief welled up in him.

"I won't bring either Great Stone to life," he said to himself. "But not because I'm afraid. I'm a prudent man, one who doesn't take unnecessary risks. If I choose not to empower one of these sigils now, it's no discredit to me. I'm only exercising discretion, as a mature man should. Who knows what I'll do in the future, when my situation changes?"

But the great predicament remained: Ullanoth barricaded in her tower, capable of anything.

If only he had more time! But he did not, and the truth of the matter was plain enough. There was no one to help and advise him: not his dead father, not the Guild officials, not impotent Kilian nor his mysterious aunt nor even the Salka. Beynor ash Linndal, Conjure-King of Moss, was alone on his throne, with no one but himself to rely on.

Abruptly, he began to laugh. He snatched Weathermaker from its nest, fitted it on his finger, then slammed shut the platinum case.

"I don't need advice on choosing a new sigil!" Beynor cried aloud. The softly shining moonstone ring seemed to gleam more brightly in anticipation. "The stones I have already are sufficient for my needs—and I've just thought of how to use this one to finish off Ulla in fine style. And if the Diddly barbarians don't appreciate my trick, then futter 'em for having no sense of humor!"

Still giggling, he hung the sigils named Subtle Armor and Shapechanger around his neck by their golden chains, then began to put on the gem-encrusted garments and jewels laid out by his servitors for the welcoming festivities. When he'd finished dressing, his young frame was oppressively weighted down by the ceremonial regalia, so for the first time he decided he would not carry the additional burden of the heavy platinum case with its two inactive stones. They would be perfectly safe left in his bedchamber, guarded by the indomitable sigil named Fortress.

"So your nerve did fail you at the end, little brother. And now, thanks be to the compassionate Moon Mother, I'll live to bring you down!"

Ullanoth momentarily relinquished the sigil named Subtle Loophole with a sigh of relief, pressing her fingers to her throbbing temples. Five days earlier she had empowered the second of her Great Stones in order to spy on Beynor while he hid behind Fortress. An open triangle with a small handle attached, through which one peered, Loophole was capable of giving her a vision—with all sounds attending, as windsight could not—of anything or anyone, even those protected by the most powerful magic. The only things safe from its oversight were sigils, alive or dead. But in Beynor's case, this mattered not. His own actions and his solitary mutterings had betrayed his fear of empowering another Great Stone.

Activating her own new sigil had sent Ullanoth reeling to her bed, afflicted by hideous dreams and an agony so unbearable she feared she would die of it. But she lived, and little by little the pain of empowerment abated, until on the third day she was able to rise and steal food, having become invisible, and begin her close surveillance of Beynor.

Ullanoth knew instinctively that either Destroyer or the Unknown Potency would be able to seek her out and obliterate her, wherever she tried to hide, so on each subsequent day of her recovery she watched her brother through the Loophole and listened to his fevered soliloquies until she could no longer stand the pain caused by the vision.

Today, with her strength almost restored, she had observed Beynor's final vacillations, praying that he would be too spineless to empower either stone. That prayer had been answered.

Having rested briefly, she lifted Loophole to her eye again, and saw—

Oh, compassionate Moon Mother! Look what that young booby was doing! If only she could act in time.

Beynor clearly intended to leave the platinum case, with the inactive Great Stones, behind in his rooms. Even now she saw him moving toward the outer door of his sitting room. *Could she use his own natural talent, with him all unaware, to solidify her Sending?*

She seized the sigils named Sender and Concealer from her purse, hung them about her neck on their chains, and ran to her slanted couch. A few moments later, after the brief explosion of pain that accompanied the speaking of the spell, she stood in her brother's bedchamber, invisible, hearing the outer door slam behind the departing Conjure-King.

It had worked! His Fortress still glowed serenely, no barrier at all to a Sending. She opened the case and removed Destroyer and the Unknown Potency from their velvet nests.

But now what?

A Sending could carry things held or worn by the original body to its destination. It could not bring any new object back nor leave anything behind.

"I don't want the awful things, anyway," she said aloud. "It's enough that he be deprived of them."

She went to the ornate fireplace, unlit on this warm day, set the little moonstone carvings on the hearth, and picked up an iron poker in her invisible hand. Inactive, the sigils were mere pieces of mineral that could be battered to bits with impunity; empowered, the tiny wand called Destroyer was an appalling weapon, while the amazingly delicate twisted figure eight of the Unknown Potency was . . . who knew what?

Ullanoth hesitated. Some day, her hated brother would be gone from Royal Fenguard and she would be Conjure-Queen. Her mother had assured her of it. Like her ancestor Rothbannon, she intended to become a scholar of sorcery; but unlike him, she would have at her disposal all the arcane libraries of High Blenholme Island—most especially those rare tomes at Zeth Abbey so jealously sequestered by the Brethren. She'd compel Conrig to give her access to them, and perhaps—just perhaps—

Why not?

Destroyer, she felt, was too dangerous to play games with; but she lifted the Unknown, stepped into the cold fireplace, reached up the chimney, and pushed the damper-plate full open. Beyond it, up the flue, was a shelflike projection having a thick accumulation of ash and soot. The castle chimneys had not been cleaned in years. She pushed the little moonstone carving into the far corner of the shelf, burying it in the powdery stuff.

With luck, it would be waiting for her when she was ready to study it.

When she emerged from the fireplace, she was amused to discover that her dirtied hand was visible as a disembodied black wraith. Well, she'd lose the mess when she sent herself home . . .

The poker made short work of Destroyer. When the deadly wand was reduced to grit, she carefully swept all traces of it into the ashpit.

Then she Sent herself back to her own tower, leaving behind only a light sprinkling of soot on the bearskin carpet in front of the hearth—too fine to be seen but still capable of soiling the bare feet of anyone who chanced to step in it.

Ullanoth returned to her own tower none too soon, for a quick glance out the window showed her that the Didionite royal flagship and its four escorting men o' war were already approaching their mooring out in the estuary. She would have to step lively in order to meet the arriving royals at the waterfront.

And leave forever this place that had been her refuge for so long.

Urgent necessity gave her fresh energy. She speedily donned her disguise, then stepped in front of the long mirror and admired her reflection for a moment. She did not intend to travel invisible all of the time, so she had assumed the aspect of a hunchbacked crone—a role suitable for the drama she had planned for the entertainment of Beynor and the Didionities. Her gown was tattered and patched and splotched about the hem with dried mud—but for all its poor appearance it was made of sturdy new wool that would keep her comfortable in bad weather. Her boots were grubby but stoutly made. She had greased and dirtied her shining hair to resemble the stringy grey elflocks of neglectful old age, and used herbal dyes to make her face hideous. The judiciously selected necessities prepared for her flight barely filled the leather fardel that would rest comfortably on her upper back beneath her hooded cloak, stained and raggedy but fashioned of heavy, water-repellent melton cloth.

The fardel contained her lone unempowered sigil—a second Weathermaker—maps and battle plans, writing materials, a few instruments of sorcery, and a tiny flask of her favorite vetiver perfume. She had no need of gold but had removed her mother's small portrait from its frame and wrapped it securely in velvet and oilskin. She intended to leave her jewelry behind, along with her fine garments. In time, all of them could be replaced.

But, oh, how she regretted having to abandon her library! At the last minute she included four precious little volumes that she could not bear to leave behind. *The Book of Prophecies,* alas, was not one of them. But she had closely studied the section dealing with the Question of Bazekoy and was fairly confident that she had deciphered King Olmigon's enigmatic answer.

It was time to go. She tucked the all-important lesser sigil named Beastbidder into the capacious belt wallet she had substituted for her gold-mesh purse. Concealer and Sender already hung around her neck, and Interpenetrator was snug in its cleverly fashioned bag up her sleeve, where a quick tug would allow her fingers to grasp it almost instantaneously.

Fortress would have to be left behind, continuing to guard her rooms at the top of the tower so that Beynor would have no hint that she had decamped. She was desolated at the thought of losing it, but if she took great care, the power of Concealer would keep her reasonably secure from both searchers and watchers.

As for her own Weathermaker, it would remain inactive until she was far away from Moss, safe in some place where the pain-price of its empowerment could be borne without jeopardizing her plans. With luck, she might not need it until Didion was conquered and it was time for her to deal with Beynor.

"Now guide me as I make my escape, dearest Mother," she prayed. "You forbade me to kill my vile little brother and I submit to your will, but I intend to leave him something to remember me by."

A tug of the string up her sleeve let Interpenetrator fall into her hand, and a windwhisper conjured Concealer. Invisible, she walked through the closed door of her tower and set off on her journey.

eighteen

The king of Didion, Archwizard Ilingus Direwold, and Galbus Peel, commander of the flagship *Casabarela Regnant* and Fleet Captain of the Realm, stood together on the foredeck and studied the waterfront of Royal Fenguard and the rainbow-haloed castle perched on the crags above it. King Achardus and the captain used spyglasses, and the archwizard his modest windsight.

"Some sort of tarted-up barges putting out now from the big dock," the king observed. "Welcoming committee, maybe."

"Your Majesty is certainly correct," said Ilingus, a middle-aged man in plain black robes, having the sad pouched eyes and pendulous flews of an old hound. His voice was high-pitched and his manner seemingly musty and pedantic. He was the King of Didion's shrewdest and most trusted adviser. "Those in the lead boat attired in violet are members of the Glaumerie Guild, Moss's highest coven of sorcerers. The leader of the delegation is one Ridcanndal, Grand Master of the Guild. You'll know him by his buck teeth and his big red nose. Looks like a bibulous beaver. Those dressed in green and black are heralds and high-ranking warlock-knights of the young King of Moss . . . Oh, dear! I'm lip-reading bits of speech from some of them. I do believe they intend for you and the rest of the royal party to go ashore in those small watercraft of theirs."

"Huh!" Achardus glowered his contempt. "No way I'm setting foot in any titchy bumboat like that. Damned thing would founder before we'd gone a half a dozen ells."

"They don't seem very sturdy, do they?" Captain Peel kept a straight face but his eyes gleamed with amusement. King Achardus weighed over three-and-twenty stone and stood six-and-a-half-feet tall. "Shall I lower our ship's boats to ferry you and the others in, sire? Of course, the Mosslanders might take offense."

"See to it, Peel, and signal our other ships as well. We're going ashore in force and in our own style. Who cares if the Mossbellies' bloody feelings are hurt? We're the ones doing them honor by coming to their bogland shindig. And speaking of honor, where's the royal whelp himself? No sign of young Beynor on the quayside, just a rabble of townsfolk, liveried flunkies, and some coaches flying our flag."

"The King of Moss probably intends to welcome you at the castle in a more elaborate setting," Ilingus said. "He and his sorcerers can perform their glamour-izing tricks more readily indoors than out."

Achardus waited until the departing captain was out of earshot, then said to the wizard, "I wish we hadn't come, Lingo. Why the hell did I let my sons talk me into this? Politics and sorcery are a devilish mix! You know it and I know it. Hon and Somar think they can manipulate this boy Beynor without having to pay too high a price for his services, but I'm not so sure. What say you?"

"I think that I'll withhold my opinion until I have more information. Ask me again tomorrow, Your Majesty, after the coronation."

"Slippery as usual, and probably with damned good reason." Achardus lifted the spyglass again and swept it over the structures on the shore. "Are you positive they've magicked up the place to make it look more presentable? Everything seems real enough to me—except for that idiotic rainbow."

"That, oddly enough, is quite real," Ilingus said with a sigh. "Its threefold nature is extraordinary, of course, but what's truly amazing is its persistence. We've viewed it for over an hour now as our flotilla moved up the channel, and the castle has remained at the precise center of the phenomenon for all of that time. Your Majesty is of course well aware that the colored heavenly arcs are pro-duced by sunlight refracting and reflecting from drops of precipitation. One would expect the arcs to fade or change their position relative to the castle as our ship sailed along, or as winds aloft carried the rainclouds northward. But that has not happened."

The king scowled. "What're you saying, man? Speak plain!"

"Some extremely powerful sorcery is controlling the wind direction, the amount of rainfall, the very size of the drops themselves, and perhaps even the direc-tion of the sunbeams. In view of your sons' report of Beynor conjuring fair winds for the voyages to and from the Continent, we must assume that he is also responsible for the peculiar triple rainbow."

"A silly enough stunt," Achardus scoffed.

"Not at all." The archwizard's voice was dark with foreboding.

The king's brow creased in perplexity. "You mean, it's a really hard thing to do?"

"To produce an *illusion* of a triple rainbow like this one would be well within the power of any competent wizard. Until today, I would have said that creating the real thing and keeping it going for such a long time was quite impossible. Yet Beynor has done it, no doubt to impress us. And I'm impressed."

"Hmmm." The king's expression of angry bafflement intensified. His brows came together to form a single hedgerow of wiry hair, and his lips tightened within a thicket of grizzled beard. He had not yet donned his massive ceremonial helmet, crested with a winged bear, and his carefully curled grey locks hung to his shoulders. He was accoutered for the occasion in a suit of dazzling silvery scale mail decorated with gold lattenwork. His surcoat was of white doeskin, emblazoned with Didion's snarling black bear's head, and he wore a cloak of heavy black-and-silver silk damask, lined with ermine.

"Your Majesty inquired about the enchantment used to disguise the town and the castle," Ilingus continued. "This is being accomplished by a more ordinary form of magic called glamour, no doubt the work of Beynor's coterie of wizards. The spell is so well-woven that I'm unable to dissolve it."

"So we won't know what's real and what's bogus once we get ashore, is that it?" the king grumbled. "They could be feeding us pig-swill and entertaining us in a mucky pesthole, and we'd never know it."

"Only the eyes are deceived by glamour, Majesty. The Conjure-King won't dare to feed us poor food, nor perpetrate any other gross imposture. I'll be on the alert every moment, you may be sure, and so will my assistants."

"You'd damn well better be."

A piping voice cried, "Eldpapa! Eldpapa! See pretty boats? Boats come! Wanna ride pretty boat!" Two-year-old Prince Onestus, son of Crown Prince Honigalus, came running across the foredeck, pursued at some distance by a red-faced nursemaid and his young aunt, Princess Risalla.

The gigantic king knelt, beaming like a jack-o'-lantern, and held his arms wide. The child leapt into them, heedless of the armor, and squealed with delight as Achardus bestowed a resounding kiss, all but burying the small face in his beard.

"Nesti! So you want a boat ride, do you, lad? But you've been riding on the *Casya* for two days now."

"*Casya* too big, like a house," the boy objected. "Wanna ride little boat like that."

He squirmed out of his grandfather's grasp and darted to the rail, which had stanchions dangerously far apart. Risalla and the nursemaid screamed a warning, still too far away to go to the child's rescue, but the archwizard, moving with surprising speed for an older man, had already laid hold of the tiny prince, scooping him safely up into his arms.

Achardus scowled at the two women, who now bobbed sheepish curtseys before him. The maid took charge of the prince, inspecting him for non-existent harm, while Risalla faced her father's anger. "Here's a pretty state of things," he exclaimed, "letting a wee lad run loose on shipboard! Where's your brains, girl? Come to that, where's his mother?"

"I'm so sorry, sire," the princess said in a tremulous voice. She was twenty years of age, the king's youngest child and as yet unmarried. Her face was wan and plain, save for eyes as blue as cornflowers, which now brimmed with frightened tears. Her honey-brown hair, partially covered by a thin white veil of sendal and crowned with a narrow golden coronet, was dressed in a multitude of thin plaits threaded with jeweled bangles. She wore a silken gown that matched her eyes and a pelisse of snow-mink.

"Dala and I were minding Nesti while Crown Princess Bryse was putting on her finery. The boy begged to come on deck and I just couldn't refuse him. It seemed safe enough, now that we're at anchor, but I tripped coming up the companionway steps and let go of his hand for an instant, and he was off . . ."

"Why wasn't the nurse holding him as well?" Achardus demanded.

"Sire, the companionway is narrow, and—"

"That's enough! You there!" The king beckoned to the nursemaid, who was now eyeing him with terror, while keeping the wriggling Onestus restrained with both hands. "Give the prince over to Her Royal Highness and come here."

When the woman was on her knees before him, he addressed her in a voice full of quiet menace. "We are about to disembark into a city crawling with sorcerers, where man-eating Salka and God knows what other fiendish beings lurk among the rocks and cessponds. Prince Onestus is your responsibility. If any harm should come to him, you will be skinned alive, then drowned in boiling oil.

Never again let the boy out of your sight and care unless his parents command otherwise. Do you understand?"

The nurse's voice was nearly inaudible. "Yes, Your Majesty."

"Now take Onestus below." He turned to the archwizard. "Lingo, go with her. Find my sons and their wives and tell Their Royal Highnesses I said to hotfoot it up on deck. The boats bearing the Mossland welcomers are almost here, and I want everyone ready to meet them."

"Yes, Your Majesty," the two of them said. The nursemaid rose, took the child from Risalla, and fled with him. The wizard followed at a more stately pace.

The princess stood with lowered eyes and hands clenched tightly in front of her. "It was my fault Nesti got away, not Dala's."

"You dare to take the wench's part?"

Risalla lifted her doleful face. She had her father's strong jaw, but her lips were budlike and soft. "Yes, Father, I do. Dala is a good woman who does her duty and loves Nesti with all her heart. She'd give her life for him."

"So she will indeed," the king said suavely, "if anything happens to the heir of Honigalus during our stay in this benighted land of Moss." Abruptly, he changed the subject. "Daughter, it's time you were wed."

She stared at him, mouth open in horror as she realized what was in his mind. "Not this Conjure-King Beynor!"

"I haven't made up my mind about him yet, but your brothers seem to believe we'd be well-advised to seek a match."

"You refused Princess Ullanoth as a bride for Somarus," she reminded him bitterly.

"Watch your tongue, madam! Sauce me and I'll flog you myself with a silken lash!"

She inclined her head in a wordless bow of submission. Tears trickled down her broad, pale cheeks.

"It's not a certainty. We'll have to see whether Beynor's as great a sorcerer as he pretends to be. But he did come up with the idea that we peddle warships to the Continent, which helped keep our people from starving, and he claims he can shut off the Wolf's Breath. What's more, he's told your brothers that he can defend Didion in case Cathra attacks us. He wants gold, of course, but he says he's willing to wait for payment until our national fortunes are restored. A dynastic marriage would cement the alliance more securely than any treaty. It's the lot of a royal princess, lass. Accept it."

"Yes, Father." She took out a handkerchief and wiped her eyes.

"If it's any comfort," the king said gruffly, "Hon and Somar say the boy-king is comely enough. Tall and skinny, black eyes, blond hair. A bit of an odd fish, but that's to be expected if he's a magicker. We'll make the betrothal contingent on his fulfilling his promise to abolish the Wolf's Breath, so you won't have to go to him right away."

"Thank you, sire."

The king gave her shoulder an awkward pat, then turned away from her, raising the spyglass to his eye again to inspect the approaching boats. "And if I don't fancy the cut of young Beynor's bloody jib, you won't go to him at all! Now go attend your mother."

The string of coaches waiting to carry the Didionite royal party to the castle had been scrubbed and polished and fitted with new upholstery. Crystal vases inside held skimpy bouquets of blue gentian, marshmallow, pink heather, and ball-buttercup. Thanks to wizards disguised as coachmen, the horses appeared to be fine matched pairs, all of them glossy black with manes and tails woven with green-and-yellow ribbons. The footmen who assisted the distinguished guests to board wore smart livery of green leather emblazoned with Moss's heraldic golden swan.

King Achardus and Queen Siry were led by Grand Master Ridcanndal to the lead coach, which was larger and grander than the others and drawn by four horses rather than two. Crown Prince Honigalus and his wife Princess Bryse, and Prince Somarus and his wife Princess Thylla settled into the second coach. The third bore Princess Risalla, Onestus and his nurse, the infant Princess Hyndry, who was the daughter of Somarus and Thylla, and a second nursemaid. Six other coaches accommodated the lords and ladies of the royal retinue, including Archwizard Ilingus Direwold and his five assistants. The Mossland dignitaries were to bring up the rear in open equipages, heavily swathed in festive bunting, that had a suspicious resemblance to gussied-up farm carts. Files of warlock-knights in fearsome black armor and emerald cloaks were poised to ride on either side of the cavalcade, while phalanxes of the Didion Royal Guard, armed in barbarian splendor and with black-and-white pennons flying, took up marching positions in the front and rear.

Queen Siry arranged her robes and peered out the coach's window at the banner-decorated buildings along the quay. They all seemed to be in good repair, and the wharves were full of bales and chests of goods, guarded by armed men.

"The place looks prosperous enough," she murmured to her royal spouse. "And have you noticed that the sky is blue—except where the stormclouds are piled up? There's no fallen ash on the ground surface or rocks, either. King Beynor told our sons true when he said that he had turned the Wolf's Breath away from Moss."

"Apparently so," the king said sourly. "But remember that the diverted ashfall landed mostly on *us!* And the young trickster was very evasive when Hon asked why he couldn't turn off the volcanos immediately, rather than doing it next spring. One might almost suspect that the eruptions are about to peter out of their own accord, and Beynor simply intends to take credit for it."

The queen frowned. The second wife of Achardus, she was an austerely handsome woman, very tall and slender, whose golden hair was fading now that she was three and forty years old. Her gown was black with panels of scarlet, and she wore a brocade cloak in the same colors. Her headdress had stiffened wings of red silk gauze springing from a crown glowing with rubies and pearls. Like her husband, she descended from the warrior queen Casabarela, who had subdued the rebellious dukedoms of interior Didion and ushered in a long period of national prosperity that had been unfortunately terminated by the advent of the lengthy Wolf's Breath.

"Look over there," Queen Siry said. "That old woman coming toward us! See how the crowd gives way before her? I wonder why?"

Some members of the Glaumerie Guild had noticed the approaching crone as well and were pointing her out to the mounted warlocks in some agitation. The knights in black armor spurred their steeds, as if to intercept the woman, but the animals only reared and wheeled about in place, neighing loudly, while the warlocks flailed the air with magical swords that obstinately refused to burst into flame.

Grand Master Ridcanndal himself came trotting up on a white palfrey when it became evident that his underlings were not going to be able to prevent the hag from approaching the coach carrying Didion's king and queen.

"Give way!" he shouted at her, brandishing his golden staff of office. His great red nose shone like a ripe apple. "I forbid you to approach, on pain of death!"

"Woe!" the old woman howled. "Woe and wrath! Terror and desolation! Death and perdition!" She held high a small thing that shone brightly green, and at the sight of it, Ridcanndal and his minions shrank back. A gasp went up from the astonished crowd. "Go home, King and Queen of Didion! Leave this place whose splendor is only a hollow sham. Go before it's too late!"

Capping her admonition with a marrow-freezing wail, she vanished.

The bewitched horses of the warlock-knights at once left off their frenzied whirling and were calm save for the odd snort and rolling of eyes. The towns-folk murmured to one another and snickered, more diverted than frightened by the spectacle. Abashed Guild members, who had tried in vain to approach the troublemaker, retreated to their carriages, leaving Ridcanndal sitting his horse, grinding his teeth in frustration.

"Fewmand me soul!" King Achardus cursed. Then he bellowed, "You, Guild-master! To me! Who the hell was that caterwauling old broomstick?"

Ridcanndal hastened to the coach window. Bowing low in the saddle, he stammered, "A m-madwoman, Your Majesty. Some deranged, malicious crea-ture from the swamps, perhaps one with a petty grievance against the Crown, who had a vain hope of disrupting the Conjure-King's peace on this historic day." He smiled in a manner intended to be reassuring, his two oversized upper teeth gleaming horribly. "But as you see, she's gone now without doing any harm." He took a deep breath. "So let the procession commence! Onward to Castle Fenguard!"

Trumpeters sounded a flourish, drummers struck up a thunderous beat, and the swords of the warlocks finally burst into flame. With a cracking of whips, the coaches began to move slowly up the lumpy cobblestone street while the populace cheered and whistled. Every one of Royal Fenguard's burghers, householders, crafters, and slaves who was not sick abed or too enfeebled to walk had been turned out to salute the guests. A few men strategically posi-tioned in the front row of spectators waved Didion's bear's-head flag. The others flapped dish-clouts or tossed up their hats as the coaches rolled by and their occupants waved from the open windows.

"Well, that was a bizarre sort of welcome," Crown Prince Honigalus said, his lips twisting with mirth. "Not exactly the best omen for a coronation. Young Beynor will hang that old biddy by her heels from the battlements when he catches her."

"*If* he does," Prince Somarus said. "Still, you have to admit the little jack-anapes brought out a decent crowd." Like their royal father, he and his brother wore parade armor and white surcoats emblazoned with Didion's bear.

"The town doesn't look nearly as decrepit and filthy as I remember it," his older brother said. "Of course, it was the dead of night when we picked up Beynor for the trip south, and we had no time to waste sightseeing before the tide turned."

Princess Thylla said, "I heard Ilingus tell Queen Siry that there's sorcery at work, making the old buildings and the crumbling castle look as good as new." She was an elegant young woman of fastidious habits, quick to find fault, and unlike her full-fleshed sister-in-law, she had not let childbirth deprive her of her willowy form. Her hair was russet, caught up in a fantastic headdress of gold net and pearls, and her gown was particolored velvet in fiery hues, embellished with jewels and trimmed with costly green vair. "Somarus, I insist that you have the archwizard inspect our quarters thoroughly before we settle in. If we're being hoodwinked and the rooms are dirty and full of spiders and mice, then I'm taking myself and our daughter back to the flagship at once—and to blazes with royal protocol!"

"I heard Ilingus speak of glamour, too," Crown Princess Bryse added. She was ordinarily easygoing and pleasant, but the harridan's tirade had shaken her composure badly. "I feel exactly the same as Thylla. How can we be sure that some Mossy necromancer won't smite all of us with infernal enchantment while we're sleeping? You men may have put your families in danger insisting we come with you to this dreary hole. Our own palace is cheerless enough these days, but at least it's safe."

"Now, love, don't fuss!" Honigalus was conciliatory, as usual. He was thickset and swarthy, like his father, but lacked the king's massive stature. Although his clean-shaven features were coarse, he had an equable disposition and an astute mind. Achardus had placed him in charge of Didion's navy, while his more volatile younger brother Somarus commanded the army.

Bryse sighed. "I'm not fussing, my darling. Only begging you to be cautious."

He gave her a comforting smile. Like himself, she was not physically imposing, nor was she fond of extravagant dress. Her gown and headdress were black trimmed with white, as befitted the Crown Princess of Didion, but she was only modestly adorned with jewels. Her marriage had been an arranged one, intended to secure the loyalty of the mighty Vandragora clan of Firedrake Water. But it had soon become evident that the prince and princess were actually a perfect match of intelligence and physical warmth. By the time Onestus was born, they were steadfast in their devotion to one another.

"I intend to be cautious," Honigalus told her. "Every bedchamber will be guarded by a squad of our own warriors and by Ilingus's assistants, on the lookout for black magic. But nothing bad will happen, be assured! Young King Beynor needs our approval and wants to impress us. That's the only reason he magicked up his town. God knows Holt Mallburn could use some serious reconstruction work after three years of the Wolf's Breath. Why, if magic could restore our capital city and lift the people's spirits, I'd bring adepts of the Glaumerie Guild back home with us in an eyeblink."

"You would, too," Somarus muttered. "Without a second thought of what else the bastards might get up to."

"Brother, let's not quarrel. You know we have no intention of allowing alien wizards inside our realm, nor has Beynor asked us to do so."

"You're too trusting," said Somarus. "I've said that from the beginning of our dealings with the boy."

"And you're too suspicious. We've already signed the Treaty of Alliance with Moss. Now it's up to Beynor to prove his worth to us. Abolishing the Wolf's Breath is all-important, but we're also counting on him and his coterie to use their scrying talent to alert us to any surprise attack by Cathra—a clear and present danger, as well you know. The Conjure-King has magical resources for oversight that poor old Lingo and even Fring can only dream about. He's already proved that to us—and to the corsair captains down in Stippen and Foraile, too."

"Oh, you're right, as usual," Somarus replied ill-naturedly. "But we ought to guard our backs every inch of the way dealing with him. And the very thought of sweet little Risalla being bedded by that uncanny twerp—" He shook his head in disgust.

Queen Cheyna Garal, Thylla's second cousin and the first wife of King Achardus, had died bearing Honigalus. Somarus and Risalla were the issue of the king's second marriage to Siry Boarsden, and the brother and sister loved one another dearly in spite of their opposing temperaments. Somarus had his mother's towering, graceful form and her chiseled good looks. Like Risalla, his eyes were bright blue. He had wavy sandy hair, a drooping reddish moustache, and eyebrows to match. His impetuous nature and ferocity in battle had caused him to be idolized by the quarrelsome warriors of the Forest Realm. Some of the dukes and robber-barons had even dared to say that he would make a better king than Honigalus . . .

"Father agrees that Risalla won't wed Beynor unless he does what he's promised," the Crown Prince said. "If our dear sister does have to go to him, we'll be sure she has a personal retinue of strong warriors to keep her secure."

"Against sorcery?" Somarus lifted one fox-colored brow in skepticism. "Don't be a simpleton, Brother."

Princess Thylla had been staring disconsolately out the open window of the coach as the princes conversed. She suddenly uttered a squeak of surprise. "What was that? Some sort of animal ran right in front of the horses!"

The team of blacks shied momentarily, making the coach swerve, but the wizard-coachman soon had them back under control.

"There's another!" the princess exclaimed. "See? Coming from between the legs of she crowd. Long and slinky, like a large brown and white weasel. I see more of them in the road. We'll surely hit one! Oh, mercy—"

Thump.

The coach bounced, Bryse and Thylla screamed, and at once a pungent and offensive odor filled the air.

"Good God!" Somarus cried. "What's that appalling stink?"

"I think we've run over a polecat," Honigalus said dryly. "In Moss, I believe they're called swamp-fitches. The creatures are supposed to be edible, once the musk-glands are removed."

Somarus was peering out his window. "The things are everywhere! I can see at least a dozen afoot and a couple that must have been crushed by Father's coach. The crowd is scattering. Those warlocks with flaming swords don't seem to be able to drive the beasts off. How the devil could—"

Thump.

"Another victim," Honigalus noted. "Perhaps it's their migration time—like lemmings."

"Bugger the lemmings." Somarus was holding his nose. "Faugh!"

The stench was becoming eye-watering. "Do something!" Bryse cried.

Honigalus began to unfasten the tapes that held the rolled window-curtains of flexible isinglass. "Tell the driver to whip up, Somar. There's plenty of room in the road now that the townsfolk are fleeing. Maybe we can outdistance the damned animals."

Certainly the leading coach carrying the king and queen was attempting to do that very thing, with heralds, musicians, and members of the Didion Royal Guard leaping out of the way of the crazed horses amid a fusillade of shouts and curses. The cobbles were littered with discarded banners, drums, and dented trumpets, as well as malodorous furry bodies.

"Faster!" shouted Somarus, and the coachman obeyed, with the result that the light vehicle began to bounce and sway so violently on the irregular roadbed that it was in peril of toppling over.

"No!" Honigalus bellowed. "Driver, pull up! We've left the beasts behind. Stop, I say!"

All of the coach teams finally halted, plunging and squealing while drivers hauled on the reins and footmen hung desperately from bridles and traces. Curiously, the once impressive matched black horses seemed to have shapeshifted into rawboned ponies of many different colors. Their formerly sleek coats were rough and shaggy, as would be natural for beasts native to the subarctic.

In the rear, the members of the parade who had been left behind were struggling to catch up. So were the carts carrying the wizards of the Glaumerie Guild and their henchmen. Almost all of the townsfolk had disappeared, except for one woman with arms raised high, standing a few ells in front of the king's coach and keening at the top of her lungs.

"It's that squalling crone again," Somarus exclaimed. "What's she saying this time?"

"His Majesty is alighting," Honigalus observed. "Perhaps we'd better get our own arses outside, Brother."

The princes hastened to join their father, swords drawn.

"Now what?" roared the King of Didion. "Get out of the way, old woman!"

"Woe! Oh, woe!" she screamed. "Woe to those who seek favors of Moss's cursèd young king! Listen to the words of Witch Walanoth, the only friend to poor murdered King Linndal. Killed by his own son! Doom and damnation and the curse of the Lights fall upon any nation that would ally with a patricide and regicide!"

"Sire, beware!" Somarus brandished his blade and strode to his father's side. "Aroint thee, beldam!" he shouted at the hag. "Begone, or I'll run you through!"

He lunged at her, but the blade passed scathelessly through her body as though it were smoke. She gave one last cry of "Woe!" and disappeared. Almost immediately, an enormous flock of gulls came diving from the sky, giving piercing shrieks. They wheeled around the king and his sons like snowflakes in a blizzard, showering the stupefied men with their excrement. A moment later the birds were gone, winging out over the estuary.

Stunned into speechlessness, King Achardus lifted one smirched silvery gauntlet and stared at the reeking mess. His regal cloak was sodden with droppings, and white ordure dripped from the rim of his raised visor into his brows and beard.

"Sire, are you harmed?" Honigalus ventured.

"I'm as well as a man can be, bathed in birdshite." The voice of the giant monarch was quiet, almost thoughtful. "Did you hear what the witch said, lads?"

They nodded.

"Conjure-King Linndal died falling down stairs late at night," Somarus said. "Easy enough to contrive."

"What are we to do, sire?" Honigalus asked.

"I'll tell Queen Siry to sit with the princesses in your coach. They can stay right here for the time being, guarded by our own warriors. You two get in the lead coach with me, and we'll go up to the castle and see what young Beynor has to say for himself. It had better be good."

He knew what she'd done. He and Lady Zimroth had watched the whole fiasco from the throne room's antechamber through windsight, powerless to prevent the indignities wreaked upon the hapless Didionites. What Beynor had not expected was for Ullanoth to appear suddenly before him, still in her guise of a hunchbacked crone.

Laughing.

"You misbegotten slut! I'll kill you myself." He drew his regal sword, advancing upon her bedraggled figure, knowing she could not harm him because of the sigil named Subtle Armor that he wore beneath his robes.

"Try!" she urged him, grinning. Her Sending was protected by Interpenetrator.

He swung the heavy blade with all his strength, taking her through the neck, but her head remained on her shoulders and the sword encountered no more resistance than slicing thin air. The sound of her laughter incensed him and he gave a great shriek of rage, flinging down the sword and going at her with his bare hands.

He ran straight through her and whirled about in consternation.

"If you need my help with your guests, Brother, I'll be waiting in my tower." Then she recited, "BI DO FYSINEK," and vanished.

Beynor was profuse in his apologies and persuasive in his explanations to Achardus and his sons. (He also used the minor sigil Shapeshifter to enhance his reedy physique and give a more mature cast to his features.) The so-called Walanoth, he explained with grave forbearance, had been none other than his estranged sister Princess Ullanoth in disguise. The pathetic creature had inherited the mental instability of their late father, and Linndal's untimely death had apparently deprived her of the last vestiges of sanity. Ullanoth possessed magical powers—but none so great as his own!—and her diabolical affront to the Didionite royal family proved that she was now trapped in the toils of madness.

"Although it breaks my heart to admit it," the young Conjure-King said, "it is my solemn judgment that Princess Ullanoth is so dangerous that I have no recourse but to condemn her to death."

"Well, I don't know about that—" Achardus started to protest.

But Beynor held up his hand. "I have spoken. As she used magic to commit lèse-majesté, so shall she perish by my own magical might! My dear elder brother Achardus: would you and your sons care to see the melancholy sentence carried out?"

Fascinated, the three Didionite royals said that they would, if they could clean up a bit first.

A short time later, Beynor led his guests, Lady Zimroth, and most of the high nobility of Moss to Fenguard Castle's forecourt and pointed to the top floor of the South Tower. Its interior was masked by the magic of his sister's Fortress. The king lifted his right hand, where Weathermaker gleamed on his index finger. Then he cried out in a loud voice for Ullanoth to surrender herself to his justice.

When nothing happened, he clenched his teeth, drew in his breath, and commanded the sigil. The moonstone ring flared with green fire.

For a moment, the setting sun continued to paint the tower with rosy light. The sky was completely clear now, and the triple rainbow had long since disappeared.

Suddenly a small cloud sprang into being overhead, black as ink and roiling like a whirlpool. It swelled, hanging above the castle like some unholy canopy. Purple flashes of silent lightning flickered within its surging heart. Achardus and the two princes felt static crackle in their hair and tingle along their exposed skin. Beynor's face was livid, contorted with repressed agony, and the moonstone sigil on the finger he pointed at the South Tower glowed like an incandescent emerald.

"Now," the boy-king whispered.

The earth shook with a stunning concussion as a blazing thunderbolt struck the upper floor of the tower. Achardus, Honigalus, Somarus, and the other spectators felt their legs buckle, and they were hurled to the ground. Only Beynor remained solidly upright, the terrible radiance of his magical tool now paled almost to imperceptibility. Debris flew from the decapitated tower. Its upper works had been completely demolished and there was a swirling mass of smoke, but no fire. The eerie black cloud began to shrink and in a few minutes it was gone.

"May the Moon Mother show mercy to my poor sister's soul," Beynor said, his head bowed.

The three shaken royals climbed to their feet and dusted themselves off. The noble Mosslanders followed suit, then burst into scattered applause. Someone shouted, "Long live Conjure-King Beynor!"

"So that's the end of her?" Achardus managed to say.

Beynor nodded. "Her body has been reduced to ashes. My slaves will cover over the roofless tower before morning, and I'll rebuild it in the spring. Shall we ride out now and conduct your ladies and children to the castle? Dinner will be served anon. You may wish to reassure the other members of your entourage that nothing else will mar their visit to the land of Moss."

A faint shadow passed unnoticed along the torchlit guardhouse wall as Rothbannon's Marvel struck the sixth hour after noon. It was full dark now but still unseasonably warm, and the windows of the great hall were unshuttered and bright. Small tubs of burning oil lined the battlements and parapets of the castle and outlined the gatehouse, making a brilliant show. The main entrance to the keep was conveniently open to accommodate the many retainers rushing to and fro between the serving kitchen and buttery on the castle's ground level and the outbuildings where the visiting warriors and retainers were accommodated.

Witch Walanoth heard music and laughter, and she smiled. The feast of welcome was in full swing inside the great hall. Again she took the sigil named Beastbidder from her belt, using it this time to summon millions of biting midges that lived in the Little Fen across the Darkling River. It would take the insects a while to arrive, but she'd wait patiently, then guide them to their portion of the feast.

Poor Beynor . . .

"No, Mother, I won't kill him," she whispered. "I'll only make him wish he were dead. Then one last blow during his coronation tomorrow, and I'll stow away on the Didionite flagship and go south to wait for Conrig and his army."

One last blow.

Shall I use rats? she asked herself. Or would swamp vipers be more appropriate?

nineteen

Red Ansel knew well enough that Princess Maudrayne's sudden indisposition was no true illness. The fact that he was forbidden by the Cathran royal family to attend and treat her was in itself suspicious. Instead, King Olmigon had thanked the shaman for his medical services, given him a large sum of gold ("for the relief of your suffering people"), and commanded him to be on board a ship of the grain convoy that was finally setting sail for Tarn on the morrow.

Deeply troubled, Ansel retired to his room in Cala Palace and windspoke his Source.

"Once again I am at a loss," he confessed, "unable to decide the best course of action, and so I beseech your advice."

Tell me your problem. Is it the wild-talented boy again?

"No, it's Princess Maudrayne. She's desperately unhappy and has discovered that her husband Conrig betrayed her with another woman—Ullanoth of Moss. She believes that Conrig intends to set her aside and marry the Conjure-Princess, and her pride is so wounded that she is determined to divorce him without attempting a reconciliation. Maude besought my help to escape from Cathra, but before I could counsel her she fell mysteriously ill and was sequestered from all visitors. I eluded Maude's guardians, came into her rooms, and found her looking healthy, but mentally stuporous. She would not respond to my questions. I believe Conrig's brother, who is an alchymist, gave her a potion to dull her wits. It was also impossible to bespeak her in her dreams, because she was transported by unnatural euphoria, unable to connect thoughts rationally. I think her husband wishes to ensure that she doesn't betray his plans to invade Didion—as well as preventing her from running away to Tarn. What I ask of you, dear Source, is whether I should help Maude escape."

Do you think her life is in danger?

"I'm certain it is not. She's finally pregnant with Conrig's child after years of barrenness. If Maude would only tell the prince of the babe, I think he would forget about Ullanoth in a trice. But she's too stubborn to follow such a course, wanting to be loved for herself—not for the wee creature she carries in her womb."

Very understandable! Nevertheless, she is no common woman, and her duty must supersede her vanity. It would be evil for her to betray Conrig's military plans out of sheer pique. And even more wicked for her to leave her straying royal husband, taking the fruit of his loins with her. She has been wronged, but she must not attempt such drastic redress—nor may you, in good conscience, assist her.

"So I am to abandon my poor young friend to her state of dazed oblivion?"

Don't think to pluck at my heartstrings, Ansel Pikan! Maudrayne's captors won't keep her drugged forever. When they leave off feeding her the potion, you must be there to talk sense into her. Prevent her from doing something so outrageously foolish that there'll be no turning back from it.

"Yes, you're right. I bow to your wisdom, Source. I'll pretend to obey Conrig's order to leave Cathra on one of the grain ships. It'll be easy enough to slip back ashore and find some place to hole up until I'm needed. Meanwhile, I'll quietly search Cala Palace for Darasilo's moonstones. Conrig never found them, and it's certain Kilian didn't take them with him—"

No! You must never think of meddling with those fatal sigils, not even for motives of safe keeping. They are forbidden to your touch. And the book that you took from the boy Deveron must remain unopened until you can hand it over to me.

"Ah! . . . How are you able to read my mind?"

No one can descry the thoughts of humankind save the gods, and I doubt whether even they would have the stomach for such a boring task, day after day. What I do read is the warp and woof of destiny's threads as it weaves the future fate of High Blenholme Island. And I tell you that you may not interfere in any matter touching upon Conrig Wincantor and his family.

"So I'm to do nothing at all for Maudrayne?"

The day will soon come when you'll be called upon to aid both the princess and your native land of Tarn. Until then, bide your time peacefully, Red Ansel—and pray that the Lights do the same.

* * *

Early on the morning that he and his Heart Companions were to depart for the north country, Conrig went to say farewell to his parents. As the lord-in-waiting opened the royal bedchamber door to admit him, another nobleman stormed out, so consumed with fury that he neglected even to acknowledge the Prince Heritor's presence.

Conrig shut the door behind him with a quizzical smile. "Lord Admiral Dundry seems to be in a fine state, sire."

Olmigon was in bed, propped up on pillows, scrawling with pained slowness on vellum, while Queen Cataldise and Odon Falmire, the Lord Chancellor, hovered over him.

"I've sacked the bastard," the king said with wry satisfaction, as he continued to write. "I gave him the chance to step down quietly from his post and retire with the gratitude of the Crown and a nice addition to his family estates. And what did he do? He had the ballocks to present me with a petition from twenty of our fighting captains, urging me to keep him on!"

"I'm amazed they'd be so bold," Conrig said.

"Easy to tell you've never had much to do with sailors." Olmigon sighed. "A naval captain is so accustomed to being a tyrant aboard his own ship, he gets to thinking that landside authorities are knaves or fools—or so sick and feeble that they can't tell good advice from bad."

"You mean, the naval officers think I've pressured you to dismiss Dundry unfairly?"

"Yes." the king scratched a few more words, signed his signature with a flourish, and passed the parchment to Falmire. "Seal that up good and proper, Odon, and deliver it yourself to Elo Copperstrand. He's appointed Lord Admiral as of now, and I want him to pick his own staff of First Captains and bring them to me for a strategy conference tomorrow afternoon."

The Chancellor took the brief, bowed, and left the room. At a nod from his father, Conrig removed the lap desk and writing materials from in front of the king and set them aside.

"I want you to attend the meeting, Con," Olmigon said.

The prince gently shook his head. "Today I leave for the north. I came to bid you farewell, sire. The naval defense of Cathra must rest in your capable hands and those of Lord Copperstrand."

The king's face fell. "Today? You can't leave now! I still need your advice on handling this cranky gang of sea-dogs. And what about the grain ships for Tarn?"

"My love," said the queen anxiously, "I told you last night that Con and his Heart Companions were ready to depart."

"You did?" A momentary trace of bewilderment crossed the old man's face. His memory, like his other faculties, was failing; only his willpower seemed miraculously rejuvenated.

The prince said, "Sire, you know far more about naval matters than I, and Copperstrand is intelligent and trustworthy. He'll know how to deploy the ships to best advantage without any help from me. But you must buttress his authority if any of Tothor Dundry's old messmates begin playing mutinous power games."

"I'll have their cods for penny-purses if they try it," growled the king.

"The grain convoy sailed on the morning tide," Conrig continued. His mouth tightened. "And I made certain that the shaman Red Ansel was aboard . . . Each skipper knows that the kingdom's fate may depend on his getting the cargo quickly to Goodfortune Bay. The Treasury has pledged to pay double the agreed-upon exorbitant shipping fee to every ship that reaches Tarnholme within eight days."

Olmigon groaned. "I suppose it was necessary."

"It was," said the prince. "The Tarnian mercenaries have agreed to weigh anchor as soon as the arriving grain ships pass inspection. They could be here in a week or less if the winds are fair."

"If," muttered the king. "It's Boreal Moon, you know. The Western Ocean can expect any sort of weather from a flat calm to a spar-cracking gale. We've even had Hammer and Anvil storms in Boreal!"

Conrig forged on, ignoring the king's pessimism. "Meanwhile, I've reinforced the coastguarding windvoices. The Acting Royal Alchymist, Vra-Sulkorig Casswell, has sent two dozen keen novices to beef up the strength at Castles Intrepid, Defiant, and Blackhorse. Besides that, he organized a squad of inspectors to vet every shipboard windvoice in the fleet, making sure they're competent. The man's turned out to be a fine replacement for Kilian. We have Gossy to thank for recommending him."

"I wish you weren't taking Stergos with you, Con," the queen said. "He has none too robust a constitution, and that mooncalf squire of his isn't the kind of bodyguard I'd choose."

Conrig took her hand and spoke reassuringly. "Gossy will never go into harm's way, Mother. I swear it on my honor. If there's fighting, I'll defend his life with my own. Better yet—I'll make certain that he stays well back out of any fray, as is proper for a man of peace. But I need him with me in this adventure, just as I will need him at my side when I become king."

"Stop worrying, Catty," the king admonished, forgetting that he had been expressing his own doubts minutes before. "Con, you must have Stergos wind-speak Vra-Sulkorig regular reports of your progress, which he'll pass on to me alone. I in turn will keep you informed of matters here in the south."

"I agree," Conrig said. "If at all possible, I'll have Gossy bespeak the news each day at sunset—and he'll inform you at once if we encounter the foe. But always remember that our plan of attack through Breakneck Pass must be kept secret. Discuss it with no one except Vra-Sulkorig." He turned again to the queen. "No one else, Mother. Not even Lady Vandaya."

"I understand." She was slightly miffed that he had admonished her, yet felt a pang of guilt, realizing that she might have been tempted to confide in her old friend. She changed the subject: "When shall we leave off giving Maudrayne the mind-dulling potion? It can't be healthy to keep dosing her with the vile stuff, no matter what Stergos and Sulkorig say."

"Stop only after I have joined battle in Holt Mallburn. After that, only keep her confined so that she doesn't run away. She must be here when I return."

"I'll see to it," Cataldise said.

"Then it's time for me to go," Conrig said. "My men are waiting and we must reach Melora by nightfall. Father, may God sustain your life until we meet again."

Conrig kissed his mother, then bent over the king's bed to press his lips to the old man's brow.

The king pulled himself into a sitting position. In the days since his return from the pilgrimage, he had lost so much weight that his skin now hung on his bones like an oversized garment. His hands trembled now when they had nothing to grasp, but his eyes had come alive again and burned with hope and determination. "We'll all be waiting for news of your triumph over Didion. And if Emperor Bazekoy should call on me to rise from this bed and assist you, I'll be ready."

In the late evening, as the *Casabarela Regnant* finally came clear of the perilous Darkling Sands and hoisted all sails for her homeward run, Ullanoth prowled the Didionite flagship, unseen by dint of Concealer.

She had found a secure place to stow away on the orlop deck, the lowest part of the huge four-tiered barque. The locked and deserted sick bay had two comfortable bunks, and food and water were easily available to her in the galley. After cleaning the stains from her face and hands and washing the grease from her hair, she went to eavesdrop invisibly on the royal family of Didion, who had fled to the ship immediately following the aborted coronation ceremony.

All of them had been well slathered with an ointment of chamomile, lavender, and pine, which gave some relief from their myriad midge bites. Queen Siry and the princesses had retired early to their beds, all save one of them nearly swooning with outrage. Risalla, the exception, was overcome by feelings of joyous deliverance, after her father informed her she would not be marrying the luckless Beynor after all.

Ullanoth found King Achardus and his sons gathered in the sumptuous cabin in the vessel's sterncastle, where they were restoring themselves by means of the traditional Didionite remedy after a bad day: getting drunk.

"More," the king commanded, holding out his cup to Somarus. "I can still feel the damned itching and see that river of red-eyed rats pouring into Beynor's throne room."

The prince obeyed with alacrity. They were drinking plum life-water, Didion's favorite spirit, prized in spite of the horrendous hangovers it caused.

"Archwizard Ilingus informed me that my wife's rat-bite was a trivial thing," Honigalus said, taking a pull from his own goblet. "It should heal quickly and leave only a tiny scar on her heel. But from Bryse's complaints, you'd think she'd taken a hit from a broad arrow. I'm never going to hear the end of this."

"You were the one who urged us all to attend that nightmare bash," his brother said waspishly. "I hope you're satisfied. At least your precious Treaty of Alliance is still in force—for whatever good it'll do us." He rose from the table and went to the great window at the stern. It was full dark now, and the ship left a phosphorescent wake as it ran across Seal Bay, flying before a chill northerly wind. The escorting vessels were visible only from their mast lights far astern.

"Beynor promises to keep a constant magical eye out for Cathran land incursions," Honigalus said. "That should give us a clear field at sea and do us plenty of good. If we sail well to the east, the Cathran magickers won't see us coming until we round the Vigilant Isles—even if they combine their windwatching talents."

"But Beynor admitted he doesn't have a moonstone amulet for scrying," Somarus said, "only the usual Mosslander sorcery."

"Which is far stronger than anything Lingo and his lot can muster. Everything will go well."

"So you lads are still determined to go ahead with your ploy?" Achardus's face was flushed and full of doubt.

Honigalus said. "Our spies in Cala City report that the Cathran fleet is still moored deep in Blenholme Roads like a flock of mud-hens sitting out a sun-shower, with small sea room to maneuver. And our mainland friends are ready. All they need are fair winds in the Dolphin Channel and a word from us."

The king wagged his gigantic head as if trying to clear his fuddled wits. "But to risk all our fighting fleet—"

The Crown Prince, who was in charge of Didion's Royal Navy, said, "The crews are sullen and insubordinate from being idle and on short rations, sire. If they have to spend the winter starving ashore, we'll lose most of them to deser-tion. Taking the fleet into action now, with the prospect of rich plunder in Cala, will lift their spirits sky-high. We'll never have such propitious conditions for a sea-strike again. Cathra's all in a lather because King Olmigon is dying. Vra-Kilian assured young Beynor of that. I daresay Conrig won't want to leave his father's bedside."

"Must keep our eyes peeled for trouble at Great Pass, though," Achardus warned blearily, surging to his feet and gesturing with his empty cup. "Keep our forces alert! Don't just count on Beynor to warn us. Sneaky rat bastard Conrig's capable of anything! Even aband'ning a dying father. What kind of a son'd do that?"

"No Didionite," Prince Somarus averred. "Only a degenerate Cathran. But we'll be ready for any trickery in the high country. I plan to collect and lead rein-forcements to Castlemont immediately. We won't be caught napping if Conrig attacks. And don't underestimate Beynor. He's a loathsome little pustule, but he's eager to earn our gold."

"What gold?" Achardus uttered a despairing groan. He was far gone in drink. "We have none left, 'cept the crown jewels. You'd think Beynor'd know that if he's such a thumpin' great magicker." He held out his cup. "More plum water!"

Honigalus poured, and refilled his own and his brother's cup as well. "Beynor knows there's gold aplenty in Cathra. And he's showed us how to take it."

"Should have figured it out by yourselves." The king's voice was slurred and lugubrious. Maudlin tears leaked from his eyes. "Not waited for a *father-killer* to tell you how to wipe your arses. Beynor murdered King Linndal! He's a monster. And he uses filthy Beaconfolk magic. He'll ruin us! Oh, gods—he'll bring the wrath of the Lights down on us, just like the old witch said!"

"We don't know that Beynor killed his father, sire." Honigalus tried to calm the agitated king. "Why should we take the word of a crazed woman? She was lying, making trouble. And now she's dead, destroyed by Beynor's thunderbolt. Here. Let me top off your cup."

Achardus batted the flagon aside and it fell to the carpeted deck, spewing colorless liquid. "Woe!" the king moaned. "Witch Walanoth howled about woe. Warned us. But we didn't listen. Woe . . ."

His huge body began to crumple. Honigalus and Somarus hastened to take hold of him, staggering under his enormous weight, and guided him to a large padded couch. Achardus collapsed on his back, and the younger men loosened his clothing and took off his boots. "Gonna puke," the King of Didion whispered. Somarus held a silver basin while Honigalus supported Achardus's head. He subsided then, bloodshot eyes half-closed and breath coming in slow, rasping surges.

"Let's cover him. Go to sleep ourselves," Honigalus mumbled. The princes finished tending to their father, then shuffled off unsteadily to their cabins.

Ullanoth watched the sleeping giant for a few minutes before going to her own secret bed. But not to sleep.

Beynor only thought to look inside the platinum case late on that awful night of humiliation, just before going to bed. He had some confused notion of comforting himself with dreams of future triumph, when he would finally empower Destroyer and the Unknown and become a sorcerer greater than Rothbannon. His brain was so addled by wine that at first he could not understand why the velvet nests were all empty. He stumbled about his chambers in his nightshirt, pawing through chests and cabinets, throwing down the contents of shelves, whimpering as the frightful realization took slow root and grew.

Gone. Both Great Stones were gone, and only one person could have taken them.

He screamed and screamed then until his throat was raw, but inside the walls of Fortress, no one could hear him.

*   *   *

"Will there be anything more, Your Grace?" Snudge waited at the open door of Conrig's room after having ushered in all of the Heart Companions for a meeting with the prince. The travelers were established for the night in the mansion of the Lord Mayor of Melora, which was a prosperous small city on the River Blen. It marked the southern terminus of the Great North Road leading to Beorbrook Hold, and ultimately to Great Pass.

Only three of the ten young noblemen who attended Conrig and Vra-Stergos knew that their party would be heading in another direction with the dawn, taking the eastern road to Castle Vanguard. It was to apprise the others of the true nature of the expedition that Conrig had called the meeting.

Snudge had been delegated to inform the armigers.

"You may go now," Conrig told him, "and see that you also make plain to the boys your special status."

Snudge bowed and withdrew, closing the door behind him, and hurried down the deserted corridor. Members of the mayor's household were discreetly absent from this part of the house.

Codders! Snudge thought. Here comes trouble! By rights Belamil Langsands, the stocky level-headed squire who attended Count Sividian, and the oldest of them at nineteen, acted as the leader of the armigers and transmitted royal commands and announcements. But Conrig had been adamant that Snudge was to do the job tonight.

"It's time the lads acknowledge your particular place in our picked body of warriors," the prince had said. "And time for you to show that you have the stones to occupy your new position. You are not merely a squire, you are my blooded man. Tell the others about your encounter with Iscannon—but not about his sigil. They must know nothing of your talent, of course, but you may make up some tale about being no stranger to magic if you think it will better dispose them toward eventually accepting you as their leader."

Taken aback, Snudge found himself gawping with astonishment. "I, Your Grace? But Belamil—"

"He's a brave young man and trustworthy, but hardly the one to lead a troop guarding Princess Ullanoth during the battle for Holt Mallburn."

"Your Grace, wouldn't it be more fitting if you assigned several of your Companions to this service? The lady might take offense at being offered an escort of mere armigers."

"It matters not how she regards you," Conrig retorted. "She's bound to come to us after we enter Mallburn Town, and I have reasons of my own for keeping her apart even from my closest friends. The boys won't dare question her and they'll keep her safe from obvious physical dangers. While you, my Snudge, oversee her magicking as best you can—more unobtrusively, I hope, than any Brother of Zeth. Thus far, Ullanoth knows nothing of your talent. I wish this state of affairs to continue."

"So . . . you don't really trust her after all." The boy barely concealed his relief.

"I trust her to do as she promised," the prince had said, "aiding us to conquer Didion. What she does subsequently, while I'm too occupied by the fighting or its aftermath to stay close to her, may be a cause for concern. Or not!" He shrugged, but his eyes were shadowed. "Perhaps our stratagem will prove unnecessary—or even impossible to implement. But I want you to be prepared, and the squires as well. I realize I've given you no clear instructions in this matter, but there can be none until circumstances dictate."

Snudge could only say, "I understand, Your Grace. Rely on me."

He squared his shoulders as he entered the common room of the mayor's household warriors, which had been cleared of furniture so that the armigers could bed down there.

"Welcome to our humble abode," redheaded Mero Elwick called out snidely. "We'd despaired of having you join us, thinking His Grace might want you to sleep on the floor outside his door like a faithful hound."

A few of the boys laughed. Snudge said quietly, "If His Grace had requested that, I would have obeyed. But instead he's sent me here with an important message for all of you."

There were surprised comments, and Saundar Kersey, Count Tayman's armiger, asked, "Does it pertain to our mission?"

"It does indeed," Snudge said. "Let's gather round the fire. It's a damp evening, with the fog coming on so thick."

"May I pour you a warm libation, messire?" Mero inquired with mock courtesy, reaching for the steaming cider-pot on the hob.

"That would be a kindness," said Snudge, giving over his new silver cup, one of the gifts of his investiture.

"Oops!" Mero let the goblet slip from his hand and ding on the hearthstone. "Not much harm done, young Deveron." He chuckled and managed to slop some of the hot drink on Snudge's wrist as he returned it.

"Thank you," the boy said, without rancor. Belamil and a few of the others scowled at Mero's spiteful display, but most of them were only interested in what Snudge would say next. "Prince Conrig has kept our true destination secret in order to foil enemy windwatchers. We are not going to reinforce Beorbrook Hold and guard Great Pass. Instead, we'll ride tomorrow to Swanwick, and on the third day arrive at Castle Vanguard, where we'll join an army poised to invade Didion over Breakneck Pass."

A tumult of shouting. Finally, Belamil cried out, "Let Deveron speak."

The others fell silent and watched him solemnly. Even Mero's usual sour expression had vanished.

"A couple of weeks ago, five of us lads accompanied Prince Conrig, Lord Stergos, and Counts Sividian, Feribor, and Tayman to Castle Vanguard. There the prince conferred with Duke Tanaby, Earl Marshal Beorbrook, and fifteen other nobles of the north country at a great council of war. It was decided to invade Didion over Breakneck Pass at the end of the Boreal Moon."

There were excited exclamations. Snudge plowed on. "The army will number only about five hundred warriors. We'll move with the greatest speed possible, riding coursers, not heavy destriers. We'll be armored only in mail but carry ample weapons. Magical allies who have created this thick fog will guide us over the mountain pass and help us to take the enemy outposts by surprise. Our army will press on to Holt Mallburn and there, with the help of more magical assistance, we will set parts of the city afire with tarnblaze as a distraction and enter the palace of Achardus through wide-open portals. This last feat will also be successfully accomplished through magical aid."

He paused, seeing round eyes and open mouths. "Any man among you who is fearful of the supernatural or less than confident of his ability to stay the course when magic is employed may feel free to leave the company and return to Cala."

A chorus of "Nay!" began tentatively, but soon shook the rafters.

Then Mero spoke with cool insolence. "Who are you to question our courage, and offer to dismiss us like children if we fall short?"

"I am Prince Conrig's liege man, sworn to his service. Some of you may know that my rank of armiger is only symbolic, because of my youth and the rules of chivalry. In truth, I became the prince's man by shedding blood on his behalf—the blood of a Mossland sorcerer spying on the council of war at Castle Vanguard, who may have had designs upon the prince's very life."

"You killed a *sorcerer?*" Saundar, a clever, dark-haired youth two years older than Snudge, was plainly incredulous.

The boy caught the eye of Gavlok Whitfell, Stergos's squire, who only shook his head. He had not passed on Snudge's confidence to the others.

Snudge spoke softly so they would be obliged to listen rather than gabble. "I stabbed him to the heart, and I'll tell you the tale anon. But first I must recount the prince's orders to you. Your duties during this enterprise will be mostly as usual—attending your masters. But His Grace has advised me that there may come a time when some members of this company of armigers may be called upon to perform an exceptional service for him. If this happens, I will be your leader."

"You!" Besides the affronted response from Mero, there were surprised protests from the rest.

"There is a reason why Prince Conrig has called on me, young as I am, rather than Belamil to lead. I have a certain acquaintance with magic. I can smell it out, if you like, and I know how to take precautions against its power."

The room had gone dead quiet except for the crackling of the fire.

Then one of the boys said, "Is that how you managed to kill the sorcerer? Tell us about it."

"Soon. But first, let those who can't bring themselves to follow my lead speak up and leave the room."

"I will follow you," said Belamil gravely. "The judgment of Prince Conrig making you his man is reason enough for me."

"And for me," said Gavlok.

One after another, the other armigers also concurred. All except Mero.

"I'm sworn to my master, Count Feribor," he said, not bothering to conceal his scorn. "Only if he commands it will I be led by a low-born grub like you. D'you want me to leave?"

"Stay," Snudge said. The last person he would choose to help guard Princess Ullanoth during a battle would be Feribor Blackhorse's cross-grained squire, so what did it matter?

"The sorcerer! Tell us!" the others demanded eagerly.

So Snudge began the highly amended tale of what he had done at Castle Vanguard.

Ullanoth windwatched Conrig's colloquy with the Companions, then Sent herself to him when the men were well gone.

"My prince," she breathed, and felt a small rush of satisfaction at his start of alarm. Conrig had been given the Lord Mayor's own fine bedroom, which was now somewhat of a mess with rugs kicked awry, chairs and stools dragged together before the fire and left every which way by the departed Companions, and tables and floor littered with the prince's possessions, sheets of parchment, and a welter of maps and equipment lists.

He did not speak immediately, but took her into his arms and kissed her. Then he said, "You need a bath. And your clothes are damp."

She gave a rueful laugh. "I'm traveling on a ship. And I had not been able to wash properly for nearly a week before embarking, since I was feeling unwell. At least my hair is clean and most of the dye washed from my face. You should have seen me in my hag disguise, berating the Didionite royals. I was a sight to brown a strong man's smallclothes."

He smiled at her crudity. "There's a tub of water behind that screen that was hot an hour ago. We could heat up a cauldron on the fire and make a tepid bath for you, at least."

She considered the matter with a whimsical smile. "If a dirty Sending washes itself, will the original body be made clean? I have no idea! Let's experiment. But there's no need to heat water. I can do that easily with my talent."

She sprawled on the hearth-rug and began stripping off her rough clothing, telling him the tale of Beynor's sorry coronation festivities. Soon they were both howling with mirth.

"If only I could have seen it," Conrig said. He gave her a cup of mead and sat on the floor beside her, admiring the rosy reflections of the fire on her slender form. "But with Beynor so humiliated, won't he be driven to empower another of his Great Stones out of sheer revenge?"

"He cannot," she said with satisfaction. Then, playing fast and loose with the truth, she told him she had destroyed her brother's two inactive sigils.

"Great God! So they can be obliterated so easily?"

"The unempowered stones, yes. I don't know what would happen if a person attempted to destroy a conjured sigil by main force. It's possible that the stone would defend itself in some deadly fashion. I do know for certain that if a person who is not the owner touches an active sigil without permission, he is severely burnt."

He gestured to Sender, which hung on its chain around her neck like a faintly glowing teardrop. "Then a sigil cannot be lent to another to use?"

"Never. Beynor had to perform a spell of abolition in order to turn his Concealer over to Iscannon. He had to relinquish ownership of it so that his minion could conjure it himself."

"I see." For a time Conrig remained silent, smiling thoughtfully as he ran one hand lightly over her pearly hair. Then he asked, "Are you safe from your brother's evil magic now?"

"I believe so. For all Beynor's hatred of me, he is still a very intelligent brat. I think he realizes that his future depends upon regaining the goodwill of Didion—not retaliating against his big sister. And don't forget . . . he believes I'm dead, blasted to smuts along with the top of my tower."

"Does he *truly* believe that?"

She frowned, then gave a sigh. "His thunderbolt was a great show of power for the royals of Didion, and Beynor will probably cling to the belief that I'm dead for a time, just to comfort his devastated pride and his rage at the loss of the two Great Stones. He won't doubt that I was responsible. But soon enough he'll begin to wonder whether I might have escaped on one of the Didionite ships, and then he'll try to find me."

"But you can hide from him, can't you?"

"Alas, the moonstone that would have veiled my presence completely and provided a sure refuge against all danger was lost in my tower's destruction. However, I still have my Concealer, which renders me invisible. Its powers are limited while I'm Sending. I must choose to conceal either the inanimate husk left behind—and this I have done tonight—or the Sending itself, as I intend to do when I assist your invasion. Beynor owns no sigil capable of pinpointing a sorceress such as I, nor can he identify me by windsearching if I'm very cautious in my own use of the arcane talents. All he can do—all any of the Guild can do—is survey every nook and cranny of the vast Didionite capital city with windsight and hope to encounter me while I'm visible, just as though they were hunting me by ordinary means."

Remembering how Snudge had followed her windtrace to Fenguard Castle, Conrig said, "But isn't it possible for a very powerful adept to scry you out if he finds the thread of your arcane speech or sight?"

"Yes," she admitted grudgingly. "But I'm surprised to find you so well-versed in thaumaturgy, my prince."

"Stergos has taught me much in the past few weeks. And what if Beynor tracks down your visible Sending?"

"To Send is far more subtle than to bespeak or descry. If Beynor chanced to discover my visible vacated body, he might be able to trace me to my Sent destination. Or if he watched us here, at this moment, he might perhaps trace the thread back on the wind to the sick bay where my invisible husk lies hidden on the Didionite flagship. But I believe there is small chance of him doing so." *And I must continue to believe it, since there's nothing I can do to change the situation.*

Conrig climbed to his feet. "Time for your bath, my lady. The Lord Mayor left me a cake of lavender-scented soap and at least half a dozen Forailean towels, soft as swansdown."

"Excellent." She rose with the sinuous grace of a meadow cat, silhouetted against the fire. Sender, the Great Stone that was actually very small in size, shone at her throat. "You shall be my attendant. And while you serve me, I'll tell you how I intend to help you conquer Didion . . . and how Honigalus plans to attack Cala by sea."

"Zeth! Have you overheard the Didionites discussing it? When will they sail? Can my army reach Holt Mallburn in time to stop them?"

"I haven't discovered that yet." She beckoned to him and moved to the tub behind the screen. "But you can be sure that I will find out. I have recently conjured a new sigil named Subtle Loophole that enables me to both oversee and listen closely to anyone, anywhere. This is a wonderful new weapon, a Great Stone purchased at the cost of much pain and suffering."

His face was troubled. "Will not such a thing put you in greater peril of the Lights?"

"Let me worry about that," she said, stepping into the now-steaming tub, which was made of burnished copper with a fine embossed-silver rim. "Forget about wars and sorcery for a few minutes, and concentrate on helping me to get clean again. And then let us take comfort in one another. I do love you with all my heart and soul, Conrig, and I long for the day when we can remain together for more than a few short hours." She tilted her head, staring at him in smiling speculation. "Do you realize we have never seen one another truly, or touched—save through magic? But we'll meet at last in Holt Mallburn, when you're victorious, and I pray we'll never be apart again."

"It will be a wondrous day, in so many ways," he said, striving to imbue the words with loving enthusiasm. Then he turned away to bring her the scented soap and a sponge, and to hang up her damp garments in front of the fire.

twenty

Beynor sulked behind Fortress in his regal apartment until all of the Mossland dignitaries had finally returned to their homes, taking with them the furnishings and appurtenances they had lent for the ill-fated coronation. Grand Master Ridcanndal and Lady Zimroth had urged him to deliver a parting speech, reassuring his vassals that the future boded well; but he was a youth of sixteen for all his kingship and magical talent, and too consumed by fury and the chagrin of his public embarrassment to accept their wise counsel. All he had done for three whole days was hide away and burn and curse his dead sister—she had to be dead!—knowing that the absurd botch of his crowning would never be forgotten by any of those attending.

He had not confessed the loss of Destroyer and the Unknown Potency to the Glaumerie Guild. Now that he was king, the wizards had no way to compel him to display the stones. He was uncertain whether Ullanoth had taken them away or destroyed them, but he did know now that she must own a Sender sigil. Its powerful sorcery was the only thing that could have penetrated Fortress; and he himself, all unknowing, had helped solidify the Sending.

His only consolation was that the Didionite royals had not repudiated their Treaty of Alliance, nor had they blamed him directly for the distressing events. So as his temper cooled, he set about to do as he had promised, shutting down Fortress for hours at a time and meticulously windsearching the kingdom of Cathra for any sign that an invasion force was gathering.

He discovered the peculiar fog.

It was confined to the northeast and north central part of the country and the Dextral Mountains, patchy but dense, and seemed natural enough. Except that it hid the principal northern roads of Cathra from his oversight, and completely blotted out the region between Elk Lake and Swan Lake that formed the crucial approach to Beorbrook Hold and Great Pass—the region that an army bent upon invading Didion would have to traverse.

Emerging at last from seclusion, he called upon Lady Zimroth and other members of the Guild highly talented in windwatching to concentrate their combined attention on the area night and day, hoping that they would descry something of importance when the mists finally broke apart. Instead, the vaporous blanket continued to expand until it began to pour over the mountainous divide into southern Didion itself.

"I'm beginning to think this fog might be magical in origin," Beynor said to Lady Zimroth. They were with eight other wizard-observers in the Guild's chapter room, seated at a great round table, and had just completed another frustrating joint survey of the enshrouded lands. It was early afternoon.

The dignified elderly woman inclined her head. She was dressed in robes, veil, and a wimple of grey silk. The skin of her face was grey as well and so full of fine lines and creases that no part of it remained smooth. Only her eyes had color, being the vibrant clear green of new alder leaves in spring.

"Boreal is the moon of mists, Your Majesty," Zimroth said. "This fog certainly might be a natural manifestation. But the fact that it hides the strategic area and persists for so long is suspicious." Her calm gaze was full of challenge. "Of course, there is one way to find out for certain if it is caused by sorcery, but one hesitates to suggest it, since you have so recently overexerted yourself using Weathermaker."

Beynor squared his shoulders and rose from his seat at the table. "I'll deal with the matter at once. You and the others wait here and keep watch until I return. I don't know how severely the sigil will incapacitate me when I use it this time. It won't be an easy job. Send Master Ridcanndal and the Physician Royal to my chambers if I don't return in two hours. I'll command Fortress to admit them."

He left the chapter room and went to his apartment in a foul mood. Even Zimroth, who'd been his dear surrogate mother, still regarded him as a shrinking child, reluctant to experience necessary pain! What would he have to do to convince them he was a man, and strong?

Weathermaker rarely left his finger now. He stepped out onto the balcony and held the moonstone ring high, conjuring a strong north wind to sweep down from the mountain heights onto the plain surrounding Beorbrook Hold. As he completed the incantation, his head seemed pierced by a lance of agony that was first blazing hot and then stunningly cold. He screamed, doubling over, and dropped to his knees. The pain swelled to a white glare, and his voice failed as his breath was choked off. His heart gave a great hurtful leap within his breast, a wave of darkness engulfed him, and he fell senseless.

When he woke the sun was lower. He lay on the moss-grown stone floor of the balcony, chilled to the bone and stiff but otherwise not afflicted. Moaning and cursing, he staggered to his feet. Weathermaker glowed wanly on his finger, quiescent again. Down in the inner ward, Rothbannon's Marvel revealed that he had been unconscious for just over an hour. He went inside, hauled on a warm robe, and made his way slowly back to the Guild chapter room where the others waited.

"Did the fog dissipate?" he asked. But their glum faces gave him the answer. He heaved a sigh of frustration. All his pain had been for nothing. "Tell me."

Two of the wizards hastened to help him into a chair, and Zimroth poured him a glass of spirits, which he sipped thankfully.

"Your Majesty, did you command Weathermaker to dissolve the mist?" Zimroth asked.

"Nay." Beynor wiped his lips with the back of his hand. "I conjured a mighty north wind to blow it away." It had seemed the easier course, but he was not about to admit that.

"I thought as much," the High Thaumaturge said. "As we watched, a gale began to push the fog down the slope before it. Great Pass was cleared and we saw no troops or other unusual activity. But upon reaching the lowlands, the wind seemed to strike invisible obstacles and form many conflicting streams of air. The fog whirled and thinned in some places, but never again did it disappear completely. Instead it seemed to become like a stormy sky brought down to earth, tumbling and chaotic. Your blast of wind then moved through the sea of vapor like a great wave—or perhaps an advancing avalanche. But when if had passed, the fog was still there. It was impossible for us to see what might be happening beneath it."

"The fog is certainly of uncanny origin," said a wizard named Makartinal. He was a craggy-faced scholar of impressive talent. "The fact that the widespread blanket was churned and thinned at times, yet was not torn open, leads me to think that it might be generated by more than one adept—perhaps by scores or even hundreds of magical practitioners who made more fog as the wind attempted to dissipate it. I believe the sorcery may be more powerful than the Brothers of Zeth can exert—or even our Guild."

Beynor frowned. "But who could be doing it? Certainly not the Salka. They would never aid Cathra."

"There are always the Green Men," Makartinal said.

Zimroth nodded slowly. "They hate the folk of Didion, true enough. But an arcane phenomenon such as this would require cooperation amongst hundreds of them. And they live in widely scattered small bands in the wolds and the Green Morass, and the groups are said to have no bonds of loyalty one to another."

Beynor sighed, rising from his seat. "My friends, I thank you for working with me. We can ponder this problem of the fog another day. I must go now and bespeak our Didionite allies, telling them what we know. And then I must rest. I'm all used up."

Lady Zimroth said, "I'll prepare a soothing draft for Your Majesty and bring it to your chamber."

"That would be most kind."

"But before you go," she added, her voice tense with foreboding, "you must see this. The foreman of the crew clearing the rubble of the demolished South Tower brought it to me while you were away conjuring the wind. It severely burnt the hands of the slave who found it. I placed it in this box for safety's sake."

She took up a small golden casket that had been on the table before her and brought it to Beynor. He opened it. Inside was a faintly shining moonstone shaped like a small octagonal plaque. He felt his heart contract as he recognized the sigil named Fortress.

Not his own Fortress, which still guarded his chambers: this one had to be Ullanoth's.

"The stone is no longer in operation, since the place it was charged to protect is gone," Zimroth said. "But it is alive, as you see, and so must be your sister, its owner. Would you have us begin to windsearch the city for her?"

"No," said Beynor, in a voice barely audible.

Alive . . . He'd deluded himself after all, and his secret fear was now confirmed. She was alive, and certainly beyond his reach. Could she have taken Destroyer and the Unknown Potency with her?

Damn Ullanoth to the Ten Hells of Ice!

"She will have gone south with the Didionites." He spoke more forthrightly. "No doubt she stowed away on one of their ships while concealed by a sigil. I must think about this very carefully. How many other people know about this Fortress stone of hers?"

"The foreman and his crew of slaves," Zimroth said. "No others, I should think."

"Kill them," said the Conjure-King. His gaze took in the group of wizards. "And all of you keep silence about this until I decide whether or not to warn King Achardus and his sons that Ullanoth may be alive and traveling among them."

Carrying the golden box with its perilous contents, he left the room, knowing what he would have to do with this sigil. If Ullanoth should discover that it was not destroyed, she could command it, even from a distance, and perhaps do him great harm. So the stone had to be abolished and then empowered to him. Immediately.

Coldlight Army, smite her! he raged inwardly. Another hideous ordeal, and this time not a relatively brief one—and all for the sake of a redundant stone that would not significantly increase his own might.

Who could tell what havoc Ulla might wreak in Didion, laying the groundwork for Prince Conrig's invasion? He doubted that she would attempt to empower his own stolen Great Stones. The risk was too formidable. But she certainly owned a Concealer; her uncanny appearances and disappearances proved that. And he was virtually certain that she possessed a sigil that enabled her body to become subtle. How else to explain his sword passing through her like a ghost, or her escape from the silken ropes? And only a Beastbidder would have enabled her to create chaos at his coronation with the fitches, gulls, midges, and rats. How many other stones did she have, and what were their capabilities? There was no way to know . . . until she used them against him.

I must find a way to kill her, he told himself in desperation. I must, or my own plans for the future will be forfeit.

But he had no notion of how to do that, short of seeking the counsel of the Lights, a prospect that caused his soul to shrivel. So from that time on, without even realizing it, he began to hate himself as much as he hated his sister, for being young and afraid.

*   *   *

After departing from Swanwick at first light, the small force of Heart Companions and armigers had ridden steadily uphill all day and were now only a few hours away from Castle Vanguard. Vra-Stergos, riding with Conrig at the head of the party, did his best to scry the fog-swathed, dripping landscape ahead of them for villains lying in ambush, while Snudge, by order of the prince, brought up the rear and took a cautious windsight from time to time, making sure that no suspicious persons came up suddenly behind them. His labors were all but useless. The mists were so heavy that one could hardly see three ells, using either eye or talent. But the prince's party was safe enough. No one traveled the road in such weather save a few peasants and other harmless persons, insubstantial ghosts in the murk who responded to Belamil's regular calls of "Make way!" by drawing respectfully to the verge while the cavalcade of anonymous-looking armed men passed them by.

At the beginning of the journey, Snudge had been full of excitement and anticipation, like the other squires. But the unending clammy gloom of the last two days had lowered his spirits. With no observation of the passing scene to distract him while riding, he was bored. The other armigers were often able to converse among themselves; but he, relegated to the tail-end of the procession by his special duty, was mostly left on his own, jouncing through white blankness, occasionally calming his horse with his talent, silently bespeaking Stergos regularly to tell him that all was well, while the other armigers had no idea what he was doing.

Only one unusual thing happened to break the monotony, a sudden roaring blast of wind that came from nowhere and nearly blew him out of the saddle. But it was gone almost as soon as it arrived, amounting to nothing.

So Snudge brooded, thinking over his life thus far, his amazing good fortune and his narrow escapes from death, wondering what future his wild talent would bring him as he served his prince. He thought of many things . . . but most of all, he thought about the sigil hanging around his neck.

Snudge wanted to try it. Oh, how he wanted to try it!

He could not resist fingering the hard lump through his mail shirt and padded leather gambeson, lying against his chest, not painful at all but alive and warm inside its thin bag. A moonstone named Concealer, the most puissant tool imaginable for a Royal Intelligencer, was now his own. The Tarnian shaman had told him it would hurt any other person who dared touch it. In the small magical book, he had read that it was possible to "abolish" a sigil—detach it from its owner and render it inactive, so that it could be re-empowered and used by another. But the spell of abolition had been long and complex (to say nothing of incomprehensible to him), and apparently involved magic that was both painful and tedious. So no sorcerer, not even Princess Ullanoth, was going to take Concealer from him easily.

The urge to make use of it was so strong that Snudge was tempted almost beyond endurance. He rode apart in the fog that hid him from his companions, so who would notice if he vanished for a few minutes, horse and all?

He was tempted, but in the end he refrained because of Red Ansel's words: *I strongly advise you not to conjure Concealer except under the most grave circumstances. Even though the Lights don't know your true name, there's still a danger of their interfering . . .*

Interfering! What did that ambiguous word mean? Was he vulnerable to Beaconfolk torture each time he made use of the sigil? That couldn't be true. The little book hadn't said so, even though it had contained an impressive list of cautions. Salka had made the moonstones and they'd evidently used them safely—during ancient times, at least. And one of the brutes he'd seen swimming in Cala Bay wore a living stone around its neck.

Beynor, in the dreams, had uttered dire warnings about Beaconfolk sorcery, but Beynor was a despicable liar who used sigils himself and even allowed his assistant to borrow one. His sister Ullanoth possessed them, too. Snudge knew now that he'd seen at least two living stones when he windwatched the princess in her tower, and Prince Conrig had said she owned others. No doubt she intended to use her sigils to regain control of her kingdom.

In his youthful innocence and frustration, Snudge asked himself why the Salka would have invented these magical tools in the first place, knowing that they were mortally perilous—but he knew the answer almost before he formulated the question:

For power.

People will risk a great deal for power—even their lives. And the greater the power one sought, the greater the risk one was willing to take.

Thinking about it, Snudge rode on, and came at last with others of the Prince Heritor's company to Castle Vanguard.

The north-country lords and the Virago of Marley had faithfully fulfilled their promises. Conrig felt his heart swell with joy as he, Duke Tanaby, Earl Marshal

Parlian Beorbrook, and the other noble leaders inspected the mounted knights and thanes massed in serried ranks in the castle's great outer ward. As the prince had commanded, each warrior was armored in a coat of mail and open helm, with steel greaves to guard the rider's lower legs. Voluminous hooded cloaks of waxed leather in drab colors concealed most of the panoply of war; shields and battle-axes were hidden by covers, and the horses' tack was unadorned.

"We have some two hundred mules and pack-ponies to carry our supplies," Duke Tanaby said, "and thirty courser remounts. Mounted thanes will lead the sumpter beasts, positioned in the middle of the column, with companies of knights at the van and rear. You realize, of course, that we will have to ride single-file on the worst sections of the Breakneck track. My best scouts surveyed the route to the summit three days ago and found it relatively clear of landslides and obstructions. There are several torrents to ford, but this time of year they have not much water in them. Of course we know not what we'll find on the Didion side of the range."

Conrig nodded. "Our magical guides will doubtless be able to tell us about the condition of the track above Redfern Castle, and whether there are other outposts of the foe closer to the pass itself."

"Where will we meet these guides?" asked Lady Zeandrise.

"At the very top of the pass," Conrig said. "I understand there is a kind of heath or meadow where we may spend the night before moving down into enemy lands."

"It's mostly a boggy mess up there at the summit," Count Ramscrest said, "But we haven't had much rain this fall, so perhaps it'll do. This fog is all very well for hiding our troop movements from the enemy, but it's going to make dicey going on a steep trail. You lowlanders don't have any notion how bad this route's going to be. In some places, we'll have to blindfold the horses. Heights and steep dropoffs tend to spook the more skittish nags, and they won't fancy loose talus skidding under their hooves, either."

Cloudfell, Catclaw, and Bogshaw, mountain dwellers like their overlord, Ramscrest, murmured their agreement.

"The mules and ponies should be fine, though," Lord Catclaw said. "They're bred for high-country travel." He was a powerfully built man in the prime of life, handsome and dashing, with thick blond hair that curled freely below his shoulders. The other nobles joked about his flowing locks, but Tinnis Catclaw claimed that braided buns of one's own hair made the best possible cushion for a war-helm.

Cloudfell, managing to look elegant even in the drab garb prescribed for the expedition, spoke languidly, as was his habit. "Perhaps we'd do better to scatter the ponies and mules amongst the steeds, once we reach the worst parts of the trail. That would help keep the horses calm."

"Good idea," said the earl marshal. He turned to Vanguard. "What kind of time can we expect to make, Tanaby?"

"Normally, in clear weather, the summit can be reached in about ten hours, riding a strong animal. With such a large army—and in the fog, of course—we'll be lucky to get to the top in fourteen hours, even if we leave before sunup."

"Must we spend the night at the pass?" Beorbrook's lumpish son, Count Elktor, didn't bother to hide his dissatisfaction.

"Oh, yes, my lord." Tanaby Vanguard's smile was ironic. "You may recall my comment at the council of war about a certain lack of comfort we might expect to endure on this adventure. Furthermore, there will be no fires—not even for cooking—unless they can be kept tiny and smokeless. Even in fog, the scent of burning wood might travel far and alert the enemy to our presence. Of course, there's almost no fuel in the summit heath except brush and dead bracken . . ."

"More likely," said Viscount Skellhaven, with an evil grin, "the air up there will be so sodden we'll be hard put to strike a light, even with tarnsticks. Oh, we're in for a foul night, my lords—unless the Conjure-Princess sends us a pack of dancing nymphs to lift our spirits as well as guide us."

"Does anyone else have a question?" Conrig asked, with some impatience. "We must dismiss the men, eat a hearty supper, and go early to bed if we intend to be off in the wee hours."

The Virago of Marley spoke up. "I have one, Your Grace. At the council of war, you told us that if any of us distrusted the aspect of the uncanny guides provided by Princess Ullanoth, we would be free to turn back. Does this dispensation still apply?"

Conrig smiled at her. "I hardly expected hesitancy in so stout a heart as yours, my lady. At the council, you seemed charged with your usual valor."

"I am responsible for the safety of my warriors," she retorted, "and I reckon each of them dearer to me than the sons I never had. Leading them into a battle that may pit them against sorcery is not the duty of a prudent mother. Please answer the question, Your Grace."

He inclined his head gravely. "I swear to you, Lady Zea—and to all of you, my lords—that so far as I know, we will fight only mortal men in Didion, not magic. The uncanny guides provided by Ullanoth will only show us the way through the mists, not fight at our sides. And, yes—if you mistrust them when we meet them, you may freely retreat. But I pray you'll all stand fast at my side as we conquer King Achardus and his sons, and free Cathra from foreign menaces forever."

The once prosperous port city of Holt Mallburn was in a lamentable state as a result of the famine. Its more wealthy inhabitants had long since fled to their manors in the countryside, leaving their townhomes in charge of servants and hired guards. But privation, the spread of disease, and violence born of the increasing desperation of the lower classes had caused numbers of these guardians to abandon their posts. Many of the fine city dwellings and business establishments had fallen prey to looters, or were used as shelter by beggars and outlaws who had formerly lived in the streets. The common townsfolk barricaded their dwellings and emerged as rarely as possible. Only a few enclaves remained completely secure, patrolled by the King's Household Guard and well-fed private forces: the palace and the parkland surrounding it, the so-called Golden Precinct where the great merchant-lords lived, and Mallburn Quay, with its all-important deepwater docks, warehouses, and shipyards.

Princess Ullanoth, using Concealer and Interpenetrator, had wasted no time once she disembarked from the Didionite flagship. Taking with her a sack of food and a blanket roll, she quickly found shelter inside a deserted warehouse. Unlike the majority of the quayside structures, which were wooden, it was sturdily built of brick, the property of the city's Guild of Winesellers. The place was mostly full of empty barrels and bottles, waiting for the day when trade in luxury items would resume; but its heavily shuttered offices had lamps, a stove with a supply of charcoal, and a few old cloaks left hanging on pegs that could be fashioned into a bed. There was even a cache of decent wine and spirits, doubtless hidden away by some of the clerks for their secret refreshment.

"Good enough," she said to herself, smiling. She could find water tomorrow. There had to be a public fountain nearby. The Sending's bathing experiment, unfortunately, had proved a failure.

When she had arranged her new quarters to her satisfaction, she took out the sigil named Subtle Loophole, put it to her eye, and began the onerous task of watching and listening.

For the first days of her vigil, she concentrated her efforts on the Didionites, passing the intelligence along to Conrig by windspeaking Stergos or Vra-Doman Carmorton, Vanguard's irascible Chief Alchymist, as the prince had instructed her to do. It was necessary, Conrig said, that her continuing participation in the invasion be known and appreciated by the other nobles under his command, so they would support him when it came time to reward her.

She saw Somarus, the second son of Achardus, assemble a company of heavily armed knights and set out for Boarsden, the strongest inland fortress of the kingdom, where he intended to gather forces to defend against the expected invasion through Great Pass. Crown Prince Honigalus busied himself supervising the provisioning of the Royal Navy, but Ullanoth was unable to determine when he intended to set sail for the south. Perhaps, she told Stergos, Honigalus was awaiting some signal from his Continental allies before disembarking. Or vice versa, since she saw that the corsair fleets of Stippen and Foraile also remained in port. Cathra's navy, on the contrary, had finally taken up defensive stations in Cala Bay, patrolling the area between Castle Intrepid and the Vigilant Isles. The Tarnian mercenaries still awaited the arrival of the grain ships, which had been slowed by adverse winds.

When she was not scrutinizing the activities of the nations, she watched her brother, and was both surprised and dismayed to discover that he was obviously engaged in the lengthy process of abolishing her Fortress sigil, even though she could not descry the stone itself. It had never occurred to her that Fortress might have survived the destruction of her tower. From her arcane studies, she knew that there were supposed to be spells for delaying or even countering abolition of a stolen sigil; but she had never seen such spells in the archives of the Glaumerie Guild, so there was nothing she could do to prevent Beynor from taking her Fortress for himself. Indeed, if the abolition process kept him distracted for some days, unable to interfere in Conrig's invasion, then the loss of the moonstone would benefit her own cause in the end.

Scrying through Loophole was far more painful and exhausting than using any of her other sigils had been, and she could not bear to do it for longer than an hour or so at a time. When she left off her uncomfortable labors, she found herself taking refuge more and more in sleep, and she had to force herself to eat. High sorcery was obviously taking a greater physical toll on her than she had anticipated, and it worried her when she chanced to think about it. But for the most part she was too engrossed in the scrying—and too consumed with relief when she let herself stop—to be apprehensive about her health.

No one disturbed her in the secure warehouse. (She had banished the rats and mice early on with Beastbidder, and got rid of the spiders for good measure.) She left the place only to find water, more food, extra blankets against the increasing cold, and to use the clerk's necessarium at the end of the loading dock. She always went invisible, and used Interpenetrator to go through the brick walls like a phantom.

I feel I'm turning *into* a phantom, she thought in bemusement, returning gratefully to the warmth of the lamplit office after a brief night excursion. I've become nothing but an observer, watching events from afar in a haze of pain and torpor, participating in nothing except information-gathering.

And there were the dreams, their details all but forgotten when she woke. Dreams of the Great Lights . . .

Reluctantly, she finally had to accept that the powerful magic was changing her mentally as well as weakening her. She could not go on like this much longer, or she would be unable to assist Conrig as she had planned. She lacked the strength to Send herself to him now, and was shocked when she realized how strongly she missed the prince.

Surely, she thought, I can't really be falling in love with the man! But Conrig persistently intruded into her thoughts, and she could not resist windwatching him, even though she now only communicated with him through Stergos or Duke Tanaby's alchymist.

Finally, on the day Conrig's army left Castle Vanguard for the pass, something happened that jolted her back to her senses. She had bespoken Stergos in the middle of the night, telling him that conditions were fair for the invaders to proceed, then gone back to bed. Now, some time in mid-morn, she woke to discover that the fire in the office's iron stove had gone out. The room was bitterly cold, and she rekindled the blaze swathed in blankets, drowsy and grumbling. It occurred to her to heat up some pea soup with sausage she had made the day before, but when she groped for the pot in the shadowy room it felt strange.

Peering into the container, she cried out, "Moon Mother, save us!"

The soup was frozen solid.

A rush of dread energized her, and she threw off her blanket cloak and began to scramble into her clothes. It could be a fluke, a brief spasm of cold provoked, perhaps, by Beynor's futile attempt to blow away the fog with a northerly gale. But what if it wasn't?

Be calm! she told herself. Even if the worst had happened, there was yet a remedy.

But first she had to discover the truth. She would not act in haste, much less surrender to panic. After donning warm clothing she heated the soup and spooned some up while the room warmed around her. Then she took Subtle Loophole, arranged herself comfortably in a chair in front of the stove, and began to study the four great volcanos of Tarn. Their names were Donor, Mornash, Goldeye, and Thunderstone. They were thickly beclouded, but Loophole penetrated the vapors with ease, as her windsight had never been able to do.

And thus she discovered that the ash-vents of each mountain were almost sintered shut, with only plumes of harmless steam rising from them, and the crater rims were already dusted with snow. The Wolf's Breath had apparently come to an end. The abnormally mild autumns and winters that had attended it would no longer occur.

Had Beynor known this would happen? Is that why he'd dared to tell the Didionites he could stop the eruptions?

The warm weather she had depended upon to support the magical fog of the spunkies was probably over as well. Hard frosts would either turn the mist into flesh-freezing billows of tiny ice crystals, or else change the moisture into hoar, clearing the air and precipitating slippery white rime on the ground and everything resting upon the ground. Either outcome would be fatal to Conrig's invasion.

She let Loophole go inactive and opened the leather wallet where she kept the sigils when not wearing them. One by one she took them out and lay them in a row on one of the wine-clerks' desks. The empowered lesser stones glowed softly: Concealer, Interpenetrator, Beastbidder. Sender shone more brightly as she took it from her neck and placed it beside Subtle Loophole. Only the one remaining Great Stone had not yet been brought to life: her own Weathermaker.

I can fend off the cold and save Conrig's enterprise with this stone, she told herself. But in my present frail condition—dreaming of the Lights!—what will the empowering do to me?

Do I need him badly enough to risk my life for him?

Do I *love* him enough?

twenty-one

The army set out from Castle Vanguard at the third hour past midnight, covering the easiest part of the journey with every other pair of warriors bearing lanterns on poles cupped in their lance-rests. They were useless for lighting the way in the fog, but at least the riders were able to keep their places in the column through following the hazy glow ahead. The lanterns were quenched at full daylight, and not long afterward the army was forced to climb single-file, strung out over a distance of over two leagues. Periodically they would stop to rest, and there was a longer halt in late forenoon—perforce with the column remaining in place along the narrow trail—when the men ate a cold meal and watered the horses from skin bottles.

At last the Cathran invasion force reached a high plateau called Eaglefell, the first spot on the Breakneck Track where the entire cavalcade was able to gather all together on reasonably level ground. According to the scouts, the summit was not quite two leagues away. Unsaid but well understood was the fact that much of that distance was nearly vertical.

"From here on," Tanaby Vanguard told the war leaders, who had gathered apart from the other men, "the way becomes very precarious. We must now remove our chain mail and other armor and lash it behind our saddles, for our horses will have to be blindfolded and led by men afoot, and we will all climb better if we're unburdened. Now is also the time to intersperse pack mules and ponies with the coursers. As we travel we must keep at least a length apart, so that if an animal stumbles on the loose wet rocks and falls to its death, others will be less likely to panic and share its fate."

Thus far, the Cathrans had been lucky. Loosened horseshoes had been nailed back on by farrier-thanes. Three mounts had been lamed by stones, another broke its leg while attempting to move through a boulder-choked ravine, and a fifth lost its footing on a switchback and tumbled down a short slope while its rider leapt free unharmed. The injured animals had been mercifully dispatched and the men furnished with remounts.

The duke continued. "However, I have to tell you that there is reason for grave concern. With the fog hiding the sky and other timekeeping methods unreliable during our travels, we can judge the hour only roughly. My alchymist, Vra-Doman Carmorton, believes it may be as late as the third hour past noon-tide. If this is true, it will be impossible for us to reach the top of the pass before nightfall, two hours from now. We have not been able to travel as rapidly as hoped, and it seems that we may require as much as four more hours to attain the summit. Furthermore, as you have no doubt observed, the air has become significantly colder the higher we have climbed. Vra-Doman estimates it now to be only slightly above the frost-point. If the trail should become icy, many lives will certainly be lost. So I put it to you all: Shall we go on?"

Ramscrest spoke up in a crotchety rumble. "Wasn't the damned Mossland witch supposed to guarantee warm weather?"

"And so she did, my lord count," Conrig replied. "Vra-Stergos windspoke her this morn before we set out, and she assured him that all was well."

"And now it ain't!" Viscount Skellhaven declared flatly.

"Vra-Doman's time estimate may be overly conservative," the duke said. "It may be entirely possible to top the pass before dark."

"Booger the time," said the buccaneering nobleman. "What bothers me is this cold air. If we climb up into a hard frost, we're dead men. Slippin' and slidin' is only half of it. My lads've not got the right clothes to stave off chilblains and suchlike overnight. We believed His Grace when he promised it'd stay warm!"

"My friends," the prince broke in, "we can solve this dilemma easily enough. Vra-Stergos will windspeak Princess Ullanoth immediately and discover what manner of weather lies above us. Her scrying talent is far superior to that of our own alchymists, who cannot see through the fog."

"Can we be sure she'll tell us the truth?" asked Earl Marshal Beorbrook. "She wants this invasion as badly as you do, Your Grace, but she might have no qualms risking our lives on this hazardous track if she thought some of us might make it through. Such a risk is not acceptable to me!"

"Nor to me," Tanaby Vanguard said. Many of the other nobles concurred.

Conrig said, "Let's deal with one problem at a time, Godfather. If the upper trail is *not* frost-covered, would our army be able to traverse it safely in full dark, using lanterns?"

"Let me summon my chief scouts," said Vanguard. "I'm almost certain that it would be possible." He went off into a nearby group of his men, who had dismounted and were resting, and returned almost at once with two leather-faced thanes—one short, potbellied, and smiling, the other tall and slit-eyed, with a straggling ginger moustache.

"Here are Jass Easterdale and Ord Sedgewick," the duke said. "They know Breakneck Pass better than any of us." He put the prince's question to the pair, who knit their brows and whispered together.

Finally the amiable Easterdale spoke. "Your Grace, Earl Marshal, my lord Duke, there's a downslope breeze started not long ago, stirring the fog. This is a very bad sign. It could likely mean that it'll get much colder very soon, even though there's no frost above us as yet. If we stop here or on top, we could find ourselves trapped by morning with hoarfrost all over the rocks, unable to move, with nowhere for man nor beast to take shelter if a real gale should rise, bringing the deadly ice-mist . . . The safest thing to do is to turn back."

"No!" Conrig said.

The scout lifted his shoulders and rolled his eyes.

The others looked at the prince without speaking, and he felt as though a fist had been driven into his belly. Striving to maintain a calm demeanor, he spoke in even tones. "I will not endanger lives needlessly, but I refuse to abandon this enterprise until all the facts are known. Look here, Easterdale—"

"Call me Jass, Your Grace," the little man said cheerfully.

"Jass. If I could assure you that there's no frost above us, can you and your mates guide us to the summit of the pass, even in the dark?"

"It'd be hard doin', Your Grace, but we could. Going dead slow. But what about frost appearing later on? Can you predict the weather?"

None of the thanes or knights bachelor were aware that Ullanoth of Moss played a role in the strategy of the invasion, although Conrig's Heart Companions and the banner knights had been told. Everyone did know about the uncanny guides who were expected, and there had been much colorful speculation as to their nature.

Conrig said, "We *can* predict the weather, Jass—with arcane talent! One of the Brothers of Zeth will try to do so at once. Meanwhile, you and Ord Sedgewick decide how best we may proceed if all is well."

"We should send an advance party ahead of the main host, Your Grace," the scout said, "to lay out the campground in the best possible place and try to gather fuel. Even without frost, we'll freeze our patoots tonight unless we find some kind of sheltered spot and have hot food. I think there's small chance of fires being spotted from the Didion side of the frontier. Breakneck Heath is a kind of bowl, out of the wind and scattered with crags. I could remain in the van of the army as usual while Ord, here, goes on ahead with a few other lads to get things ready. They might even be able to ride part way to the top if they saddled up mules— though I wouldn't risk it with war horses."

The prince said, "Go ahead and get the mules ready, Jass." He turned to the nobles and spoke quietly. "I'll find Stergos and have him bespeak Ullanoth, and let's hope for the best."

The royal brothers went to a place apart and crouched together on inhospitable bare rock. Nothing grew on the plateau but yellow and black scabby lichen, reindeer moss, and a few alpine herbs. Fog eddied closely around Conrig and Stergos, and except for the reassuring sounds of the invisible men and their animals, the two of them might have been alone in a formless wasteland of grey.

The Doctor Arcanorum closed his eyes and let his head drop into his hands. After time had passed, with the prince waiting impatiently, he looked up, lids still shut. "She gives you greetings. She was asleep when I called."

"Ask her why in hell it's so cold up here," Conrig demanded baldly. "Tell her the air is nearly freezing and we face the prospect of having to turn back and abandon the invasion."

Stergos nodded. His lips tightened, and in spite of the chill his brow glistened with sweat. After remaining quiet for some minutes he opened his eyes. They were dark with concern.

"Con! Princess Ullanoth believes that the Wolf's Breath has ceased abruptly, with the result that the warm dry air of the past three autumns is being displaced by the arctic winds normal to this time of year in the north."

The prince started to his feet, cursing, but Stergos quieted him with an uplifted hand. "Don't despair. She says she possesses a Great Stone, a sigil called

Weathermaker, capable of temporarily holding back the cold until we have taken Holt Mallburn. The stone is not yet alive. If we decide to go forward, she will begin the empowerment procedure at once, and then immediately conjure the return of clement airs. The process will require about an hour, she says, although the warmth will take longer to reach us—perhaps three to four hours."

"Thank God we can proceed," Conrig cried, sinking back onto his haunches.

"There will be a price," Stergos went on. "Bringing a Great Stone to life causes atrocious suffering to the magical practitioner. She has only recently recovered from activating still another important sigil, one which enhances windsight, and she is debilitated from scrying our enemies with it. Empowering and then immediately using Weathermaker will probably leave her incapacitated for days. She'll be unable to Send herself to Redfern Castle's windwatchers and kill them while invisible, as she had originally planned. We'll have to manage it somehow ourselves."

"Snudge!" said the prince, brightening. "We'll send him in after the magickers. You know his trick of hiding . . ."

"There's also the matter of opening the gates at Mallmouth Bridge and the palace's gatehouse to our troops. The princess would have been able to perform both deeds, using other sigils of hers. But if she is disabled and helpless abed—"

"We'll find another way. Maybe she can advise us when we're outside the city. But if she doesn't use Weathermaker soon, we all could die up here on this thrice-bedamned mountain pass! Tell her that."

Stergos nodded, closed his eyes briefly, then opened them to stare at Conrig with an expression that combined anxiety and reproach. "Ullanoth says she will empower the Great Stone immediately. She . . . sends you all her love."

The prince said, "Tell her that I count the minutes until we are together again. Give her my heartfelt thanks for her loyalty and sacrifice. Say I will soothe her hurt with my own hands. Say anything, Brother, that will convince her to use that sigil!"

The alchymist bowed and resumed windspeaking at length. At last he opened his eyes with a deep sigh. "It's done."

"Good." Conrig assisted the alchymist to rise. "I'll inform the others. You find Snudge and tell him he's to accompany the advance party of scouts to the summit. One of Vanguard's men named Ord Sedgewick is saddling mules to push on ahead of the main body of the army. Tell the boy I expect him to bespeak you a report on what he finds up on top of Breakneck as soon as he arrives. I want to know just what kind of uncanny guides await us. I've had enough of nasty surprises this day."

Sedgewick and the four thanes who made up the rest of the advance scouting party were openly contemptuous when Snudge came and told them he would be going with them.

"Can't be lumbered with a green lad on a job like this," Ord said, not even bothering to look at Snudge. The chief scout was laboring to control a balky, powerful-looking mule that had been relieved of its pack. Three other animals, more placid of disposition, were still being unloaded by his men. "You go tell your prince we'll do fine without the likes of you giving us orders, messire."

"His Grace has commanded me to go," Snudge said humbly, "and we may not gainsay him. But I promise I won't be a burden. I'm not nobly born, you see, and I'm quite willing to follow your commands on the trail. I was a stable lad before Prince Conrig dubbed me his liege man, and I have a certain way with animals." Without asking leave, he took the bridle of the fractious mule, caught its eye, and stroked its head. Instantly, it left off misbehaving and stood as docile as a sheep, blowing gently.

"Frizzle me pizzle!" exclaimed Ord Sedgewick. He hastened to slap on a pad and saddle and tighten the girth. "The sod's not even holding his breath to bloat up and loosen the cinching."

"He wouldn't do that," Snudge said, scratching the beast's neck. "What's his name?"

"Primmie," said the scout. "Short for Primrose. Guess it's because he's a yellow dun. Picked him out because he looked big and strong, but he might not be fit to ride."

"I'll ride him," Snudge said. He began adjusting the stirrups, speaking softly to the animal, then swung up into the saddle, wheeled the mule easily about in a small circle, trotted to and fro in the fog, then dismounted and patted Primmie's flank. "He'll be fine. Shall I strap on my bags and bedroll and other things?"

Sedgewick studied the boy for a moment, frowning and tugging at his moustache. Then he said to one of the other scouts, "Rando, leave that mule for me and go tell Jass you're staying with him and the army. I guess we'll take this stable boy lordling along with us to the summit after all."

*   *   *

Except for distant glimpses when he had traveled with Prince Conrig's party to Castle Vanguard for the council of war, Snudge had no experience of mountains. His life had been spent in the coastal city of Cala, mostly in the environs of the palace. As the prince's footman, he'd accompanied Conrig on short trips to southshore castles such as Eagleroost, Defiant, and Intrepid, where there were soaring headlands and sea cliffs, moors and rolling hills. But never had he known the grandeur of real mountains, masses of living rock thrust from the bosom of the soil-covered land and only sparsely covered with trees and other plants, where level footing was hardly to be found.

The other armigers had told him he had something fine to look forward to.

Yet here he was, among some of the loftiest peaks on the island, unable to see a thing. Riding higher and higher, leaning so far forward in his saddle accommodating the steep angle of the dreadful track that his head nearly rested on the mule's mane, he knew nothing at all of his awesome surroundings. Now and then the beast put a foot wrong, but it never fell. Primmie didn't even need his soothing talent; the mule knew its business and ignored his efforts to prompt its movement.

Snudge rode at the tail-end of the small train, sunken in gloom, cold and aching in every joint, especially his knees, wondering whether the rest of the war was going to be as miserable and boring as this.

Stergos bespoke him silently twice, but there was nothing to report, not even the cry of a raven or an eagle. The only sounds were hooves clopping on wet rock, the creak of harness, the blowing of the four laboring animals, and the occasional rattle of stones falling into misty emptiness.

Finally Ord Sedgewick turned about in his saddle and called out, "It won't be long now. See how the track is less steep, and wider? Perhaps a quarter of an hour to go."

Snudge grunted. He was half asleep, having forgotten completely about the uncanny guides.

Until he heard them.

He jerked bolt upright, bringing a snort from Primmie, listening.

Windspeech! Not the human sort, but a murmurous piping whisper of alien talents bespeaking one another. There were far more than he could count, and after a bit he could distinguish what they said, even though the language was not his own.

Four humans. Ah!

Not the most succulent sort, but in this barren place perhaps the best we can hope for.

Hungry! Hungry!

NO.

We've come so far, Shanakin, fasting, fasting!

Not even furry animals here to slake our need. They all hide in the rocks from the cold and the oncoming night. Give us leave to take these men and their beasts.

NO.

Hungry! Hungry! These four come ahead of the others. They won't be missed. The lady will never know. We beseech you, Shanakin!

NO. I have promised her.

We must, we must! Our Lights grow faint. We are weak from making the fog. And hungry. So hungry.

NO. Wait. You must wait.

Monsters! Snudge sat petrified with fear, jaws clamped tight to keep from moaning aloud. His nearly invisible companions rode on unconcerned, speaking about the welcome prospect of soon being able to dismount and make a fire, not knowing that their lives were in peril from the very beings that Princess Ullanoth had entrusted their safety to.

Hungry. So hungry! These four won't be missed.

Wait. You must wait.

Who were these creatures? Not Salka, certainly, for their windvoices were very different from the brutes of Cala Bay, but some sort of maneater nevertheless.

Hungry.

NO. Wait!

A moment later Snudge heard the windvoice of Stergos bespeak him: *Deveron! Deveron, answer me.*

He almost responded with a frantic warning—catching himself just in time. What if the demonic things overheard him and were provoked to strike?

God's Teeth! he thought. What shall I do?

Then he saw the tiny white light, hanging an arm's length above his head, and stifled a shriek as Primmie braced all four legs and skidded to an abrupt halt.

You are different from the others, aren't you, boy? Interesting! I am Shanakin, ruler of the Small Lights. Bespeak me wordlessly, so as not to alert your companions.

Hoping to conceal his talent, Snudge whispered, "My lord, please don't eat us!"

The spunkie darted at him, striking his hooded head with a blow as sharp as a flung stone. Snudge muffled a yelp.

Did I not tell you to use windspeech, clodpate? Obey me!

He did so. "Yes, my lord. I'm sorry, my lord."

A wild talent. Very rare indeed. Does Princess Ullanoth know that you serve Conrig?

"No, my lord. Please don't tell her!"

Hah! Small chance of that. What's your name?

"Snudge." But not really . . .

Well, Snudge, you may rest assured that you and your companions will not be harmed by us so long as we are treated with respect. We are here to guide you. Our feeding will come later, as the Conjure-Princess has promised, but that needn't concern you.

"No, my lord. May I inform Prince Conrig of your presence here? He was anxious to know whether you and your—your subjects had arrived. That is why he sent me ahead with the scouts."

I have a better idea! Ride on now with your companions, and when you reach the summit I'll tell you about it.

Below, Prince Conrig struggled along leading his blindfolded courser, almost at the end of his strength. Every breath was painful. He could hardly lift his feet and found himself clinging to the reins, letting the blinded horse drag him as it was forced along by Stergos's beast pressing close at its heels. Only profane urging of the animals by the men afoot kept the column moving at all.

The lanterns had been lit. The sun was well down now and the last pinkish glow had faded from the shrouded sky. Though there was still light enough to see the ground beneath their feet, darkness would be upon them soon. So confusing was the fogbound terrain that not even Jass Easterdale and the experienced highland guides could estimate how far they were from the top of the pass. They could only guess that it must be fairly close now.

"Try to windspeak Snudge again," Conrig hissed to Stergos, who trudged miserably behind him.

"I've done nothing but try," mumbled the Doctor Arcanorum. "There's no answer. I even attempted to bespeak Princess Ullanoth, with no result. All we can do is continue on. At least it has not grown much colder."

Perhaps not, the prince thought in dejection, but neither was it any warmer. Men and beasts exhaled great clouds of vapor, and ominous white patches glittered here and there among the dark rocks when beams from the lanterns swept over them.

"Column, halt and stand easy," came the command, passed man to man down the line. Conrig, Stergos, Tanaby Vanguard, Beorbrook, and the Heart Companions were near the head of the force, preceded only by Count Ramscrest, a score of his handpicked knights, and the scouts.

Duke Tanaby's place was just ahead of the prince, and he drew close to the royal brothers so they could converse without being overheard.

"Godsons, we are coming to the end of our tether. Even the most valiant of the men are losing heart. Before long, they will start dropping from exhaustion and the army will be stalled dead on the trail, perhaps only a short distance from the summit. We should have sent either Vra-Doman or Vra-Stergos ahead with the scouts rather than your squire Deveron, so that we might keep in constant contact via windspeech at this crucial part of our journey and bolster our failing courage and strength. I know you didn't want to put either of the Brethren in peril, but—"

"We dared not send one of them," Conrig cut him off. "Neither is a man of action, with the stamina to keep up with your scouts, and I swore not to endanger their lives if it could be avoided."

"We should have brought along more talented men," the duke said wearily.

"I considered it, and I know that having only two alchymists accompany us was a calculated risk. But the gamble seemed necessary for security's sake, since we knew not how far Kilian's tentacles might have extended in the Order of Zeth. But so that you may not be anxious, Godfather, I'll confide in you: there is a third man of talent accompanying us, and he *did* go with the advance party."

"Bazekoy's Bones!" the duke exclaimed. "Surely you don't mean the boy—"

"Yes. My young liege man, Deveron, is a secret wild talent. This is how he was able to ferret out the spy at our council of war, and how he also confirmed my suspicion of Kilian's treachery. Deveron is not only capable of windspeech, he can also exert uncanny influence upon horses and move about so stealthily that only the keenest adept will notice him. I appointed him my intelligencer. Please tell no one of his talent, not even the earl marshal, for he is my private confidant as well as my secret weapon. He was instructed to bespeak Stergos frequently and survey the top of the pass for signs of our uncanny guides. He has not reported back for over an hour, however. God only knows why."

"I thought there was something odd about that lad! I'll say nothing of his talent, of course, but I pray he's worthy of your trust."

Conrig chuckled wryly. "So do I. And God help us all if he's a rogue, for he knows almost every detail of my strategy for Sovereignty." He wrapped his waterproof leather cloak more tightly about him. "The devil take this cold and damp! Even if there is no frost, we'll perish if we spend the night marooned on this track—"

"Con!" Stergos cried, in a voice suddenly full of joy. He had moved back at the duke's approach, but now slithered forward again, around the prince's blindfolded horse.

"What is it?" said Conrig eagerly. "Have you windspeech from Snudge?"

When Stergos's face fell in dismay at having the boy's secret spoken of before the duke, Conrig hastened to reassure. "Our godfather now knows that I employ a wild talent, Gossy. Speak freely."

"He's at the head of our column, come down from the summit on muleback, while leaving the other scouts to organize the camp! We have less than three hundred ells to go before reaching the top! Even now, the good word is traveling down the column."

"God be thanked!" Tanaby cried. Other happy exclamations could be heard echoing among the rocks above.

"The boy says he brought our guides with him," Stergos continued. "Let's go forward and see."

Newly energized, they gave the reins of their mounts over to others and struggled up the exiguous trail. They collected Beorbrook as they went, passed Ramscrest's knights and the scouts, who were laughing and chattering with relief, and finally reached the thickset count himself, clad all in waxed leather and standing with his back to a tall rock at a sharp turn in the trail where there was a bit more room. His arms were crossed over his chest and he glowered fiercely at Snudge, who sat his mule.

"Your Grace, Lord Stergos, Earl Marshal, my lord Duke," Snudge said solemnly, bowing in the saddle. "Since the day is so far advanced, our good guides agreed to accompany me, so that our forces may be brought safely to the summit even in full darkness. The track ahead is very difficult."

"But where the hell *are* the guides?" Ramscrest bellowed. "This young knave refuses to tell me!"

Abruptly, the fog seemed to explode with a thousand sparks of golden light. They wreathed Snudge and his stolid mount and extended in a sinuous dancing swarm along the zig-zag switchback trail above the halted army. Where the bits of brilliance hovered, the fog now began to vanish, leaving a tunnel of clear air no higher than a horse's head. As Conrig and the others watched open-mouthed, the flood of tiny glowing things flowed over and past them going downhill, banishing both fog and darkness for the cheering warriors following behind.

"God's Breath!" Beorbrook exclaimed. "They're spunkies!"

One of Ramscrest's knights, an ox-like young stalwart named Ruabon Lifton, gave a loud, uneasy guffaw. "Swive a swan, lads! It's the silly little bogles our mums and nursemaids used to threaten us with when we were naughty children! Remember how they said spunkies'd carry us off and drain our blood if we stayed too long outside in the evening? And now the same willy-wisps will light our way to camp. Spunkies as guides! What a great joke!"

The tiny sparks flared and a tinkling hiss, oddly menacing, filled the frigid air.

"They prefer to be called Small Lights," Snudge announced. "The other name they consider offensive."

Ruabon went off into gales of near-hysterical mirth, joined by a few of his companions. "Do they! Well, futter me if I give a damn, though they're well-met in this fog, for all that."

Even Conrig was smiling as he turned to Vanguard and Ramscrest. "What do you think, my lords? Will the Virago and our other wary friends be satisfied with the benign aspect of our guides?"

"I can't think why not," Tanaby said.

"It's incredible!" the earl marshal exclaimed. "They can dissolve the bloody fog!"

"That's because they made it, my lord," said Snudge.

"You can talk to them?" Tanaby Vanguard said, amazed.

"To their leader only, lord Duke, who awaits you at the summit meadow, where you may speak to him, too, if you wish. May I suggest that you now mount up and follow me? The trail from here on is very steep but not as narrow as previously, and your horses should not be distressed with their eyes uncovered, moving inside the lighted tunnel. They won't be able to see much outside of it." He wheeled about. "Follow me when you're ready."

Ramscrest asked the prince, "Who the hell is this armiger of yours? A wizard in disguise?"

"Only a brave and intelligent young man," Conrig replied easily, "whom I value highly. Fall in close behind me, Munlow, and I'll tell you something about him as we go."

It was very late when the entire army finally gathered safely on the summit, not that the time could be ascertained with any accuracy, save by the empty bellies and sore muscles of the men. The spunkies arranged themselves in a low dome above the campsite, obliterating the groundmist beneath and providing dim illumination to the area. Snudge had been given assurance that the glow of the uncanny creatures would be imperceptible to an enemy windwatcher because of the thick layer of fog remaining overhead.

The high meadow had proved to be strewn with large rocks, but was mercifully free of boggy ground. Because of the dampness of the air, the scouts had thus far been unable to light any fires. Stergos and Doman ordered the men to whack down more brush and dead bracken with their blades and axes, making twenty or so sodden heaps scattered about the site. Then the two alchymists gingerly broke apart several tarnblaze bombshells, distributed the contents, and ignited chymicals and wet fuel with their talent. While the army huddled near the fires, volunteers cooked up cauldrons of hot oatmeal porridge, which was served with ample quantities of cold meat and mead. Nobles and thanes received identical meals, including a tot of spirits as a nightcap.

There was insufficient burnable material to keep fires going long for warmth, so the warriors made do as best they could laying out their saddles as pillows, improvising groundcloths from their leather cloaks, and donning all the clothing they had brought with them. The lighter-clad seagoing warriors took the spots nearest to the fires and commandeered the smelly load-pads of the sumpter beasts for mattresses and coverings. A single small tent was set up to shelter the non-combatant Brothers of Zeth, who were unused to sleeping rough, but everyone else—including the prince—was resigned to a cold night in the open.

Before the army retired, Conrig gave a brief speech.

"We've successfully covered the worst terrain in our journey without losing a man. Well done!" There were perfunctory cheers. "Redfern Castle, a small Didionite fortress, lies about five-and-twenty leagues away downhill. Tomorrow, we'll set out as soon as the track can be seen, guided by our uncanny allies, the Small Lights. They have assured me that no other outposts of enemy warriors are emplaced between the pass and the castle. A force of fifty knights led by Lords Cloudfell and Catclaw will descend first, hooves muffled, and array themselves out of sight in the fog, near the castle's drawbridge. Another magical ally of ours, who is already hidden inside the castle, will lower the bridge and open the gate for our attacking force. This ally is already known to some of you: she is Ullanoth, Conjure-Princess of Moss, a great friend of Cathra, whose help will enable us to conquer Didion."

The thanes, who had not known the identity of the mysterious "magical ally" assisting Conrig's cause, although they were aware that the person had recruited the spunkies, greeted this information with ambiguous murmurs.

Conrig continued. "Redfern will fall into our hands like an overripe fruit. And we need not worry that its windvoices will warn Holt Mallburn of our invasion— for the same powerful princess who opens the castle gates to us will already have silenced those voices. Once we have secured Castle Redfern, we'll rest for a day before moving on as swiftly as possible to Holt Mallburn. That's all I wish to say to you men tonight. But before we sleep I will introduce you to the being responsible for bringing us safely to this place—who also caused the magical fog that has shielded us from the windsight of our foe."

Conrig paused, looking up. From the fuzzy glowing dome above came a whirling ball of several dozen golden sparks, looking like a swarm of incandescent bees. The ball hovered before the prince, who inclined his head politely, whereupon the golden bits of radiance were extinguished, leaving a single blue-white Small Light floating alone.

"I am Shanakin," said a distinct high-pitched voice. Conrig felt the flesh at the back of his neck crawl, remembering what Snudge had told him about these creatures. He wondered whether anyone else had experienced a similar touch of grue, and cursed Ullanoth for not telling him the truth about the spunkies— whatever it might be.

"My people are not friends of humankind," Shanakin said. "For the sake of the Conjure-Princess only are we here, serving you. Remember that and have respect! We are Small Lights, but we have our ways—as many humans know to their everlasting sorrow."

The ball of sparkling attendants reappeared, hiding their tiny ruler, and all of them wafted up into the formless glowing dome.

The men remained still as statues for a moment, then relaxed and began to laugh nervously and whisper among themselves.

"Go to your beds now," Conrig told them. "All will be well." He turned to the collection of nobles and the two alchymists standing behind him at the central fire. "Lady Zea, my lords, you should also retire . . . Vra-Doman, I have brief need of the tent you and my brother will occupy tonight. Please remain here for a few minutes while I confer in it with Vra-Stergos."

"Certainly, Your Grace," said the long-faced magicker, heaving a put-upon sigh. "I'll just say my night prayers—if I can recall them after that unsettling exhibition. Spunkies! Saint Zeth preserve us!"

Conrig took his brother's arm and guided him to the small canvas pavilion, on the way passing Snudge and the other armigers. "You there, Deveron! Come with me and the doctor. I have an errand for you."

"Yes, Your Grace."

There was scarcely room inside the tent for the two bedrolls already laid out. Conrig sat on one and gestured for Stergos to take the other. Snudge crouched between them at the closed doorflap. "Scry the area to be sure that no one comes near," the prince ordered, and the boy nodded. Then Conrig told Stergos, "Please attempt to bespeak Princess Ullanoth."

The alchymist closed his eyes and remained motionless for many minutes. Then he whispered, "She is silent. It was to be expected. The woman is doubtless totally prostrate with the effort of empowering her third Great Stone."

Snudge gasped at the appalling news. "Prostrate? Not even able to wind-speak us?"

"It's what we feared might happen," said the prince grimly. He explained to the boy how the Conjure-Princess had used her Weathermaker to foil the onset of the deadly cold, even though she was already weakened by bringing the Loophole stone to life. "So it's obvious we can expect no help from her silencing the wind-voices at Redfern Castle or opening its gates to our troops. We must devise an alternative plan."

"You want me to do it," Snudge said, without surprise.

"Your talent for hiding was good enough to deceive Vra-Kilian's novices and the Royal Guard at Cala Palace. It's unlikely that powerful adepts will be stationed at a minor fort such as Redfern . . . Of course, the enemy windvoices cannot merely be captured and bound."

Stergos gave an involuntary cry of dismay. "Con—he's only a boy!"

Snudge's voice was remote. "I understand, Your Grace. They must be absolutely prevented from using their talent."

The prince said, "You are a man, Deveron, not a child, as both of us know, and must do a man's hard duty. The windvoices are not warriors, but neither are they innocent bystanders in this war. They *must* be silenced."

Snudge said nothing.

"Do you think you can get inside the castle?" Stergos asked anxiously.

"I've just thought of a scheme that might work, my lord. And with luck, hardly any of our people need know that it was not Princess Ullanoth who quelled the windvoices and opened the castle gate." He hesitated. "Will she have recovered by the time we reach Holt Mallburn?"

"God only knows. Tell us your plan for Redfern."

The boy did, omitting only the way he intended to deal with the castle's magickers, knowing the prince would say him nay. "I'll have to work out some details. But I'm a harmless-looking young fellow, and if I can be certain of offering an irresistible bribe—"

"See Duke Tanaby tomorrow morning before you leave," Conrig said. "Tell him I said to give you anything you want."

"Thank you, Your Grace." Snudge opened the tent flap. "I'll try to get some sleep now, if I can . . . And to think I was bored nearly to death just this afternoon!" He disappeared.

The Doctor Arcanorum could no longer hold back his indignation. "Con, he's only sixteen! He slew the spy Iscannon in self-defense, but you've just ordered him to kill unarmed men in cold blood."

"Pray to Saint Zeth for him," the prince said without emotion, climbing to his feet. "Pray also for Ullanoth. If she doesn't recover promptly, we may be forced to call upon poor Snudge for even more crucial assistance. Just think about it, Gossy! The Emperor Bazekoy said that my hope for Sovereignty depends upon the help of a dying king. Is it any more preposterous for the key factor to be a wild-talented stable boy? . . . I bid you good night."

With that, Conrig pushed out of the little tent and went towards the central fire to tell Vra-Doman that he could retire.

But he stopped short at the sight of Munlow Ramscrest. The stout count stood there in the golden murk, flanked by two of his knights, holding a large, sagging bundle in his powerful arms. Conrig realized that it was a body wrapped in a military cloak. "What's happened?" he demanded.

"It's Sir Ruabon, my youngest knight," Ramscrest said, "a brave lad with an over-ready tongue. These two friends of his found him when they went to make water behind yonder crags. Uncover his face, my prince."

For a moment, Conrig was frozen with apprehension. Then he lifted the flap of leather. The burly knight's countenance was shrunken and stretched tight over his skull. He looked like a wasted invalid, nearly fleshless and as pale as clay.

Ramscrest said, "There is no mark on his body. Yet he's little more than skin and bones."

"God grant him peace." The prince met the older man's eyes. "We know who must have committed this savage deed. What would you have me do, Munlow?"

"Only we four know of this," Ramscrest replied. "Poor Ruabon was a fool to insult the spunkies, yet did not deserve to die like this. But I can't condemn our great enterprise to failure on his behalf . . . most especially since there is no way of taking vengeance on the wee shites who murdered him. The lad's death is part of the fortunes of war. We'll bury him quietly 'neath a cairn and carry on. We can do naught else." He fixed Conrig with an adamant eye. "However, Princess Ullanoth must admonish her uncanny minions to make certain this doesn't happen again. Please see to it, Your Grace."

"My brother Stergos will windspeak her in the morning and transmit my command. As for Ruabon Lifton, his family will share equally in the reward given to all by my Sovereignty. We'll bring home his ashes when our army returns to Cathra victorious."

Ramscrest only grunted.

"I have good news that you may spread among the men," the prince added. "Within an hour or so, this cursèd cold should be completely gone. Ullanoth is conjuring it away at this very moment. Nothing should impede us in our march to Redfern Castle."

"More bloody magic!" the mountain lord growled. He bared his teeth in a snarl of frustration, then spat out an oath. "Why can't we fight this war like honest warriors?"

"Because we'd lose," the prince told him. "Come. I'll help you bury Ruabon, and then we must try to sleep."

twenty-two

Ullanoth dreamed of them. They were enormous: so bright, so terrible, so eager to engulf her suffering self. Her anguish fed them in some arcane fashion, and they drank of her for hours on end and then let her go, laughing at her relief, dancing off into the night sky, shrinking, vanishing. Leaving only stars above her and that marvelous freedom from excruciating pain.

Still dreaming, she lay on a flat rock at the water's edge, dressed in a thin sendal shift, not daring to breathe, knowing that the respite couldn't last, exposed as she was to the icy Boreal wind that swept in from the sea. She felt gooseflesh rise and her teeth begin to chatter, and fought not to inhale for that meant surrender. But a terrible shudder suddenly racked her, forcing her to fill her lungs with air so frigid that the tender membranes kindled with agony. As though this were some perverse signal, the rest of her body started to afflict her all over again: the pounding head, the aching muscles, the fierce gnawing in her belly.

Soon they'll be back to feast again, she realized in despair. They gave and now they take. The balance is in the exchange, and to submit is to survive. I willingly endure this only for the sake of my great goal and not for his sake. Never for his sake. Never . . .

"Never!" she cried aloud, and at the sound of her own voice, Ullanoth woke.

The cracks between the closed shutters of the warehouse office showed a faint grey light; it had to be nearly dawn. She had more than slept the clock around. The only sounds were the creak of the cooling iron stove and wind sighing around the eaves of the building. For the moment she was free of the pain of Weathermaker's empowerment—but still not without a certain nagging discomfort. Dazed from sleep (she had forgotten the dream), she was at a loss to understand what was wrong with her until her guts writhed insistently, reminding her that the Great Stone's ordeal had its ignoble aspects. There was no helping it. Weak as she was, she'd have to go outside. With a muttered oath she emerged from her cocoon of warmth and began to draw on clothes, stockings, and boots. Then she took up Concealer and Interpenetrator and hung them about her neck.

Invisible, she passed through the locked and barred door that gave onto the quay and made her way very slowly to the necessarium overhanging the water at the end of the winesellers' pier. No trading ships were docked there. With the near-cessation of normal commerce on account of the famine, this southernmost area of Mallburn Quay near the great river was virtually deserted. Even the stews and taverns were boarded up, and only a few small coaster vessels were tied at the adjacent slips and wharves belonging to other merchants. A lamptender with a ladder, accompanied by an armed guard, was extinguishing the tall streetlights along the waterfront one by one.

She took care of her body's needs, then let her disinterested gaze roam about the big harbor. She'd never seen it at dawn, and its aspect was oddly unfamiliar. The tide was high and the sky to the east, above a fog bank at the mouth of Didion Bay, glowed a muddy crimson. Thanks to her magical labors of the day before, the air was only moderately chilly. In spite of the brisk breeze from the west, a thin mist blurred the scene, but the far shore where the shipyards and naval installations lay was distinct enough in the half-light. The uncanny dense fog generated by the spunkies had not yet reached the city, but it would surely do so by tomorrow.

The princess hobbled back toward her sanctuary, stopping frequently to rest, wishing she had thought to bring some sort of walking stick. Every step brought increasing pain in her legs, and her head had begun to throb, perhaps from lack of food. She would scratch up a simple meal of biscuit, dried meat, and wine, eat it in bed, then sleep again even though she knew she would suffer while dreaming. The debt must be paid, and as quickly as possible.

Behind the semicircular quay, the rising expanse of Mallburn Town revealed streetlights only in the privileged Golden Precinct. The rest was dark, having been abandoned at night to the lawless and the desperate. Holt Mallburn Palace, situated high on a parklike wooded hill a league inland, had its walls and battlements ablaze with fire-baskets. She paused and automatically attempted to wind-watch the palace's inhabitants, but her unaided talent was now too diminished to penetrate the massive stone walls of the fortress. The Loophole sigil was no option for spying, either. In her present weakened state, the pain of its conjuring would probably render her senseless.

You pathetic thing! she thought. Wobbly as a newborn lamb, and about as dangerous! How can you hope to help Conrig take this huge city? All of the plans they had made earlier were rendered useless by her disability. The Cathran army was due to arrive in two days, but she would hardly have regained her full strength by then. Who would open the gate for Conrig at the great bridge on the River Malle? Who would admit his force to Holt Mallburn Palace itself?

Yesterday, bespeaking Stergos before empowering the new sigil, she had been optimistic. But she had badly underestimated the price Weathermaker would extract from her already weakened body.

I'm no good to him now! The thought came to her without volition as she leaned against the wall of the winesellers' warehouse and stared blankly at the harbor. His invasion will fail through my fault. He'll either die in battle or retreat to Cathra in defeat, and meanwhile the Royal Navy of Didion will sail south, link up with the Continental fleet, and—

Navy!

Comprehension hit her like a thunderbolt. She'd been too thickheaded to appreciate what her naked eyes had already shown her: the forty-odd warships that had been moored in the harbor and tied up at large piers on the northern end of the quay were no longer there. Conrig's slim hope that his invading army might arrive in time to stop the fleet from moving against Cathra was dashed. The armada of Crown Prince Honigalus had sailed on the dawn tide with a fair wind to carry it out of the bay.

I must warn him!

She re-entered the warehouse and collapsed on her improvised bed, clawing at Concealer and Interpenetrator to get them away from her body, sparing herself that insignificant discomfort at least. But the consequences of the empowerment once again began to overwhelm her, even before she fell fully asleep. The stabbing in her belly, the dizziness, the crushing weakness, the irresistible compulsion to yield to unconsciousness and pay the Great Lights their due of pain . . .

I can't! Not yet!

She fought with all her will to remain awake, demanding that her body obey. Focusing whatever mental strength remained to her on that single need, she cried out and felt her muscles convulse, then subside into a deadly languor—no longer hurting.

Oh, yes! Thank you, Mother!

Her breathing had become shallow and rapid. Fever burnt at her temples and flooded down her neck, engulfing her body, but she was awake. She reached for a nearby beaker of water. Her trembling hand upset the pottery container, causing it to tip and spill its precious contents onto the dirty wooden floor.

Very well, forget that. Concentrate on windspeaking the message! It would be impossible to reach Vra-Sulkorig in Cala Palace, so she must tell Stergos. First, visualize the countenance of the Doctor Arcanorum, target of the bespeaking—

Oh, Moon Mother, have mercy. *I can't see him.*

Try as she might, she could not bring Stergos's gentle round face to mind, much less the face of the other alchymist accompanying the army. Even her memory of Conrig was dimmed to nullity by her dazed brain. The realization sent a gush of stark terror through the pain-free lethargy that temporarily sheltered her.

Mother, what am I to do?

There was only one hope. She could attempt a general outcry on the wind. It was a form of bespeaking that might be overheard by any adept within range, more tenuous than directed communication, susceptible to blockage by dense matter such as solid rock. The brick wall of the warehouse would be relatively transparent to it, but not Holt Mallburn's granite bastions, nor the keeps of the other Didionite castles within range. She must make the message brief yet unmistakable. The enemy would probably not overhear her, but if Conrig's magickers had already crossed the massif of the Dextral Mountains at Breakneck Pass, there was a good chance at least one of them might understand.

I'll put all the power I have left into the one cry, she decided. For now, it's all I can do.

The two Brothers of Zeth, relegated to the Cathran army's rearguard to protect them from danger, were still in the bowl-shaped summit heath, shielded from the flimsy windcry by the intervening rocks. Prince Conrig, riding with Cloudfell and Catclaw so as to be in the fore of the assault, possessed too meager a talent to grasp the message. The only one who heard was Snudge—far ahead of the others, being guided by spunkies to Castle Redfern in the first light of dawn. That faintest of bespoken cries came to him:

Warships gone.

"Codders!" The boy hauled on Primmie's reins, and the mule halted so abruptly that he nearly flew over its head.

The handful of dancing sparks that surrounded the mounted boy began to cheep and squeak like a nest of disturbed starlings. Unlike their ruler, they did not speak the language of humankind, although an adept could understand their windspeech readily enough.

"Oh, be still!" Snudge hissed at the tiny beings.

He closed his eyes, slumping in the saddle, and attempted to follow the strange cry back to its origin, but it was less a thread than an amorphous web, and might have come from anywhere. After that failure he tried to windsearch Didion Bay for a sight of the fleet, but the waters a few leagues east of the enemy capital city were heavily shrouded in a dense fog that was creeping toward the land. If the ships were out there, no ordinary windwatcher could see them.

He bespoke Stergos, who was dozing in his saddle alongside Vra-Doman Carmorton, waiting for his turn to take to the trail.

"My lord, wake up! Don't disturb your companion. Wake up, I say, and respond to me stealthily in windspeech. It's Snudge. I believe I've received a message from Princess Ullanoth!"

There was a silence on the wind, broken by an incoherent murmur that eventually resolved itself into a bespoken reply.

Snudge? What are you telling me?

"Lord Stergos, I heard a peculiar undirected message on the wind: *Warships gone.* I believe it can only have come from the princess. We know she is very weak after empowering her Weathermaker. Perhaps she could only transmit those two words, without aiming them at a specific person. I think she meant to tell us that the Didionite fleet has set sail for the south. You must alert the Royal Alchymist at Cala Palace. Say that you were the one who received the message: *Warships gone.* Let them make of it what they will."

Oh, Blessed Zeth. This is dreadful! I'd better press to the front of the column and tell the prince and see what he thinks. He hoped we might reach Holt Mallburn in time to stop the fleet—

"My lord, no offense. Stop waffling! Tell His Grace later if you must, but pass on the information to Vra-Sulkorig at Cala without delay. Is that clear?"

The reply was surprisingly meek. *Quite clear, my boy. Thank God you were able to receive it . . . You know, I'm praying for the success of your own mission.*

"Thank you, my lord."

I also pray—I mean—oh, Deveron! Are you certain that your scheme will enable you to accomplish your task without shedding the blood of Redfern's wind adepts?

"As I told you, with luck—and with the special goods I packed on my mule— I'll manage."

I know my brother charged you with a warrior's duty, but he's a ruthless man and you're—ah, you're—

"I'm Conrig's liege man. Farewell, Doctor. If you do speak to His Grace, tell him he can depend on me."

Snudge opened his eyes to the ghostly mountainside and thumped Primmie gently in the ribs. Obediently, the loaded mule continued downslope on rag-wrapped hooves. It was an intelligent beast for all its bad temper, and it had quickly learned to follow the parade of five glowing specks that wafted just ahead of it, floating a foot or so above the ground.

Queen Cataldise opened the door to the king's bedchamber when she heard the gentle scratching. "Vra-Sulkorig. It's rather early. Has something important happened?"

The Acting Royal Alchymist's face lit up at the sound of notes being plucked expertly from a lute. "His Grace is awake, then?" The time was shortly after dawn.

The queen sighed. "Revising his Deathsong again. He slept poorly last night and did not wish to waste the time. I've also had very little sleep. What do you want?"

"I do have significant news, Your Grace."

The lute music stopped. "Well, come and tell me about it, man!" growled the king.

Sulkorig approached the enormous bed. The ailing monarch was propped up on a pile of pillows, holding the stringed instrument. His lap table held parchment and writing materials, and he was surrounded by ranks of lighted candelabra on silver-gilt stands.

"Lord Stergos has received a two-word windspoken message: *Warships gone.* He believes it came from Princess Ullanoth in the Didionite capital city, but cannot be sure. The lady herself is supposedly in ill health after accomplishing some notable feat of magic. The Doctor Arcanorum believes we must take the message very seriously and presume that the war fleet of Crown Prince Honigalus has set sail from Holt Mallburn and intends to attack Cala."

Olmigon nodded slowly. He began to retune one of the lute strings, picking at it in a finicky fashion. "Did you have our own Brothers scry up Didion way?"

"Your Grace, the distance is too far, even for our most talented windwatchers working in unison. If the winds are favorable to them, the enemy ships might reach the vicinity of the Vigilant Isles in four to five days." The alchymist tactfully accommodated the king's failing memory. "Didion's fleet strength, as you know, is around forty men o' war, with at least eighteen triple-tier barques carrying up to sixty guns apiece and more than twenty two-decker frigates with twenty-six guns or more. All of the heavy warships might not have sailed, of course."

Olmigon finished his tuning and strummed an ominous minor chord. "What about the damned Continentals?"

"Teams of adepts riding small sloops have been plying the Dolphin Channel, keeping watch twenty-four hours a day, as closely as their powers allow. So far, there seems to be no suspicious movement of ships from ports in Stippen or Foraile."

"And the Tarnian mercenaries?"

Sulkorig's grave expression brightened. "There, at least, we have good tidings. I didn't wish to disturb your rest unnecessarily, but late last night we were bespoken by the shaman of Sealord Yons Stormchild. Our grain ships have made port, and he has ordered twenty well-armed frigates, carrying extra supplies of tarnblaze, to sail south on the dawn tide."

"Thank God!" cried Cataldise.

Olmigon glowered. "You should have come and told me—whatever the hour."

"Of course, Your Grace. From now on, it will be done." The wizard's eyes slid reproachfully toward those of the queen, who looked innocent. On her orders, the king had remained undisturbed.

"See that our captains at sea are informed."

"It's already done, Your Grace."

"Very well, you may leave us."

The alchymist bowed and made his exit. King Olmigon gave his wife a level stare and then bent over his lute, playing a brief, haunting melody as nicely as any court minstrel. By ancient custom he was forbidden to sing the song aloud until the time that he felt death approaching. "What do you think?" he said. "Isn't that tune better than the old one?"

She had seated herself in an easy chair near the candles and opened a book. Now she looked up at him with tears glinting in her eyes. "My love, you must satisfy yourself. The song is your own to compose, and I know you are obliged to do it. But the thought of your singing it breaks my heart."

"Sweet Catty!" The king chuckled. "I need a more stringent music critic for an honest opinion. Bring Maudrayne to see me later today. She's never shy about telling me what she thinks."

The queen gave a little start. "But . . . our daughter-in-law is ill, as you know. A weakness of the chest brought on by the long journey to Zeth. She still cannot leave her apartment."

"Then I'll go visit her. I'm feeling lively enough today. You come, too. We can all have tea together. Why, I haven't seen the dear girl in over a week."

"No!" Cataldise said wildly. "I mean—she is in no condition to receive us. The alchymists have forbidden her visitors."

Olmigon frowned, setting his lute aside. "If Maudie is so seriously ill, why wasn't I told? You know how I feel about her. What the hell's wrong?"

The queen burst into tears.

"Stop that!" the king thundered. "Madam, tell me at once what ails the Crown Princess!"

After much sniffling into her lace handkerchief, Queen Cataldise confessed what had been done on Conrig's orders. "Maudrayne threatened to leave him, to run away to Tarn. Con even feared she might compromise his invasion plans out of spite. She thinks he betrayed her with another woman, but it's all nonsense—"

"What other woman?"

"Ullanoth of Moss," the queen admitted reluctantly. "But Con assured me it wasn't so! He's a faithful husband who only wishes to protect Maudrayne from her own folly."

The king lowered himself to his pillows, groaning. "The witch! Of course it would be the witch." He hauled himself up again, eyes burning. "Who's giving Maudie the vile potions? That sour-faced old prune Sovanna Ironside?"

"Stergos gave Lady Sovanna appropriate medicines for the princess before he left the palace. He assured me they were entirely harmless. Vra-Sulkorig has also attended Maudrayne when it seemed . . . when she was too apathetic to eat. But she is in excellent health now, except for being languid and disinclined to cause trouble."

"Maudie? Languid? Great God, woman! The drugging must stop at once. I command it."

"She'll run away." The queen's dolorous face took on an obstinate expression. "That must not happen. I promised Conrig that his wife would be here when he returned victorious."

"Then lock her in her bloody chambers," Olmigon raged. "But no more filthy poisons. Swear it to me!"

More tears began to trickle from the queen's eyes. She nodded blindly. "I swear on my soul that I'll do as you say. But we can't allow her to run away to Tarn and put Con to shame on the very eve of his Sovereignty."

Olmigon's face had gone red and his eyes bulged in fury. "Humiliate Conrig? What about poor Maude's humiliation if our son lied about Ullanoth? What about—" He broke off with a sudden cry, more a cough than a grunt, clutching at his upper arm. When he was able to speak again his voice was querulous and nearly inaudible. "Catty. Oh, God, how it hurts."

Queen Cataldise leapt up from her chair and came to him. "Husband?"

But he had fallen back onto the pillows, his eyes half-closed and his lips gone blue. The queen fled from the room in a panic, screaming for the alchymists.

twenty-three

*W*e have reached the ruined outpost, human. It lies on your left, halfway up the wall of the ravine—what's left of it.

Hee hee! You can't see in the fog, but a great rock came down on the guardhouse roof and smashed it to flinders. This is the place where you wanted to stop. We're about halfway to the place you call Redfern.

Snudge reined in Primmie. "We'll rest for a while, old boy. There's a bit of grass and you can have some water." He dismounted and led the mule to the stream that paralleled the downhill track through the gorge. The mist was thinner there and a sizable pine tree grew on the bank. Bending and stretching, he smote his aching inner thighs with closed fists. After a cold drink, he sat down on an exposed tree root and began to chew on a piece of sausage.

Between bites he addressed the spunkies: "My friends, two of you please go on ahead and look for enemy humans on the trail. I doubt any patrol will venture far from the castle in this fog, but we have to be sure. Douse your lights and fly as fast as you can, and return quickly to tell what you've found."

Tinkling giggles. *And if we find a wandering Didionite patrol, may we eat it?*

"No, God damn it! Remember what Shanakin told you. No feeding! If you must, frighten the soldiers back to the castle or lead them astray to their doom. But if you drink their blood, I'll see that your master punishes you severely."

Spoilsport!

Two sparks winked out and Snudge presumed the little beings were on their way. He hoped they'd follow orders and restrain themselves.

In spite of attempts to keep Sir Ruabon's murder secret, numbers of the knights had found out about it from the dead man's two friends and reacted with both anger and apprehension. The mutinous undercurrent was halfhearted thus far. But if the attack force, which had set out from the summit an hour or so after Snudge, should chance upon a heap of eerily drained Didionite corpses, the consequences might be disastrous.

"You other Small Lights," Snudge said, beckoning, "gather near me. I have something to show you."

The three remaining spunkie guides hovered expectantly before the boy. For this special mission, he had left his armor, gambeson, military cloak, and armiger's weaponry with Ord Sedgewick. He wore his spare outfit, a simple wool tunic and trews, and had a raggedy pony-blanket as an improvised cape. He pulled from his shirt a small thing that hung on a thong around his neck and slowly removed its covering. The sigil named Concealer glowed softly in the murk.

Yeee! squealed the creatures. *A Hiding Stone!*

"So you know what this is. Good! I'm going to use it to accomplish my task at Castle Redfern. As a matter of fact, I intend to make myself and the mule invisible from here on during our journey, so that I can get used to it. I've never done this sort of thing before."

There followed a distressed chittering. *Bad magic! Great Light magic! You'll be sorry if you use it, human.*

Snudge felt his heart thudding in his breast. I'm not afraid! he told himself, and turned his back on the agitated spunkies, tucking the sigil into his clothing so that it rested against his bare flesh. Then he swung himself back into the mule's saddle and spoke the words that would render him and the animal invisible.

"BI DO FYSINEK. FASH AH."

The commotion made by the spunkies was cut off as by a slamming door. Night fell abruptly: black, icy, star-strewn. Overhead hung a single slow-blooming patch of gauzy scarlet radiance shot through with restless beams of pale green. A sepulchral voice—one he'd heard before—spoke from the sky.

CADAY AN RUDAY?

Oh, shite!

Panic seized him. It wasn't supposed to happen this way! Red Ansel had never warned him he might have to speak to the Light again when he first used the sigil . . . What were the bloody words? What what what?

Yes!

"GO—GO TUGA LUVKRO AN AY COMASH DOM."

KO AN SO? Asking his name.

"Dev—" No, you dungpoke, not your true name! "SNUDGE. SNUDGE."

MMMMM. A very long, portentous silence. Then, almost in a tone of disappointment: *THASHIN AH GAV.*

Had this been some sort of a test? Did the Beaconfolk suspect the earlier subterfuge when he'd used his nickname, and were they now attempting to get a stronger hold on him? Perhaps. But this Light had apparently accepted his answer.

Now to say thanks. "MO TENGALAH SHERUV." And please—oh, God, please!—send me back to my own world.

Dank grey fog lapped his face, while three fuzzy Small Lights danced anxiously around, buzzing like midges. He sat in the saddle and felt his mount stamp one muffled hoof, felt the stirrups supporting his booted feet, sensed the sloshing of the kegs in their nets tied fore and aft of his thighs. A vaguely uncomfortable warmth rested against his breastbone.

He lifted his mittened hand in front of his eyes. It wasn't there—any more than the rest of him was, or Primmie.

"I'm gone!" he chortled, and the spunkies gave a shrill squeal of consternation and fled into the fog. "No, wait! Come back!" he called. "It's all right. I'm only using magic to hide from the enemy. Come back!"

A faint windspoken statement: *You are a sorcerer. Like the lady!*

"Only a very young one. A beginner. Going invisible is the only important spell I know. Please come back. I won't hurt you." Some impulse made him add, "If you don't hurt me."

The three Small Lights reappeared. One of them pointed something out to the others. *Look very closely! See? The mist outlines his body and that of the animal. Oooh!*

Damn, Snudge thought. I'll have to remember that. And Iscannon had cast a shadow when he hid behind Concealer. He said to the spunkies, "My friends, you're far more clever at magic than I am if you can see me in the fog. Let's just travel on to the castle with no more delay."

You promise to do no more Great Light magic?

"I promise," Snudge said. With a few disgruntled chirps and jingles, the three Small Lights took up their position just above the ground and floated off down the track. Primmie followed without urging.

* * *

Snudge never did get a good look at Castle Redfern, although he was later to discover that the place was very small and poor. The fog surrounding it was the thickest he had yet encountered, rendering indistinct any object more than an ell distant. The ravine where the castle was situated was a muddle of spectral shadows. After being assured by the uncanny guides that no enemy warriors were on duty outside the stronghold, the boy had them lead him to the ramp of the fort's raised drawbridge, which spanned a steep-walled watercourse that would have made a formidable barrier had it not been nearly bone-dry.

"Can you thin the fog just a bit between here and the castle's gatehouse?" he asked the spunkies. "I want the guards to be able to see me when I go visible again and call out to them."

. . . There!

"Excellent. Now fly to the windvoices in the army following after me. They must approach with no noise at all and position themselves here, hidden in the fog and ready to attack when the drawbridge lowers and the gates open. Tell them that'll probably happen very suddenly."

The spunkies peeped and disappeared.

As Snudge prepared to speak the words that would render him visible again, he wondered whether he would face another confrontation with the Great Light. It would be horribly inconvenient if that happened each time he used the sigil—and probably fatal if the insubstantial monster in charge of lesser sigils asked him a question he couldn't answer.

Well . . . "BI FYSINEK. KRUF AH."

No mystical darkness, no querying Light. Only the swirling white fog of noontide and he himself, a drably dressed youth sitting on a big dun mule draped with cargo nets bulging with small kegs. Primmie's hoof-muffling rags had been removed.

"Hello, the castle!" Snudge shouted. "Hoy, hoy, hoy! Castle Redfern!"

He had to continue for some minutes before a voice yelled from the blurry battlements above, "Who goes there?"

He had his story ready. "I'm Lunn, son of Rek Warmergill, Royal Customs Officer of Rockport." He gave them the name of the coastal town that was the eastern terminus of one fork of the Breakneck Track. "I'm sent with provisions you'll welcome gladly! Five kegs of fine Langford malt spirits, part of a cargo

taken from a Cathran coaster off Skellhaven by our valiant local sailormen. Good
King Achardus has ordered the frontier garrisons at Redfern and Highcliff to
have a share of the loot as a token of his gratitude for loyal service."

The glaring improbability of such largesse from the notoriously stingy
monarch during a time of naval blockade was lost on the sentry.

"Spirits!" the awed man cried out. "Stand fast, lad, whilst I get the sergeant of
the guard."

After a few minutes another voice, more authoritative and suspicious, called,
"Are you all alone, then, young Lunn?"

"Well, the load's not large," Snudge admitted, "although the proof of the
liquor's supposed to be superbly high. Dad sent me out when the royal order
disposing of the contraband came through yesterday. My brother Rado went to
Castle Highcliff, the lucky duck. The fog's not nearly so bad near the coast. It took
me forever to get here. I had to sleep rough on the trail last night, and I was
sore tempted to broach one of these kegs to keep me warm. But I didn't. Dad
would skin me alive for messing with a royal gift."

"Wait," said the voice, laughing.

He did, and for a considerable time, praying that the lord of the castle would not
think to have his wind adepts scan him, since he would not be visible to their talent. It would be even worse if the alchymists bespoke the authorities in Rockport
to confirm his story.

Evidently nothing of the sort happened. There was a great grinding noise
and a scream of poorly greased windlasses. The drawbridge was coming down.
Quickly, Snudge dismounted. He snatched a sixth keg of liquor from one of the
nets and a coil of strong rawhide lashing that had been looped over the pommel,
then rendered himself and his burden invisible and moved back until he was well
into the fog. The bridge grounded with a thud, the castle gates opened, and a
squad of guards marched out with halberds at the ready, led by their sergeant.
They surrounded Primmie and examined the load.

"Damn my eyes if it isn't Snapevale Stillery malt!" The sergeant was overawed. "Booze fit for a king! But where's that lad gone? Holla, boy!"

"Prob'ly answering nature's call," said one of the soldiers.

"Well, to hell with him," said the sergeant. "Let's get this treasure safely in. If
the stupid juggins gets caught outside when we lift the bridge, it's his lookout."

He took the mule's reins and led it through the gate. Snudge followed after, unseen. After a few tentative shouts for the missing "Lunn," the sergeant ordered the drawbridge raised and the iron portcullis lowered.

Primmie clopped decorously into the bailey of Castle Redfern and was immediately surrounded by a noisy mob. Some of the men had tears of joy running down their cheeks. Snudge's windsight had revealed to him that the garrison's strength was small—no more than two score and ten warriors, nearly half of those either elderly or very young, and all lean to the point of emaciation. If these defenders of the realm were nearly starving, what must be the condition of the ordinary folk living in Didion's capital city?

"You men!" bellowed the sergeant. "Hands off the kegs until His Lordship gives leave to pop the bungs! Warlo, go fetch Baron Maddick."

Snudge waited. The unimpressive small keep was an unadorned two-storey block of stone with a single watchtower on the right and only a few little unglazed windows. After ten minutes or so the lord of the castle came striding out the entry, followed by six knights in house garb and a pair of men wearing black hooded robes who had to be the resident wind practitioners.

Snudge's prey! But not to be slaughtered as Prince Conrig expected, if the plan succeeded.

Baron Maddick was a greying man of slight stature who possessed an incongruously loud and sonorous voice. "Have patience, all! First, let's see whether this unexpected bounty is as advertised. Wizard Hiblesk, tap one of the kegs and sample it."

The tallest man in black bent to the task. When the tap was in place his colleague handed over a wooden cup, which the wizard filled to the brim. Then he rose to his feet, sniffed the cup's contents, and addressed the baron. "As you are aware, my lord, members of our sacred cohort are forbidden to quaff ardent spirits. It is only to reassure Your Lordship of the wholesomeness of this beverage that I dispense myself from the obligation."

A few titters came from the crowd of soldiers. Hiblesk swept them with a glare, then sipped gingerly from the cup. He frowned, and grumbles of incipient dismay arose. Then he sniffed the liquor again, drained the cup in two strong pulls and lifted it high. "It's good," he declared, and the assembled men raised a thunderous cheer.

Baron Maddick said, "I claim this keg for my high table. The other four will be shared out immediately in equal portions to all fighting men of this garrison. Sir Evolus, supervise the distribution." He turned on his heel amidst more cheers and returned to the keep followed by five of the knights (one carrying the tapped keg), the windvoices, and invisible Snudge.

The great hall of Castle Redfern was stark and incredibly dreary, its windows shuttered against the cold and damp. Smoking torches and hanging cressets furnished illumination. The central hearth was unlit and the floor strewn with rubbishy dried grass and trampled weeds that had obviously not been changed for weeks. Snudge trailed the two adepts to the upper floor, where they evidently had their chambers. As soon as the baron and his knights were out of earshot, a quarrel broke out between the wizards.

"You could have shared, Hiblesk!"

"Nonsense. You know the Rule."

"Look who's talking! You needn't have filled your cup to the brim to do the test! And the Rule can be relaxed in times of great hardship. You know that as well as I do."

"I'm your superior, Coxus. I'll interpret the Rule!"

Still bickering, they reached a door at the end of the corridor. Hiblesk unlocked it, and the pair entered. Snudge slipped in after them. Most of the sizable chamber was dedicated to alchymy. It was neat enough, with tattered woven mats on the floor. Bundles of dried herbs hung from the rafters, tables were strewn with arcane equipment made of copper and glass, and the walls were lined with shelves holding books and all sorts of containers. A huge soot-stained fireplace burned merrily, almost making the place comfortably warm. On the hearth stood a glowing charcoal brazier with an alembic distilling some potion. Both wizards went to inspect it.

When their backs were turned Snudge placed the keg that he carried on the floor and stepped away from it, uttering the visibility command in silent mind-speech: KRUF AH.

As he'd hoped, it worked . . . like a charm. The small wooden cask appeared out of nowhere, and when the younger wizard named Coxus turned around he caught sight of it at once.

"Great God of the Heights and Depths!" he bleated. "A miracle!"

With his hood lowered, Hiblesk proved to be a bald, eagle-beaked man, having very little chin, a defect he had attempted to remedy by growing a little white goat beard. His pale eyes bulged as he spotted the keg and he struck a magical pose, held out hands with stiffened fingers aimed at the eldritch container, and pronounced a lengthy spell to banish demonic illusions.

The keg of spirits remained in place.

"It's real!" Coxus knelt reverently beside it. "And it's ours."

Snudge held his breath. Would Hiblesk succumb to temptation?

"We must report this singular occurrence to Baron Maddick at once!" the bald wizard intoned.

"Codders," Snudge muttered in disgust. He pulled out the sock full of coins he'd prepared and coshed the bald alchymist neatly behind his ear. The man dropped to the floor, moaning. "Stand still, Coxus," the invisible boy said. "Clasp your hands behind your head and don't dare to speak on the wind or you will die."

The young wizard, paralyzed by fright, gibbered, "Who—who are you?"

"A mighty sorcerer, come to give you a choice. Your colleague has already chosen wrongly, by the way, and when he wakes up he faces a very unpleasant fate unless he changes his mind."

"W-what k-k-kind of choice?"

"I must prevent both of you from windspeaking for two days. A sure way to do this would be to strangle you." Snudge flung a length of the invisible rawhide lashing around the wizard's neck and tightened it gently. The man stood stock still, hands at his sides.

"I p-presume there is an alternative."

"Oh, yes." Removing the thong. "From personal experience, I know how the arcane talents are gummixed up by the consumption of spirits. But perhaps the prospect of a two-day spree violates your tender conscience."

"I wouldn't say that!" The young wizard smirked. He would have been handsome had his face not been scarred by acne. "Why do you want Hiblesk and me wind-silent?"

"None of your business. But I promise you'll be better off for it in the long run. Do you have your beds in this room?"

"Behind yon curtain."

"Help me carry your friend. Take his shoulders."

"He's not my friend, he's my boss. And a bloody-minded one, at that."

Snudge and Coxus took Hiblesk by the arms and legs and dumped him on one of the narrow raised palliasses. He was already regaining consciousness, and he whimpered and struggled weakly as the invisible boy bound his crossed wrists and ankles securely with the rawhide.

"I'll have to tie you up, too," Snudge told Coxus. "Just sit on the edge of the bed. When you're wrapped tight I'll give you a nice big beaker of booze, and you can savor it at your leisure while I deal with your master." To be on the safe side, he intended to pour them twice as much as he had drunk the night he'd killed Iscannon. Men unaccustomed to strong drink would either puke it up or fall asleep. Snudge devoutly hoped for the latter.

"You'll never get old Hiblesk to swallow any liquor if he sets his mind against it," Coxus warned.

"Maybe not. But I noticed some soft tubing and a funnel amongst your alchymical equipment. They'll do the job for me if he decides to balk. But I reckon he won't."

Hiblesk didn't. When he came to his senses and the horrid alternative was explained to him he capitulated without argument, swilled the fine malt with a fatalistic shrug, suffered a brief bout of hiccoughs, relaxed on his pillow, and began to snore. Coxus drank more slowly, smacking his lips and humming.

"I know who *you* are!" he said in a playful sing-song tone, as Snudge retrieved the empty beaker from him. "Y're invashioners! Cathran booze, Cathran invashioners. Right?"

"Right," said the boy amiably. "And when Didion joins our new Sovereignty, we'll see that all of you starvelings get decent food as soon as possible."

The young wizard giggled. "Food and *drink!*"

"I'm going to lock your door, but someone will come and look in on you in a few hours, after we've stormed the castle. You'll be well taken care of."

Coxus didn't reply. He had passed out and was snoring in chorus with his colleague.

Snudge paused for a moment, closing his eyes, and windwatched the area of the drawbridge ramp in front of the castle. There were bulky shadows lurking out there, and a myriad of faint little golden lights. The advance force led by Prince Conrig had arrived.

"Time to go," he told himself. "I hope most of the garrison has a nice buzz on by now. Maybe they'll surrender instead of taking a futile stand."

He poured himself a small tot from the broached keg, tossed it down, and went to lower the drawbridge.

twenty-four

Leading the force of fifty knights on his ebony courser, Conrig thundered over the drawbridge of Castle Redfern as the gates swung wide. Like the other charging warriors, he howled "Cathra!" at the top of his lungs and swung the curved blade of his varg in deadly arcs. The slightly tipsy garrison, taken completely by surprise when Snudge did his work invisibly in the gatehouse, had only begun to scramble for their weapons when the invading knights trampled them in a screaming mêlée, exulting in the first taste of battle. The active defenders were hacked down without mercy until a trumpet-like voice cried out: "We yield!"

Baron Maddick had appeared in the open entryway of the keep, sword in hand, transfixed by horror at the carnage in the bailey and the rampaging invaders on horseback. He cast down his blade and raised both hands, shouting again, "We yield! Redfern yields!" Six white-faced knights of the household, standing behind him, also threw down their unbloodied swords and fell to their knees.

The prince wheeled his mount about and cried, "Cathra! Leave off! Have done! They have surrendered." He rode up to the lord of the castle, who still stood on his feet. "I am Prince Heritor Conrig Wincantor, and I claim this fortress as the first prize of the Sovereignty of High Blenholme."

"I am Maddick Redfern, holder of the fief. We yield without condition. Will you grant mercy and allow us to tend our wounded?"

"I will indeed . . . On your honor, my lord: how many gates in your curtain wall?"

"Besides the main gate, only a small postern on the downstream end of the bailey near the kitchen shed, through which we cast refuse and slops."

Conrig turned to Lords Catclaw and Cloudfell, who sat their horses close by. Both were grinning and splattered with gore. "Tinnis, have your men seal the postern shut and collect the weaponry. Wanstan, set a close guard at the drawbridge and send off a messenger to inform our force of the victory. Have them advance with all speed." Then to Maddick: "Where are your wizards?"

The baron shrugged. "In their chambers, I suppose, squawking on the wind like rooks warning of a falcon's presence."

"Not so, Your Grace," a quiet young voice said. Snudge stepped out of the shadows of the stable annex. "I've seen them to their rest."

"You!" Maddick uttered a groan. "The lad with the lovely presents! But how in hell did you lift the portcullis and let down the bridge with six men on guard in the gatehouse? Even half-drunk from your gift, they should have been a match for you. How did such a young sprout overcome them?"

"How indeed?" murmured the prince.

But Snudge only smiled.

Much later, when the main body of the Cathran army was safely ensconced in the secured castle, Conrig sent for his intelligencer. Snudge found the prince walking the torchlit battlements above the drawbridge, watching as ten gangleshanked nags and two draft oxen with ribs as prominent as slats—the sole occupants of Redfern's stables—were led outside into the mists.

"You summoned me, Your Grace."

"There's something important to discuss. Have you spread word of Princess Ullanoth's secret departure, as I asked?"

"Yes, Your Grace. It wasn't possible for me to deny being here and assign the princess total responsibility for opening the castle. Too many of the defenders had already spread the tale of the lad with the booze-laden mule. But I gave the lady credit for silencing the windvoices and pretended she helped me subdue the men guarding the gate. Only Duke Tanaby knows that Ullanoth was never here. I had to tell him the truth this morning before he would give me the casks of spirits."

The prince grunted, turning away to gaze over the battlement. "Look down there."

The boy peered through one of the crenels. Cathran thanes were turning the scrawny animals loose into the gorge, where the foggy gloom was eerily illuminated by thousands of bobbing golden sparks. The oxen lowed and plodded off once the ropes were removed from their nose rings, but the castle's horses pawed and snorted and hung about the bridge nervously until given whacks on the rump, after which they trotted off to temporary freedom.

"We would have had to dispose of the enemy's mounts anyhow," the prince said somberly. "Can't have one of the resident knights galloping off and giving the alarm when we quit this place tomorrow. So I decided to give our uncanny guides a small treat. Can you hear them on the wind? My own talent is too feeble to distinguish more than a horrid faint piping sound that causes my flesh to creep."

Snudge heard only too well. "They say they're hungry, Your Grace. These mountains lack their natural prey, the night creatures of the fens, ponds, and ditches. And creating the fog has made them more ravenous than usual." He hesitated. "Are you aware that our thanes have learned that Sir Ruabon was killed by the Small Lights?"

"The nobles and knights are attempting to calm the men's fears. All the same, tonight we'll shelter inside the keep except for those guarding our own stock—and they'll have bonfires and torches to discourage wandering spunkies. Stergos and Doman will alternate in keeping windwatch from the top of the tower as well. I presume there's no danger of enemy forces discovering that we're here?"

"No danger at all, Your Grace. I've thoroughly searched the two roads leading from this place and the mountain paths as well. No one is abroad this evening in the fog save the Small Lights."

Prince Conrig was silent for some time, watching the gyrating fuzzy glimmerings. Then: "Why did you disobey my order to kill Redfern's wizards, Snudge?"

The boy said coolly, "You gave no such order. You told me only to silence them, and that I did—with the bonus of rendering most of the rest of the garrison pissy-eyed as well. Regular doses of liquor will keep the adepts incapable until their talent no longer threatens our invasion. Lord Stergos said he'd have his squire Gavlok see to it."

"I stand corrected," Conrig retorted, none too graciously. "But your soft heart will have to yield to mortal expediency very soon. Not long ago, Stergos attempted to bespeak the Lady Ullanoth. She did not reply, and we can only assume she's still very weak from having empowered Weathermaker and banished the freeze. Now, our army is due to enter Mallburn Town during the wee hours of the day after tomorrow. By then we may hope that the princess will be recovered to a certain degree. Unfortunately for us, she will probably not have the strength to Send herself handily about, abetting our forces as she'd planned. Stergos believes, as I do, that she can't possibly perform both of the strategic tasks she originally set herself. She will have to choose between opening the gates at the Mallmouth Bridge and admitting us to the stronghold of Holt Mallburn Palace."

"I see." He did, too . . .

At that moment a stomach-wrenching shriek rang out from below, the sound of a horse maddened by terror. Conrig flinched. "Bazekoy's Bones, there goes the first of them." The cry was cut short, only to be followed by a drawn-out bovine bellow that culminated in a mournful gurgling tremolo. "We needn't stay here. Let's go inside the keep."

He led the way along the curtain wall parapet to the rickety wooden stairs that gave access to the crowded bailey. The Cathrans had compelled their prisoners to gather much of the castle furniture to make fires upon which cauldrons of savory pottage were simmering. Other men in leg-fetters were demolishing the worksheds and other wooden structures inside the walls to make more fuel. The army's huge herd of horses, mules, and ponies was picketed closely but still filled the greater part of the ward. Thanes were seeing to the animals' feed and water, farriers were checking hooves, and here and there knights or their armigers gave personal attention to specially favored steeds.

After the fight, Snudge had found Primmie the mule in the castle stable, ensconced in a stall like some equine guest-of-honor, munching a small manger of fresh hay that was evidently the best the castle had to offer. The boy had groomed the big yellow brute fondly and secured proper oats for him once the sumpter ponies arrived.

"The Didionite prisoners seem unusually cheerful," Snudge observed, as he and the prince passed among a group nailing together improvised water troughs.

"Only fifteen of the castle's men-at-arms died in the skirmish, for all the blood, and none of the castle workers received a scratch. They've been subsisting here on dried fish and thin barley gruel. We fed them meat pottage and decent bread. If I asked it, every surviving Didionite warrior would probably pledge heartfelt allegiance to Cathra."

"And the baron and his household?"

"Sulking and not yet willing to take the oath of fealty. But our lenient treatment may predispose them to accept the Sovereignty later, as well as pass on tidings of my clemency to their peers. They'll have little enough choice. By the time we leave this place, there'll be neither food nor firewood left. We're feeding Redfern's barley stores to our own beasts. After we move on, the baron and his folk will have to abandon the castle and flee to the coast on foot. Thank God there are no women or children here."

The victorious Cathrans who were not on duty had taken over the great hall, where a roaring blaze at the center and replenished wall-cressets cheered and warmed the scene. Even if most of the food and drink on the trestle boards was cold, there was plenty of it.

The smallish high table was already filled by Catclaw and Cloudfell and their roistering knights, celebrating the abbreviated combat. Conrig and Snudge sat down on stools by the fire that had been hastily vacated when the prince approached.

Cloudfell's armiger came running from the table with a crock of steaming spiced wine. "Your Grace! My lord urges you and your squire to come sit with us."

"Nay, lad, we're fine right here. But search out Duke Tanaby and the earl marshal and bid them join us."

When the armiger dashed off, leaving the jug behind, Conrig spoke in a low voice to Snudge, who was filling both their cups. "As I understand it, your talent for hiding is based upon misdirecting observers rather than true invisibility. Furthermore, you once told me that the trick is impossible to manage if more than two or three persons are watching."

Snudge nodded.

"Yet you overcame six gatehouse guards, by Maddick's own admission. How?"

"I lifted their helms and whacked them on the head with a sock full of coins. It works fine, even through a chain mail hood."

"And not a single man saw you?" Disbelief curled the prince's lip.

Sighing, Snudge unbuttoned his shirt, drew forth the bagged moonstone sigil and let its pale green glow shine for an instant behind his cupped hand. "I was quite invisible. As you doubtless suspect by now, Iscannon's amulet, the one called Concealer, is fully empowered and bonded to me. The Tarnian shaman Red Ansel helped with the conjuring."

"God's Teeth!" the prince hissed. "You told me you threw it in the sea!"

"Ansel also cautioned me to use the sigil only under the most grave circumstances, lest my soul be endangered by the Beaconfolk. Your Grace, I debated long with myself before deciding not to tell you that Concealer was alive. You may recall that I beseeched you to trust me. Now, of course, you must know about the stone, since I presume you wish me to undertake another special mission: opening the Mallmouth Bridge gate."

Conrig took a deep pull of wine, trying to calm his anger, trying to be fair to the youth who had just enabled the first victory of his campaign against Didion. But his pride was sorely wounded, and he felt that his ability to control this all-important enterprise had been flouted by a lowborn boy. "Never presume to deny me such knowledge again!" His whisper was grating and his face dark with suppressed anger. "I am your liege lord, and it's you who owe *me* trust!"

Snudge lowered his head. "I'm sorry, Your Grace. I feared . . ."

"You feared I would make frivolous use of your sigil! You played me false, Deveron Austrey. I did trust you, but you had no faith in me!"

The boy said nothing, nor did he raise his eyes. He pushed the bagged moonstone into his shirt and fastened the buttons.

"I forgive you," Conrig said, in a voice that was still unsteady, wondering whether he spoke the truth. "Drink up. Here come Beorbrook and Vanguard, slowly pushing through the crowd. The duke already knows the truth about your talent. Now is the time for the earl marshal to know as well—and about the Concealer sigil. We four must decide how to effect the conquest of Holt Mallburn, now that we can no longer depend fully upon the assistance of Princess Ullanoth."

Snudge drained his cup and wiped his mouth with his cuff. He was confident again as he looked the prince in the eye. "Do you recall how you planned for me and the armigers to guard the Conjure-Princess during the battle for the city? I think you might use us to much better advantage in another way." He explained what he wanted to do, and what he would need.

"I can obtain a map of southern Didion for you easily enough," the prince said, frowning. "As for a diagram of the Mallmouth Bridge machinery—such a thing must exist in the Cathra University library at Greenley. I'll have Stergos bespeak them, get a description, and sketch it for you . . . But you must find a way to open the bridge by yourself, Snudge, as you did here today at Castle Redfern. I refuse to let you reveal your wild talent to a mob of boys! They'd never be able to keep the secret. It would put paid to your future usefulness to me as an intelligencer."

"I won't need all of the armiger cohort, Your Grace, but I will require help. The bridge defenses are bound to be much more complex and difficult to overcome than those of this small castle. Concealer is capable of rendering invisible persons who stand close to me. I could take just three squires—"

Conrig broke in. "But must you tell them of your arcane abilities? The boys have no notion of the way sigil magic operates, that it can only serve the talented. Can't you say that the Concealer stone never lost its power when you took it from Iscannon?"

"I could do that," Snudge agreed, "and caution them to tell no one about it." And perhaps they would obey.

"If Vra-Doman or another Brother of Zeth should learn of your using the sigil, they would realize the truth. So would Ullanoth. And I think your life would not be worth a mouse turd if the Conjure-Princess should discover that you have the talent and own a Concealer."

"She can't windwatch me, so she'll only learn of my talent and possession of the stone if someone tells her. I can swear my fellow squires to secrecy, in your name. Then I'll conveniently 'lose' the sigil during the battle. If the Brethren hear rumors of it later, their tender consciences will not oblige them to report the matter to Abbas Noachil. As for my alleged wild talent"—the boy shrugged—"how can it be proved, and why would loyal adepts wish to expose me?"

"Hmmm," said Conrig. "This could work. Let's put it to the duke and the earl marshal, to make certain we haven't overlooked some crucial flaw in the plan."

"They probably won't like it," Snudge predicted. "Laying such a great burden upon the shoulders of mere squires won't sit well with older warriors."

"Then let them come up with an alternative," said the prince, with a dismissive flip of his hand.

The Didionite wizard Fring Bulegosset, principal talent accompanying the armada of Honigalus of Didion, swept into the Crown Prince's day-cabin on the *Casabarela Regnant* with a supercilious nod.

"Your Royal Highness, how can I serve you?"

Honigalus and Fleet Captain Galbus Peel were seated at a table where charts and navigational instruments were laid out. The morning sun shone brightly outside the stern windows of the great barque. Three hours earlier, the fleet had emerged from the fog that had shielded it while it sailed out of Didion Bay.

Unfortunately, the fair wind that had speeded the fleet's passage on the previous day immediately dropped to a light breeze once the ships reached the open sea and turned south.

"Fring, I want you to bespeak King Beynor of Moss," said the prince, "and try to get him to pump up the damned wind for us. You can see how we've lost way in the last few hours. While he's at it, ask him to shift the wind direction from west to northeasterly, and bring back the fog so the enemy can't scry us. We're already nearly abreast of the Cathran shore. You can take a seat over there in the aft corner, by the windows, while you work."

"Well, I'll do the best I can, Your Highness," the wizard said tetchily, "but the young Conjure-King was uncommonly brusque when I last bespoke him, requesting his estimate on our time of arrival in the Dolphin Channel. One is tempted to think that our request for changes in the winds may be straining his abilities."

Fring seated himself, drew the hood of his black robe over his face with a dramatic gesture, and silently began the magical communication. He was a well-fleshed, pasty-faced man in his fourth decade of life, with a small tight mouth and beady blue eyes as pale as watered milk. His windwatching talent was the most powerful in Didion, equaled only by the towering arrogance of his manner. Even though the naval officers and men were on iron rations (and fair-minded Honigalus himself shared their fare for the sake of morale), special delicacies of food had been quietly brought aboard the flagship to keep this all-important wizard in good humor; he had also insisted upon traveling with his personal cook-slave.

Captain Peel said to the prince, "Do you think Fring could be right about Beynor not being able to pull his oar strongly enough, performing weather magic?"

"I don't know. Maybe these extraordinary feats are harder on a boy than on a grown man. There does seem to have been something strange about his behavior the last few times we've bespoken him. He's been evasive about the nature of the widespread landside fog, for one thing, not seeming to know whether or not it's natural or produced by Cathran adepts to hide troop movements. Still, my brother Somarus's scouts haven't found any evidence of forces assembling around Great Pass, and no Cathran infiltrators have been seen or captured by the outposts above Castlemont."

"This clear blue sky is unexpected." The captain was offhand, but Honigalus understood his implication immediately.

"And we know what it must mean! I doubt Beynor would admit that the Wolf's Breath has ceased of its own accord, and we certainly won't point it out to him while we still have a use for his magical services. But if the volcanos have gone quiet at last, there'll be no need to pay the young knave the outrageous tribute he squeezed out of my father. We won't deny him completely, lest he retaliate. But appropriate renegotiations will be called for."

Peel chuckled. "It's only just. I wouldn't be surprised if Beynor already knew the eruptions were nearly over when he pledged to stop them with sorcery."

"We can't trust him an inch, Galbus. But we don't dare antagonize him yet. We'll need fair winds in the Dolphin Channel to take on the Cathran fleet—and our allies in Stippen and Foraile must be able to join us without delay once we round the Vigilant Isles."

"This time of year, we're likely to get fair winds down there even without resorting to magic. Let me show you." The stalwart Peel began to demonstrate tactical technicalities on a channel chart, using tiny model ships, and the two men remained completely absorbed until the wizard rose from his seat, threw back his hood, and approached. His countenance was baleful.

"I've spoken to King Beynor," he announced, interrupting the captain's lecture without apology. "It seems His Majesty is temporarily indisposed, due to magical overexertion on our behalf. He tells me he'll perhaps be recovered later, when we can expect the wind to rise. Restoring the seafog, unfortunately, is not possible at this time. He gave me a complicated explanation involving arctic air masses and other meteorological twaddle that I'll spare you."

Honigalus uttered a disappointed curse. "There goes any hope of postponing the Cathrans spotting us."

"If we sail well away from the coast," Fring said, "we'll be out of their range. Only Mossland wizards, Tarnian shamans, and a handful of other adepts can windwatch or search beyond twenty leagues or so, even with combined talents." He paused and looked away modestly. "I, of course, am able to scry nearly thirty leagues, over open water."

"Which is why we are so fortunate to have you with us," Honigalus said tactfully.

"Don't worry, Highness," Peel said, flicking an indifferent glance at the wizard. "Even if the Cathrans do scry us, our strategy can accommodate it."

"But," intoned Fring, almost with malicious glee, "can it also accommodate a squadron of twenty Tarnian frigates racing to Cathra's aid? King Beynor assures me it is on its way. The ships left Tarnholme yesterday morning, driven by strong natural winds. We're actually racing them to Cala."

"Bloody hell!" groaned Honigalus. "How long before the Wave-Harriers make Intrepid Headland and Cala Bay?"

"Perhaps as little as four days, given the expertise of their crews," Fring said. "The Conjure-King may be able to delay them—but only at the cost of giving less impetus to our own fleet."

Galbus Peel was rummaging in a drawer of the chart table. He found more model ships and began deploying them in Tarn's Goodfortune Bay with a mordant smile. "Our upcoming sea-war looks more and more interesting. Any other bad news, wizard?"

"If you require some," Fring replied loftily, "I can always have my colleagues intensify their windscrutiny of the shore. Perhaps we'll detect a group of Cathran adepts scrying us from Skellhaven."

Honigalus said, "Do what must be done. And bespeak our spies in Cala City again. I must know whether Prince Conrig is still in the palace attending the dying king. Tell them to exert their talents to the utmost and find out for me."

Fring sniffed. "If King Beynor has thus far failed to discover Conrig's whereabouts, I doubt whether our people on the scene in Cala will have much better luck. I'll urge them to do their best, but I can't promise success." He gave a curt bob of his head and left the day-room.

"Prickly bastard," the Fleet Captain observed. "But he seems to know his job."

"Just as you do, my friend." Honigalus went to the expanse of windows at the ship's stern and looked out at the Didionite navy surrounding his flagship. The vessels had raised every scrap of canvas in hopes of utilizing the paltry breeze. "With Tarnian mercenaries augmenting their fleet, the Cathrans will have far the advantage of numbers until our allies from Stippen and Foraile arrive."

"But not a tactical advantage," Peel said comfortably. "Our men o' war are bigger, faster, and better armed, and we've forgotten more about naval tactics than those poxy southerners ever knew. With or without the aid of our Continental friends, we'll whip the cods off the lubbers."

*　　*　　*

For the first time in many days his body was free from pain, and the terrifying dreams had finally ceased. Let the Didionites wait until tomorrow for their high wind. He had other business to accomplish—out on the Darkling Sands.

The Conjure-King ordered his skiff to be prepared, then had himself driven down to the harbor in a two-wheeled pony carriage. Most of the fishing fleet was away, but six large sealers from Thurock had come up from the south and were unloading bales of raw furs and casks of oil at the commercial dock. A single fast schooner of the Fennycreek Company was taking on a cargo of amber, walrus ivory, and medicinal herbs, risking one last profitable run to the Continental markets before winter closed in. Beynor had the coach stop at their warehouse store, where the manager presented him with three small, lumpy leather sacks. He scrawled his signature on a receipt and ordered the carriage driver to proceed to the royal boathouse.

The day was brilliantly sunny and crisp with a smart offshore breeze, ideal for his day-trip. Alighting at his private dock, he greeted Opor, the grizzled old retainer in charge of small craft who had first taught him to sail when he was a tiny lad. "Is everything ready?"

"Aft'noon, Majesty. Got your oilskins stowed aboard. You'll need 'em out in the channel. It's chilly. Sand-gliders, too—but you take care if you go for a stroll on the flats today. Tide's dead low now, but she'll come in three foot over normal."

"Thanks, Opor."

"Sail's still under cover. Didn't figure you'd need it."

"That's fine." The king hopped aboard the skiff and stowed the three sacks while Opor cast him off. A few minutes later the boat was moving down the Darkling River, impelled by the regal talent, while Beynor sat at the tiller and gazed over the sparkling expanses of black sand.

He deliberately emptied his mind and tried to relax, keeping as close as he could to the southern shore, which was bereft of human habitation above the isolated village of Gonim. Area creeks draining the Little Fen made a maze of confusing channels accessible only to shallow-draft watercraft, such as his own skiff.

He steered up one of those creeks, past desolate marshy islets where recent hard frosts had rendered the rice-grass and bulrushes lifeless and brown and driven away most of the birds. It was cold, even with the windproof oilskins, and he hoped he wouldn't have to wait too long at the lake.

Two leagues inland, he reached the first of the Forbidden Lakes, linked dark mirrors of water having a reputation so sinister that not even the most intrepid fowlers and herb-hunters ever came there. Only Beynor came, and then only when he needed to converse face-to-face with the Darkling Sands Salka.

He liked to think that this particular band of monsters were his friends. They were much less sophisticated—and less contemptuous of humanity—than the Salka of the Great Fens or the Dawntide Isles. When Beynor was twelve, just entering manhood, two of the frightful creatures from the Forbidden Lakes had inexplicably rescued him from death on the tideflats. In the years that followed he'd visited their scattered settlements along the chain of lakes, bringing gifts and soliciting counsel on magical matters.

The Salka were the ones who had first recognized his tremendous talent and suggested that he might be able to master the Seven Stones of Rothbannon, even though his parents had failed so disastrously. The Salka had shown him how to convince Lady Zimroth (and ultimately, the entire Glaumerie Guild) that he was worthy to be trusted with the sigils. They'd guided him through his first encounter with the Lights when he'd activated Subtle Armor, the least of the minor stones. They'd advised him on the safe use of Shapechanger, Concealer, and Fortress. But when it came to the three Great Stones, the Darkling Salka had turned reticent. They provided only reluctant advice about Weathermaker—and would say nothing at all about Destroyer or the Unknown Potency. Whether their silence was prompted by fear, or by an unwillingness to permit a human to control high sorcery that should have belonged to their own race, Beynor did not know.

He *did* know that they were his only hope in overcoming the new crisis that faced him.

The familiar Salka lair lay within the high bank of a hummock at the last lake's far end, concealed by a growth of scraggly willows. The monsters who dwelt there had never invited him into their abode. Perhaps the entrance was underwater, as in a beaver's den. He guided the skiff to a point some five or six ells away, where the still, black water was very deep, and paused to listen. The only sound was a faint hiss of wind in the dead rushes.

Using the Salka language, he bespoke them.

"Great Ones of the Land and Water! It is I, Beynor, your friend. If this is a propitious time, I beseech you to please emerge and give me your excellent advice, for I am sore troubled."

He waited for what seemed an interminable time. It was always like that. Sometimes, especially during the past three years, after he'd empowered Weathermaker, the monsters had declined to meet him—not saying a word, simply refusing to come out.

"Please don't deny me today! I have gifts . . ."

Ha!

First, a few bubbles, then a roiling of the water, and finally an upsurge and a fountaining splash that would have drenched him had he not worn the protective oilskins. The huge sleek form with the burning eyes opened his snaggle-toothed maw and uttered a conversational roar. He wore a sigil the size of a razor clam on a woven strand hung about his thick neck.

Beynor smiled and held out two of the leather bags. "Arowann, my old friend! Thank you for coming."

Boneless arms with tentacular fingers clasped the gifts. The monster's voice, although harsh and overloud to human ears, was amiable enough. "What have you brought us?"

"Beads of finest amber in many colors, pierced and ready to be strung." The king lifted the third bag. "And ivory love-rings, so that your sweetings may long delight in your attentions."

"Good." The Salka dropped the bags of amber into the water, where they were doubtless retrieved by one of his fellows, and did the same with the ivory. Then he sank neck-deep, blinked, and said, "Let me know your trouble, Beynor."

"Arowann, recently I've suffered agonizing dreams of the Lights. They seem to feed on my pain and demand more and more of it as I use my one Great Stone."

The monster considered the matter gravely for some minutes. "Do you use the Weathermaker sigil often?"

"Yes," Beynor admitted. "To aid my human allies in Didion, who are waging war on Cathra."

"Ah . . . a war. And have you also used the Great Stone in other ways?"

Beynor's reply was defiant. "I used it to make a triple rainbow at my coronation. It was necessary to impress the Didionite royal family with my abilities. To gain their respect."

"And how else?"

He flushed and looked away from the blazing red-gold eyes. "To create a great thunderbolt. It demolished the tower where my treacherous sister Ullanoth lived. But she was not inside, as I'd thought."

"In your dreams, did the Lights approve your actions?"

"It's hard to remember," the boy-king admitted nervously. "I think—I think they were scornful and laughed at me! But why should that be? Aren't the stones mine to do with as I like?"

The Salka's booming voice was caustic. "Only a fool, or a child, would ask such a question. The Great Stones extract enormous power from the Coldlight Army, and the conjurer must pay their price. If the Lights despise the use to which their power is put, or if they decide that the sorcerer is using the power frivolously, they may exact penalties."

"Worse than the pain-debt?"

"Much worse." Arowann shook his enormous crested head. "Beynor, my young friend, you said you came for advice. Here it is: leave off using the sigils vaingloriously. Approach the Lights in the way Rothbannon did—as a meek pupil—and do it very slowly."

"But I've made promises to my allies! And my sister will find a way to steal my kingdom if I don't destroy her. Is there no way I can make the Lights understand?"

"No," said Arowann. "There is no way any of us mortal beings can sway them. The Coldlight Army does as it pleases, and we deal with them circumspectly, and always at our peril. Farewell." He sank out of sight.

Beynor stared at the place in the water where the monster had been, wishing his advice had been different. Then he took the tiller and steered the boat back in the direction it had come. On his right index finger, the glow of the knobby moonstone ring was lost in the Boreal sunshine.

twenty-five

Red Ansel had easily beclouded the minds of two Cathran grain-ship captains, making each think that the other one had taken charge of him. By the time the corn fleet reached Tarn and the truth was discovered, neither man wanted to admit being duped. So the shaman's continuing presence in Cala remained undiscovered.

He modified his appearance somewhat and took a room in a sailors' lodging above a cookshop on the waterfront, where he pretended to convalesce from recurrent ague, a common affliction of seafarers visiting southern Continental ports. His dinghy, disguised with a new sail and a repainted hull, was tied up at a nearby slip. On moonless nights when the landlord and his wife were too busy with trade to notice his absence, he prowled the bay, committing to memory its tidal vagaries and hazards to navigation, while he easily scried the maneuvers of the Cathran fleet and judged the competence of the different squadron leaders.

On the day that Didion's navy emerged from the fog and became visible to his powerful oversight from Cathra, Ansel was ashore. Events were fast coming to a head, and his great premonitory talent warned him to remain alert. He had spent long hours eavesdropping windspoken orders that had been flying between Cala Palace and the patrolling vessels like frantic clouds of bats. Ever since Ullanoth's message about the Didionite armada had been received, Cathra's leading naval captains and Lord Admiral Copperstrand had been arguing about what to do.

Coming himself from a race of expert fighting seamen, Ansel could scarcely believe what happened next. Cutting off all debate, Copperstrand divided his strung-out force of fifty-two warships into two equal groups. The first, under the command of Vice Admiral Woodvale, headed for western Cala Bay off Castle

Defiant to safeguard the capital from attack from the Continent. The other half of the fleet, led by the Lord Admiral himself, began to gather below the Vigilant Isles some two hundred leagues to the southeast, evidently intending to engage the oncoming force of Crown Prince Honigalus.

Oh, badly done! the shaman said to himself. Unless the Tarnian mercenaries arrived to save the day, Copperstrand had just ensured that one half of his fleet would be outnumbered by Didion, while the other half faced an uncertain (but probably large) number of corsairs sailing up from Stippen and Foraile.

Red Ansel debated with himself whether to advise Vra-Sulkorig or the Prince Heritor's brother about Copperstrand's dubious action. But he feared that the alchymists would never understand the blunder; they might even think dividing the fleet was logical. And the only person having the knowledge and authority to countermand the Lord Admiral's decision was King Olmigon, who was resting after his heart spasm the previous evening, tended ably enough by his alchymists but in no condition to issue orders.

In the end, the shaman decided that all he could do was wait.

He left his room and went to the Chandlers Market, intending to buy neat's-foot oil to dress his boots, as well as to sample the mood of Cala's waterfront denizens as the nation braced for war. He was surprised to discover that commerce seemed to be proceeding at its normal autumnal pace, with no one particularly worried about possible threats from Didion. The shoemaker who sold him the oil opined that Cathra's magnificent warships were more than a match for the starving barbarians. Venders who peddled roasted chestnuts, sweet apples, and pies to eat out of hand confessed that nobody seemed to be buying up food to hoard against a siege. Others that Ansel gossiped with seemed to believe that the so-called Didionite threat was only propaganda instigated by Prince Heritor Conrig, with the motive of raising taxes for his Sovereignty scheme once he succeeded to the throne. As for the Continentals, everyone knew they were too lazy to disturb the status quo—especially in an alliance with those pathetic losers from Didion.

It all made perfect sense, Ansel realized, unless you knew the truth. But when had the common people ever been privy to the dark secrets of the state?

With a spicy venison pie in his scrip for supper, and munching on hot nuts, he was about to leave the market and go down to his boat when he spotted a familiar face critically surveying a tray of late-season table grapes. Rusgann

Moorcock, the loyal maidservant of Princess Maudrayne, was perhaps in search of a treat for her ailing mistress. Ansel felt a guilty start as he realized he had neglected to windwatch the princess for the past several days, having been distracted by Conrig's invasion and the events taking place at sea.

He approached the strapping, broad-featured woman and addressed her politely. "Goodwife Rusgann? Perhaps you remember me. I'm Ansel Pikan, the shaman, a friend of Princess Maudrayne. May I inquire about Her Grace's health these days?"

The maid turned slowly, fixing him with a sharp look. "You were supposed to've been shipped back to Tarn."

He smiled. "But as you see, I'm still here. I knew what had been done to the princess, poor soul. And while I could not alleviate her condition, neither could I abandon her. I've remained in Cala hoping so be of help to her when the time was ripe."

Rusgann appeared to be thinking deeply. After a moment, she beckoned. "Come take a sup of ale with me. I've something to tell you."

Maudrayne's alchymical confinement was like a life lived underwater, a bright, viscous world where movement was slowed and senses lacked their normal acuity, where shapes and colors were blurred, sounds were distorted and indistinct, and her lips formed words that never quite translated into speech.

The princess had been at peace, even happy in that state of easy lassitude. She did as she was told when she was told, obeying Lady Sovanna or Vra-Sulkorig like a puppet. Her mind was intact except for its total lack of volition. Most of the time she sat motionless by the fire or at the large window in the room she called her studium, where the two younger ladies-in-waiting would read aloud, or make music, or simply chatter to one another as they played games or embroidered, while paying no more attention to their helpless mistress than to a piece of furniture.

She was never left alone, except after they put her to bed.

While she slept, she soared amidst memories of her happy childhood— sailing her little boat on a summer sea dotted with bergy bits, flying on skis down the frozen Donor River, pulled by a horse shod with spiked iron, gathering cloudberries on a hillside bright with the luscious pink flowers of dwarf willowherb, sitting by the roaring hearth on blizzard nights with her brothers, listening to Eldmama's tales of ancient heroes battling demons . . .

But the calm strangeness was ebbing away now, leaving unwelcome reality in its wake.

Last night, the dreams of her youth had been fragmented by intermittent hints of dread, of another life tainted by sorrow and rage that awaited her beyond the comfort of sleep. This morning, when she woke and the maids came to dress her in an overly ornate gown chosen by Lady Sovanna, she managed to utter a small sound of disapproval and attempted to push the garment away.

"Let's have none of that, madam," said the chief lady-in-waiting, gesturing briskly for the women to continue fastening her into the billowing garnet-colored silk. "Today the King's Grace is coming to visit, and we can't have him see you lolling about in a shift and wrapper like some invalid, with your hair undone and your face pale as a sheet."

So they adorned and primped her and skillfully used cosmetics to give her complexion and lips a simulated bloom of health, and all the while she felt the drugged lethargy continue to fade. At breakfast, she ate without needing to be commanded. By mid-afternoon, with Rusgann hovering excitedly near her, pressing her to drink cup after cup of small beer to flush the remnants of the soporific physick from her body, she was returning to herself and could speak in a fashion that was nearly normal.

They put her in an armchair in the sitting room, lighting every candle because the day was overcast and dreary, and there she waited half-dozing until King Olmigon, borne in a litter and attended by his lords-in-waiting, entered the room.

Blinking uncertainly, with a tentative half-smile on her face, she rose and dipped a small curtsey to her father-in-law.

"Your Grace."

The king uttered a cackle of feeble triumph. "So you *are* getting well, Maudie! I didn't know whether to believe it or not." He snapped at the footmen, ordering them to bring him close to her chair. "Now everyone get out! I'll speak to the princess alone."

Lady Sovanna opened her mouth as if to object, then shut it again, frowning. She herded courtiers and servants out of the sitting room and closed the door.

Olmigon leaned toward Maudrayne, extending a trembling hand. She took it, searching his ravaged face with bewilderment, seeing the dulled eyes more deeply sunken, the cracked bluish lips, the furrowed cheeks now tinged with the grey pallor of fast-approaching death.

She said, "I'm . . . recovering, sire. And you . . ."

He sighed. "It won't be long, lass, but I'm not on my deathbed yet. Old Bazekoy will have to wait a bit. The doctors got all miffed when I insisted on coming to see you, but I had to make certain Sulkorig and Sovanna obeyed my command." A spark of anger lit his eyes. "That they were no longer drugging you to make you docile."

She looked away. "Is that what it was? I felt very strange, but there was no discomfort."

"You know why Conrig had it done?"

"I . . . can't remember."

"Because you were angry at him and threatened to run away. We can't have you doing that, Maudie. Not while Con's fighting the war for Sovereignty. It would devastate him if you weren't here when he returned victorious."

"Ah." But her air of puzzlement remained. Why had she been angry at Con? What had he done? Why—

Oh, God!

Her hand flew to her mouth, and she knew everything once more. A soft moan escaped inadvertently as she thought of the babe. Was it still safe within her womb, in spite of the poisons they'd given her? It was too new yet to make itself felt.

"Don't worry about Conrig," the king said, misunderstanding her sudden anxiety. "He'll be back soon. Meanwhile, I'm afraid you must stay in your rooms. But if you would, I'd like you to visit with me every day. I've missed you."

"Of course I'll come," she agreed. She fell silent, but her pensive frown betrayed the fact that she was consumed by thought. "Sire? May I ask a small favor of you?"

"Of course."

So she did, and after a brief demurral during which she became more and more insistent, the king finally agreed. His smile was wry. "Now I'm certain you're getting better. You have the strength to argue, and I'm too decrepit to stand up to you!"

They laughed together, and Olmigon bade her join him and the queen and little Prince Tancoron for an early supper. "Sir Hale Brackenfield will come to escort you around the fourth hour."

"The Master-at-Arms?" She lifted a brow. "Am I in danger then?"

The king looked sheepish. "Certainly not. Just come along with him and we'll have a nice meal. I'll make a little music for us with my lute, and Prince Tanny will sing. I'm afraid I can't tell you much about Con's doings in the north. The past few days I've been too . . . tired to deal with affairs of state."

"I understand." She had tended her dying mother, who had had the same aura of mortality about her as the end neared. But this failing old man still possessed a store of uncanny strength. The princess, deeply in touch with the arcane as were most of her people, wondered if Emperor Bazekoy could be responsible.

The king lay back on his litter cushions and allowed his eyes to close. "Now call the others back, if you please. I need a nap."

She rose and summoned the royal attendants, who entered along with Maudrayne's own people in a bustling, solicitous horde. After Olmigon was taken away, the princess stood by the window for some minutes, looking out without saying a word. Her ladies-in-waiting and maids hovered, clearly at a loss how to react now that she seemed to have regained her wits. Many of them no doubt dreaded the reappearance of her famous temper.

Finally Maudrayne said, "You may all withdraw save Lady Sovanna and Rusgann." When they were gone, she said to the maid, "I'll have another cup of beer." And to the noblewoman: "Please come into my studium."

The two of them moved into the inner chamber. The princess left Sovanna standing, went to a press, took out a portfolio, placed it on a worktable, and began to leaf slowly through the pages, which held mounted specimens of dried flowering plants.

"Beautiful, aren't they?" she remarked. "Still very lifelike. I understand that certain of them were fumed by alchymists to prevent their fading. The Brothers of Zeth are so clever with their elixirs. So many mystical potions with so many wonderful uses!"

"Yes," Sovanna said uncertainly.

"Since the king has told me I must temporarily remain in my rooms, I've decided to organize my botanical collection. Perhaps I'll begin a small book about the wildflowers of Cathra."

"A fine idea!" said the lady with forced heartiness. "The project will occupy your mind as you regain your usual good health. Just let me know how I may help."

"Sovanna, I know I have you to thank for taking such excellent care of me during my late illness. You and Vra-Sulkorig. The King's Grace explained it to me."

The woman became very still. Only the tightening of her thin lips showed that she understood. Her small dark eyes glittered in the candlelight.

"I intend to live very simply and quietly until the return of my royal husband. With King Olmigon's permission, I'll no longer require highborn ladies to assist with my social affairs."

"Nevertheless—"

The princess gazed at her steadily. "Rusgann and the chambermaids will serve me well enough from now on. I have no doubt that Queen Cataldise will reward you for your years of devotion to me, and I will, of course, add my own token of appreciation to your boon."

"But Prince Conrig himself charged me to take care of you—"

The princess spoke in a voice of ice. "If you stay, I shall not eat or drink. And King Olmigon will know the reason why. I accept being imprisoned behind locked doors, but no power on earth will compel me to endure your odious presence any longer. Now go away and never let me see you again."

Sovanna inclined her head stiffly and swept out of the room. A moment later, the outer door slammed.

Rusgann peeped around the doorframe, grinning. "That's telling the wicked old bladder!" She brought in the cup of beer.

Maudrayne laughed, but there was no joy in her eyes. "Now that my brain is no longer so muddled, I must make plans for my escape. But first, I must know whether or not my . . . secret is still safe. And unharmed."

"It is, thanks to a little flagon of chicken blood I smuggled in here and dripped on the bedding!"

"Clever Rusgann."

A ferocious scowl twisted the woman's features. "To tell the truth, I worried about the health of the babe when they fed you that ungodly shite. But it's fine." The frown turned to a smug grin. "We oldwives have ways of knowing."

"Bless you for your kind reassurance! Now tell me how I'm guarded."

"Well, the door to the corridor is locked and barred now, with two sentinels on duty at all times. I heard one of them say you'll only be allowed out of here accompanied by an armed escort. You won't escape easily, my lady."

"Hmmm." Sipping from the cup, the princess moved back into the sitting room. "Bring me the ivory casket where I keep my diary, and I'll show you something."

She took a seat by the fire, and when the maid returned with the box she opened it and removed a tiny green-glass phial. "I had this sleeping potion from my friend Ansel the shaman when I was troubled by melancholy. But I found I didn't need it after all. If you somehow persuade the guards outside my door to drink it, then you and I can escape in disguise while they and the castle sleep!"

Rusgann's eyes shifted. She reached into the pocket of her skirt and drew out a folded scrap of grubby parchment. "I don't know what this says, for I never learned to read. But it comes from Red Ansel. I met him by chance in the market yesterday. He was supposed to've been sent back to Tarn, but gave the king's men the slip and stayed to keep an eye on you. When I told him the alchymist and Lady Sovanna had left off dosing you with that devil's brew, he gave me the message."

Maudrayne opened it and read:

Stay where you are until I come. This is vitally important to both of you.

"Both of you," the princess whispered, knowing at once that Ansel was not referring to Rusgann. "Futtered again!"

With a snarl of resignation, she wadded up the parchment and threw it over-hand into the fire with a powerful gesture. "My friend, we'll have to wait. Ansel is up to something, and he wants me to stay here until he comes to get me. Be assured you'll be going along, too. Meanwhile, collect the things we'll need for a long journey and hide them securely. When we do leave this damned place, we won't ever be coming back."

twenty-six

Mero Elwick, armiger and cousin to Count Feribor Blackhorse, had celebrated the taking of Castle Redfern with as much enthusiasm as the rest of the Cathran army. All throughout the previous day of rest, while the army and its animals recovered from crossing the mountains, he'd drunk and caroused with the best of them. But unlike many of his less fortunate fellow-squires, Mero was one of those hardheaded souls who rarely suffer a thick head after overindulgence. Instead he slept well, until he was jolted into alert wakefulness by the small sounds made by Snudge and his three companions as they rose before dawn.

"Hoy!" The big redheaded youth hauled himself onto his elbows. "What're you up and about for? We're not due to leave here until noon."

A fitfully burning candlestub lit the scene. Four shadowy figures were tying up their bedrolls and gathering gear, while seven other man-sized lumps lay on the floor with Mero, snoring in their blankets.

"Be still!" Belamil whispered. "Go back to sleep."

The privileged squires serving the royal brothers and the Heart Companions had been quartered in the small but relatively dry and flea-free chamber that had once housed Redfern's castellan, while that worthy had spent the past two nights shackled in the remnants of the stable, along with the other prisoners of middle rank.

One of the prowlers cursed under his breath. "My damned gauntlets have gone missing."

"Better find them, Saundar," Snudge advised, "or you'll have a devilish time with the cables and heavy chains."

"What chains?" Mero demanded. He was wide awake now, shrugging into his tunic, pulling boots on over bare feet, and rising from his pallet. "Where do you think you're going?"

"On Prince Conrig's business," Snudge said, "and none of yours."

"Ooh! I'll bet you're off on the mystery mission, right? The one you nattered on about that night in Melora. Come on, stable boy, you can tell me!" Fast as a stoat, Mero hopped over a sleeping body, took hold of Snudge's right wrist and elbow, spun him around, and hauled the pinioned arm up tight behind the boy's back in a painful hammerlock.

Mero laughed at Snudge's stifled groan. "Tell me all about it."

"Stop that!" Belamil grabbed Mero by the hair and jerked his head back sharply before the taller armiger broke free, still with a tight grip on Snudge. Saundar came running with a fist cocked, but stopped short at Mero's warning whisper.

"I could break the knave's arm before either of you land a punch. Tell me what's up!"

Gavlok's mild, clear voice said, "We four are going to Mallburn Town in advance of the army to prepare the way. Princess Ullanoth of Moss is there already and requires help with her beneficial magic. We're going to assist her to open the town's bridge gate. Now let Deveron go without harming him."

"Oh, why not?" The bully chortled. "I mustn't deprive you of your gallant leader." He flung Snudge away from him with such violence that the boy fell to the floor. Some of the slumbering squires had begun to stir and mutter.

Belamil said, "That was ill done, Mero. Your master will hear of it."

The redhead sketched a mocking bow to Snudge. "I humbly beg your lordship's pardon for damaging you a wee bit in our friendly tussle. All in good fun, of course! I'll leave you to get on with packing while I go take a piss."

He left the chamber with surprising speed.

Belamil said to Snudge, "Are you all right?"

"Yes. Let's hurry and get out of here before the whoreson comes back. I think he may have more on his tiny mind than satisfying his curiosity."

"My lord. Wake up. It's Mero."

Feribor and the other Heart Companions were sleeping in the castle's cramped solar, next to the baron's single private chamber, which had been taken over by Conrig and Stergos. The count roused himself with difficulty, blinking at the youth who knelt beside his pallet. "What the hell? Is something wrong?"

Mero spoke very quietly so as not to wake the other nobles, but he could not keep the excitement from his voice. "Not wrong. But four armigers, including the wretch Deveron Austrey, are about to leave the castle on what they say is an important secret mission for Prince Conrig. It's to do with aiding our assault on Mallburn Town. They go to meet Princess Ullanoth and assist her with some magical conniving. There was talk of opening the city's bridge gate to our army. I thought you should know."

Feribor cursed luridly. "For this you interrupted my rest? I ought to—" He broke off, seized by some arresting thought, then whispered, "You say Deveron is leading this foray?"

"Yes, my lord. He's chosen Belamil Langsands and Saundar Kersey to accompany him—both great-hearted lads, you will agree. But his third choice is that wispy beanpole Gavlok Whitfell, who serves Vra-Stergos. The dreamy oaf can barely swing a sword! He's not fit for combat. He'll endanger the mission, whatever it may be. I beg you to speak to Prince Conrig. Let me go in Gavlok's place! You know I'm the tilting champion amongst the armigers."

Feribor gave an evil chuckle. "Scheming young glory-hog! Aren't you afraid to get mixed up in magic?"

"Nay, my lord. Why should the Princess Ullanoth wreak harm upon her helpers?"

"Not Ullanoth, you young dunce. Deveron Austrey, Conrig's secret wild talent!"

The armiger was aghast. "Deveron—a magicker? My lord, are you jesting?"

"I wish I were," Feribor said viciously. He sat up and began donning his clothes.

"The young mutt did lead the spunkies to our army when we were struggling to reach the top of the pass," Mero recalled. "Everyone was talking about it. But we thought—"

"Do you know that Deveron single-handedly managed to open Castle Redfern to us as well?" Feribor hissed. "Oh, there was some tale spun about Princess Ullanoth already being inside the castle and the boy merely plying the garrison with liquor. But I chanced to hear two of Catclaw's knights talking in their cups. They said they found six fully armed guards knocked colder than codfish, lying within the gatehouse after the castle fell to us. This was supposedly done by Ullanoth's magic—yet not a single prisoner I spoke to saw hide nor hair of the witch, nor any sign that Mossland sorcery was at work. The six guards were bludgeoned about the head, not sent sweetly to sleep by magical means. I don't believe Ullanoth was ever here! But if she was not, then how did an ordinary youth overcome six armed men? There's only one answer: he's not ordinary. He has a wild talent that enables him to approach persons with uncanny stealth."

"But can you be sure, my lord? Perhaps—"

"There's no doubt. I was told of the brat's talent by a close and trusted friend, one who had suffered greatly because of him." The tall count rose to his feet, drawing his cloak about his shoulders. "Your boyish lust for adventure is very stupid, Mero. Any sensible warrior will tell you never to volunteer for a mission in which you will very likely perish. Nevertheless, I'm going to do my best to grant your foolish request."

The armiger came closer. His eyes were alight with slyness. "You wish me to observe Deveron's tricky ways and advise you what he gets up to in Mallburn Town?"

"I want more than that from you, my lad. Much more." Feribor laid his hand on the brawny squire's arm. His voice was barely audible. "Deveron's dangerous. The prince has no notion how perfidious his little pet can be, but *I* know! And as Conrig's loving friend and Heart Companion, I must do what I can to alleviate the danger—even if it means acting without the prince's knowledge, to save him from his unwisely given trust. Can you be my agent in this grave matter, Cousin?"

"With the greatest pleasure, my lord."

"Of course, nothing must happen to our talented stable boy until his mission has been accomplished. And the other armigers with you must never know his fate—nor Princess Ullanoth, either, if she should present herself to you lads during the fight for the city."

"The low-born wight may be her secret minion!"

"Find that out if you can, before you move against him. Now go gather your things with all speed and meet me down in the bailey. I suspect Prince Conrig is already there."

It was the hour of dawn, but the everpresent fog enveloping the small castle, and the deep gorge wherein it was situated, caused darkness to linger within Redfern's ramparts. Working as quietly as they could, Snudge, Belamil, Saundar, and Gavlok saddled their horses and strapped on their equipment—which included a tarnblaze bombshell for each, hidden inside sacks. They had been given surcoats and shield-covers with the armorial bearings of Lord Maddick's household knights, along with a lance bearing Redfern's pennon. A case full of important-looking documents—scrawled up by Vra-Doman on the previous day and sealed with the baron's own ring—was addressed to court officials at Holt Mallburn. It was hoped that the dispatches and the armigers' disguises would prove sufficient to deflect unwanted attention from them once they reached the Didionite capital. Unlike Conrig's army, which would invade the city after midnight on muffled hooves, the boys had to move about the approaches to Mallburn Town during the early evening, when soldiery and townsfolk would still be about. Even the thick fog could not hide them fully—or so all of them believed, except Snudge.

"I still don't understand how we're going to get close enough to the bridge works to bollocks them up," Saunder grumbled. "There'll be plenty of light around such an important structure. The guards are bound to be suspicious of young fellows poking where they have no business."

Count Tayman's squire was perhaps the brightest of the wellborn cohort, handsome, dark-haired, and deliberate in temperament. He was eighteen years of age and second only to Belamil in the respect of the other armigers.

"I have a way to get us close without notice, and in safety," Snudge reassured him. "I can only beg you to trust me. My plan's bound to work if you all do exactly as I say."

"We will," Belamil said firmly.

Gavlok uttered a gasp of dismay. "Bazekoy's Beard! Here comes Prince Conrig—and look who's with him!"

To avoid the most crowded part of the ward, where watchfires tended by squads of thanes still burned among the ranks of picketed horses and mules, the four had been making preparations near the closed inner portcullis of the gate-house. Conrig and his companion moved purposefully through the throng of men and animals.

"It's Mero." Saunder's voice was full of disbelief. "And he's armed and carrying his gear!"

They waited in stunned silence. Finally Snudge stepped forward to greet the prince, hoping desperately that he was not about to hear the thing he feared. "Your Grace, we're ready to depart. Do you have any final orders for us?"

"A slight change of plan." Conrig flashed an easy smile. "It's been pointed out to me that Gavlok might be better employed in his usual task of guarding

Vra-Stergos. Now that we're about to ride into combat, the Doctor Arcanorum must be shielded from any possible peril, since he's our principal windvoice link to Cala Palace. I've decided that Mero will take Gavlok's place in your company. As you know, he's a splendid young warrior. He'll serve you in good stead and follow your orders faithfully." He turned to the armiger, who stood blank-faced at his side. "Isn't that so?"

"On my honor, Your Grace!" Mero avoided catching Snudge's eye.

"Splendid! Gavlok, strip off your surcoat disguise and shield cover. Help Mero transfer his things onto your mount . . . Deveron, step over here. I have instructions for you."

"Yes, Your Grace." He couldn't hide his dismal expression.

When they were beyond the others' hearing, Conrig said, "This is for the best. I know Gavlok's your good friend, but I had doubts about his suitability even before Count Feribor spoke to me."

"Prowess in martial arts isn't the skill most important to this mission. To make a success of it, I need people with brains . . . and loyalty."

"Feribor is one of my staunchest Companions," the prince said stiffly. "Mero is his cousin, for whom he has extremely high hopes. The boy swore to me he would follow your orders as he would my own. And he's not stupid, even though he's over-fond of brawling and a bit too ready with the rough edge of his tongue."

"I understand, Your Grace. We'll take Mero with us." And leave him trussed in a ditch if he makes trouble . . .

Conrig clapped Snudge on the shoulder. "I knew you'd accept the change in good spirit. Here is the map you requested, and a diagram of the bridge machinery."

Snudge took the folded parchment and tucked it into his belt wallet. "Is there anything else?"

"The Princess Ullanoth bespoke Vra-Stergos late last night. Her windspeech was still weak, but she says she's recovering and will surely be able to open the palace stronghold to us. I've told her I'm sending infiltrators to deal with the bridge gate, but she doesn't know you're the one leading them. Don't go anywhere near her during the fighting! Even though our own alchymists are unable to recognize your talent, we can't be certain about her."

"Beynor knows all about me," Snudge reminded the prince glumly. "But I doubt he'd tell his sister. Still, Red Ansel the shaman had no trouble at all spotting me as an adept. A Mossland sorceress might do the same thing if I came close to her."

"After you lads hit the bridge, attempt to discover if Ullanoth is also doing her part at Holt Mallburn. She may be too occupied to keep in constant wind-contact with us. She intends to approach the palace while invisible, but in the fog, you may be able to scry her body's outline, knowing what to look for."

Snudge nodded. "Inside the lighted palace gatehouse, she'll cast a shadow. It may take some time for a single person to disable the portcullis machinery, open the gates, and contrive to keep them open—even using sorcery. I'll know if she's at work because of the commotion amongst the guards and palace engineers trying to repair the damage. And I'll also know if she comes to grief . . ."

"Bespeak tidings of your progress and that of Ullanoth to Stergos when you can. He'll keep you notified of the army's position. We hope to arrive at the riverside about an hour after midnight. The palace is only a league or so from the river. Coordinate your effort with that of the princess if you are able."

"Your Grace, what if she should prove after all to be too frail to accomplish her mission?"

Conrig took a deep breath. "Then we'll contrive another way to take the palace. But above all, you and your mates must open Mallmouth Bridge to our army. Unless that's done, the invasion is doomed to fail. Come now. I'll speak a few words to your companions."

Together, they returned to Redfern's gatehouse. Gavlok was gone. Belamil and Saundar already sat their horses. Mero climbed into his saddle, smiling in triumph, carrying the lance with Redfern's device.

Snudge said to the thane in charge of the guard detail, "Open the gates and lower the drawbridge. We're sallying forth." He mounted his own horse and wheeled it about to face the prince.

"Young men," Conrig said, "much is depending upon your bravery and daring. Follow Deveron's lead and carry out your mission. Tonight, shortly after midnight, the army of Cathra will be poised to invade Mallburn Town. God grant success!"

"God grant success!" the boys chorused. Then Snudge led them through the gatehouse and over the drawbridge into the fog—where a cluster of several dozen fuzzy yellow sparks waited.

*　*　*

It was a cold, clear dawn in Royal Fenguard. There had been a layer of frost on the balcony outside the closed tall windows of the Conjure-King's suite, and Beynor decided to perform his windsearch indoors, even though it would decrease the keenness of his scrying. He deactivated both Fortress sigils, not caring whether Ullanoth or anyone else watched him, then overviewed Great Pass and Holt Mallburn and discovered that both remained heavily fogbound.

He was no longer surprised. Yesterday, after doing much research, Lady Zimroth had told him that the Small Lights were fully capable of performing such magic. The young king had received the news with a sudden bitter comprehension: Years ago, his sister had responded to his own childhood cultivation of the Darkling Sands Salka by becoming friendly with the abhorrent spunkies.

Beynor decided it would be politically disadvantageous to pass this information on to the Didionites. Instead, he bespoke Honigalus's wizard and confidently announced that he was about to generate the promised gale to speed the war fleet more swiftly southward.

The Crown Prince is deeply grateful for your efforts, Fring replied. *He also requests that the Conjure-King create a storm to delay the Tarnian mercenaries . . . unless, of course, such magic is beyond Your Majesty's powers.*

The insolent weevil! But Beynor could hardly admit that yesterday's sudden favorable wind had been entirely fortuitous and none of his doing, and that he was nearly paralyzed by dread at the thought of what the Lights might do to him following today's use of Weathermaker.

"Of course it's not beyond my powers to delay the Tarnians. As a matter of fact, I'd already thought of doing so myself! Tell the Crown Prince to trust me and get on with his war. And stop bothering me with superfluous requests!"

Beynor cut the windthread before the imperious bastard could begin arguing. Muttering, he restored the spells of the two Fortress sigils, went to a velvet couch in his sitting room, and flung himself onto it.

Curse the Didionites! He was endangering his life for them and still they treated him like a hireling hedge-witch, never offering him the deference that was his due. It was all the fault of the coronation disaster, of course. All the fault of Ulla!

Who had also invaded his private chambers and stolen his two remaining Great Stones. He had not dared confess to Arowann the Salka that he'd lost them.

If only he'd had the courage to empower Destroyer! If only he'd sent the bitch to the Hell of Ice where she belonged!

He groaned, knowing in his heart that recriminations were futile. He must get on with his work, conjure Weathermaker twice, endure its pain, pray that the Lights wouldn't penalize him too drastically, then get on with trying to find a way to outwit Ullanoth. She had to be hiding in Holt Mallburn. Perhaps he should go there secretly and try to hunt her down before Conrig of Cathra started his war. Perhaps—

I'm dithering because I don't want to be tortured. Because I'm afraid I might suffer my mother's unspeakable fate and never even understand what I'd done to offend the damned touchy Beaconfolk . . .

Craven!

He lifted the ring-sigil and began to pronounce the spells that would create gale winds on opposite sides of the island.

But even as he did so, before the anticipated hammerblow of agony rendered him senseless, the startling realization came to him: *Ullanoth could not have taken his Great Stones away*. A Sending could carry nothing new back to its point of origin. Either she had destroyed the two sigils while inside his rooms, or else she'd hidden them, hoping to come back for them some day.

Hidden them?

Crushing pain and blackness were claiming him. Blackness . . . he remembered it on the soles of his feet the morning after he'd discovered that the Great Stones were gone. At the time, he'd been too distraught to understand why there should have been soot on the floor of royal chambers kept immaculately clean by his slaves.

But now he knew what his foolish sister must have done, and falling into the abyss, he smiled.

When she woke in mid-morning, Ullanoth gave grateful thanks to the Moon Mother. Her body was fast recovering. She suffered no ache in her head or belly and she was very hungry, an excellent portent. She made a pottage of barley, bacon, and chopped hard cheese and put it on the fire to cook. Sipping watered mint-angelica liqueur from the clerks' cache to soothe her nerves, she dressed and painted her face, then greased her hair into straggles with the bacon rind. The reflection of Witch Walanoth grinned back at her from the water bucket.

She took up the minor sigil named Beastbidder. Its pain would be minimal, and if it was able to assist her, the journey to Holt Mallburn would be less arduous and she'd have more strength to devote to her task. She conjured a spell, then restored the small animal-shaped stone to her pouch. Time would tell if the sigil's magic had been successful.

By the time she had packed everything she intended to take away from the warehouse, her food was ready. She ate slowly, feeling better every minute, a glow of hope and expectancy lifting her soul. Conrig was coming with his army. By tomorrow at this time—please, Mother!—they would be together, victorious.

It was time to depart. Cautiously, she eased open the side door of the clerks' office, peered out into the fog . . .

Could not resist giggling with delight. Beastbidder had done its work.

A scrawny dapple-grey mare wearing a battered saddle stood there, reins trailing, lathered with sweat and blowing clouds of vapor. The princess knew that somewhere in Mallburn Town its owner must be lying in a gutter, cursing the silly nag that had abruptly thrown him and run off.

"I'll call you Mist," she said, patting the animal. After retrieving her fardel and lashing it to the saddle, she adjusted the stirrups and mounted. Her cloak hid details of the mare's tack in case the Town Watch were looking out for her, so there was no need to go invisible as yet.

She called out on the wind. "Shanakin! Are numbers of you ready to follow me? I'll require special service of you very soon."

We're here, lady, as you commanded. More of us arrive in the city with every passing moment, now that we need no longer create the widespread fog beyond the mountains. We're very hungry.

She laughed aloud. "Soon. Tonight! Even the most cautious townsfolk will flee their homes and fall helpless into your power. But even better will be the well-fed prey at the palace! It will be the greatest feast you've ever known. But you must not harm the Cathrans. Never—if you hope to keep my friendship."

We understand.

She rode off into the grey fog at a slow walk, ascending the winding maze of streets that led from the waterfront to Holt Mallburn. Now and then tiny points of golden luminosity were perceptible in the darker byways of the city, but none of them were visible near the old crone who rode along as confidently as a queen.

twenty-seven

With unaccustomed forbearance Mero remained silent, riding in the rear while the spunkies created the now familiar fog-free tunnel and guided the four armigers down the sharp switchbacks toward the great valley of the River Malle.

As the falcon flew (if one had dared the murky sky), the distance from Red-fern to the capital was less than thirty leagues along this shortcut trail. But the terrain was so steep, descending a perilous escarpment, that most who traveled between the castle and Mallburn Town used a second road that followed the gorge to Rockport and then joined the Coast Highway, even though the distance was nearly doubled thereby.

After seven hours the boys finally arrived in the lowlands, having met only a goatherd with a single goat, some gaunt-faced children gathering fagots, and a pair of old women carrying a basket of some wild edibles they'd gathered off the mountainside. All of these persons plunged away from the trail with squeals of terror, thinking they had encountered phantoms, when the troop loomed up behind them in the fog, eerily lighted on its way by the spunkies.

A thin drizzle had begun by the time the narrow track turned into a sem-blance of a road and the armigers entered the first Didionite village. It might have been a fairly prosperous place once, but the famine had reduced it to a squalid ruin. Most of the roadside cottages had been sacked and burnt. If folk still lived thereabouts, they were silent and secretive for fear of raiders. The village inn, built sturdily of local stone, still had its roof, although the door and the shutters for the upstairs windows were gone.

Snudge dismounted, handed his reins to Belamil, and went to the inn entrance to inspect the interior with his windsight. "Nobody there," he announced. "It's dry, there are scraps of wood about from broken-down walls and such, and the hearth seems undamaged."

"How can you tell?" Mero inquired innocently. "It's almost pitch black inside."

"I've got eyes like a cat! We could do worse than stop here to rest and eat. If the chimney's not clogged, we could even chance a fire. No reason why the horses can't come in, too, out of the wet."

"But not the willy-wisps!" said Saundar with a shudder.

Mero was the only one who laughed, but he clamped his jaws almost at once, remembering the rumor about Sir Ruabon—and the cries of the sacrificed livestock outside Castle Redfern.

"I'll tell the Small Lights to remain without," Snudge reassured the others.

"How do you talk to them?" Mero asked. "They don't speak our language. All they do is squeak and chitter."

"When I whisper, they understand," Snudge lied. "But I suggest you don't start giving them orders. They only answer to me because their leader Shanakin commanded them to obey." And warned them not to drain our blood on the way to Mallburn Town . . .

Snudge produced a tarnstick, which miraculously lit in spite of the pervasive damp, with only a small assist from his talent. Tinder and twigs blazed and smoke went properly up the inn's chimney. Snudge and Saundar broke up wood for fuel, while Belamil used a bunch of dead weedstalks to sweep the area in front of the fireplace. Mero meekly filled the horses' nosebags and gave them water from a leather bucket.

They roasted fat sausages, spread toasted chunks of bread with soft cheese, and finished off with honeycakes made of oats, raisins, and filberts. A skin of ale, passed from hand to hand throughout the meal, almost made them forget how cold and clammy they felt. The horses munched their grain, stamped and whiffled, and filled the derelict tavern with the pungent scent of their droppings. It was all rather cozy until Snudge took out the map parchment and spread it on the hearthstone, preparing to describe the next phase of the mission. The others gathered close.

"I think we're right here, in a hamlet called Brayshaw. From now on, we travel as fast as possible so as to reach the River Malle by eventide. About ten leagues from here there'll be another village, Hoolton, that's larger and very likely inhabited—but most of the people will probably be locked safely inside their houses because of the fog. We'll gallop right on through, and if anyone peeks out and spies us, they'll be too frightened by the ghost riders to do anything about it."

The others chuckled.

"We keep going to this T-junction with the highway, where there's a sizable place called Bardsea, and turn left. Fortunately for us, most of the town lies off the main road, down by the shore where there's a harbor. The Coast Highway goes directly to Mallburn Town, and once we're on it we have to change tactics, since we're bound to encounter sophisticated travelers or even Didionite patrols."

Belamil drawled, "No more spectres enveloped in glowing vapors, scaring the wits out of the simple peasantry?"

"No," Snudge agreed, with a thin smile. "I'll command the Small Lights to stop creating the uncanny tunnel and just carry on leading us through the fog, glowing dimly and floating an ell or so in front of each courser, down close to the surface of the road."

Mero was incredulous. "The horses will never follow spunkies!"

"Yes they will. Prince Conrig told me it would work, after being reassured of it by Princess Ullanoth. I tried it out successfully on my trip down the mountain to Castle Redfern, riding a mule. Of course, mules are often smarter than horses, but just keep spurring your beast on, and after a while he'll get the idea and trot after the guiding Lights like a sheep."

"I hope you're right," the redhead growled. "What happens if we meet Didionites?"

"It probably won't happen too often. If it does, the Lights will go dim and squeak a warning well ahead of time. Rein up, get off the highway, and wait in the fog till the enemy riders pass. The Lights will extinguish themselves without being told."

"Is that why we haven't seen the others?" Saundar inquired thoughtfully. "The creatures generating all this magical fog?"

"Yes," Snudge said. "They shine only when they want to."

"The rest of the time," Belamil said with grisly relish, "they lurk. And not timidly, either, like the spunkies down south in Cathra! There are thousands and thousands of them up here in the north country, infesting the swamps, waiting for unwary prey. My granny told me so."

"The devil take your granny," Mero grumbled.

Snudge continued. "We should reach the river by dusk—or what would be dusk if there was no fog. We'll send our weird little friends away then, ignite torches, and proceed to the bridge as though we were a legitimate troop of dispatch riders. If the guards at Mallmouth accept our pose, we'll ride into the city like we own the place, find a spot to hide the horses, and get on with our job. Mallburn Town is supposed to be half deserted because of the famine. Only the docks, the precinct where the rich merchants live, and the great Malle Road leading from the bridge to the palace are well lit at night."

"What happens if the guards at the bridge gate don't want to admit us?" Mero asked.

"We get righteously huffy, wheel smartly about, and warn them we'll be back in the morning to make big trouble. Don't worry. I have another way of getting us inside the city if it becomes necessary."

"How?" Mero persisted.

"Ask me after we're turned away—but be sure your shoulders are well limbered up for rowing against a tidal current." He flipped the map, revealing a diagram of the bridge fortifications on its reverse side. "Now, take a careful look at this, lads. I've been told the Mallmouth Bridge is a great wonder of engineering, much more impressive than any bridge in Cathra. The Diddlies may be barbarians, but they're very clever barbarians."

The others studied the drawing in silence. The bridge was over five hundred feet long. The four fixed spans closest to the city shore were supported by three massive stone piers rising from the riverbed. Only small boats could pass beneath the arches. Taking the place of a fourth pier was a fortified tower, also with its foundations in the water. It contained the bridge gate, which consisted of two heavy iron portcullises at either end of the central passage. Within the tower was also the machinery that lifted a movable span linking the bridge to the opposite shore, where there was a small guardpost and a tollbooth.

Saundar poked the parchment with a finger. "This final section of the bridge lifts to let tall ships through. And look: when the leaf is up, the city's neatly isolated from invaders like us coming from the south."

"Right," said Snudge. "The next bridge over the river is nearly sixty leagues upstream, at Mallthorpe. Between there and Mallmouth, the people must use ferryboats to cross."

Belamil was frowning at the diagram. "But how does the movable span lift? There are no chains coming from the tower to the end of the leaf, so it can't be a regular drawbridge. And the leaf is so long!"

Snudge nodded. "Nearly ninety feet. It's called a bascule, and it lifts like a kind of gigantic one-sided see-saw. Look here at this smaller sketch. There's a counterweight inside a great vault attached to the southern side of the tower, along with a pivot—something like a huge cart-axle—that enables the bridge-leaf to move up and down."

"I see it now." Belamil almost had his nose to the parchment. "And once we disable the counterweight machinery, the bridge gets stuck in the down position."

The counterweight was only partly made of caged granite blocks. On its upper side was a large iron chamber that was pumped full of water or drained dry when it was time to raise or lower the bascule. It took two dozen men to operate the pumps.

"As you may have guessed," Snudge said, "it strongly behooves us to launch the first part of our attack when the bridge is down. I could get us across the water gap in a small boat and into the tower while the bascule leaf was raised— but there's no way just the four of us could pump out the counterweight chamber and lower the bridge again."

"Deveron." Saundar's intelligent brow was deeply furrowed. "I know we promised not to question your plan—but this task seems less and less within the realm of possibility, the more you tell us about it."

"I'll say!" Mero chimed in.

"The task can be achieved," Snudge insisted, "and by us. Four tarnblaze bombshells exploded within the counterweight water-chamber will crack it badly and damage the pump mechanism so that neither one can be fixed for days—even weeks. We accomplish that task first, then jam open the two portcullises of the bridge gate. They are raised and lowered with ordinary chains and windlasses located on the upper floor of the tower."

"Sounds easy as pie," Mero said in a scathing tone, licking honey off his big fingers. "We'll just marshal up a thousand spunkies and order 'em to drink the blood of every foeman inside the bridge tower."

"No," Snudge said equably. "My plan is quite different, and it doesn't include magical mayhem."

"But there will be some sort of magic at work, I presume!"

"There will," Snudge agreed.

"Then tell us what kind!" Mero demanded, jumping to his feet with hands clenched. "And what about Princess Ullanoth? Is she going to help us with sorcery?"

Snudge shook his head. "You'll hear details of the plan when I'm ready to tell them. Do you intend to dispute my leadership, even after promising Prince Conrig you'd follow without question? Or does the thought of magic frighten you?"

The big armiger's face went dark with fury. "Are you calling me a coward—" He broke off, his jaw dropping, as a high-pitched, wavering screech came from outside the inn. "Futter me! What the hell was that?"

Belamil dashed to the open doorway. "Nothing outside but fog. Our guiding spunkies seem to be gone."

"The murdering wee wankers are probably killing someone," Mero growled. "We could be next!"

Snudge said, "The Small Lights aren't dangerous to human beings in daytime. Even at night, when they're strongest, it takes large numbers of them to overcome a grown man or woman. Of course a small child, in thick fog . . ." He trailed off uncomfortably.

"Perhaps the noise was just a fox taking a hare," Saunder said, clearly believing nothing of the sort.

"I think it's time for us to press on," Snudge decided. "Pack up. And collect some wood we can use for torches. I have a pot of pitch we can dip them in later."

He folded the parchment and put it into his belt-pouch, then went outside to call the missing spunkies back from whatever mischief they had been up to.

Even with the mare named Mist moving at a snail's pace, Ullanoth arrived at the great hill-park surrounding Holt Mallburn palace in early afternoon. Its wrought-iron gates were locked, but she rode boldly up to the sentinels on duty and addressed them in cracked, querulous tones.

"How does one get an audience with King Achardus?"

The armed men regarded her with amused scorn. "These darksome days, one doesn't," said the sergeant. "I'm surprised you don't know that, Gammer."

"I've come a distance," she admitted, "all the way from Highcliff hoping to appeal our baron's unjust sentencing to death of my grandson. Poor Nallo never burnt those hayricks! They only blamed him because he's not quite right in the head. I realize my appearance is not prepossessing, messire, but I'm not without means. I hoped His Majesty would accept a nice token from me and look kindly on my petition for clemency."

The sergeant's eyes shone with greed. "You could give the petition and the token to me. I'll take it in straightaway."

"Then His Majesty *is* in residence?"

"Where else would he be?" The man was getting impatient. "Well?"

She feigned concerned thought. "Oh, dear! I'd set my heart on seeing the king myself. If you could but arrange it, messire, there'd be a lovely token for you, too."

"King Achardus doesn't see the commonalty. Give over your petition and coin, woman, and stop wasting my time."

"I must go back to the inn and fetch them," she said. "Expect my return in an hour or so."

She dug her heels into the mare's ribs and cantered away into the fog before the guards could restrain her. "Or better yet," she murmured to herself, "expect me when you least expect me!"

The princess turned into a narrow alley between tall, shuttered shops, a place she had scouted out before approaching the Royal Park. She dismounted and removed the fardel she had lashed to the saddle.

"Now you must go back where you belong, Mist," she informed the dapple grey, and commanded the moonstone named Beastbidder to find the mare's rightful home and compel her to return there.

"Small Lights?" she called on the wind. "Shanakin?"

A swarm of golden sparks with a single blue-white one among them winked into view. *Yes, lady?*

"I require you now to travel with this mare to her home and keep her safe from human villains."

We would rather suck the juices from the beast, lady. And the villains, too.

"Do as I say! All of you leave me now. I intend to rest for some hours. Await my summons outside the main gatehouse of Holt Mallburn Palace at midnight."

The mare pricked up her ears as though listening. A moment later she trotted off downhill, in the direction of the city center. The spunkies had vanished.

Ullanoth replaced Beastbidder and readied Interpenetrator. It would make short work of the iron fence around the park—to say nothing of the palace walls.

Yes, she would rest—but not before using the enhanced viewing powers of Subtle Loophole to study everyone who interested her. Too much time had passed without her being able to scrutinze the play-actors in her great drama and make certain that all was well.

She intended to oversee Achardus in his palace, her wicked little brother Beynor, King Olmigon of Cathra, the fleet of Tarnian mercenaries, the distant Southern Continent where the corsairs of Foraile and Stippen were gathering, Crown Prince Honigalus and his armada, and Conrig and his invasion force.

It would be an uncomfortable session that might lay her low for hours, but performing the difficult oversight within Holt Mallburn itself would be deliciously satisfying. Before undertaking the work she'd savor fine food and drink from the royal kitchen and buttery, take a much-needed bath, and wash her hair. Snooping about hidden by Concealer, she'd surely be able to find suitable fresh garments for herself in the wardrobe of one of the Didionite princesses. It would never do to welcome Conrig wearing the rags of Witch Walanoth. Later, when the ordeal of scrying was over, she'd take her repose in one of the palace's elegant guest rooms.

How ironic it was that she should come so harmlessly into the innermost stronghold of Didion! Invisible, able to pass through the thickest wall or the most secure door, she could kill Achardus Mallburn as easily as a rabbit, opening the veins of the giant monarch's throat with his own purloined dagger. But she would not. Such a gross deed was not fitting for a future Conjure-Queen, nor did she have any personal animosity towards Didion's king. Vengeance belonged to Conrig Wincantor. All Ullanoth intended to do was make that vengeance possible, with the help of her friends.

Subtle Loophole showed Achardus Mallburn, his Privy Council, Archwizard Ilingus, and Queen Siry Boarsden wrangling over penalties to be imposed on the treacherous timberlords of Firedrake Water, who had refused to send troops to join Prince Somarus's defense force at Great Pass. How boring! But it was interesting that the tall queen favored the most drastic punishment of the rebels, and the men seemed inclined to let her have her way. The royal women of Didion were far from being mere political pawns or broodstock . . .

Beynor lay unconscious in his bed, tended by Zimroth, Master Ridcanndal, and the Royal Physician, who had been granted permission to penetrate the spells of couverture generated by his two Fortress sigils. Her brother was in a sorry state after using his Weathermaker to conjure a strong fair wind to speed the Didionite armada and a strong foul one to delay the Tarnians. The doctor opined that the Conjure-King might not recover for two days. Good! Beynor's antics would not distract her during the battle for Holt Mallburn . . .

The sigil showed King Olmigon of Cathra looking like a man at death's door, but nonetheless giving crackling orders to his anxious windvoices. He was attempting to regroup the divided Cathran navy into a single force, and complained bitterly about the alchymists' inability to maintain reliable communication with ships on the high seas. Vra-Sulkorig blamed malignant magic. King Olmigon himself voiced suspicions that his admirals were determined to fight the Didionites in their own fashion, without being distracted by royal meddling . . .

The Tarnian frigates were shortening sail and putting out sea-anchors to counter the savage tempest now assaulting them off the Stormy Isles. Viewing them with concern, Ullanoth hoped she would not have to use her own Weathermaker to help them reach Cathra in time . . .

The Continental ships were gathered in the Stippenese port of Nis-Gata, their crews carousing ashore and their captains showing no immediate intention of putting out to sea. Strange . . .

Crown Prince Honigalus and Fleet Admiral Galbus Peel were playing chess and chewing hard ship's biscuit aboard the south-charging *Casabarela Regnant*. Peel was winning the game, but the prince didn't seem to mind. During the brief time of her oversight, neither man discussed the upcoming sea battle, except to say that it might take place on the morrow if Beynor's driving gale remained constant . . .

Last of all (as she thought), she focused the sigil on Conrig. Her breath quickened and her heart leapt when she saw him again. She wondered how she could ever have forgotten his face. His uncovered wheat-colored hair sparkled with droplets of moisture as he conferred with the leading nobles of the invasion force in the ward of Redfern Castle. His cheeks were flushed, his lips bore a confident smile, and his dark eyes blazed with confidence as he reviewed tactical assignments. She felt a deep warmth stirring within herself and recalled how good it had been when they were together.

Yes, she told herself. If I have it in me to love any man, I will love Conrig

Wincantor. Together we'll conquer and rule this island. And if anyone can help him to aspire beyond the Sovereignty of High Blenholme and equal Bazekoy's glory, I am that person!

But what was the prince telling the Cathrans now?

She was first disbelieving, then shocked to hear Conrig say—and the other leaders agree—that the opening of the Mallmouth Bridge gate by a certain band of armiger infiltrators was more crucial to the success of their attack than her own role admitting the army to Holt Mallburn itself . . .

Trembling with anger, as well as with the worsening pain and weakness caused by use of the Great Stone, she aimed Subtle Loophole at the mysteriously important boys and found them riding toward the Coast Highway, guided through thick fog by spunkies. The four youths were under the age of twenty, all of them squires who had been at Castle Vanguard during Conrig's council of war. They were disguised as Didionite knights and spoke not a word to one another.

Why on earth had the prince entrusted these ordinary lads with such a vital mission? How could they possibly hope to open a fortified bridge guarded by dozens of armed men? Had Conrig made some foolish miscalculation?

Ullanoth forced herself to scry the quartet more closely. A burly older boy with a truculent air, having a fringe of brick-red hair straggling out from beneath his chain mail hood. A stocky, well-muscled youth who was singing bawdy ballads in a fine tenor voice to lighten the tedium of the ride through limbo. A tall clever-looking boy who sometimes sang along with his companion. And the youngest of the party, slender and broad-shouldered, with comely but forgettable facial features—

Forgettable save for his eyes, which the uncanny clarity of Subtle Loophole revealed were a vibrant blue . . . and afire with the unmistakable gleam of a powerful wild talent.

"What do you mean—the Continentals refuse to rendezvous with us off the Vigilants?" Honigalus smashed his fist down on the chessboard, sending the pieces scattering in all directions.

Fring the wizard blinked at this unusual display of agitation from the normally phlegmatic prince. He stood with folded arms thrust up the sleeves of his black gown and assumed an irksome expression of long-suffering. "Royal Highness,

I don't presume to analyze wind-messages from our allies. I only report them. May I continue?"

Regaining his self-control, Honigalus sighed. "Proceed."

"A conference of corsair captains has unanimously agreed to delay joining with our fleet until after we have successfully engaged the Cathrans for the first time. Until then, their fifteen frigates and thirteen corvettes will remain in Nis-Gata, a port some seventy leagues south of the Vigilant Isles. They intend to send out a squadron of fast cutters, forming a windvoice relay, to observe and report upon the battle."

"Putting me to the test, the slimy bungholers! Making absolutely certain Didion has the upper hand before finally committing themselves."

"Apparently, Highness."

"So much for Beynor of Moss and his precious Treaty of Alliance. Damn— if only the pirates of Andradh had agreed to join us! The Harriers are not nearly so lily-livered as their neighbors to the east." Honigalus turned to Fleet Captain Peel, who had remained seated at the chart table on the opposite side of she chessboard, keeping his expression unreadable. "What do you think of this development, Galbus?"

"The Continentals are a wily lot. It'll do us no good to attempt to pressure them. All we can do is acquit ourselves valorously against the foe, and pray that the Continentals never learn that Cathra is expecting reinforcements from Tarn."

twenty-eight

For most of their journey along the Coast Highway, the four armigers met no one. Even the usual wandering packs of curs that infested the approaches to large cities were absent, perhaps having been trapped and eaten by the famished countryfolk. The fog was as thick as ever, smelling of the sea, which was now closely adjacent to the road. Mercifully, the cold drizzle had stopped. As they neared the great river they were aware of occasional walled manor houses on their left, with gate-flanking firebaskets shining dimly through the greyness. Finally, when the sky overhead ahead began to darken, they heard the faint slow tolling of a great bell marking the fifth hour after noontide.

"The city must be very close," Belamil said.

At that moment the spunkies began to squeak and grow dim. The boys hastily drew aside as a fine coach, escorted by eight armed linkmen trailing sparks from their firebrands, came up from behind them and thundered past.

"I was beginning to wonder if any Didionites were left alive in this infernal fog," Saundar muttered.

"I'll wager the coach is hurrying to get through the bridge gate before it closes for the night," Belamil said. "We should waste no time ourselves."

"Let's stop here and get our own torches ready," Snudge said. He dismounted and extracted the pitch pot from one of his saddlebags. "Take care of it, lads, while I go down to the shore and reconnoiter. Maybe the mist is thinner over the water and I can catch sight of our goal."

He withdrew, moving cautiously until he heard waves dashing on rocks, then sent his windsight due north across the estuary, like a gull skimming the surface of the sea. No human eye could see much of anything, but his talent scried the

shadowy silhouettes of docks and buildings along the immense quay, which curved
for nearly three leagues along the opposite shore. Sighting along its frontage, moving toward the river, he perceived at last the outline of the Mallmouth Bridge.

It was enormous, longer than any span he'd ever seen before. Even obscured
by mist, the fortified tower seemed the size of a small castle keep. The leaf of the
bascule was still down.

But how long would it stay that way?

"Small Lights!" he called. "Are you with me?"

The luminous swarm winked into existence. *Some of us are, human. Most of
our number have already gathered inside the city to await the great feast promised to
us by the lady. The bridge you seek is very near. With torches, you should not require
our assistance to find it. Give us leave to join Shanakin and our fellows.*

For a feast!

Our reward!

"Go. But remember to harm none of my people!"

We obey Shanakin and the lady, not you. Fight your fight and be damned, human.

Snudge felt his gorge rise, wondering again whether Prince Conrig knew
how Ullanoth intended to secure his victory, and whether he cared.

He ran back to the others, vaulted into his saddle, and accepted a torch from
Saundar. "Only a league left to go now," he said. "I could see the bridge lights
across the water. Spur your horses to a gallop!"

In the end, it was almost laughably easy to pass through. The small guardpost on
the southern shore was manned by hollow-eyed troops whose sergeant studied
their forged papers with apathy, then ran a dirty hand along the sleek damp flank
of Mero's horse. The big armiger had taken the leadership role, since he bore the
barony's pennon. He was the only one of the group without a torch.

"Looks like Castle Redfern's hardly feeling the famine at all, from the looks of
your mounts," the Didionite observed, not bothering to conceal his envy. "Better
keep a sharp eye out for gangs of starving desperados once you get inside the city,
messires. They'll cut you down in a trice just to get their teeth into this juicy
horseflesh."

Mero lifted the banner in salute. "Thank you, sergeant. We'll stay alert. Come
along, men!"

They trotted across the bascule and into the fortified tower. Snudge counted at least twenty-five armed warriors inside the well-lit structure, but no one there possessed talent. He noted with his windsight the passages leading to the counterweight vault and the upper storey where the portcullis machinery was. As in most well-designed gatehouses, the roof of the area between the iron grates was perforated with scores of murder-holes. Anyone trapped between the two lowered portcullises risked being arrow-shot or pelted with deadly missiles.

But that didn't worry Snudge. The real cause for concern was his windsight of the vault, where engineers were obviously preparing to man the pumps and lift the bascule for the night.

When the armigers rode out of the tower they continued on only until they reached the first of the three bridge piers, where Snudge signaled a halt. He could detect no one else crossing in either direction, and they were beyond the view of anyone in the tower.

"I've decided we must leave our horses here," he said, "rather than take them all the way across and hide them inside the town. We're fast running out of time. The Didionites are preparing to raise the bridge."

"How do you know that?" Mero demanded.

Snudge didn't answer the question. Dismounting, he snuffed his torch and ordered the others to do the same and tie their mounts to the bridge railing. Each squire then removed the sack holding tarnblaze from his saddle and refastened the awkward load to his belt.

"We'll not use our swords during this mission unless it becomes absolutely necessary," Snudge said. "I have special weapons for us that are more likely to convince the foe that supernatural beings are on the loose." He handed around thick wool socks half-filled with copper coins, which the other armigers regarded at first with bemused disbelief. "A smart blow on the head from this, swung wide, will render the strongest man senseless, even if he's struck through a mail hood. Try to hit behind the ear rather than on the top of the skull."

"But the guards are sure to see us coming at them!" Belamil protested.

"No, they won't." Snudge pulled the leather thong holding his bagged sigil from beneath his armor and uncovered the moonstone. It shone pale green in the golden haze emanating from the widely spaced bridge lamps. "Here is a powerful amulet of invisibility that I took from the dead body of the sorcerer I killed at Castle Vanguard. Prince Conrig knows all about it. I have dedicated the amulet to his service. It will shield all of us from the eyes of the enemy."

"Codders!" murmured Saundar. The others stared goggle-eyed.

"Step close," Snudge commanded, "one beside me and the other two directly behind. The amulet's magic hides its wearer and anyone else within four ells of him, if commanded to do so."

"Show us," Mero demanded. He took a place as Snudge's left, while Belamil and Saundar perforce had to fall in behind.

"Best cling to one another's surcoat tails," Snudge said. "We'll be invisible to each other as well as to the foe. Let's start off moving slowly back along the bridge, then speed up once we get the hang of staying together. While we're within thick fog, our outline is dimly visible. Once inside the lighted tower, we'll cast faint shadows. No need to worry overmuch about that, though! With the guards getting ready to lock up, there'll be other shadows aplenty. Remember: if you move four ells away from me at any time, you'll become visible again and vulnerable to the enemy. I'll take us directly to the vault entry, which is near the southern portcullis, on the right side as we approach. If anyone gets in our way, push them gently aside. No violence unless I give the command . . . Are you ready?"

Three voices muttered "Aye."

"BI DO FYSINEK. FASH AH."

Three yawps of astonishment from three invisible mouths.

"Are those the words of the magic spell?" Mero asked softly.

"Yes," Snudge said. "Now hold tight to each other and let's go."

After some initial stumbling and cursing, the boys settled into a steady lope that swiftly brought them back to the tower. No one spoke.

Mero was wild with an excitement that had nothing to do with the upcoming action. An amulet of invisibility! Count Feribor had said nothing about Deveron possessing such a thing. Feribor probably knew nothing about it—nor need he ever know.

Before I kill the young bastard, Mero thought, I'll force him to show me how to work the amulet. The other two will have to die also, of course, but such things happen during battle.

The boys moved without hindrance down into the pumping area beneath the bridge deck, which was accessed by a flight of stone steps. There, as Snudge had predicted, they found the team of twenty-four workers already manning a line of twelve stout pump handles. Water drawn from the river passed through a great hosepipe made of tarred leather into the huge metal chamber mounted atop the main counterweight, pushing it down into the vault as the chamber filled. As the counterweight sank, the bascule leaf pivoted upward.

The weight was already starting to edge downward.

"Quick!" Snudge whispered. "Stand abreast and strike them down!"

The workers dropped, four at a time. A few uttered cries of surprise and confusion as they saw their mates mysteriously stricken, but most fell without a sound. The last to drop were the two stupefied engineers, who had stood rooted to the spot as the pumper team was dispatched, only to attempt to escape up the steps at the last minute. Unseen armigers tripped the fleeing pair, then clouted them as they lay sprawled on the damp stone floor.

"KRUF AH. BI FYSINEK."

The four boys reappeared, grinning at each other. But Snudge sobered quickly as he took a better look at the great water tank, which was almost the size of a small cottage. Its top lay about six feet below the level of the pumping platform and was separated from it by a gap of nearly ten feet.

"Damn it! I didn't think the water-chamber would be completely lidded over with metal, except for the place where the hose goes in. We'll have to cut the hose with our swords to get the tarnblaze bombshells inside. A pity no one carries a battle-axe."

Saundar said, "Belamil and I have the heaviest broadswords. We'll do the job."

Snudge nodded. "See that catwalk along the wall of the vault? Go along it to the opposite side, climb over the pivot housing, and then down onto the top of the tank. All we need is a hole in the hose large enough to drop the bunched shells through. Be careful! The hose might spew water when you hack through it. Don't slip and fall into the vault . . . Leave your sacks of tarnblaze here, and I'll get the shells prepared."

Mero was assigned to guard the stairs, with orders to get close to Snudge if he heard someone coming so that they could both defend themselves while invisible. The great vault was poorly lit by torches, so there was a good chance the two boys working on the hose would not immediately be seen by the guards.

Snudge unwrapped the tarnblaze bombshells, black iron spheres about two handspans in diameter, with long wicks protruding from their iron necks. Each shell was enclosed in a net made of stout cord for easy handling. The infernal devices were usually used in siege engines or in naval catapults when an explosive effect was required, rather than a gout of unquenchable fire.

Snudge used leather thongs from the sacks to tie two of the shells to his own swordbelt. The others he lashed together and slung about his neck. They weighed at least ten pounds apiece.

Saundar and Belamil reached their goal and began chopping. The hose was twice as thick as a man's leg. Though flexible to accommodate the movement of the counterweight, it was obviously extremely tough.

"I'm going to cross over," Snudge told Mero, "to be ready as soon as they finish making the hole."

"Why not leave your invisibility amulet with me?" Mero suggested. "You won't need it—and I might."

"The magic only works for the stone's owner. I'm able to use it only because Iscannon the sorcerer died. It burns any other person who touches it."

Mero's eyes narrowed a fraction. "But I tried to take it from you once when we were horsing around. Remember? You kneed me in the balls! I'm sure I touched the amulet then."

And so he had—before it had been empowered.

"No, you couldn't have done." Snudge's tone was offhand. "I'll send Belamil and Saundar back before I toss the bombshells into the water-chamber. All of you take cover in the alcove behind the stairs when I give the signal. I don't think the explosion will blast the counterweight to pieces and kill me, but if it does, the rest of you will have to secure the portcullis machinery as best you can."

Mero gasped. "Saint Zeth! . . . But how shall we do it?"

"With luck, there'll be so much confusion after the blast that no one will pay much attention to you, even if you're visible. Just take off your knightly surcoats so you're not obvious outsiders. Climb to the upper floor, strike down anyone you find there, and barricade yourselves in. Then lower both portcullises and keep them down until Prince Conrig and the army arrive. There'll be the usual weapons stockpiled above to shoot with or drop through the murder-holes. Use them if the trapped guards refuse to surrender. Just be damned certain that no foeman gets out of the tower and across the bridge to give warning in Mallburn Town."

"Very well . . . You seem to have thought this out rather thoroughly."

Snudge shot a glance over his shoulder as he headed for the catwalk. "Stable boys have their share of low cunning."

"You're more than that, Deveron," Mero said smoothly, "as you've reminded the rest of us often enough." He drew his razor-sharp varg sword and strode through the collapsed bodies of the pump workers to take up his position near the stairs.

"Ready?" Snudge called. "Take cover, everyone! I'm lighting the bomb wicks."

He had tied all four of the wax-soaked fuses together. After igniting them with his talent, he balanced the net-covered iron spheres on the ragged edge of the hose-cut until the flames disappeared into the necks of the shells. Then he pushed the deadly load into the hole and scrambled for his life.

As he dove behind the bascule pivot, a devastating thunderclap of sound deafened him. He felt the massive iron housing lurch and sway like a speeding cart hitting a pothole. Water rained down on him, and the entire vault chamber was instantly filled with an opaque cloud. Snudge lay flat, covering his head with his arms, while echoes of the explosion reverberated from stone and metal. The entire tower shuddered. A single fragment of broken iron clanged down, narrowly missing his body.

Then it was over. He heard distant shouts from the bridge deck above, a stifled groan that was much closer, and the continuing sound of rushing water leaking from the great ruptured tank. The wall-torches had been extinguished and the only illumination came from the staircase opening. Trembling, filthy, and soaking wet inside his chain mail, Snudge struggled to his feet and attempted to use his talent to scry the others in the misty shadows on the opposite side of the vault.

Another low groan. He searched the alcove where his companions had taken refuge and saw a single figure standing upright amidst the swirling steam clouds. A second crouched on the floor, bent over a third, who lay prone and motionless.

Snudge felt his way back to the pumping platform along the catwalk, which had remained intact. From above, a Didionite shouted, "Hoy! Down there in the vault! What in God's name has happened?"

Snudge yelled, "Don't come down! Danger! Don't come down!"

"Deveron?" A voice called softly from near the stairs. Mero.

Snudge scried that the bully still held his sword, and its tip rested at the back of the crouching squire's neck. Whoever that other boy was, he had lost both his helmet and his mail hood.

"Are you safe, Deveron?" Mero called out again. "I can't see you. Come across.

I think Saundar was hurt by a piece of falling iron and Belamil may be injured, too. Come and help us."

Oh, shite . . .

Snudge grasped Concealer and silently bespoke the spell. He reached the platform, where a few of the bludgeoned workers were stirring and moaning. The cloud of vapor dissipated rapidly, revealing Mero's burly figure looming above the other squires.

"What have you done?" Snudge said quietly. He had come to a halt a dozen feet away from the trio. Slowly, he drew his own sword.

Mero chuckled. "Ah. So you've gone invisible, have you? But I'm certain you can see me—with your damned wild talent, if no other way. Belamil will die in the next instant, unless you cancel the amulet's spell and show yourself. Do it now!" The blade of the varg glittered wickedly.

"BI FYSINEK. Don't harm him!"

Belamil lifted his head and stared at Snudge with eyes bereft of hope. "He's gone mad. He coshed us both with a sock before you set off the bombshells. When I woke after the blast, I saw he'd slain poor Saundar—"

"Shut up!" Mero barked. To Snudge: "Cast down your sword." After that was done, he said, "Take off the amulet and put it on the floor. Carefully."

"Don't!" Belamil shouted.

But Snudge obeyed. Mero nodded in grim satisfaction. "Now step back from it ten paces and get on your knees." Again, the younger boy complied. "Good."

"You can't use the stone yourself," Snudge said desperately. "It only responds to persons of talent. If you touch it, you'll be burnt!"

"Liar."

"I've done what you asked. Let Belamil go free!"

"Yes. I'll give him his freedom."

Mero thrust the varg into Belamil's nape with a single savage thrust, killing him before he could utter another sound. Snudge screamed in horrified disbelief. "You murdering whoreson!"

"Don't move!" Mero bellowed. He let the body fall. Three swift paces brought him to the green-glowing sigil. With a crow of triumph, he scooped Concealer up by its thong and held it dangling from his left hand. His right still gripped the hilt of the bloodstained varg. "Now it's time for me to go invisible and finish you off . . . BI DO FYSINEK!"

Nothing happened.

Mero cursed in a good-natured fashion. "Of course! I forgot one important detail. First, the former owner must die!" He flipped the sigil on its thong, intending to stuff it into his belt-pouch, and grasped the moonstone in his bare fist.

His shriek of agony echoed in the vault. Snudge smelled something like burning pork. He rolled frantically sideways as Mero reflexively brought down the varg with all his strength, still voicing that hideous scream. The fine steel blade struck the stone floor, missed its intended target, and broke in half. The sigil flew from what had been Mero's hand and struck the wall beside the stairway alcove. It fell, blazing like a green meteor, and came to rest less than two feet from Saundar's corpse.

Protruding from the left sleeve of Mero's mail shirt was a blackened mass of nearly fleshless bones. He staggered about like a drunken man, never ceasing his howling, as Snudge retrieved his own blade, sprang to his feet, and dashed back to the comparative safety of the catwalk.

Mero ignored him. He had caught sight of shining Concealer and lumbered toward it. "You won't have the amulet either! I'll destroy the cursèd thing." Bending, he drew Saundar's broadsword from its scabbard, swung it high, and brought the heavy blade down with practiced accuracy on the moonstone.

Open-mouthed, Snudge saw the tall armiger bathed in emerald incandescence, suddenly frozen in place, a statue clad in chain mail and a tattered, filthy surcoat, clutching a lowered sword. A moment later the dank air was filled with a shower of bright particles, fiery embers that once were flesh and bone, cloth and leather and forged iron. The embers faded to a scatter of cinders that did not quite conceal the foxfire glow of the sigil partially buried beneath them.

Snudge came off the catwalk and trudged through the fallen bridge workers. He seemed to view the terrible scene from a far distance. It could not be real. Later, he told himself, he'd surely discover that his two friends were not dead, that brutal Mero had never attempted treachery.

Later—after he'd taken care of the portcullises and finally secured Mallmouth Bridge for Prince Conrig and the Cathran army.

He picked up Concealer and wiped it clean. The sigil would need a new thong. For now, he thrust it behind the collar of his padded gambeson, beneath his shirt, where it rested warm against his bare skin. He spoke the spell of invisibility, then mounted the stairs swinging his sock full of coins.

*   *   *

By the time he had struck down the last of the stubborn ones and herded those who had yielded into the custom clerks' small chamber, the head of the Cathran column, with the prince in the lead and Vanguard and Beorbrook attending him closely, had crossed the bascule and was waiting at the closed southern portcullis. It took the last of Snudge's strength to operate the great windlass and haul up the counterweighted iron grate. Then he made himself visible, slipped the sigil into his boot, and trudged wearily down to hold his master's horse while he dismounted.

"Well done, Deveron!" Conrig exclaimed heartily, and the other two great nobles also added their congratulations. The prince continued in a low voice. "We have let it be known that Princess Ullanoth's magic was responsible for taking the bridge, and you and the armigers merely assisted her . . . Where are the other boys?"

Snudge's eyes welled up and he was too spent even to wipe away the tears making runnels on his sooty face. "Alas, Your Grace. It grieves me to inform you that they have perished."

"Great God!" said the duke. "This is melancholy news."

"We must retrieve their poor bodies before quitting this place," the earl marshal said.

"Where do they lie, lad?" the prince asked. "I'll send my Heart Companions to retrieve them. Your three brave friends shall still ride with us as we conquer Didion."

"Only the remains of Saundar Kersey and Belamil Langsands can be so honored," the boy muttered. "The armiger Mero Elwick was—was destroyed utterly by evil magic. All that is left of him is ashes."

"God's Breath!" Vanguard whispered. "And you: are you hurt?"

"Only slightly, lord Duke."

"How did this come to pass?" the earl marshal demanded. "If the Mossland witch was not actually here—"

Conrig held up his hand. "My lords, now is not the time to question Deveron. He has accomplished his task and is plainly near the end of his tether. I must confer with him myself before we continue on into Mallburn Town. Godfather, please see that the northern portcullis is also opened so we may proceed across the river, and demolish the winch mechanism so that the grates cannot be lowered again. The prisoners must also be secured. Earl Marshal, bid all of our troops to take brief ease and inspect their mounts and weapons. Array the advance force that is to engage the Town Guard garrison on the opposite shore. And find my brother Stergos and send him to me to tend Deveron's wounds. Inform the other noble leaders that we'll sally forth as soon as we receive word from Princess Ullanoth."

The two nodded and turned their mounts back towards the column of warriors, which waited silently in the murk.

Conrig spoke curtly to Snudge, "Hobble my horse, and give an account of your actions as you do so. I want to know everything—particularly why you deemed it necessary that the other armigers should die. It's true that I commanded you do all possible to guard the secret of your sigil and talent, but there will now be inconvenient inquiries made, especially by Feribor Blackhorse."

Snudge held the prince's eye without flinching, even though tears continued to course down his face. "It was Count Feribor's squire, Mero, who murdered the other two, not I. He slew Saundar out of hand, even as I blasted the bridge machinery with tarnblaze. Then he threatened to murder Belamil unless I turned over to him my Concealer sigil. When I put down the stone so he could take it, he killed Belamil with a single thrust of his varg. We fought. He attempted to command Concealer and failed. He tried then to destroy it. Instead, it engulfed him in green flame . . . and vanished from my sight. I know not what has become of the stone. Perhaps the Beaconfolk themselves have taken it back. If so, I'm glad of it, for it was a thing accursèd."

The prince gave a sharp inhalation of breath. He was silent for a long time. "I beg your pardon for accusing you unjustly."

Snudge nodded. "There's something else I must tell you. Mero knew that I am a wild talent. He made sly insinuations during our journey and accused me of it openly before he died. I've cudgeled my brain, trying to think how I might have betrayed myself to him—indeed, how he might even have come to know such a phrase, which is not commonly known, except among magickers. I did not betray myself, Your Grace. I can only conclude that Mero learned of my wild talent in some other way."

"But can you be absolutely certain of this?" the prince asked, understanding well enough what the boy implied, yet not wanting to accept it.

"No." Snudge spoke dully. "I can't be certain."

"And the Concealer sigil: will you swear to me on your heart and soul that it's truly lost?"

Snudge did not immediately answer. He hated the moonstone because it had been the death of his two friends. He hated it even more because of what he had seen in the prince's eyes when he asked about it. Concealer was truly a thing accursèd, and he wanted nothing more to do with it.

And yet he had not thrown it into the river, as he had almost done after lifting the portcullis to Conrig and his army. The Salka would surely have found it in the water, he told himself with facile reasoning, and taken it to Conjure-King Beynor. So Snudge kept the stone, convincing himself it was necessary to do so until he had a safe way to dispose of it.

"Your Grace," he said earnestly, "I swear to you by all that is sacred that the stone is truly lost to the sight of men—although mayhap the Beaconfolk, or the Salka who made it, or even Princess Ullanoth do know where it is. Sigils are evil things, just as the princess warned us. We're well rid of it, believe me."

Conrig's dark eyes with their glint of talent bored into his, seeking the truth. But Snudge stood fast, and at last the prince turned away and spoke of the matter no more.

twenty-nine

Ullanoth awoke in the guest room as the bronze bell in Holt Mallburn's highest tower tolled the first hour after midnight. She felt quite well, even jubilant, and ignored the pain of Subtle Loophole as she first scanned the vast palace with its mostly sleeping inhabitants, then observed the vanguard of Conrig's army, led by young Baron Pasacor Kimbolton, move silently across the fog-bound span and prepare to fall upon the unsuspecting Town Guard barracks down by the riverside.

The prince himself waited with his other noble leaders inside the bridge tower, until they should receive the signal to charge into the city. Hovering unobtrusively near Conrig, having minor wounds tended by Vra-Stergos, was the wild-talented youth Deveron, disheveled and somber. She'd have to find out exactly what he'd been up to, although from the admiring remarks of the others, it was obvious that he and his companion armigers had been successful in taking the bridge.

She took time to comb her hair and attire herself in a sable-trimmed over-robe of wine-red velvet filched from the quarters of Princess Risalla, the youngest child of King Achardus. Then she bespoke Shanakin, ruler of the spunkies.

"The time has come. Are you ready?"

Waiting for you, lady.

"Do not enter the central gatehouse of the palace until I give the command."

Impatient evil chitterings polluted the wind.

Moon Mother! she prayed. Let Shanakin be able to keep his subjects under control. If only there had been another way . . .

Conjuring her Concealer, she hurried down the dark and silent corridors.

Only a few household knights and men-at-arms seemed to be keeping watch within the central keep where the regal apartments were. Holt Mallburn was not as splendidly furnished as Cala Palace, but it was much more strongly fortified—and magnificent enough to prick her envy and bolster her resolve to restore Fenguard, once she deposed Beynor. She would live in Cathra with Conrig only during the dreary winter months, returning to her home in Moss when spring greened the marshes and the swans flew north . . .

She came at length into the massive gatehouse, which was set into curtain walls twenty ells thick. Most of the palace's troops were quartered in huge towers flanking the gatehouse's central passage. At this hour of the night, with Holt Mallburn secured and presumably impregnable, less than two dozen armed men were on duty.

"Shanakin!" she called. "Bring your Small Lights over the walls into the outer ward and attend me! All human beings within the gatehouse and its towers, excepting only those I keep close to me, now belong to you. Begin your feast!"

She became visible, conjured Interpenetrator, and strolled into the guard-room at the inner end of the gate passage. A middle-aged captain, seated at a table with two of his sergeants, leapt to his feet, exclaiming in astonishment.

"Lady! What are you doing here so late?" He scowled. "And who *are* you?"

"I am Ullanoth of Moss, the Conjure-Queen," she replied. Why not style herself by her rightful title? "And I am here to claim Holt Mallburn for my own. Every warrior dwelling within this fortress will yield up his life to my sorcery this night . . . saving only those few who surrender themselves to me and agree to do my bidding."

"Kill her!" roared the captain, drawing his sword and rushing at her. The others also sprang to the attack, but gave shouts of dismay when their blades and then their grasping hands passed through her slender body as though she were a ghost.

"Stand still!" she commanded. "Listen!"

"No!" the wild-eyed captain cried, still brandishing his weapon. "Outside, men, and sound the tocsin!"

She stood in the guardhouse doorway with hands held high. "Fools! Listen, I say! If you cross the threshold, you're dead men."

The three of them hesitated, heads cocked, as a curious rustling sound, almost like the stirring of rats in a granary, began to fill the air. The noise swelled in intensity, becoming an unearthly hissing hum that almost drowned out the sounds of screaming.

"What's happened?" quavered one of the sergeants, potbellied and having the hectic complexion of a heavy drinker.

"They're dying." Ullanoth spoke without emotion. "Your fellow-warriors. Those lying abed and those standing nightwatch. The warm red blood is draining from their helpless bodies."

"No!" croaked the captain, approaching her and making another futile jab with his sword. "Follow me, men! We'll walk right through the witch—" He uttered a startled curse as she stepped aside and gestured wordlessly at the great cloud of golden sparks now whirling outside in the passage like a swarm of infuriated hornets. They filled the broad corridor from one side to the other.

"God a' mercy!" The second sergeant, tall and thin, let his sword fall from his hand as he gaped in terror. "Spunkies! But I never saw so many . . ."

"As you know, they sup on blood," she said. "They are my servants. Relatively harmless in small numbers—but I have summoned them from all over the island to feast tonight in Mallburn Town. Shall I invite them into the guardroom, or will you surrender to me and keep your lives?"

"What do you want?" the captain asked. His face sagged with despair.

"Place all of your weapons on the table, then come with me."

They complied. She commanded the hovering, hissing Small Lights to vacate the passage. The creatures receded into the ward as Ullanoth and the men emerged. Two bodies in armor lay on their backs beneath a torch on a wall-bracket. The tortured faces within the open helmets resembled skulls wrapped in crinkled pale parchment.

"Swive me!" the lanky sergeant wailed, as he caught sight of the remains. "We're goners!"

His big-bellied mate turned aside and vomited.

"I swear to you on my honor," Ullanoth declared, "that if you obey me I'll spare your lives."

The captain asked, "What must we do?"

"Open the palace gates. All of them."

"Even if you spare us, King Achardus will have us drawn and quartered—"

"Your king, all unknowing, is certain to die this night. He sealed his fate when he rejected Cathra's Edict of Sovereignty and slaughtered the delegation presenting it. Now Conrig Wincantor, my ally, is advancing on Holt Mallburn with an army. Tomorrow you and whoever else survives will be subjects of his Sovereignty—like it or not."

Mallburn Town was on fire.

Conrig rode through the night, surrounded by his Heart Companions, leading the principal Cathran host up the broad boulevard called Malle Way. Squads of thanes guided by spunkies had already gone ahead into the sidestreets with crocks and bombshells of tarnblaze, setting buildings alight to sow panic amongst the enemy.

After the brief, decisive fight down by the riverside, no more Didionite troops came forth to oppose the invaders. Any townsfolk abroad in the streets, fleeing the flames, remained well hidden—or else had fallen prey to the bloodsuckers. Spreading scarlet billows warmed the air and began to melt the uncanny fog, so that the main body of the army no longer required guidance by the Small Lights as it approached Holt Mallburn Palace. Only now and then were indistinct yellow sparks visible on either side of the advancing cavalcade.

Duke Tanaby Vanguard and a second large force were en route to the Golden Precinct, further east, to engage the private guards who protected the dwellings of the wealthy merchants and guildsmen, while Viscount Skellhaven, his cousin Holmrangel, and their seagoing warriors were galloping toward the harbor, ready to torch the quay and seize whatever ships were in port.

It was all happening as Ullanoth had predicted.

Conrig smiled, recalling the jubilant face of his brother Stergos as the doctor relayed the windspoken message of Princess Ullanoth: *The gates of the palace are wide open, and most of its garrison has fallen to my sorcery. I await your coming, my dearest prince—and so does King Achardus Mallburn.*

By the time the Cathran host reached the Royal Park, the vapors had so thinned that the watchfires of the palace ramparts were clearly visible at the top of the wooded hill. Overhead, low clouds reflected hellish tints of blood-red and orange onto the scene below.

The army came to a halt. The park's sentry post had been abandoned, but the tall wrought-iron gates were shut with six large padlocks. Conrig and the Companions rode aside as thanes from Parlian Beorbrook's cohort used bombshells to topple the ornate supporting columns and bring the gratings down. As the twisted fragments were being dragged aside by horsemen, the earl marshal himself rode up to the prince, followed closely by his son Count Elktor and the alchymist Vra-Doman Carmorton.

"We're finding no opposition to our march at all," Beorbrook announced. "Aside from the Town Guardsmen Kimbolton cut down at the river, the city seems unpatrolled. It's damned eerie."

"There'll be troops defending the Golden Precinct where the well-heeled trader-lords dwell," Conrig said. "Vanguard and his lads will be a match for them. But I wish I knew what to expect at the palace."

Conrig rode a short distance away from the Companions, motioning for Beorbrook, Elktor, and Vra-Doman to follow. In a low voice, he asked the earl marshal, "Have you had further windspeech from Princess Ullanoth?"

"Not yet. Your brother is engaged in other arcane business, bespeaking news of our advance to King Olmigon in Cala, so I thought you might wish Vra-Doman to query the princess again . . . or even call upon the resident wizards of Holt Mallburn, to see if Achardus might be of a mind to surrender."

Conrig nodded. "Attempt Ullanoth first, Brother."

The alchymist's expression was fretful and his eyes darted nervously about. "Someone please hold my horse and help me to dismount. I'm not feeling at all well! There are extremely malign influences abroad on the wind tonight."

Young Elktor assisted the adept, while Conrig and the earl marshal exchanged glances. "Our tiny collaborators," the prince murmured. "I presume they must have helped Ullanoth subdue the palace garrison, but she gave no details."

Beorbrook grimaced. "There's wickedness in the air, all right. Even I feel it."

Vra-Doman sank onto his heels, ignoring the puddles amidst the cobblestones, and drew the hood of his habit over his head. After some minutes had passed, he looked up at Conrig.

"The princess doesn't respond, Your Grace. Shall I bespeak the Didionites?"

"Please."

This effort took longer. When Vra-Doman finished, his face was blanched and his eyes glazed. "They—they refuse to yield to a force in league with—with the Beaconfolk."

"God's Breath!" Conrig exclaimed, astounded. "What the hell do they mean by that?" *And what has she done? . . .*

"I have bespoken one Ilingus Direwold, Archwizard of Didion," Vra-Doman continued. "He speaks for King Achardus, who declares the following: 'The atrocities committed by the Witch of Moss cry out to the God of the Heights and Depths for just retribution. I will never consign the people of Didion to a liege lord who avails himself of the depraved sorcery of the Coldlight Army. I pledge that I and my sons will oppose the Sovereignty of Blencathra with all our strength until the moment of our deaths in battle.'"

Even thickheaded Count Elktor was struck speechless.

The earl marshal murmured, "I wonder if the prospect of imminent defeat has caused the mind of Achardus to founder? Failing that, Your Grace, we may have come to a pretty pass, relying on Princess Ullanoth."

"Damn the woman!" Conrig muttered. "And damn that hypocrite, Achardus, who was willing enough to use *Beynor's* Beaconfolk magic!"

"Nevertheless," Beorbrook warned, "sufficient numbers of your loyal subjects agree with Achardus's opinion of the Lights, so that it would be unwise to publish his statement abroad. My son and I will keep silent, of course."

Conrig inclined his head in agreement and turned to the alchymist. "Vra-Doman Carmorton, I charge you also to tell no one else of this. And I avouch to you, my friends, that if Ullanoth has indeed committed an atrocity, it was never done at my behest. She promised me she would never use Beaconfolk magic as a weapon."

"Perhaps she did eschew the evil of the Great Lights," Vra-Doman whispered, "but what about the Small?"

Conrig drew a breath. "Whatever else she's done, Ullanoth has opened the stronghold of Holt Mallburn to my army. We must put all else aside and seize this moment. Later, after the conquest, I'll decide what must be done about the princess."

"There are those," Beorbrook said, "who believe you are considering taking her to wife."

"I would as soon wed one of the Beaconfolk." The prince wheeled his horse about, drew his sword, and shouted to the assembled warriors, "Cathra! Follow me to the palace, and to victory!"

No enemy troops hindered the progress of the invaders as they moved forward to attack Holt Mallburn. They surged through the open gates to the outer ward and then the inner, and only Baron Catclaw's men, assigned to take the gatehouse towers and the troops garrisoned within, knew early on of the appalling massacre perpetrated by the spunkies. Beorbrook's followers, along with the knights and thanes loyal to Conistone and Silverside, charged about on horseback, pursuing and cutting down any castle inhabitants who dared confront them with weaponry in the open courtyards between the three great wings of the sprawling pile.

The barricaded towers in the curtain wall were the objective of Ramscrest, Bogshaw, and Cloudfell. Under cover of their shields to avoid the rain of arrows, their warriors blasted open the tower entryways with tarnblaze shells. Smoky fires set at ground level soon routed out the beleaguered defenders, who were rounded up and placed under guard.

Conrig, the Companions, Beorbrook's thanes, and the fighters following the Virago of Marley attacked the main keep, where resistance was expected to be most fierce. Surprisingly, after a brief but ferocious skirmish on the broad stairs leading to the great hall, the palace defenders seemed to lose heart.

"Companions, to me!" Conrig shouted. "Forward to the royal chambers—but remember that Achardus Mallburn is mine!"

Following him, a mob of Cathran nobles, knights, and thanes went howling along the carpeted corridors of the keep's upper floor, kicking in doors and using tarnblaze on those that were barred. Most of the Didionites they encountered fell to their knees and begged mercy. Those who fought were swiftly overwhelmed, and there were few casualties among the invaders. It soon became evident to Conrig that the huge palace was largely empty of non-combatants. He discovered the wives of Honigalus and Somarus and their tiny children cowering in a wardrobe and set two Companions to guard them. Princess Risalla, the king's daughter, was found with her ladies in her bedchamber, waiting calmly by the fire. She greeted the bloodstained Cathran Prince Heritor with dignity, but refused to say where her father Achardus might be hiding.

A shout rang out as Conrig quitted Risalla's apartment. Feribor Blackhorse and Sividian Langford were ascending a staircase giving access to the southeast tower. "Your Grace! There's a locked iron door up here. Perhaps it leads to some strongroom where the royals have taken refuge."

Baroness Zeandrise Marley lifted a baldric with a pendant pouch from her mailed shoulder and handed it to Conrig. "I still have my small bombshell. Take it with my compliments."

The prince grinned at her, snatched the baldric, and ran to join his friends at the top of the steps.

"Hang it from the latch, right on top of the lockplate," Count Sividian urged excitedly.

The prince uncovered the neck and wick of the iron sphere and arranged the leather baldric against the door. "Who has a tarnstick to light the bombshell?" he asked. But neither man did. "Never mind, I'll find one somewhere. Go down again, both of you, out of danger."

When the pair were below in the corridor with the others, all looking up in anticipation, Conrig knelt and struck a light with his talent, as Snudge had taught him. A tiny flame sprang from his fingertip and ignited the fuse. He ran down the stairs, reaching the bottom just as the explosion flung him onto his face and filled the place with smoke.

Someone screamed, "Your Grace!"

"I'm fine, not a scratch." He got to his feet, drew his sword and felt his way up the stairs. Feribor, Sividian and the Virago were at his heels.

The door was open. Torchlight from within illuminated the clouds of smoke in a confusing manner, reflecting from countless objects of polished gold and silver. The place was clearly a storeroom for the palace plate and other precious items. The gigantic king of Didion stood there among the treasure chests and laden shelves, barefoot and in his black-and-white striped nightshirt, holding the five-foot-long Sword of State in a two-handed grip. The sword hilt blazed with jewels, but the blade, wavy-edged and etched with intricate designs, was of the finest Forailean steel. Behind him, in the shadows, stood a wizard in black robes and Queen Siry, wrapped in a voluminous cloak of snowy fur.

Achardus roared, "Bastard son of a Cathran sow!" He moved forward as Conrig advanced, swinging his long blade in a heroic arc. The prince skipped aside, ducking beneath the stroke, and upset a spindly stand holding a tray of gem-studded golden goblets. The cups went bouncing and clanging over the wooden floor.

The king trod on one, lost his balance as the thin metal buckled beneath his great weight, and crashed onto his back like a felled oak. But he still grasped the jeweled sword in one hamlike hand, and as Conrig sprang at him he aimed its point at the prince, intending to spit him as though he were a charging boar.

"Con—no!" Count Sividian leapt at Conrig, bowling him aside. Both men fell to the floor beyond the reach of Achardus, who bellowed like a bull in tor-ment, rolled over, and attempted to regain his feet. But long years of feasting and indolence had weakened the leg muscles of the mountainous body. It was too ungainly to rise without help.

Conrig was upright again in an instant, stamping the king between his shoulder blades with one thick-soled boot. Achardus gave a great whooping exhalation of breath, like a surfacing grampus. The blade fell from his fingers.

In one swift movement Conrig straddled the king's head and lowered the point of his own sword into the thick roll of fat hiding the neck of Achardus Mallburn.

"Yield, Didion! Yield to my Sovereignty!"

"Go to hell," said the king wearily "and take the Mossland witch with you to the Cold Lights."

Conrig thrust downward with all his strength. The steel passed through flesh and spine and into the planks of the floor, where it stuck fast.

Queen Siry uttered a piercing scream, throwing off her fur cloak as she rushed toward the man who had slain her husband. In her right hand was a rapier, and in the left a misericord, one of the thin elongated daggers used by plate-armored combatants. Momentarily overcome by surprise, with his weapon immobilized, Conrig hesitated. Feribor and Sividian seemed equally dum-founded and stood as though turned to stone, as Siry came at the prince with both blades.

It remained for the Virago of Marley to take a great running leap, her varg a shining blur, and sweep off the Queen of Didion's head with a single blow.

thirty

In mid-morning of that Leap Day of the Boreal Moon, when the tumult of battle had subsided, Cathra's wounded received succor and her dead were wrapped in shrouds and laid out on individual funeral pyres in the palace's outer ward: nine knights from various households, the two nobly born armigers slain at Mallmouth Bridge, and twenty-two thanes.

The low-riding sun shone brilliantly and the air was very cold. Snudge stood among the other squires of the royal cohort assembled to pay tribute to the fallen. When the alchymists had completed their prayers and the flames were leaping high, the boys and the Heart Companions gave a final flourish of swords in tribute and prepared to accompany Conrig back into the palace, where he would hold audience and deal with necessary business devolving upon the conquest.

"Deveron, you are excused from attending." The prince spoke privily to the boy as they ascended the great staircase leading to the presence chambers of Didion. "Rest and recover in the apartment set aside for me and Vra-Stergos in the west wing. My trussing coffer is there. Take fresh clothes for yourself. Later, if you have the strength, undertake a windsearch for Princess Ullanoth, whose whereabouts are still unknown, and then attempt an overview of events taking place at sea off Cathra's southern coast. My brother has been unable to obtain any detailed information from the windvoices at Cala, nor do we know how the Tarnian mercenary fleet may be faring."

"I'll find out what I can, Your Grace."

"Await my coming. Tell no one else what you discover." He pulled a distinctive sapphire ring from a finger of his right hand. "Show this to Lord Bogshaw's men, who secure the door to my rooms, and they will admit you."

"Yes, Your Grace."

The palace was now surprisingly quiet, with tired-looking sentries standing guard in critical areas. A few servants with haunted faces crept about the corridors on domestic errands, shepherded by armed Cathran thanes. Only sanded-over stains on the floor and occasional piles of broken furniture and other debris pushed into corners gave evidence of the fighting that had taken place during the night. Didionite prisoners of war had removed their own dead. On Conrig's orders, the wounded defenders were being given the same care as his own men.

At the opulent guest chambers the prince had appropriated, Bogshaw's men recognized Snudge at once as the hero of Mallmouth Bridge. The young knight in charge of the guards smote his breast in an affectionate mock-salute as the boy showed him the ring, then admitted him to the royal suite. The sitting room and two adjoining bedchambers were deserted, but quaint tiled stoves standing in all three rooms contained briskly burning fires, so the place was warm, in contrast to most of the rest of the palace. Conrig's armor and coffer had been left in the larger bedroom. The boy helped himself to a set of fine linen smallclothes, a simple black tunic, a pair of scuffed leather trews, and thick wool stockings. He stripped naked and washed his bruised and battered body, then dressed in the fresh clothes.

Exhausted though he was and aching in every muscle, he knew that the last thing his royal master really expected was for him to take his ease. He pulled a truckle-bed out from beneath the prince's own canopied bed, sprawled on it fully dressed, and undertook a windsearch for the Conjure-Princess. In spite of her promise to meet Conrig, no one had yet laid eyes on her, nor had she bespoken either alchymist since giving notice that the gates to Holt Mallburn were open to the Cathran army.

Snudge's first cursory search revealed no trace of Ullanoth, which did not surprise him. Nevertheless, he felt certain that she was still in the palace and began a more methodical inspection of the huge fortress, beginning with the central keep, scrying every room, closet, and cubbyhole. He forced himself to persevere in the tedious work until his fatigued brain would have no more of it. The reality of his task changed into a dreary dream of it, and dreaming passed in turn into welcome oblivion.

*   *   *

It was only a matter of convenience that Conrig Wincantor sat upon the throne of Didion during his first official audience following the conquest. Honigalus, the new king, had thus far refused to respond to Cathran windspeech, and there could be no capitulation of Didion to the Sovereignty unless its legitimate ruler formally submitted.

Conrig's invasion of the enemy capital had succeeded, but the war was not won—and the fact that King Achardus had chosen death over the Sovereignty of High Blenholme had been a severe blow to the Prince Heritor's overall strategy. His small army could not possibly hold Didion over the winter; there was not enough food. Unless Honigalus was quickly defeated at sea or persuaded to accept vassalage, the Cathrans would have to withdraw ignominiously, with their tails tucked between their legs.

None of his lords had voiced this unpleasant contingency to Conrig, but all of them knew it to be true. The prince had yet to decide what he would do next; nevertheless he showed a confident face to all of those assembled in the throne room, and commanded Earl Marshal Parlian Beorbrook to make the first report.

The marshal informed Conrig that the toll of mortality among the combatant warriors of Didion was unexpectedly modest. Those slaughtered by the spunkies might have numbered in the thousands, but no one could now say for certain. By dawn, when all traces of the uncanny fog had melted away, the terrible little creatures had disappeared—and so had the remains of those they had feasted upon. Nothing was left of the victims but the empty garments and armor they had worn, lying in drifts of dust.

"We will speak no more of those slain by the Small Lights," Conrig told Beorbrook quietly. "Few of our people witnessed the blood-drained bodies last night, and in time they may come to believe that the awful sight was only imagined, not real."

"Or that the wasted corpses were merely those who had starved to death in the famine," Beorbrook suggested. "I'll deal with any who persist in saying otherwise."

"I place the military occupation of Mallburn in your able hands," the prince told him. "Ramscrest will serve as your principal deputy, arranging for the defense of the city against any Didionite forays from the countryside. Somarus and his force at Boarsden probably pose the only serious threat against us. Persuade members of the late king's Privy Council to tell you how many warriors he has under his command. Their lives depend upon their cooperation. When your plan of occupation and defense is complete, come and inform me of the details."

"Very well. But before I go, Your Grace, I think you should interview the Didionite archwizard. My men have him here in custody, and he's given his parole not to attempt any magical mischief. He says he has a message from Honigalus."

"Bring him forward," the prince said.

Ilingus Direwold stood defiant before the conqueror, his hound-dog features radiating something very close to triumph. "I have recently bespoken King Honigalus. Even as we speak, his armada is engaging your own navy in a fierce sea-battle east of Cathra's Vigilant Isles. Your ships are strongly outnumbered and are in the process of being defeated."

Those standing close to the throne uttered gasps and cries of consternation.

"Go on," Conrig said flatly.

"After his victory is accomplished, King Honigalus will be reinforced by over two dozen heavily armed frigates and corvettes commanded by Continental corsairs. They'll make short work of the rest of your navy and then commence bombarding Cala Palace without mercy. King Honigalus invites you to transmit word of your surrender via my windvoice, at your convenience. If you do so promptly, he will spare the lives of King Olmigon, Queen Cataldise, and your wife Princess Maudrayne."

Conrig inclined his head in a gracious gesture. "Thank your king for his suggestion. Please tell him to go to hell." And to Beorbrook: "Lock this man in the dungeon with his fellow magickers. My brother tells me that these Didionite adepts have fairly weak talents and are unable to bespeak or windwatch through a dense burden of rock and earth. If Honigalus has any more messages for me, let him send them through the Brothers of Zeth."

"You condemn your family to death!" Ilingus cried.

"Take him away," Conrig said wearily. "I'll hear Duke Tanaby's report next."

Vanguard, his three fighting sons, and their considerable force of warriors had rounded up the officers of the great guilds and the city's merchant-lords almost without bloodshed and marched them to the palace in chains. Conrig now interviewed each Didionite magnate briefly, assuring them that they would eventually be allowed to continue in business under the Sovereignty if they cooperated with Vanguard's inventory of their treasure, food supplies, and weaponry.

He then beckoned Viscount Hartrig Skellhaven to approach the throne, the last of the principal Cathran battle-leaders to render his report. But before the seagoing noble and his associates could make their way across the crowded room, there was a commotion at the door and the sound of female voices raised in sharp protest.

Conrig rose to his feet and commanded silence.

"It's the three Didionite royal ladies," Count Sividian called out, "demanding audience with Your Grace."

"Let them enter." The prince resumed his seat.

Uncrowned Queen Bryce and Somarus's wife Thylla were like dead women walking, their faces ravaged by shock and grief and their hair hanging in snarls. They still wore rumpled nightrobes and shuffled forward as if they were dazed sheep, driven by young Princess Risalla. She was dressed in a black gown, simply cut but of rich fabric. Her pale hair was arranged in neat coils and covered by a black veil.

"Prince Conrig!" Risalla cried out boldly, stepping ahead of the other two. "We've come to beg a boon of you. Give us the bodies of King Achardus and Queen Siry, so that we may prepare them for burial in the ancestral crypt."

After their brief encounter the previous night, Conrig had dismissed the youngest child of Achardus as a meek, colorless creature of no great beauty. But the woman who confronted him now had no aspect of fear or diffidence about her. Risalla's eyes were alight with courage and determination, giving her plain features an aura of strength and magnificence beyond mere comeliness.

He said quietly, "The brave queen's remains you may certainly have, Princess. But why should I grant honorable repose to an uncivilized brute like Achardus, who flouted every norm of chivalry by murdering Cathra's peaceable delegation?"

"I know it was ignoble of my father to have killed your people, cast their bodies into the sea, and piked their heads above Mallmouth Bridge," Risalla said. "And you would be within your rights as our conqueror to treat his poor corpse in a similar manner. But I beseech you to show mercy and kindness instead, if you hope for our fealty within your Sovereignty."

Conrig sighed. "And *would* you accept the Sovereignty of High Blenholme, madam, if fate decrees that my victory over your nation shall stand?"

"With all my heart," said Risalla. "It would be my duty, which I value above any other consideration."

Conrig lifted his gaze to Sividian, who stood behind the royal women. "Give them the bodies and see that they have what is needed."

The count nodded and ushered the three of them away.

Viscount Skellhaven finally approached and reported that he had made short work of the handful of naval vessels deemed too unsound to join the armada and the few merchantmen tied up at the docks, arresting their officers and sending their crews fleeing into the ruins of the city.

"But the harbor spoils were as paltry as we feared, Your Grace. Most of the warehouses are empty. Of the captured ships, only a single Stippenese transport carrack was well found and decently armed with a dozen culverins. She's a strong, speedy clipper about a hundred fifteen foot long, displacing five hundred tons. Her name is *Shearwater* . . . and I want her!"

The prince laughed. "Draw closer, Hartrig. The ship is yours—but not yet to keep, until you and your brave seamen have done a necessary service for me."

Skellhaven climbed the dais. He spoke low. "What is it?"

"I must finish the job I began, taking on King Honigalus, or else our victory here in Holt Mallburn is an empty sham. Can you provision and crew this *Shearwater* before nightfall? I intend to leave for Cathra as soon as possible."

The viscount nodded slowly. "Aye. Between us, Cousin Holmrangel and I've enough hands for a fighting crew. We'll press a few willing Stippenese officers as well from the gang of prisoners. It'll save time, shaking the ship down, although she's not that different from Cathran carracks . . . But it's five hundred fifty hard leagues to Blenholme Roads. Even with the fairest winds and no storms, the voyage could take nearly four days this chancey time of year."

"What if our sails are stiffened by a magical gale created by Conjure-Princess Ullanoth?" the prince inquired softly.

"Depends on the condition of *Shearwater's* bottom," Skellhaven said. "But if she's clean below, and doesn't dismast or fall apart under the strain, and if we avoid digging her bow and flipping fore-and-aft—we might just be able to make it in thirty-six hours."

"That's more like it!" Conrig's grin was reckless. "Are you game to try, my lord? The fate of the Sovereignty—and Cathra itself—may depend on your answer, for our new Lord Admiral Copperstrand has played the fool and split his force in two, counter to King Olmigon's express command. I've been told by the enemy's archwizard that our warships are badly outnumbered by the fleet of

Honigalus in a battle now taking place off the Vigilants. I have no windspoken word of the outcome as yet, but we must prepare for the worst. I intend to take command of what's left of our fleet myself—if any vessels remain afloat upon our arrival."

"That futterin' great booby Copperstrand!" Skellhaven exclaimed. "What did he think he was doing—holding ships in reserve, in case the Continentals snuck up behind him into Cala Bay?"

"I presume so. I've been informed that the southern corsairs are still in port, no doubt waiting to see how Honigalus fares."

"I'll wager they won't stay there for long . . . Well, I'll be on my way back to the quay. I'll leave it to you to whistle up the magical gale. Count on me to take care of everything else."

"I will," said Conrig.

He watched the tattered, indomitable viscount stride from the throne room, then summoned Tayman and Feribor, who waited with most of the other Heart Companions for the prince's orders. Swiftly, he informed them of his decision to sail south, delegating each a particular area of preparation. "We'll take the surviving armigers with us, but no one else save my brother Stergos. Find him for me, Feri, before you undertake your other tasks, and send him to my private chambers. I must know how that damned sea-battle is going."

The count's saturnine face showed a flicker of irony. "I should think the Lady Ullanoth could give you a better account, using her superior sorcery."

"So she could," Conrig retorted grimly, "if I could only find her! The woman seems to have vanished."

Conjure-King Beynor woke from his latest dream of pain just before noon. He lay motionless in his bed, hardly daring to believe that the agony inflicted by the Lights was temporarily in abeyance, savoring the small comforts of being horizontal, warm, and cradled in softness.

His eyes opened. Sunshine shone through the windows of his chambers. Through the open bedroom door he beheld the reassuring sight of the twin guardian Fortresses, glowing in the golden monstrance out in the sitting room. His hand groped for the two chains hanging about his neck: Subtle Armor and Shapechanger were there and safe, as was the Great Stone Weathermaker, which he kept always on his finger.

She had not stolen them while he slept.

Stolen sigils . . . and soot on the soles of his bare feet!

The memory returned like a crash of cymbals, the remarkable insight that had struck him as he lost consciousness the day before. With caution, he levered himself upright and lowered his feet to the floor, where fur-lined slippers waited. Still pain-free. Was he growing stronger, becoming inured to Weathermaker's baneful side-effects?

The temperature of his room was still reasonably comfortable, but the fire was almost out. Good! His windsight showed only blackness inside the chimney. If the sigils taken by Ullanoth were concealed up there, they were buried in cinders and soot.

He slipped on a velvet robe and went to the hearth, where he easily quenched the last glowing peat coals with his talent. Nevertheless, he'd still be forced to wait a bit until the iron damper and the firebricks of the flue were cool enough to permit him to search.

He rang for breakfast, then poured some of Lady Zimroth's nerve-stimulating elixir into an emerald-encrusted goblet and drank it down. Immediately, he felt energized and decided to discover what events had transpired while he slept. He put on a heavy fur coat, shut down the Fortresses, and went out onto his balcony to scry.

The day was clear and extremely cold, with a light northerly breeze. It was, he realized, Leap Day of the Boreal Moon—traditionally a portentous time for the island of High Blenholme, when significant things might be expected to happen . . . such as a victory at sea for the navy of Crown Prince Honigalus!

Closing his eyes and bracing himself against the stone wall, he sent his windsight soaring southward. And there it was: Copperstrand's eight barques and eighteen frigates engaged in a desperate mêlée against forty Didionite men o' war, and clearly getting the worst of it. As Beynor watched, enthralled, fusillades of tarnblaze bombshells from three fast-moving enemy two-deckers raked the Cathran flagship, toppling its tall mainmast. A few moments later, the Conjure-King's windsight was blinded by a spectacular silent explosion that virtually obliterated the crippled three-tier barque, beyond a doubt killing every soul aboard.

"Cathra's whipped!" the delighted king whispered. He refocused his overview again and again from differing perspectives, watching the Cathran battle line break in three places. Some defending ships allowed themselves to be trapped between the island reefs and the onrushing foe and were being driven onto the rocks. Others, outmaneuvered by the more agile vessels commanded by Honigalus, had been devastated by tarnblaze and were sinking or being forced to surrender. At length, when the scene was almost entirely masked by clouds of smoke, two barques and three frigates flying Cathran colors burst out of the turmoil and fled westward toward Cala Bay. No Didionites followed.

Beynor cut off his scrying and excitedly bespoke Fring, the Crown Prince's windvoice.

"Is the battle over? Has Honigalus won? I oversaw Cathran ships running away!"

The laconic reply was some minutes in coming. *The fighting is not quite finished. But Didion is triumphant, King Beynor, beyond any doubt. Not a single ship of ours has been lost. Twelve of the foe have been sunk—including their flagship—five have surrendered, and five more have fled.*

"Excellent! Convey my congratulations to Prince Honigalus. And ask him what he intends to do next."

Again there was a delay. Then:

Didion's battle losses are minor. Three of our great ships-of-the-line suffered consequential damage and will have to retire to Continental ports for repairs, taking our wounded with them. The rest of our war fleet will await the arrival of our allies, who are expected to bring provisions and fresh stocks of munitions. After the rendezvous and reinforcement, we will proceed to Cala Bay and bombard the Cathran capital of Cala. We will avenge Prince Heritor Conrig's attack upon Holt Mallburn last night, the city's fall to our enemies, and the sad demise of King Achardus and Queen Siry.

Hearing these tidings for the first time, Beynor felt his heart contract within his breast. So Conrig had mounted a successful land invasion in spite of all his efforts! But the situation was far from hopeless. Didion would never surrender while its new king lived and was poised to fall upon Cala. And the second son of Achardus, Prince Somarus, still headed a sizable army capable of retaking Holt Mallburn.

"Please convey my condolences to King Honigalus upon the death of his royal father and the queen. I can only presume the villain Conrig was abetted in his conquest by malign Beaconfolk sorcery. No commonplace magic could possibly have hidden his invading army from my scrutiny."

So you say, Conjure-King . . .

Beynor winced at the windvoice's cynical tone. But there was no way the Didionites could know for certain that Ullanoth and her sigils were assisting Conrig. Curse her! What would she do next? It was imperative that he track his sister down and devise some way to destroy her, perhaps using Weathermaker. Might it be possible to direct the Great Stone's thunderbolt at her without knowing her precise location? Nothing in Rothbannon's writings indicated that the sigil was capable of such a deed, but—

King Honigalus of Didion presents his compliments to the Conjure-King of Moss, and assures him of his continuing goodwill and deep regard. When the time is appropriate, please initiate a brisk wind out of the southeast to speed our Continental allies to us. Needless to say, these fair winds must be judiciously sustained to assure the final vanquishing of our mutual enemy.

The pitiless bastards! Would they never allow him a single day to recover?

Beynor managed to say, "When it's convenient, I'll consider the request of my esteemed fellow-monarch, Honigalus. Meanwhile, let him savor the triumph which I already helped him to achieve."

In a smoldering fit of pique, he cut off the windspeech dialog with Fring and put all thought of the Didionite armada out of his mind. Let them wait for their bloody wind. He had more vital matters to consider.

Sweat beaded his brow and drenched his fur-swathed body. His earlier sense of well-being had totally evaporated, and he stood trembling in reaction to the terrible news of Holt Mallburn's fall and the sure knowledge that Ullanoth had brought it about.

"Shall I scry the city and learn the truth of what she's done?" he asked himself aloud. "No. Better use Weathermaker against her without delay."

He re-entered his chamber, shut the balcony doors, closed his eyes to shut out the brilliant sun, and forced himself to breathe slowly and deeply, all the while trying to suppress the uneasiness that burgeoned within his breast.

"But what if I'm asking the Lights for the impossible? What might they do to me then? Father confessed that an arrogant demand made by Mother, using Destroyer, brought about her appalling death . . ."

Beynor heard a laugh. It was light, feminine, familiar.

Falling to his knees, he was almost paralyzed by a premonition of what was about to happen. Haltingly, he began to speak the spell reactivating the Fortresses.

Then he'd retreat behind Subtle Armor so that even her Sending would be power-less to harm him—

Beynor! I have something important to say to you.

As her voice came to him on the wind he uttered a mewling cry, like a fretful infant, and clapped his hands over his ears. "No, damn you! I won't listen!"

But his sister bespoke his reeling mind, and he was helpless to ignore her.

Our own conflict is nearly over, Brother, and you are defeated. Think on it! There is now no place in the world where I may not reach you. Your Fortresses are no barrier to me. Even if you remain inside their spell of couverture, you still solidify my Sending, which you cannot harm because of Interpenetrator. Furthermore, I have empowered a new Great Stone named Subtle Loophole that now enables me to watch you, wherever you may hide, and also listen to every word you speak . . . True, you may shield yourself temporarily from my wrath by activating the Armor sigil— but its spell is no more than a prison. Enveloped within it, you are deprived of food and drink as well as all physical contact with the world around you. You cannot wear Subtle Armor for a single day, much less for the rest of your life.

"Go away," he moaned. "Sky Father! Moon Mother! Have mercy!"

Her windvoice was kind. *It is I who will have mercy on you, Little Brother, although you murdered our father and deserve none. If you hope to live, you must make public confession of your crime, atone for it, and relinquish the crown of Moss and all of your sigils to me.*

"Never!" he screamed. "I'd rather die!"

I'll give you a single day to consider the matter. No more. Farewell.

He lay in a heap, almost senseless, until a warm hand touched his brow and caused him to start up in a panic. But it was not Ullanoth's terrible Sending standing beside him, only the grey-robed form of Lady Zimroth, the High Thaumaturge, who had his permission to penetrate the Fortresses. Her lined face was suffused with tender concern.

"Your Majesty! Oh, my poor dear boy, how can I help you? Did I not warn you against overuse of the Weathermaker stone? Is it the Lights who have stricken you?"

"Just . . . help me to a chair. I'll be all right soon. The Lights haven't harmed me." He managed a feeble chuckle. "No more than they ever do. I was only over-come for a moment."

She assisted him to his feet and led him to a seat by the dead fire. "Your chambers are freezing cold. I'll call the slaves to stoke up a blaze—"

"No!" he said. "Not yet. But do give me a sip of your invigorating elixir, and then go and bid the kitchen hasten with some hot food."

She poured the medicine and held it to his lips. When he had drunk it, she patted his shoulder. "Just sit quietly, dear. I'll be back immediately."

When she was gone, Beynor rose on unsteady legs and stepped into the ashes of the cavernous fireplace. He pushed the damper wide open and thrust his hand up into the filthy opening, scrabbling blindly.

A shelf, piled deep in soot!

He searched the mess, feeling from one side to the other and finding nothing. But then, almost out of reach back in the far left corner, his fingers touched a single small thing, smooth and hard and oddly shaped. Not the wand-shaped Destroyer, but . . .

He drew forth the Unknown Potency with a blackened hand and stared at it. Exerting his talent, he banished the soot to the ashbed, then stepped out of the fireplace and dropped into a nearby chair.

The twisted ribbon of moonstone gleamed clean in his upturned palm: the sure answer to all his prayers, if only he had the courage to make use of it.

"Snudge! Wake up!"

The boy groaned. Someone was shaking his shoulder, and none too gently. It was the prince, with the somber-faced Doctor Arcanorum at his side.

"Forgive me, Your Grace. I worked for some time on the task you assigned me, but with no success. I'm afraid that I fell asleep." He hauled himself into a sitting position, noting that the day was now far advanced. "All the same, I'm certain that she is somewhere close by." He lowered his voice to a whisper. "We'd be well advised to keep that in mind."

"Con, I told you so!" Stergos said.

The prince pretended not to understand. "No doubt she's engaged in important business of her own. But we must hope that the lady reveals herself soon— for I'm heading back to Cathra immediately, sailing on a Stippenese vessel commandeered by Lord Skellhaven, and I'm counting upon the princess to supply us with the necessary fair winds."

"Are you indeed!"

Both Snudge and Stergos uttered cries of alarm as Ullanoth—or was it her Sending?—abruptly became visible before them. Conrig took her hand and brushed the back of it with his lips, while giving every evidence of happy surprise.

"Welcome, my dear! And thank you, from the bottom of my heart, for all you have vouchsafed to me and my people. I had hoped to express my gratitude privately before this. Are you well?"

She nodded rather distantly. Snudge and the doctor she totally ignored, as though they were nothing but faithful dogs keeping the prince company. "I'm rested and almost recovered from the stress of empowering the Loophole and Weathermaker. There's a bit of bother involving my brother Beynor, but it needn't concern you at present. Tell me more about your plan to return to Cathra. I presume you intend to take personal charge of the defense of Cala City."

"I must. Lord Admiral Copperstrand is dead. His deputy, Zednor Woodvale, concurred in the disastrous decision to split our fleet and shares responsibility for a disastrous defeat off the Vigilant Isles. God knows what Woodvale will do when Honigalus is reinforced by corsairs from the Continent. A windspoken message from King Olmigon has informed us that my father's admonitions to the fleet officers are still being ignored." He smiled grimly. "But they won't ignore me."

"The Continentals gathered in Nis-Gata have not yet left port," she said. "Rumors have reached them from Andradh that a force of twenty strongly armed Tarnian frigates is coming to the aid of Cathra. Unfortunately, I know for a fact that the Tarnian ships are still delayed in the Western Ocean by bad weather generated by Beynor."

"Can you do anything about it?"

"Perhaps," she said, shrugging, "if my recovering strength is not exhausted by other difficult magical endeavors. You say you wish me to propel your ship southward at speed. This is no trivial request."

"But a vitally important one, my lady! And I must leave at once. This evening. I hope you will accompany me and lend your good offices as I confront Honigalus—"

"This is not possible. My brother must be dealt with. Beynor poses a grave threat to all of us, and not only because of his continuing assistance to Didion. At the moment, I have him off balance and vulnerable, and I must press my advantage."

An emotion that might have been relief touched the prince's features. "But I need you at my side, lady!" he protested.

She made a quelling gesture. "I dare not take myself far away from Moss at this time. Not when the regaining of my stolen throne is within my grasp." She came close to him and placed one hand on his heart. "Conrig, I've vowed to assist your cause. I've already risked my life for you. Trust me."

"Of course," he said, embracing her. "As you must trust me."

She lifted her face to be kissed, and after the chaste salute, whispered, "I love you, Con, and it breaks my heart that we must part, even for a brief time. But both of us have kingdoms to secure. My homeland must seem a poor place to you, compared to the grandeur of Cathra. But I will have it. I must have it! So I leave you now, but I shall grant you the magical winds you need—and return to you as soon as possible to guarantee your victory."

"I understand," he said, letting his arms fall and stepping away from her. He still smiled, but there was only emptiness in his eyes.

He does not love me, she realized.

Had she ever truly believed it? But neither did he love his barren wife. Perhaps he was one of those who are incapable of surrendering to another, as she once believed herself to be before her traitor heart betrayed her.

She asked herself: *Does it matter?*

That remained to be seen.

She turned, seeming to take notice of Vra-Stergos for the first time. "Doctor, perhaps you will be so kind as to bespeak me in two days or thereabouts, with news of Cathra's struggle against Honigalus."

"I will do my best to contact you, lady," the alchymist replied anxiously, "but our ship will have traveled far to the south by then, and my talent may be insufficient to bridge the leagues."

Her glance flickered toward Snudge. "Then perhaps you will have to seek help from others with more strength."

She smiled at the startled look on the faces of the brothers, then vanished.

thirty-one

The volcanos of Tarn belonged to the planetary realm, outside the dominion of the Beaconfolk and beyond their power to coerce.

For this reason the fire-mountains had been able to besmirch the northern sky with impunity, diminishing the Lights' glory in the sight of lesser entities as well as affronting the dignity of the great beings themselves and making them peevish. Only in lowly Moss, where the talented human boy had deflected the clouds of ash with his sigil, had the aurora borealis shone on unimpeded.

In their toplofty way, the Lights had been appreciative of Beynor's effort. They granted his increasingly impudent requests and withheld their anger, even though he misused his Great Stone for petty purposes.

But now the forbearance of the Beaconfolk was wearing thin.

The noxious eruptions were over, the heavens had cleared, and the Great Lights once again blazed supreme in the Northland, paling the stars of winter as they basked in the awe and admiration of monsters and men alike.

Yet here came that tedious boy again, with more inappropriate demands!

Secure in his royal apartment, certain that Ulla would not violate the grace period she'd given him, Beynor held high the finger wearing the moonstone ring. He uttered the two incantations and awaited the green flares of fulfillment and the necessary pain.

Nothing happened. Instead, windspoken words roared unexpectedly in his mind.

CADAY AN RUDAY?

He was taken aback. Not since his activation of Weathermaker over three years ago had the Coldlight Army asked him the ominous ritual question. He replied as confidently as he was able, using the language of the Salka to praise the Lights and abase himself before getting down to business.

"Great Skylords! I ask two favors of your Weathermaker stone. The first is fair southerly winds in Cala Bay, to assist my allies in their attack upon Cathra. The second—"

WHAT YOU ASK IS INCONVENIENT AND UNTIMELY, CONTRARY TO THE NORMAL COURSE OF EARLY WINTER AIRS IN THOSE WATERS. WE HAVE ALREADY CONDESCENDED TO GRANT THIS DIFFICULT REQUEST ONCE. FOR YOU TO DEMAND IT AGAIN IS INSOLENT.

"But necessary! I beseech you! I conjure you! . . . Please?"

PLAY YOUR SILLY HUMAN WARGAMES WITH LESSER SIGILS. YOU ARE TESTING OUR PATIENCE SEVERELY. REMEMBER THAT WE KNOW YOUR NAME, BEYNOR SON OF LINNDAL!

"Then—then fulfill my second conjuration, at least. The most important one. It should be an easy thing for you. An insignificant drain on your mighty powers."

Silence.

Heartened, he lifted the moonstone ring once again and spoke the spell: "Let a black thundercloud form above my sister Ullanoth, wherever she may be. Let its whirling winds create an imbalance between the humors of the earth and air, so that a colossal stroke of lightning reduces her body to its elements and scatters them, never to be reassembled!"

WHY?

Why? . . . The terror and sense of impending disaster he had thus far been able to repress welled up and threatened to unman him. He took a long moment to formulate his reply. He had to make them understand!

"Because Ullanoth dares to use your magical gifts against me. I am the Conjure-King of Moss, the true heir to Rothbannon. My sister threatens my life and my reign. I can only be safe if she is dead."

Again there was the long, portentous silence. When the response came, it was unexpectedly reasonable in tone.

YOU TOOK THE CROWN OF MOSS BY REGICIDE AND PATRICIDE, DID YOU NOT?

What should he say? The Lights weren't human! They themselves never scrupled to kill persons who offended them. Why should they feel bound by the moral constraints of mankind? Would the simple truth suffice to justify him?

"Great Lords of Light—my poor father the Conjure-King was afflicted by madness, subject to drastic swings of emotion. His will swayed like a willow in a gale. He affirmed me as his heir to the throne, but he might well have changed his mind the next day—"

SO YOU SLEW HIM. AND NOW YOU ASK US TO COLLUDE IN YOUR CRIME, KILLING YOUR LEGITIMATE RIVAL—SHE WHO SHARED YOUR MOTHER'S WOMB, WHO HAS NEVER YET USED OUR SIGILS IGNOBLY, WHO HAS EVEN VOWED NEVER TO TAKE YOUR LIFE.

"Has she indeed?" Beynor cried out. "The more fool she! But what does my life matter if I lose my crown to that perfidious whore and stand despised before my people and the world?"

Even as this furious and despairing outburst of his rang on the wind, he knew he'd finally gone too far.

The Lights laughed.

WHAT DOES IT MATTER, BEYNOR OF MOSS? YOU ARE ABOUT TO FIND OUT! BUT BECAUSE IT AMUSES US TO SOW UNCERTAINTY AMONG HUMANITY, AND BECAUSE AN ACTION OF YOURS, ALTHOUGH ALL UNWITTING, ONCE REDOUNDED TO OUR SPLENDOR, WE WILL LEAVE YOU WITH A SINGLE TOKEN OF OUR MERCY—WHICH YOU ARE FORBIDDEN TO USE!—AFTER REQUITING YOU LESS PUNISHMENT THAN YOU DESERVE.

They struck him down then with a crushing avalanche of pain, and he thought he was finished, damned to suffer forever.

Instead he woke at length to find himself lying on the bearskin hearth rug of his sitting room, nearly frozen to the bone and feeble as a nursling babe, but otherwise unharmed. Icy drafts rattled the windowpanes and fluttered the undrawn drapes. Outside, the Beacons rioted in the black evening sky, casting faint shadows on the walls of the room. Aside from that flickering cold brilliance, there was no other illumination save a few dying coals in the fireplace.

No reassuring emerald glow from the Fortress moonstones. The tall monstrance that had held both of them was empty.

Still sitting on the rug, he raised his right hand and discovered that

Weathermaker was gone from his finger. The twin golden neckchains where Shapeshifter and Subtle Armor had hung now lay tangled uselessly against the skin of his breast.

"I have nothing left," he whispered, knowing even as he voiced the self-pitying statement that it wasn't true. He still possessed his considerable natural talent. The Lights had not deprived him of that. But it was insufficient to save him. When Ulla confronted him tomorrow, as she'd promised to do, she'd know instantly that his sigils were gone. That he was helpless to oppose her.

With great effort he rose to his feet, took blocks of peat from the basket beside the fireplace, and used tongs to set the fuel carefully among the embers. Flames blazed up almost at once, warming him and casting more light about the room. Something made of metal gleamed on the shadowed mantel: the handsome platinum case that had held the Seven Stones of Rothbannon. He gave a despondent laugh, reached for it, opened the catch, and cried out in astonishment.

All of the small velvet nests were empty except one. It held a peculiar amulet carved in the shape of a twisted ribbon with a single surface and a single edge, the only sigil of its kind ever fashioned. The Unknown Potency was still lifeless, but it reflected faint intriguing glints from the fire.

We will leave you with a single token of our mercy, which you are forbidden to use . . .

"But what good is it, then?" he groaned. "Where is the mercy?"

The answer stole into his mind.

Over and over again, from their earliest childhood, Beynor and his sister had been told the tale of how Rothbannon had received his wonder-working sigils from a certain Salka of the Dawntide Isles—a venerable, high-ranking shaman reviled by his fellows for having been too faint-hearted to activate the Unknown Potency himself, who had nevertheless, for some perverse reason of his own, given the enigmatic Great Stone and six others to a human sorcerer.

Would those monsters, driven from their original home by encroaching humans, welcome one who restored their lost treasure to them?

His friend Arowann, of the Darkling Tribe, might know!

He composed himself and sent out a call on the wind, but there was no reply, perhaps because the amphibious being and his kin were fast asleep in their subterranean lair among the frozen Forbidden Lakes.

I can't wait until tomorrow to bespeak Arowann, he thought in a panic. Ulla will come for me! I don't dare waste a single minute.

He'd have to try the others. It was a risk—the brutes could play him false, knowing he was helpless now—but he had no other choice.

He bespoke the Salka of the Dawntide Isles, begging the attention of the Master Shaman Kalawnn, who had dismissed his earlier plea for advice and heartlessly told him to grow up before attempting high sorcery.

Somewhat to his surprise, there was an answer.

Speak, boy.

Insolent as ever, the conceited troll! But at least the creature seemed willing to listen.

Kalawnn made no comment as Beynor poured out a frank description of his predicament, then offered to return the Unknown in exchange for sanctuary. As an additional incentive—and in hopes of preserving his life after handing over the sigil to the monsters—the boy-king spoke of his knowledge of Darasilo's trove of ancient moonstones hidden somewhere in Cala and his opinion that the disgraced Cathran alchymist Vra-Kilian, now imprisoned in Zeth Abbey, possessed two books that might reveal hitherto unknown secrets of Coldlight sorcery.

"Kilian still has reason to be friendly toward me," Beynor said eagerly. "If you grant me your protection, Master Kalawnn, I'll not only give the Unknown Potency to you, but also do all in my power to persuade the alchymist to share his knowledge with us. He hates Conrig of Cathra from the depths of his soul. Who can say what fruit an alliance with Kilian might bear?"

Beynor had said all he could safely say. Now his fate rested with the Salka Master Shaman. He waited for a response, and the time seemed to stretch interminably.

Finally Kalawnn said: *Do you still have the large ship gifted to you by the princes of Didion?*

"Yes, for all the good it is to me. The barque's name is *Ambergris*. She's moored in the Darkling River estuary, but with only a few watchmen aboard to keep an eye on her throughout the winter. She cannot be used in high winds and freezing weather."

Listen to me, boy. Dress in your warmest garments, go to the vessel, and get rid of any humans who are there. Is that clear? You must be alone on the ship.

"But *Ambergris* needs nearly two hundred men to crew her!"

The inhuman windvoice sneered at him. *Do you wish to live?*

"Yes," he replied humbly. "Yes, Master Kalawnn."

Then do as I say, and leave all the rest to me.

From her hiding place in the topmost chamber of Holt Mallburn's deserted Wizards' Tower, where she rested invisible under Concealer's spell, Ullanoth watched her brother through Subtle Loophole and smiled.

Let him go off in his empty ship propelled by monsters. Let him think himself safe from her, and let the Salka do as they pleased with him, poor gullible child! It was as good a solution as she could hope for now. In time, she'd find out what Beynor and Kilian Blackhorse had connived at together, discover the secret of Darasilo's moonstone trove, and scry out whatever mischief the Dawntide Salka decided upon.

Meanwhile, she intended to conjure her own Weathermaker three times, in ways that she hoped would not offend the Lights: to send Conrig's ship south, to dissolve the storm frustrating the Tarnian mercenary fleet, and to conjure a blizzard to trap the force of Prince Somarus in Boarsden Castle, so that he might not soon threaten the occupation of Holt Mallburn. None of those requests demanded weather that was inappropriate to this time of year. North winds, precisely directed, would take care of everything.

Her Weathermaker debt to the Lights was still a light one, and she'd pay it gladly. Perhaps it might incapacitate her for a day, even two—but she'd be safe here in the tower, thanks to Concealer. When she recovered, she would Send herself to Royal Fenguard dressed in regal garments. The Glaumerie Guild would by then be frantic at Beynor's abrupt disappearance. Her own reasonable proposal should find a ready reception.

Why should Moss settle for an infant monarch and a regency when it could set the rightful royal heiress on its throne? An heiress, moreover, who commanded sigils more powerful than those of the departed usurper, who could guarantee Moss First Vassal status in Conrig Wincantor's new Sovereignty of High Blenholme, and who would in good time bring a dowry of Cathran gold along with her!

Of course they'll accept me, she told herself. And when my throne is secure, I'll Send myself on to Cathra . . .

Outside the round Wizards' Tower, the wind already blew gently out of the North. Ullanoth went to the window that overlooked Mallburn harbor, more than a league away, and lifted Loophole to her eye. The conquerors had restored the lights along the quayside, and torches illuminated the dock where the captured Stippenese merchant clipper *Shearwater* was tied up. The provisioning was now complete and the ship ready to sail.

The sigil gave Ullanoth a close view of Conrig, his Heart Companions, Vra-Stergos, and their armigers approaching the quay on horseback. The squire named Deveron Austrey rode unobtrusively among the other boys. She scrutinized his person with the greatest of care. There was nothing at all unusual about him—saving only his eyes, still dulled by enormous fatigue but betraying a wild talent so powerful that it even rendered him imperceptible to ordinary scrying, as though he were one of the great shamans of the Northland.

What else might Deveron's talent be capable of?

When she had Sent herself to Conrig and Stergos and found the young armiger with them in their quarters, she had experienced an unsettling disturbance in her own arcane equilibrium. Some hours earlier, moving invisibly about Holt Mallburn and taking stock of the occupation, she had overheard rumors of how this same Deveron had played strangely crucial roles in the taking of Redfern Castle and Mallmouth Bridge.

Conrig was clearly using the boy's talent for his personal advantage. It remained to be seen whether that talent posed a danger to *her* . . .

She lowered Loophole with a sigh of relief and tucked it into an inner pocket of her gown. The problem of Deveron Austrey could wait, but Weathermaker's conjuring could not.

She had brought food with her to the tower, and the wizards' refectory cupboard was well supplied with all manner of drink. She supped on cold roast capon, a pear tart with cinnamon, and mead mulled with a hot poker. The simple pallets in the wizards' cells were unappealing places of repose, so she gathered numbers of feather ticks and pillows into the archwizard's cozy study, where there was a padded long chair, and made up a bed near the ceramic stove. It seemed a peculiar heating device, fueled by charcoal and pellets of resinous heartwood; but she soon discovered that it was a very efficient generator of heat.

She made everything ready for the inevitable ordeal, slipped Weathermaker on her finger, then looked out the tower window one final time. The ghostly gleam of the aurora was just beginning to rise above the horizon to the north, and frost whitened the palace's roofs and parapets.

Perhaps I won't need to create a magical snowstorm to maroon Somarus after all, she thought. Nature may just do the job without Weathermaker's help!

But Conrig still needed his strong north wind, and so did the beleagured Tarnian mercenaries. She returned to her bed and conjured the Great Stone.

Dancing in the sky above the frigid wastes of the Barren Lands, the Beaconfolk responded amiably to the appeals of the sorceress.

Then they added a few meteorological embellishments of their own.

thirty-two

Against the urgent advice of his worried alchymists and physicians, King Olmigon personally presided over a meeting of his Privy Council with the great peers who by tradition shared the defense of Cathra's south coast. The two council members who were at Sea—Prince Heritor Conrig and the newly promoted Lord Admiral, Zednor Woodvale—participated through windvoices.

It was the king's hope to persuade the nobles to send armed merchantmen and small fighting craft from their private fleets to reinforce the decimated Cathran navy. But in spite of his best efforts, the conference degenerated quickly into a bootless wrangle when it became plain that most of the Lords of the Southern Shore thought such an action would be unwise.

"Is it not true," asked Count Chakto Cranmere, whose commercial fleet was the largest in the kingdom, "that the Tarnian mercenaries have finally broken free of the storm that delayed them?"

Olmigon said, "This is what the windvoice traveling with them has told Vra-Sulkorig. Their ships are now flying down the Westley coast, driven by a strong north wind. However, it's uncertain what conditions they'll meet once they round Flaming Head and enter Dolphin Channel—and this is why I've decided to seek additional reinforcements of you, my lords."

Count Brinmar Woodvale, brother to the admiral, spoke to the king. "With respect, sire, more ships are surely not needed. Even with headwinds, the Wave-Harriers are bound to arrive in time to save the day. Tarnians are the finest sailors in the world and the best marine warriors as well. Let them earn the reward we've already paid them."

"The Crown paid," Chancellor Falmire reminded the count, "not you Lords of the Shore."

"As was only proper," Duke Nettos Intrepid snapped, "since it was the Crown's negligence that let the Royal Navy fall below strength in the first place."

"You refused to tax yourselves for new capital ships!" the king retorted. "And all of you denied there was any danger from the sea, even when the Prince Heritor warned you of Didion's secret alliance with the Continentals. And now half our war-fleet is destroyed and Cala City itself stands in danger."

"If Your Grace had not dismissed me from my post," Lord Dundry said, forgetting that he had been one of the loudest to dispute the threat from the sea, "I might have led our navy to victory in the Vigilant Isles. Young Elo Copperstrand displayed a fatal lack of experience. It was ridiculous to divide the fleet—"

"My late son acted as he thought best!" shouted Duke Bandon. "Damn your self-serving hindsight, Tothor Dundry!"

Insults flew until Vra-Sulkorig broke in with a windspoken observation from Lord Admiral Zednor Woodvale.

My lords, leave off quarreling and listen to me! We face sure defeat if the Tarnian frigates are delayed. I must have some sort of reinforcements at once. No other considerations are important.

"He's right," said Count Haydon Defiant, who had thus far made no comment. He was a few years older than King Olmigon, whom he had known since childhood. Short-clipped snowy hair and long white moustaches gave his broad face the look of an intelligent walrus. In contrast to most of the other nobles attending, he was a firm supporter of the Sovereignty. "I for one intend to send the Lord Admiral every small fighting vessel at my disposal—sloops armed with springals and cutters carrying tarnblaze bombards."

"Your merchantmen mount more effective mortars and culverins," the king pointed out to his old friend. "What about them?"

"Well, most are already laid up for the winter and the crews dispersed landside." The count refused to meet the gaze of the monarch. "The small boats will serve better, sire."

And more cheaply, was the unspoken thought.

Duke Nettos Intrepid agreed it would be insanity to pit slow-sailing merchant ships against men o' war. "But can sloops and gunboats make a tactical difference fighting Didion's three-tier battleships and heavy frigates—to say nothing of a vicious pack of Continental corsairs? Perhaps we should consider suing for peace. Offer to send food trains to Great Pass if Honigalus agrees to withdraw."

Why should he do so, the Lord Admiral interposed bleakly, *if victory at sea and the corn stores of Cala are within his grasp? No, my lords! We must fight—and pray the Tarnians arrive in time.*

"Even with fair winds, the Wave-Harriers face a full day's sail to Cala Bay," said gloomy old Duke Farindon Eagleroost. His fortress, together with that of Shiantil Blackhorse, defended the approach to Blenholme Roads and Cala City beyond. "Honigalus and the Continentals will probably fall on the Lord Admiral's fleet in half that time. Need I remind you that Cathra's next encounter with the foe will pit more than sixty enemy men o' war against our paltry twenty-nine? Even with the twenty Tarnian frigates, we're still outnumbered."

"Sue for peace," Cranmere said. "It's the only solution."

"Nay!" cried the king. Beads of sweat glistened on his face and his voice faltered. "You're wrong! We must call out every vessel capable of hurling tarnfire or other missiles at the foe . . . Even light fighting craft can perform a useful delaying action! I . . . I have a daring plan. Only . . . let me explain it . . ."

But his strength was fast failing. He slumped back into the litter that had borne him to the council chamber, and the physicians gave him water to drink and applied cool cloths to his brow.

Count Haydon Defiant spoke firmly. "We have yet to hear from Prince Heritor Conrig on this matter. Vra-Sulkorig, be so good as to invite His Grace's comments."

Conrig addressed them through the windvoice of Stergos: *My lords, I beg you not to give in to pessimism. All is not lost. The strong winds now filling the sails of our Tarnian allies—and speeding my own fast ship toward the waters of home—are being generated by the magic of Cathra's good friend, the gracious Princess Ullanoth of Moss. Thanks to her, the winds in Cala Bay will soon shift to the north. They will be unfavorable to Didion's huge first-rate ships and frigates, and give a powerful advantage to our defenders. The idea of the King's Grace to use small fighting craft to harry the enemy force is an excellent one. Listen to him and have courage! Emulate the example of our fearless warriors who captured Holt Mallburn.*

The lords murmured uncertainly. Before Conrig could say more, Duke Shiantil Blackhorse spoke up in a manner that was both offhand and calculated.

"It is well-known that Beaconfolk sorcery invoked by Conjure-Princess

Ullanoth enabled the Prince Heritor to overcome King Achardus of Didion. Vra-Sulkorig, I urge you to ask the prince if more of the witch's black magic is poised to shield our Lord Admiral's fleet from the wrath of Achardus's son."

"For shame, Blackhorse!" cried Haydon Defiant.

"Slander!" Eagleroost roared. "What has this to do with the danger facing us now?"

At least one person in the chamber knew. Lord Chamberlain Flintworth, who had been a crony of the deposed Royal Alchymist, hid a tiny smile of secret satisfaction. His intensive coaching of frivolous Duke Shi-Shi in recent weeks seemed not to have been in vain after all.

Blackhorse said, "My beloved uncle Vra-Kilian tried to warn our king that the Prince Heritor was in thrall to the Conjure-Princess. For his pains, he nearly lost his head and has been banished! I feel it is my duty to inform this assembly of the truth. Before you agree to follow any recommendation of Prince Conrig, consider what manner of man he is. And what future Cathra may face if he becomes its king—and Ullanoth its queen."

"This is lunacy!" King Olmigon gasped. "What in God's name are you playing at, Shiantil? Making such accusations now, with our nation in imminent peril!"

"I think I know," Eagleroost said.

"And I," muttered Defiant.

But Blackhorse persisted. "Does the Prince Heritor deny that Ullanoth gave him his northern victory and that he intends to share the throne with her?"

"Lies, foul lies," King Olmigon croaked. "Tell them so, my son! Tell them— ah!—tell them." He fell groaning back into the litter.

Vra-Sulkorig raised both arms. "My lords! Listen to Prince Conrig's own words, spoken to me on the wind."

Sire, my lords—I swear on my royal heritage and on the Halidom of Saint Zeth that my victory over Achardus Mallburn was achieved through honorable means and not through dark sorcery as certain false reports have put forth. It is true that Ullanoth of Moss has been Cathra's ally, assisting us through her benevolent magic, and for this the Sovereignty intends to reward her well. But I never promised to marry her or set her on Cathra's throne. And as God witnesses, it was the strength and valor of our warriors that vanquished Achardus Mallburn and gave Holt Mallburn into my hands—not uncanny powers. He who claims otherwise is a liar and a traitor!

Farindon Eagleroost began to applaud. He was immediately joined by Defiant, Vigilant, and Count Woodvale. The others, with the exception of Shiantil Blackhorse, who only smiled and shrugged, eventually joined in.

King Olmigon's voice now had renewed vigor. "My lords, thank you for your expressions of goodwill. Will you now put aside your differences so that we may work together defending the realm?"

"Aye!" came the nearly unanimous response.

Eagleroost said, "I'll have my windvoice transmit orders at once. Following the good example of Count Defiant, I'll send every suitable gunboat at my disposal to join the Lord Admiral's fleet."

"So will I," said Lullian Vigilant.

"And I," Count Woodvale added.

The others, even glowering Shiantil, added their affirmations. The small fighting craft would set out as soon as their crews could be assembled. Those based in Cala Bay could be expected to reach Woodvale by dawn.

None of the Lords of the Southern Shore had volunteered to risk any valuable merchantmen, however. Whispering among themselves as Olmigon lay back in evident relief and commanded Vra-Sulkorig to bespeak the good tidings to the Prince Heritor and the Lord Admiral, the lords quietly concluded that even if Honigalus and the Continentals licked Woodvale and wreaked havoc on Cala, they could gain no lasting foothold in Cathra nor do much damage to the lords ensconced in their strong castles. Winter storms would soon force the enemy armada to retreat. And in spring, the situation might be very different . . .

The king said, "My lords, I thank you and beg that you keep in mind a fact that every naval strategist knows: numbers are not everything in sea warfare. Bravery, the cunning use of resources, and luck can conquer even the most overwhelming odds."

Murmurs. They would have liked to believe it.

"This conference is now adjourned," the king went on. "But before I leave you, I wish to share the great secret which I have thus far kept to myself—the response of Emperor Bazekoy's oracle to my one Question."

Suddenly, every man in the room was silent and motionless, with all eyes fixed upon the dying king.

"I asked Bazekoy if my son Conrig could succeed in uniting High Blenholme in a great Sovereignty. The oracle said it could be done, provided that I myself fulfilled a certain very strange condition. Last night I dreamed of the emperor. The time has finally come for me to obey his dictate. My friends, believe that Cathra will win this war and the Sovereignty will come to pass. And now I bid you farewell, for it's unlikely we'll ever meet again."

He gestured to the litter-bearers, and they began to carry him from the council chamber.

"But, sire!" Count Brinmar Woodvale cried out uncertainly. "What is this condition of the emperor that you intend to fulfill?"

"Muster your small craft to defend Blenholme Roads," the fading voice said from the corridor, "and you'll find out."

"Oh, no!" The sweet face of Queen Cataldise stiffened in disbelieving horror as Olmigon explained what he was going to do.

"I beg you to be reasonable, Your Grace," Vra-Sulkorig implored, speaking for the cadre of physicians and alchymists who stood aghast at the king's bedside. "Your heart-pains are nearly constant now. Any exertion will surely be the death of you. Why, I feared you would never survive this afternoon's conference! For you to leave the palace is unthinkable."

"Emperor Bazekoy told me that Conrig would unite our island only if I rose from my deathbed to assist him." Olmigon's lips had gone bluish again, his face was mottled, and his burning eyes were sunk deep into his skull. "I'm ready. Order my carriage and have my gentlemen prepare suitable garments. I'll need heavy wool underthings, for starters."

"Husband, stay!" The queen had begun to weep. "Stay if you have ever loved me."

"I love you," came the implacable response, "and I'll do as I was told. Bring me a waterproof leather jerkin and trews . . . high boots, fur-lined . . . a long sealskin cloak with a hood edged in wolverine . . . fur mittens on a long string."

Sulkorig hesitated, then inclined his head in agreement. "I'll summon the lords-in-waiting at once, sire. They'll bring everything you need."

The queen rounded on him in a fit of anguish. "You can't let His Grace do this!"

The Acting Royal Alchymist took her arm and pulled her insistently to the door, whispering, "Let be, let be! We must humor him in this sad obsession. In a short time he'll tire and accept the sip of poppy he refused earlier, and it will make no difference how he's attired. He'll sleep—and when he wakes tomorrow he'll realize that it's too late for rash action. If God wills, he may not even remember that we thwarted him."

"Yes, I see." The queen dabbed at her eyes with a handkerchief. "How sensible of you."

"Catty!"

She spun around as Olmigon called out and returned quickly to his bedside. "What is it, husband?"

"I want to say farewell to dear Maude. I won't be coming back from this jaunt of mine, you know."

Cataldise swallowed her fresh distress and forced a smile. "Shall I fetch our daughter-in-law? I'm sure she can be here by the time you're dressed. I'll go myself, and there'll be no need to summon the Master-at-Arms."

The king lifted a trembling hand and touched her cheek. "Don't grieve for me, dear heart. I'm a happy man, going to battle again after sitting helpless on the sidelines for thirty years."

She steeled herself to leave him. "Lie easy then, and don't quarrel with the alchymists while I'm gone. They only wish to help."

"Let them help me take one last piss like a man!" the king said, glaring at the doctors. "Do you hear? Then swaddle me well and wrap my loins in oilskin, so my damned leaking bladder doesn't wet me down and bring on a fatal chill. I will not die before my time! Bazekoy would be furious."

As the guards announced the queen, Princess Maudrayne's dour maidservant was trimming wicks and getting ready to light the lamps and candles against the setting of the sun.

"Take me to your mistress," Cataldise demanded, before Rusgann could even rise from her curtsey.

"She's working in her little study-room, Your Grace. Please to follow me."

There were no other attendants in the apartment. The place was cluttered with stacks of books, baskets containing parchment rolls, stoppered glass containers with peculiar things floating in them, and pieces of scientific apparatus. Some of the brass objects reminded the queen of the disused navigation instruments that were now only ornaments on the shelves of the king's sitting room.

What a mess! Cataldise thought. The girl has let her quarters become positively squalid since Sovanna was dismissed. Whether Maude likes it or not,

I'll have the place tidied up, starting tomorrow. What would Conrig think if he returned and found things in such a state?

"The Queen's Grace to see you," Rusgann announced to Maudrayne.

"Leave us," Cataldise told the maid, who shot her a saucy look before withdrawing.

The queen and princess exchanged cool nods, then sat down opposite one another at a large table piled with tomes and notebooks. Maudrayne had been watercoloring an ink sketch of a flower on a sheet of vellum. She wore a splattered apron over her gown, and her fingers were stained.

"I have some good news, Daughter. Conrig is sailing south and may arrive in Cala Bay tomorrow or the next day if he's not delayed by bad weather. Of course he probably won't come immediately to the palace. I believe he intends to visit Admiral Woodvale on his flagship first and instruct him how to dispose of Honigalus and his nasty band of raiders."

"I look forward to seeing my husband," Maudrayne said. "Thank you for coming to tell me of him."

"There's something else." Cataldise bit her lip to forestall tears. "The king has taken a turn for the worse. He wishes to see you."

"Oh!" Genuine concern furrowed the brow of the princess. "Of course I'll come at once." She rose and untied her apron.

"Listen to me first, Daughter. His Grace is not himself. He's been seized with a crazed notion and refuses to abide by the advice of his doctors. He won't even heed me. You'll have to help us calm him or—or the consequences could be mortal."

"What is this notion?"

"His Grace is determined to leave the palace this very night and take personal command of our war-fleet. He has no confidence in Lord Admiral Woodvale's ability to engage the Didionites in battle. He truly believes that Emperor Bazekoy wants him to rise from his deathbed and direct the defense of our kingdom."

"Great God!" Maudrayne could not help smiling. "But who can say if the king's desire is madness or sanity? If Copperstrand and Woodvale had not ignored him when he attempted to windspeak them, perhaps we would not have suffered such a terrible drubbing at the Vigilant Isles. What other way can His Grace guarantee that his orders are carried out, than by taking command?

I've read accounts of his youthful naval exploits against the pirates of Andradh—"

Cataldise was on her feet, livid with anger. "Don't talk like an idiot! Sulkorig told me that the least exertion will stop my dear husband's faltering heart. He *cannot* leave his bed! I came here hoping for your help, madam, knowing that you love Olmigon. If you intend to encourage him in his pathetic fantasy, then damn you for a heartless fool—and be sure I'll tell Conrig how you failed his father in his last hours."

Maudrayne went white. "You misunderstand me, Your Grace. I was only speaking rhetorically. Foolishly also, I confess. I scarce know what I'm saying, being so shaken by what you've told me. I beseech you to forgive me for being so thoughtless at this difficult time."

The princess had come around the table and taken the queen's hands in her own. Her sea-blue eyes were brimming. "I do love the King's Grace deeply, as you know. If you'll allow it, I'll accompany you to him and do my utmost to soothe his troubled mind and distract him from sick fancies."

"He insists on saying good-bye to you," Cataldise said tiredly. "To humor him, I'm letting his gentlemen dress him in outdoor clothing, as though he were truly going to sea. You'll have to go along with the charade."

"Of course . . ."

Behind Cataldise, the door to the sitting room opened slowly without a sound. Rusgann was there, grinning. Beside her stood the shorter, more ample figure of Red Ansel the shaman, holding a finger to his lips. He winked. A moment later, the door swung nearly shut again.

Maudrayne embraced the queen, her heart wildly pounding. "I understand perfectly, Mother. Wait here just a moment while I instruct my maid."

The princess rushed from the studium. She found Ansel holding out a small green glass phial he had removed from the ivory casket where she kept her diary.

"Take this with you," he whispered. "It's time for us to leave this place. But our manner of departure will be more memorable than any of us ever dreamed."

"What must I do?" Maudrayne said breathlessly. "Oh, hurry, or the queen might discover you!"

"No, she won't," said the shaman. "Return with her to the king and contrive to give her a few drops of this sleeping potion. It has no taste and won't harm her. Rusgann and I will meet you at the royal bedchamber very soon."

"But what about the king?" the princess said.

"I thought you understood." Ansel's dark eyes were dancing. "He's going to escape with us."

"They all think I've lost my mind, lass," Olmigon said to Maudrayne in a quavering voice.

"Oh, husband!" The queen sighed.

"It's true. My dear wife and the wizards and that morbid old raven Falmire all believe I'll turn up my toes if I leave the palace. But they thought the same when I told them I was going to Zeth Abbey to ask my Question of Bazekoy. And I lived through that, didn't I?"

"So you did, sire." The princess leaned forward from her stool beside the king's bed and gripped his hand.

He lay atop the swansdown comforter, completely dressed except for his heavy cloak and mittens. Only Maudrayne and Cataldise now attended him. At Olmigon's insistence, the alchymists and the others had withdrawn. Vra-Sulkorig had left behind a tall crystal tumbler containing a poppy draft, which sat on a nightstand along with a pitcher of water, a basin with washcloths, a decanter of wine, three unused goblets, and a burning candle. The only other light in the room came from the hearth.

"They're taking too long with my carriage," Olmigon complained.

"It'll be here soon," the queen said. "Don't be impatient, love. Remember there's your yacht to be readied as well. You don't want to be kept waiting at the dock when you can rest more comfortably here. Are you sure you don't want us to take off your boots?"

The king grunted. "I'm fine, damn it."

Cataldise lifted the crystal tumbler and offered it to him again. "You really ought to take your tonic. You'll need your strength."

But he turned his face away. "Not yet. I'll drink it at the last minute before I go, so its benefits will last longer."

Cataldise rolled her eyes. "You know best."

"Damned right I do! If I could only have convinced my jackass admirals of that, I wouldn't have to take charge of things myself." He began to cough, and both women sprang up to lift his head and shoulders. The queen tried once more to hold the tumbler to his lips, but at the first bitter taste he knew what it must be and began to curse and splutter. "Take it away, woman! Didn't I tell you I won't have the vile brew yet?"

He calmed down as the queen began to sniffle and told her he was sorry for losing his temper. "It's just that this delay is vexing the hell out of me, Catty. Find out what's delaying the carriage."

"Perhaps Maudrayne could go—"

"She's still under arrest," the king reminded his wife coldly. "You do it. Please. You can make them hurry."

"Very well." She left the chamber, moving reluctantly, and Olmigon said nothing more until the outer door closed behind her. Then: "Maudie, they're playing games with me, aren't they!"

"I'm afraid so, sire."

His voice dwindled to near inaudibility. "God help me. I thought I could pull off Bazekoy's trick, but they've flummoxed me. I'm too far gone to make anyone obey. It's over. Nothing left to do now but sing the Deathsong and polish my sorry excuses for the emperor."

"Sire—"

"Woodvale's bound to bungle it, you know. He's a professional naval officer with no idea how to utilize a flotilla of cockleshell irregulars. You see, by all conventions of modern warfare, large ships only battle large ships, while cutters and other light craft only fight with each other or act as runabouts in service to the big men o' war. But it doesn't have to be that way! I could show Woodvale how to use our small fry against enemy ships-of-the-line and frigates . . . like hornets harrying a herd of bulls! But I'll never get him to understand, talking to him through the bloody windvoices."

"Your Grace, listen—"

But he swept on in a tone that was weighted with a certain gloomy relish. "If Con were only here, I might get the message across through him. He has no preconceived notions of proper naval tactics, and he wouldn't take any guff from Woodvale and his captains. But there's only me."

"And me," she said. "And my friend Red Ansel Pikan. Sire, your oracle of Bazekoy is a hard thing for sophisticated Cathrans to believe in. But we Tarnians are different. And because we are, Ansel and I intend to flout the queen, the wizards, and all the Cathran court if need be. Your idea of taking charge of the Cathran fleet is magnificent folly . . . and Ansel and I will do everything in our power to help you carry it out."

Olmigon stiffened. An odd sound came from his throat, and for a moment the princess feared she was hearing his death-rattle. Then she realized that the king was laughing.

"How do we manage it, lass?"

Maudrayne took the tumbler with the poppy mixture and flung its contents into the fire. "We pretend you've drunk that. You feign deep sleep when the queen returns."

She took the green glass phial from her bodice and poured four drops into one of the empty goblets on the nightstand. "This is a harmless soporific given me by Ansel. The queen and I will share a welcome bit of wine, watching you snore—and when she begins to lose her senses I'll help her safely to a couch. Then you and I will wait for Ansel, and trust that his magic suffices to get us both past the guards and out of this cursed prison."

"Bazekoy's Brisket!" he crowed. "Can you really do it?"

"Only if you promise not to drop dead on me as we try," she said, smiling demurely. "In which case, I'm off to Tarn—and your unfaithful son can win his war as best he can."

Olmigon's elation vanished. "Ah, Maudie . . . Is there no way to reconcile the two of you?"

"Not unless he renounces the Conjure-Princess. And small chance of that, I think, with him counting on her sorcery to gain him the Sovereignty."

"He swore to us this very day that her magic is benign."

"He lied," Maudrayne replied somberly. "I have it from Ansel that Ullanoth uses moonstone sigils that call on the power of the Beaconfolk—those inhuman creatures we Tarnians call the Coldlight Army. Such magical tools inevitably put the wielder's soul at risk, as well as the souls of those around them. Conrig knows this, but his ambition won't permit him to admit the truth. I don't believe he loves Ullanoth. But he intends to use her. If it suits his purposes, he may even make her his queen."

The old king's eyes squeezed tight shut as she spoke and he gave a soft groan of pain. "No! He insisted he would not! Such a thing would taint the Sovereignty beyond repair. Can't you convince him—"

"He'd never listen to me, sire. Perhaps he'd listen to you."

"But is there time?" Olmigon's eyes opened again, leaking tears. She took a washcloth and wiped his face.

"Only God knows," she said. "And perhaps a certain emperor dead for ten centuries and more."

"I dreamed of him last night," the king whispered. "I saw Bazekoy's head afloat in its crystal urn. He said: *They're coming: cold iron and cold iron clashing. Warn your son to take refuge then, forsaking victory, for these two are the foe no man can defeat.*"

Maudrayne's eyes widened. "What does it mean?"

"I don't know. I feel that I ought to know—but my wits are so skimble-skamble these days."

Before he could say more, the latch on the corridor door clicked. Queen Cataldise came tiptoeing back into the royal bedchamber.

"Finally asleep!" she whispered happily, bending over her husband and kissing his forehead. The king's eyes were closed and he breathed slowly. "I see he's drunk the potion. Oh, well done, Daughter!"

The princess took up the decanter and filled two goblets with red wine. "Share this with me, Mother. Then we'll undress His Grace and sit quietly here through the night, knowing we've done the best we can for him."

Veiled by the shaman's magic and carried in his muscular arms, the dying Olmigon Wincantor was successfully spirited from his rooms to the palace stableyard, trailed by the princess and her trusted maid. An unloaded cart, one of many that nightly brought in firewood, awaited them near the Dung Gate. None of the guardsmen, porters, or other lackeys working nearby seemed to notice the Tarnian as he rearranged sheets of canvas to cover the lumpy shapes now resting inside the cartbed. As for the rig's former owner, he was already returning afoot to his hut in the countryside, thinking how he would spend the bag of gold hidden under his smock.

"Are you all ready?" Ansel inquired as he checked the harness of the draft-mule.

"As we'll ever be," came Rusgann's truculant reply from beneath the concealing canvas.

"If only my dearest Catty could have heard me say farewell," said the king.

"She'll find your note in her pocket tomorrow," Maudrayne said. "It will suffice."

The shaman climbed into the driver's seat and took the reins. A click of his tongue urged the mule off at a smart trot, and the cart rumbled out the gate and headed down the cobblestoned street to the harbor.

Maudrayne's sloop-rigged yacht, only slightly disguised, was tied up at Red Gull Pier. She gave a cry of delight when she caught sight of the fine-looking craft, bobbing in the dark water at some distance from the other sailboats and dinghies, and oddly requiring no watchman to keep it unmolested by the dockside skulkers and roistering seamen.

"It's my own *Fulmar!* I never thought I'd see her again. Conrig was supposed to have ordered the yacht sold."

"And so she was," Ansel said dryly, tying the mule to a bollard. "To me."

Olmigon had mercifully fallen asleep. Maudrayne and Rusgann climbed out of the cart and began unloading bundles of supplies they had brought along, provisions of every type gathered and hidden for their great escape. None of the roughnecks wandering about paid the slightest attention to them, although they were the only women on the pier.

"Let's get everything aboard quickly," the princess urged, "and cast off before some busybody reports us to the Harbor Patrol."

"No one will," Ansel said. "We're not really invisible, but you needn't be concerned that anyone will try to stop us. Not even those who spy from strange places!" He peered over the edge of the dock with a sly smirk. There was nothing to be seen among the pilings in the dark water but seaweed and the usual floating bits of rubbish.

"Who do you mean?" Rusgann asked, scowling.

"Never mind. There's nothing to fear."

It was not quite midnight and the great quay seethed with activity. Sheltered by the hills north of the capital, the harbor air was cold and almost dead calm. A shallow blanket of mist hung above the water, which was still fairly warm close to the shore.

Rumors of an impending naval attack upon Cala had caused many panicked merchant captains to abandon the commercial docks and put out to sea, or else move their vessels up the Blen or Brent River estuaries out of harm's way, in spite of the danger of grounding at low tide. The skippers of some smaller craft, heeding the Crown's call to arms, were installing simple artillery capable of hurling tarn-blaze shells at the foe. The distinctive sulphury smell of the infernal chymical mingled with the usual harbor odors of decaying fish, tar, stale beer, and human waste.

The king was not to be moved until the other contents of the cart were unloaded and the sloop made ready. Maudrayne had laid a gangplank and hopped aboard *Fulmar*. She was catching bags of supplies tossed to her by the maid and stowing them below in the yacht's tiny cabin.

During one of the intervals when the princess was out of sight, Rusgann said to the shaman, "I hope you don't intend for my lady and me to go aboard some Cathran warship and sail into battle! It's the king who's mad—not us women."

Ansel chuckled. "Nay, goodwife, you and your mistress will be let off safely ashore before Olmigon meets his destiny. The Lord Admiral's fleet awaits the enemy in the waters between Eagleroost and Castle Defiant, some seventy leagues to the south. We'll zip handily down the coast and land you in a likely spot. Our voyage will last only three hours or so, and will be as blithe as my magic can make it."

King Olmigon had finally roused at the sound of their voices. He said to the shaman, "Duke Farindon Eagleroost is a loyal friend, and his wife is Tarnian. She'd welcome Maudie. I could rest briefly at the castle, then sail away and deliver my great surprise to Admiral Woodvale at dawn! Perhaps small craft from Defiant's flotilla might even ferry me to the rendezvous. Then you yourself would be able to remain with the princess and keep her safe until the final victory, after which I pray you help my son and his wife mend their differences—"

"I will see you to the Lord Admiral's flagship myself," the shaman said, "as is my solemn charge." His face was no longer mild and good-humored but had assumed an expression of profound sadness. Arcane talent glimmered in his black eyes. "The rest of it is not for you to command."

"I see," the king whispered.

"No, you do not." Ansel had climbed into the back of the cart and spoke close to the king's ear, so that he alone might hear. "Bazekoy is not the only uncanny entity taking an interest in the fate of High Blenholme Island. There are others, both kindly and malevolent, who hope to influence its future. Your son, his wife, and their unborn child loom large in this conflict—but not, I fear, as the happy family you might have hoped for."

The full import of Ansel's statement escaped Olmigon. The king had grasped only one thing, and his ruined countenance was illuminated by sudden joy. "A *child?* Maude carries Con's child?"

"A son. I tell you this, old man, to give you comfort as you approach your end. But you must keep it secret, especially from the Prince Heritor. He will soon face terrible choices, and his decisions—unlike most of your own—must evolve from cold reason, not the sentimental promptings of the heart."

The king's face fell. "And Maudie?"

"A prideful woman, obstinate and strong, one of those whose cleverness can be honed to wisdom only through suffering. Her son will have formidable enemies. He will not survive, nor will the Sovereignty, without his mother's governance and good counsel."

"We're ready," Maudrayne called. "Bring him aboard."

The Tarnian gathered the frail body of the king into his arms. "How are you feeling, old man?"

"Like death," Olmigon said. "But that's as it should be. Let's be on our way."

thirty-three

The easy triumph that had seemed well within the grasp of King Honigalus yesterday was now looking much more difficult to achieve. And it was all Beynor's fault.

The steady southeasterlies requested of the young sorcerer had prevailed nicely enough while the Continentals sailed up from Nis-Gata, but the wind dropped away to nothing within an hour of the corsairs' joining the armada. At first, the flat calm seemed fortuitous. It eased the transfer of munitions and much-needed foodstuffs from the newcomers to the nearly empty holds of the Didionites and enabled the king's fleet commanders to confer face-to-face with their Continental counterparts. Battle-plans were coordinated, stores of food and water secured, magazines filled, and cannons readied. The Didionite captains and their allies enjoyed a fine meal in the royal saloon of *Casabarela Regnant*, then prepared to cross Cala Bay and make short work of Woodvale just as soon as the wind picked up again.

But it did not pick up. And frantic appeals to Beynor went unanswered.

King Honigalus and his officers stood glum on the quarterdeck of their huge flagship beneath a full spread of sails that only fitfully filled with gentle breezes. Instead of coming out of the southeast, the light airs blew from the north. After seven hours creeping to windward, the armada had moved less than fifty leagues toward their encounter with the foe.

"Where's that damned Fring?" Honigalus demanded. "Surely he and his clutch of magickers must have found out some news of Beynor by now. It's impossible that the entire Glaumerie Guild of Moss should have no notion of the boy's whereabouts. We must have a favorable wind!"

Galbus Peel threw a brief glance at the overcast sky. "This morning we had a red dawn, Your Majesty—not a thing that mariners traditionally welcome. But it might signify an important change in the weather."

"The wizard comes!" one of the young lieutenants announced, and a bulky black-robed figure emerged a moment later from the companionway and came on deck.

Fring bowed to the king and made his report with a long face. "There is grave news from Moss, Majesty. Ridcanndal, Master of the Glaumerie Guild, finally admitted that Beynor has disappeared from Royal Fenguard. So has the barque that was Didion's gift to the king. No one has any notion of the missing young man's destination, nor can they explain why he should have gone away. All Ridcanndal will say is that baleful thaumaturgy is at work, clouding the guild's oversight."

Honigalus spoke a weary obscenity. "Beynor has let us down. The brat over-reached himself, just as we feared, and now he's gone into hiding."

"Beg pardon, Majesty." Fring's lips displayed a grimace that might have been a smile. "If the Conjure-King had merely failed to fulfill his boastful promises to you, there would have been no good reason for him to flee Fenguard—especially since a terrible blizzard is now raging throughout the northland."

"It matters not," Honigalus said, shaking his head in disgust. "The whole pack of bogtrotters can go to the Hell of Ice for all I care! Were your scryers able to locate the Cathran fleet? And what about the Tarnians?"

"The effort was one of the most difficult we have ever attempted. However, we did obtain the information following an intensive—and, I might add, painful—conjunction of minds. As Captain Peel predicted, Admiral Woodvale has taken up a position just south of the entrance to Blenholme Roads. The Tarnians have met with light, variable winds, just as we have. They are now making their way across Tunny Bay, moving very slowly. Unless conditions change drastically, we are bound to reach the Roads many hours ahead of them."

The king's face cleared. "Excellent! After we smash Woodvale's force, the Harriers are bound to turn tail for the Western Ocean. Why should they risk themselves in a futile cause? They aren't fools."

"No, Your Majesty." Fring was smug. "Do you have further orders for me?"

When Honigalus shook his head, Galbus Peel said, "Bespeak our people at Sorna on the west coast and Castle Highcliffe on the east. I wish to know the wind direction up there and its force—and if there is any sign yet of snow-clouds coming southward over the sea."

Just before sunup, with the weather around Bluefish Bay partly cloudy and the wind no longer so strong as to preclude any sort of delicate maneuvering, Hartrig Skellhaven suggested to Prince Conrig that they might risk taking *Shearwater* through the tricky channel separating the mainland from the Vigilants, rather than skirting the islands as prudent navigators invariably did.

"We could save nearly two hundred leagues, using the shortcut," the viscount said. "But I don't think we should chance it unless Stergos bespeaks Ullanoth. We need to be certain that her rambunctious magical gale doesn't return unexpectedly while we creep through the shoals."

"Very well," Conrig said, rising from the table in the officers' mess, where he had been conferring with Skellhaven and Baron Ingo Holmrangel, who served as First Mate. "I'll ask my brother to attempt to reach the princess. But she warned me she might be too weak for distant windvoicing after conjuring yesterday's big northerly blows on either side of the island."

Holmrangel shook his head slowly, frowning. "A wierd thing, that, and nothing any seaman familiar with Cala Bay wants to get on the wrong side of, this time of year. Still, the air's nowhere near the frost-point yet, and the gales have petered out, so I guess we needn't worry."

The baron was a rough-featured, bearish man with a distinct family resemblance to his older cousin. He had proved himself to be impressively efficient at organizing the makeshift crew of *Shearwater,* and had personally beheaded a Stippenese bosun caught attempting to sever the clipper's fore-topmast stay early on in the voyage. After the execution of the saboteur, the other Continental crewmen pressed into service had cooperated meekly with their Cathran captors.

Conrig found Stergos on the poop deck, staring morosely at the passing scene of Bluefish Bay. The Doctor Arcanorum had declined to join the prince and the Heart Companions at breakfast earlier, saying that he preferred to take some fresh air and pray, now that the violent wind had finally fallen off. The precipitous voyage down Blenholme's eastern coast under straining sails had badly shaken the nerves of the sensitive alchymist, as had his almost continuous duty of maintaining communication with the windvoices at Cala Palace and those of Admiral Woodvale.

"It's no use, my trying to bespeak Princess Ullanoth," Stergos said, after Conrig had made his request. "I attempted to reach her a short time ago with no success. She may still be recuperating abed—as poor young Deveron is—and with us so far away from Holt Mallburn now, my voice is not strong enough to penetrate her slumber."

"Snudge!" Conrig brightened. "He's rested long enough. Let's wake him and have him try for Ullanoth. She made it plain enough that she knows of his talent." He took Stergos by the arm and drew him toward the companionway. "I wish we could have kept his ability secret from her, but I feared she'd learn of it if she ever got close to him."

"Do you think she also suspects Deveron of using Iscannon's sigil?" the doctor whispered, following Conrig down the ladder to the middle deck, where the squires had been given sleeping space among the merchant ship's single line of cannons.

"Who can say? I only wish I knew whether Snudge told the truth when he claimed the Concealer was lost at Mallmouth Bridge." His face twisted. "Damn him if he still has the thing, but quails from using it out of cowardice!"

"Cowardice? How can you say such a thing?" Stergos hissed, seizing his brother by the upper arms as they gained the middle deck. "He saw his friends murdered before his eyes, and their killer burnt to cinders by the moonstone's sorcery. He has told me of this to ease his mind, weeping like the devastated child he is. But no coward opened the bridge-gate to your army."

"Snudge swore fealty to me and dare not abjure his duty," said the prince, his face adamant. "If you know that he still has the Concealer stone in his possession, you must tell me."

"I don't know it." Stergos met his brother's hard gaze without flinching, even though there was desolation in his own eyes. "Neither will I question him about it, lest he be tempted to lie to me."

"So! But you care not that the boy lies to *me?*"

"Con, I love you and will give my life for you. But you can't demand that I compromise the conscience of another person. No liege lord on earth can ask such a thing. I know that Deveron has begged you to trust him—"

"As has Ullanoth," the prince muttered. "Trust! It's a luxury few princes can afford."

"But the boy is worthy of it. If he does still have the stone, perhaps one day he'll feel strong enough to use it again in your service. Until then, I beseech you not to press him. It will do no good."

"Ah, Gossy!" Conrig made a gesture that mingled exasperation and surrender. "You and Snudge are alike in so many ways. I swear I'll ask no more of either of you than you will freely give. Forgive this black humor of mine. It's the war . . . my fears for the Sovereignty and for Cathra itself . . . the quirk of fortune that allowed Honigalus and his armada to escape Mallburn Town before we could stop them . . . the stupidity of our own admirals. And here I am, with all my hopes now dependent upon the powers of a fickle sorceress—"

"And perhaps also upon our poor dying father," Stergos added. "But he believes the oracle that said all would come right in the end. What can we do but try to believe it, too?"

They were gentle waking the boy, who had dark circles beneath his eyes and was so sluggish that he could barely emerge from the blankets of his hammock. He had slept for more than twelve hours and eaten nothing since *Shearwater* had quit Mallburn harbor, but if he suffered nightmares he said nothing of it to Conrig or Stergos.

"You need warm food and drink more than anything," the alchymist decided, after he and his royal brother had helped Snudge into his clothes. They draped his arms over their shoulders, hauled him to the petty officers' mess next to the galley, and sat on either side of him at the splintery table. A fat Stippenese cook dished up fried ham and warmed-over wholewheat porridge laced with dried apricots to Snudge, and served all three Cathrans heated wine from the private stock of the ship's dead captain.

"Now, before you drink down too much of that awful vinegar-blink and blur whatever talent remains to you," the prince said, once the cook had retreated, "try to bespeak the Conjure-Princess in Holt Mallburn. Ask her if she can maintain a gentle wind in the channel north of Terek Island in the Vigilants, so our ship can shortcut through it to Cala Bay. Ullanoth may be asleep, recovering from her magical labors."

Snudge nodded and hunched forward with his head in his hands. The brothers sipped the wine, which was actually an outstanding vintage.

After a while Snudge sighed and lifted his face. He was smiling wanly. "I did have to wake her, and she wasn't pleased. But she assures me that whatever winds prevail here now will continue for at least half a day more. Later, the weather may change due to natural causes. There is nothing she can do to influence it through magic at this time—not, she says, without risking harm to herself."

Stergos rose. "I'll inform Skellhaven." He hurried away.

"The Conjure-Princess wasn't surprised to have me voice her," Snudge said. "She also told me that King Beynor has fallen afoul of the Beaconfolk, who were so angry with him that they took Rothbannon's sigils away. The king has fled to the Dawntide Isles to live with the Salka. Ullanoth assures you that her brother will no longer assist Honigalus through his sorcery."

"Futter me!" the prince exclaimed. "There's good news for a change. Maybe our navy has a chance against Didion and the Continentals after all . . . Did the princess tell you whether she plans to join us soon?"

"No, Your Grace. And I didn't think to ask her. All she said was that she needed to rest. She commanded me not to bother her again before evening."

Conrig sat back with a sigh of disappointment. "Ah, well. Drink up, lad. And get that food inside you. When you're stronger, I'd like you to scry what the enemy armada may be up to."

"I'll do my best, Your Grace."

Conrig sat silent until the boy had finished his meal, apparently lost in thought. Finally he said, "Are you truly feeling better? I realize that the affray at Mallmouth Bridge was a terrible thing. Terrible! You were like one sleepwalking for much of the time after."

Snudge sipped wine, making no reply.

The prince rose. "Perhaps you'd like to get a little more sleep in my cabin. It's a tiny place, but God knows it's warmer and drier than that cramped coop on the gundeck."

"It's best that I sleep with the other armigers. But perhaps a short stay in a more private spot would be best if I must attempt scrying."

Conrig said, "I'm afraid you must. Stergos can bespeak our own war-fleet and even contact the Tarnian windvoice traveling with the mercenaries. But I must depend on you to give us oversight of the foe, even though the work drains your strength." He hesitated. "Is it very hard on you, Snudge?"

"I can bear it, Your Grace, for duty's sake."

*   *   *

Shearwater threaded her cautious way through the rocky channel, aided by a spring tide, and finally gained the open waters of Cala Bay. Meanwhile, with Snudge overwatching and giving periodic reports to Conrig and Stergos, the advancing armada of Honigalus made better time as the wind veered to the east and blew more steadily. By sundown, the sky was heavily overcast and a cold drizzle brought misery to seamen forced to climb the rigging of the tall ships to shorten sail. Honigalus and Peel plainly intended pressing on through the night, but the individual ships of the armada now gave each other wide sea-room and proceeded with great caution.

"They'll hit the Lord Admiral's force in the morning, after they pull together again into battle formation," Skellhaven predicted. "But we still have the advantage, Your Grace. We're bound to reach Woodvale first. Too bad about the Harriers, though."

The Tarnian frigates pressed on doggedly toward Intrepid Point, but none of their skippers would predict when they might reach Blenholme Roads and join the Lord Admiral's fleet.

Snudge and Skellhaven departed the captain's cabin to their separate duties, leaving Conrig and his brother alone, brooding over a chart by lamplight. The night was full of the distinctive sounds made by a great ship under sail: the creak of timbers, the squealing of spars and booms, the slap and hum of rigging, and the continuing rush of water sliding past the hull.

"Brother," the prince said after a time, "bespeak our father. We may as well find out whether the king's brave attempt to educate the Lord Admiral and his captains in the niceties of small-craft warfare has failed or succeeded."

"And we must learn how he fares bodily as well," the alchymist said in quiet reproof, "although the ship's doctor professed to be amazed at his unexpected vitality."

The chief windvoice aboard Woodvale's flagship *Princess Milyna* was a cheerful young alchymist named Vra-Bolan.

Ho, Gossy! So it's you again, is it? There's really no news. We're riding in midbay, waiting and praying. I can hear the men below singing loud songs. The Lord Admiral ordered an extra ration of grog to cheer them up.

"Bolan, the Prince Heritor would talk to King Olmigon, if His Grace hasn't retired for the night."

He's actually in remarkable fettle. He came aboard this morning with no crown or other symbol of royal authority, and an hour or so ago the fo'c'sle gang decided something had to be done about that before tomorrow's battle. So they crowned the old man with the iron band from a tarnblaze cask!

Stergos passed on this bit of intelligence to Conrig, who burst out laughing.

It took Vra-Bolan only a few minutes to reach the cabin where the king lay, and then father and son conversed haltingly on the wind. Conrig soon learned that Olmigon's scheme for the small-boat flotilla had finally been accepted by the admiral and his commanders, although they still nursed serious doubts. The outlook now seemed so grim that almost anything was worth a try—even sending sloops and cutters to attack men o' war.

I had to demonstrate the damned maneuvers over and over again, the king complained, *first to Woodvale, then to the fleet captains, and finally to the shallop skippers themselves, maneuvering squadrons of dried beans around tiny warship models on a tablecloth. The little fellows know what they have to do, though, and they intend to do it well . . . You realize, of course, that most of them will die.*

"Yes, sire," said the prince.

Take care of their people.

"Of course."

Is there any hope of magical assistance from Ullanoth?

"I fear not. She gave us gales on either side of the island when we needed them and calmed the winds that favored our foe. It exhausted her. We bespoke her not long ago. What strength she can summon she intends to use tomorrow to Send herself to Fenguard and claim the crown of Moss. That's her highest priority. I can hardly fault her."

No . . . Con?

"Yes, sire?"

You should know that if my insane deathbed ploy does help launch the Sovereignty, much is owed to your wife Maudrayne and to the shaman Ansel, who enabled me to reach Woodvale. Show them your gratitude also.

"I will. And I intend to acknowledge the emperor's role as well. The entire island will hear of his oracle and marvel at it. Perhaps I'll put Bazekoy's face on the coinage of the Sovereignty."

He'd probably think that a great joke . . .

"How do you feel, Father?"

Tired. Content. There's not much pain. Did I tell you that I dreamed of Bazekoy only a day ago? That was how I knew my time had come, that I must leave my deathbed and take action. But the emperor also spoke strange words to me that pertained somehow to you. He said, "They're coming: cold iron and cold iron clashing. Warn your son to take refuge then, forsaking victory, for these two are the foe no man can defeat." . . . *I couldn't fathom what he meant.*

"I don't understand it either, sire. Was he saying that Cathra cannot win the upcoming battle? If so, that contradicts his response to your one Question. It puts paid to all our hopes."

No. I think it must mean something else entirely. If only I could grasp the damned slippery thought and force it to yield up its gist!

"Take heart. Perhaps this dream of yours was just a dream, and no arcane portent at all. Put it from your mind and rest. Tomorrow, when I see you again, we can speak more of this if you wish."

The king bade both of his sons good night, but they still sat at the chart table, reluctant to go to their cabins. With the index fingers of either hand, Conrig idly traced the rugged coastline of High Blenholme—from Tarn in the far northwest, from Moss in the northeast. The two fingers came together in Cala Bay.

He gasped as the realization came to him. "Oh, God, Gossy! Could that be it? The Hammer and Anvil?"

The brothers regarded each other for a moment in a dread surmise. Then the alchymist said, "Since the Wolf's Breath, our winters have been mild, without great storms in the south. But the volcanos are calm now. And Ullanoth's twin gales . . . might they act as inadvertent precursors? If our father's dream was indeed warning that Hammer and Anvil storms are sweeping down from the Barren Lands—"

"But *when* will they clash?" The prince's eyes glittered as he moved one finger up the chart, northward between the promontories of Blackhorse and Eagle-roost, into the comparative safety of Blenholme Roads. "When?"

Stergos said, "We know a blizzard rages in Moss, and Prince Somarus and his army are trapped by heavy snow in the northern interior. Yet it could be days before the storms reach Cala Bay—if they come at all. You said it yourself, Con: Perhaps Father's dream was only a dream, and nothing more."

The Prince Heritor's body relaxed. His hands fell into his lap and he sighed. "In any case, we can't let such a thing influence our strategy. Tomorrow we fight

Didion. And who knows? By the time we meet the King's Grace, he may have had another dream that will explain it all to us."

But there would be no meeting and no explanation.

Much later, when Conrig was finally preparing to go to bed, Stergos entered his tiny sleeping cabin without knocking. The alchymist's robes were awry and his face streamed with tears. He seemed unable to speak and only stood helpless until the prince took his shoulders and shook him.

"Gossy, what is it? What's happened?"

"Vra-Bolan just bespoke me the news. Our father is dead, peacefully in his sleep. You are the King of Cathra." As his younger brother stood frozen, Stergos knelt and kissed his hand. "I—I've not yet told the others."

Conrig pulled the alchymist to his feet. "Nor will we tell them. Not until we reach the Lord Admiral's flagship and see Father's body with our own eyes. Only then will I be willing to don the iron-hoop crown he wore and undertake the duties of a king."

"Oh, Con. He never was able to sing his Deathsong!"

"He sings it somewhere. Don't worry." He drew the weeping alchymist to the cabin door and thrust him into the corridor. "Leave me alone now, Gossy. Pray for our father's spirit, but pray especially hard for me."

When Conrig was alone again he took a bottle of malt liquor from his trussing coffer, filled a beaker to the brim, and downed it, hoping to silence the gush of speculation that rose like a black tide in his brain. But the remedy was futile and so he drank more, cursing beneath his breath, and finally fell insensible into the cabin's mean, narrow bed.

thirty-four

Viscount skellhaven brought *Shearwater* alongside *Princess Milyna* as another scarlet dawn broke over Cala Bay. The waters were choppy, and bursts of chill rain drenched Conrig and Stergos as they transferred to the Cathran flagship. The Lord Admiral and his officers had prepared a solemn reception, but the new king brushed aside all ceremony and said that he and the Royal Alchymist would view the remains of their father at once, escorted only by Woodvale.

Olmigon was laid out in the admiral's sleeping-cabin. They had dressed him in plain robes, placed two candles beside his head, and assigned four knight-lieutenants as a guard of honor. The improvised crown, a slightly rusted circlet, lay on his breast.

Stergos knelt at the foot of the bier and drew the scarlet hood of his habit over his head. As the Lord Admiral hovered uncertainly and the guards presented their swords, Conrig regarded the late king's body in silence for a brief minute. Then he took the iron cask hoop and set it upon his own wheaten hair, which was still wet with rain.

"This is the only coronation I shall have . . . Whether I retain the throne of Cathra at the end of this day now depends upon you, Lord Woodvale, and the brave seamen under your command. Are your windvoices ready to transmit orders to the other ships of the fleet?"

"Aye, Your Grace. Save for the small craft, who have no adepts aboard. They'll be signalled with flares when the enemy heaves into view. The light forces know their role and need no further direction. King Olmigon spent many hours coaching their skippers in naval tactics, as he did my own commanders."

Conrig smiled thinly. "Whatever Olmigon advised—no matter how much his ideas contradict conventional naval practice—that you must do. Those are *my* orders."

"Aye, Your Grace."

Vra-Stergos uncovered his head and said, "I was just bespoken by Princess Ullanoth. She says that the armada of Didion is coming at us. They are less than thirty leagues distant."

Woodvale nodded. "Time to attack, then—cockleshells in the van. There are thirty-seven of the small gunboats, sire, augmenting our twenty-nine men o' war."

"And sixty-five warships of Didion, Stippen, and Foraile," Conrig said, smiling without humor. "Which gives us the advantage of a single craft. Carry on, my lord."

Skipping away close-hauled on the rising east wind, the small boats moved to the right flank of the lumbering, overconfident enemy, then turned west and ran among them out of the misty rain. The result was everything Olmigon might have hoped. The masthead lookouts and scrying adepts aboard the ships of the armada saw the approaching sailboats, but had no idea what they were up to. Even shrewd Galbus Peel believed that the ragtag flotilla must consist of a mob of panicked fishermen, hoping to reach the coves below Eagleroost ahead of a strong squall.

When the Cathran boats opened fire, the great ships of Didion and their allies manned their own guns. But the attackers were so small and fast-moving that they could hardly be targeted. Warship after warship, hampered by their innate clumsiness, was struck at close range by bombshells and fire-casks of tarnblaze—not fired in wasteful random broadsides but aimed with frugal precision near the waterline or at critical structures on deck. Fourteen of the proud corsairs were holed so badly that their crews abandoned ship. Six more frigates—and two huge Didionite barques—lost their masts or saw their sails consumed in tenacious sheets of unquenchable flame. The four-decker *Casabarela Regnant*, looming above the rain-pecked waves like some monstrous floating fort, was singled out for special attention by tiny marauders who slipped beneath her guns and bombarded her rudder. With steering damaged, she lost way and was soon nearly dead in the water. Fires dotted her from stem to gudgeon, and black smoke poured from her ornate sterncastle. Frantic figures swarming on the forward boatdeck were attempting to lower the captain's gig, so that King Honigalus, Fleet Captain Peel, and the all-important cadre of wizards could transfer to another ship. For a deadly half-hour, like wolves slashing at the heels and underbellies of giant elk, the small craft darted among the enemy vessels as if daring them to retaliate.

They did, of course, once the initial element of surprise was lost.

Agile as the fighting sailboats were, the sheer number of guns firing on them guaranteed their eventual doom. When their limited supplies of munitions were exhausted, they attempted to run away, but less than a dozen escaped the infuriated Didionites and Continental corsairs. The few that did attempt to surrender were blown to bits.

There was a lull, after which Honigalus and Peel, newly installed aboard the barque *Riptide*, regrouped their disheveled fleet. Nearly a third of the original force was unfit to fight and began a retreat to the Continent. The others pressed on toward the twin lines of Cathran warships that Fring and his cohort of scryers had overviewed standing before the entrance to Blenholme Roads.

"The Tarnians have just bespoken me that their adverse winds have suddenly reversed themselves." Vra-Bolan reported to the Lord Admiral. "They are now charging past Intrepid Head with half a westerly gale in their sheets, and estimate that they will come up behind the foe in less than three hours."

"Westerly?" Woodvale frowned. "How strange, with east winds so strong hereabouts. But it's welcome intelligence all the same, if we can only hold out until the Harriers arrive. Inform King Conrig of this development, and see if he has further tidings from the Mossland sorceress."

The original plan devised by the Lord Admiral and his staff for the defense of Blenholme Roads was in a classic mode: two battle lines, the longer and stronger in the vanguard, strung out between the opposing headlands, would stand and repel enemy attackers. King Olmigon had insisted that this plan be abandoned— simply because it was so tried and true as to be obvious.

As Didion swept up the bay, also arrayed in two lines, the Cathran ranks suddenly broke and erupted into a bizarre free-for-all advance. Some angled east and others went west, engaging the smaller enemy warships on either wing, while leaving the great capital ships of Honigalus at the center of the line with no one to fight at first. It was an audacious trick and one that again took the invaders by surprise. What followed was a fierce, messy mêlée scattered over many square leagues along either shore, dragging on for more than three hours in shallow, treacherous waters, where Cathran knowledge of local navigational hazards counted more than the superior firepower of the enemy. As more and more Didionite ships were cut to pieces, their corsair allies lost heart and began to retreat—only to run head-on into the guns of approaching Tarn.

As the battle drew to its climax, Woodvale and his captains blessed the madness of dead Olmigon, who had demanded that they throw away the rulebook of conventional naval warfare. *Riptide,* the substitute flagship of Honigalus, was being chased northward up the Roads by the *Princess Milyna* and two heavy Cathran frigates. The Cathrans were gaining steadily. Before night fell the contest would be decided.

Wrapped in stormgear against the rain and wind, Conrig stood on the quarterdeck with the Lord Admiral, Stergos, and a gaggle of jubilant ship's officers and windvoices, debating with himself whether to demand Didion's surrender or simply blow Honigalus's barque apart. He burned to revenge himself against his royal antagonist. But if he did, then Prince Somarus would inherit his brother's throne.

The war would remain unwon.

The king cupped his mouth in his hand and spoke into the alchymist's hooded ear. "Gossy! It's time to bespeak Fring and his master and put an end to this."

Before the Royal Alchymist could respond, a green-glowing figure appeared on the streaming quarterdeck before them. Woodvale and his officers jumped back in stunned amazement; but Conrig and Stergos recognized Ullanoth.

"My Sending is weak and can only last a few moments," she said urgently. "Listen! You and your people are in terrible danger. The great storms you Southerners call Hammer and Anvil are converging on Cala Bay. There will be devastating wind, freezing rain, and snow when the tempests clash. If you hope to live, command your ships to take shelter. I have already told the windvoice of King Honigalus of the impending calamity, but he does not choose to believe me. In Didion, sailors dismiss tales of the Hammer and Anvil as myth."

The apparition flickered and vanished.

"Did you hear?" Conrig shouted at the Admiral. When Woodvale nodded dumbly, he continued. "My father warned me this might happen. He had a final dire premonition."

"The Hammer and Anvil!" The young alchymist Vra-Bolan repeated the words, stricken with awe. "Not since the advent of the Wolf's Breath have we suffered their fury."

As if to confirm Ullanoth's words, a sudden fusillade of sleet swept over the warship. Then, paradoxically, the wind began to fall off. The Lord Admiral began to issue terse commands to the windvoices and officers.

Conrig said to Stergos, "Bespeak the King of Didion. Confirm Ullanoth's warning. Tell him I offer honorable terms of surrender if he will accept the Sovereignty and become my vassal. *Riptide* may precede us into the harbor at Eagleroost, while other vessels of his fleet have my permission to take sanctuary in whatever Cathran port they can safely enter, provided that they strike their colors."

The reply was slow in coming. But in the end, whether he believed in the Hammer and Anvil or not, Honigalus of Didion could not dismiss the reality of the three enemy warships hard-charging in his wake.

Fring spoke: *His Majesty King Honigalus is pleased to accept the Sovereignty, given one final demonstration of goodwill by King Conrig of Cathra.*

"Ask what he wants," Conrig said.

Stergos did, and when the answer came, he was surprised to see a sardonic smile upon his royal brother's face.

"Tell Honigalus that Cathra graciously condescends to agree," Conrig said.

The ships caught in the great tempest were drenched in freezing rain and battered by hurricane blasts. Hopelessly topheavy as their rigging took on a burden of thick ice, they foundered and sank without a single survivor. A pitiful handful of men o' war belonging to Cathra and Didion, along with three Tarnian frigates, reached safe havens. All of the Continental corsairs still in Cala Bay were lost.

Hours later, when the sleet storm was over and snow sifted gently down on the battlements of Eagleroost Castle, Cathra accepted the surrender of Didion. Sitting in a simple chair in Duke Farindon's crowded little presence chamber,

Conrig wore the Iron Crown that would afford him his popular nickname, but no other emblem of royalty as Honigalus kissed his hand and signed the Edict of Sovereignty. Fleet Captain Galbus Peel repeated the gesture of fealty and also signed, acting as the proxy of Prince Somarus, who participated in the ceremony through the wind-talent of Fring, not bothering to hide his fury at the craven behavior of Honigalus, who had declined to die for Didion.

To accommodate the custom of the barbarians, a declaration of surrender was signed in the blood of both Conrig and Honigalus, and Duke Farindon Eagleroost and his two adult sons contributed drops of their own blood as witnesses. Then there remained only a single thing left to be done.

"Let the Princess Maudrayne be admitted to the presence chamber," the duke said with evident reluctance.

His wife, Duchess Sotera, whose hair was almost the same rich auburn shade as that of her distant kinswoman, led Conrig's wife into the assembly of nobles and high naval officers. Sotera's face was red and swollen from weeping, but Maudrayne seemed so coolly serene that most of the men believed she knew nothing of what was about to happen.

Without prompting, Maudrayne strode to Conrig, knelt, and kissed his hand. "My liege," she murmured with eyes cast down. "My husband. I congratulate you on your great victory."

"Thank you, madam. My late father informed me of the way in which you helped him. For this I will be eternally grateful."

Maudrayne lifted her head and looked him full in the eye. "And how will your gratitude be shown, Your Grace?"

"First we must speak of another matter." Conrig's voice was remote. He held out a hand and Stergos, his lips quivering, gave him a document, which the king passed in turn to the woman kneeling before him. "Please read this. You may rise. If you understand what is written, sign your name to it."

She stood, and her gaze flicked over the parchment. "A bill of divorcement. They tell me you intend to make a marriage with the sister of Honigalus, Princess Risalla, so that Didion's place in your new Sovereignty is affirmed."

"That's true. Will you sign the bill?"

She said softly, "And what does the other lady think of this alliance?"

Conrig frowned. "If you speak of Princess Risalla—"

"Not she. The *other*."

"The newly crowned Conjure-Queen of Moss has already pledged to me her fealty. As First Vassal, she rejoices that Didion and Cathra are to be united in a dynastic family. And when the great benefits of Sovereignty are fully understood by your uncle, the High Sealord of Tarn, I'm confident that he will also pledge. A new era is about to begin on our island of High Blenholme, one bringing prosperity, peace, and security to all four of her sister-nations. I ask you again: will you sign?"

Maudrayne gripped the vellum so tightly that it began to crackle. She turned about, letting her gaze sweep over those present in the room. All of them, excepting Duchess Sotera, who had buried her face in her hands, seemed to be holding their breath.

"How can I not agree to sign the bill, knowing the great good that will come of it?" She went to the side table where pen and ink waited and scrawled her name. Then she took the document to Conrig, dropped it at his feet, and screamed out: "Now pay the price!"

She turned and ran from the room like a deer, leaving the men shouting, Sotera collapsed in the arms of the duke, and Conrig on his feet, flushed with rage.

"Go after her!" he cried.

Four of Eagleroost's household knights dashed for the door. Stergos hastened with them, desperately calling, "Maude!"

The rest of them waited, some displaying shock and bewilderment, others plainly sharing the king's anger and muttering of lèse majesté and even treason. Count Feribor Blackhorse picked up the bill of divorcement and handed it over to Conrig, smiling enigmatically.

Then Stergos returned. His normally pleasant features had turned into a mask of stone. "She has leapt from the parapet into the waters of the bay," he told his brother. "May God have mercy on her—and upon you."

"Fool," said Red Ansel the shaman. "What if I had not been anchored nearby in *Fulmar*? Not even a Tarnian could survive more than a few minutes in these icy waters. You and the unborn babe might have died—and what would I tell my Source?"

"Shut up," said Maude, drawing the blankets more closely around her nakedness and crouching closer to the sloop's tiny galley stove. "If your precious Source had wanted me dead, I'd be lobster-food by now. Suppose you do something worthwhile by making me a hot drink. I've never been so cold since I fell through the ice of the River Donor when I was twelve years old."

"They're coming down to search for your drowned corpse," Ansel warned her. "Look—you can see torches on the steps leading to the dock."

"First my drink, then you can up anchor and set sail for home. The snowfall has stopped and the night's clearing nicely now that the Hammer and Anvil have done their work."

"What a piece of work!" the shaman muttered. But Maude knew he was not speaking about the storm.

Conjure-Queen Ullanoth of Moss put aside Subtle Loophole and let the sight of softly falling snow outside her tower window ease the pain of her watching. Conrig had temporarily slipped away from her control. She feared that might happen if she did not accompany him on the journey to Cala, but she had had no choice. Her own kingdom must come first. There would be time for the Sovereign of High Blenholme later.

After she dealt with runaway Beynor . . . and found a way to obtain the great collection of sigils hidden by his exiled co-conspirator, Kilian Blackhorse. The young fool had babbled the secret to his Salka captors in the Dawntide Isles, and she had heard and seen, nearly overcome by a burst of wild exultation as she realized what those sigils might do, were they in her own hands.

Maudrayne and her unborn son were a delicious paradox. The Tarnian woman had been transformed from an antagonist into a potential ally the moment she had signed the bill of divorcement. According to Cathran law, her son had first claim to Conrig's throne, having been conceived in wedlock. The proud Sealords of Tarn would find a way to use Maudrayne's son against the man who hoped to force them into vassalage. And she, Ullanoth, would use the lot of them in turn.

It would be so very interesting to mull over the possibilities during the long winter nights, thinking and watching and listening and planning. When spring came, unlocking the icy fastness of the Boreal Sea, she'd know the best way to act.

The sloop, its sails filled by the magical airs of Red Ansel, was long gone by the time searchers from Eagleroost Castle reached the shore. They launched rowboats, combed the black waters, and clambered over the snow-slippery rocks, but in the end they found nothing.

Stars came out in the sky above Blenholme Roads, only to be overwhelmed when the Great Lights appeared in the north. Bright shimmering curtains, thrusting lances, and slow explosions of red and green and golden radiance stretched from horizon to horizon, whispering about what they might do next.

F MAY

May, Julian.

Conqueror's moon : the
boreal moon tale #1